I0611337

CHERYL AMMETER

IVEY AND THE AIRSHIP

IVEY AND THE AIRSHIP

Copyright © 2016 Cheryl Ammeter

All rights reserved. No part of this book may be reproduced in any form or by any means without the written permission of the publisher.

Cover illustration by Wylie Beckert
www.WylieBeckert.com
in collaboration with Bob West.
Creative direction, writing consultation,
identity design, diagrams and interior design by
Bob West / Thought Nozzle™
www.ThoughtNozzle.com

Pantala Press
689 Lockhaven Dr.
Pacifica, CA 94044
www.PantalaPress.com
www.AethersEdge.com

ISBN-13: 978-0-9848035-2-1
ISBN: 0-9848035-2-1
Library of Congress Control Number: 2016913032

FIC 028060 FICTION/Science Fiction/Steampunk
FIC 009020 FICTION/Fantasy/Epic
FIC 027120 FICTION/Romance/Paranormal

DEDICATION

This book exists because
Ebrill first imagined it
And my family never stopped believing in it.

From the farmlands of Iowa and the Blue Ridge Mountains of North
Carolina, to the plains of Texas and the sea cliffs of Pacifica,
this generational tale was built on the framework of a loving,
beautifully complex family.

Ivey and the Airship is dedicated to the memory of

Richard Ammeter

Syvalia Owen

Etta Owen

Brandan Owen

Bill McEvoy

Rachel Hasler

TABLE OF CONTENTS

~

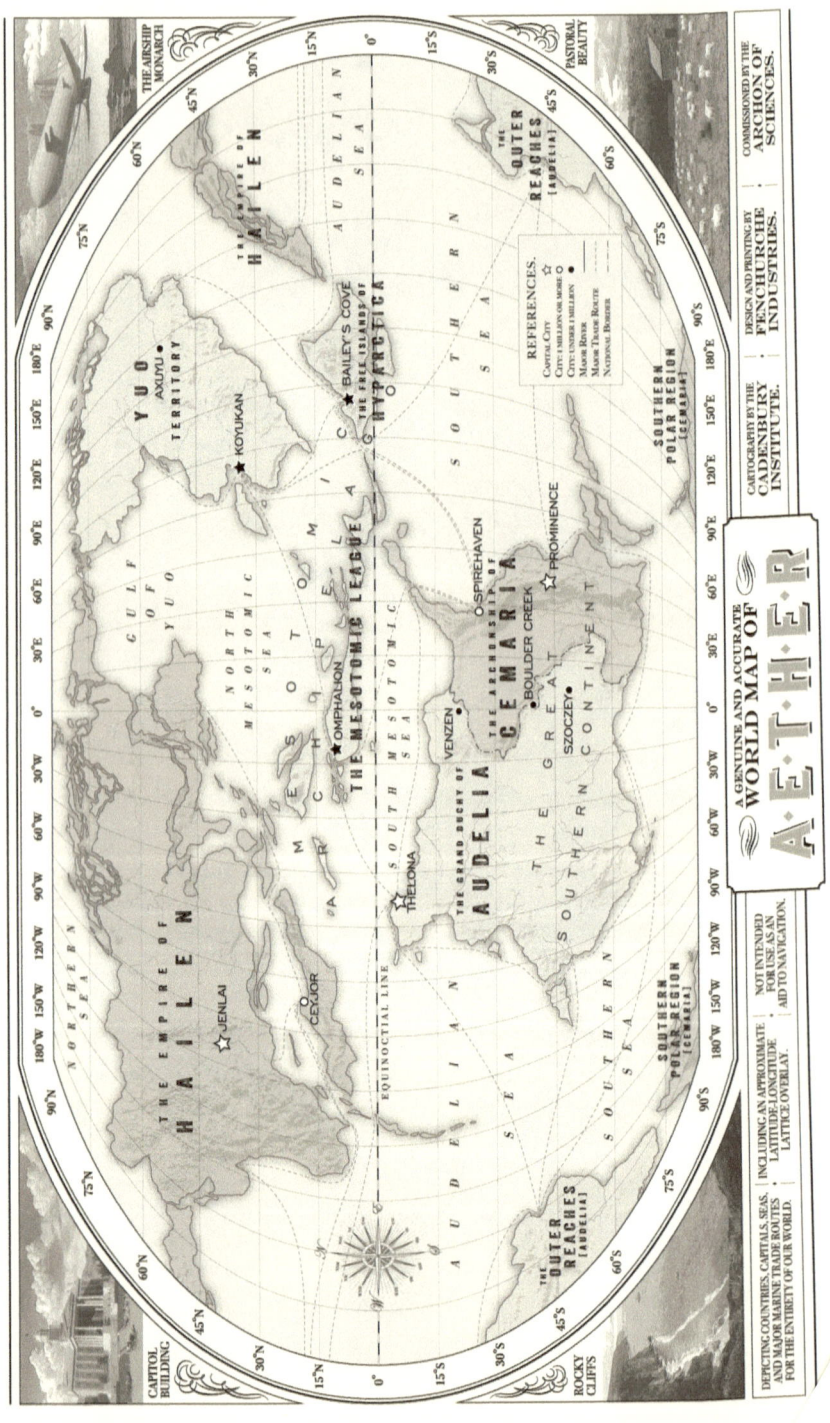

A GENUINE AND ACCURATE
WORLD MAP OF
A·E·T·H·E·R

THE AIRSHIP
MONARCH

PASTORAL
BEAUTY

CAPITOL
BUILDING.

ROCKY
CLIFFS

DEPICTING COUNTRIES, CAPITALS, SEAS, | INCLUDING AN APPROXIMATE | NOT INTENDED
AND MAJOR MARINE TRADE ROUTES | LATITUDE-LONGITUDE | FOR USE AS AN
FOR THE ENTIRETY OF OUR WORLD. | LATTICE OVERLAY. | AID TO NAVIGATION.

CARTOGRAPHY BY THE | DESIGN AND PRINTING BY | COMMISSIONED BY THE
CADENBURY | FENCHURCHE | ARCHON OF
INSTITUTE. | INDUSTRIES. | SCIENCES.

REFERENCES.
☆ CAPITAL CITY
☆ CITY 5 MILLION OR MORE
● CITY UNDER 1 MILLION
— MAJOR RIVER
— MARINE TRADE ROUTE
····· NATIONAL BORDER

THE EMPIRE OF
H A I L E N

THE EMPIRE OF
H A I L E N

YUO
TERRITORY

AKAYU ●

KOYUKAN ★

G U L F
O F
Y U O

NORTHERN
SEA

N O R T H
M E S O T O M I C
S E A

M E S O T O M I C

A R C H I P E L A G O

SOUTH MESOTOMIC
SEA

SOUTH MESOTOMIC SEA

THE MESOTOMIC LEAGUE

OMPHALON ★

THE FREE ISLANDS OF
H Y P E R T I C A

BAILEY'S COVE ★

A U D E L I A N

S E A

S O U T H E R N
S E A

THE
OUTER
REACHES
[AUDELIA]

VENZEN ●
OSPREHAVEN ●
THELONA ☆

THE GRAND DUCHY OF
A U D E L I A

THE ARCHENSHIP OF
C E M A R I A

BOULDER CREEK ●

PROMINENCE ☆

SZOCZEY ●

T H E
G R E A T

S O U T H E R N
C O N T I N E N T

SOUTHERN
POLAR REGION
[CEMARIA]

JENLAI ☆

CEYJOR ●

EQUINOCTIAL LINE

A U D E L I A N

S E A

S O U T H E R N
S E A

SOUTHERN
POLAR REGION
[CEMARIA]

THE
OUTER
REACHES
[AUDELIA]

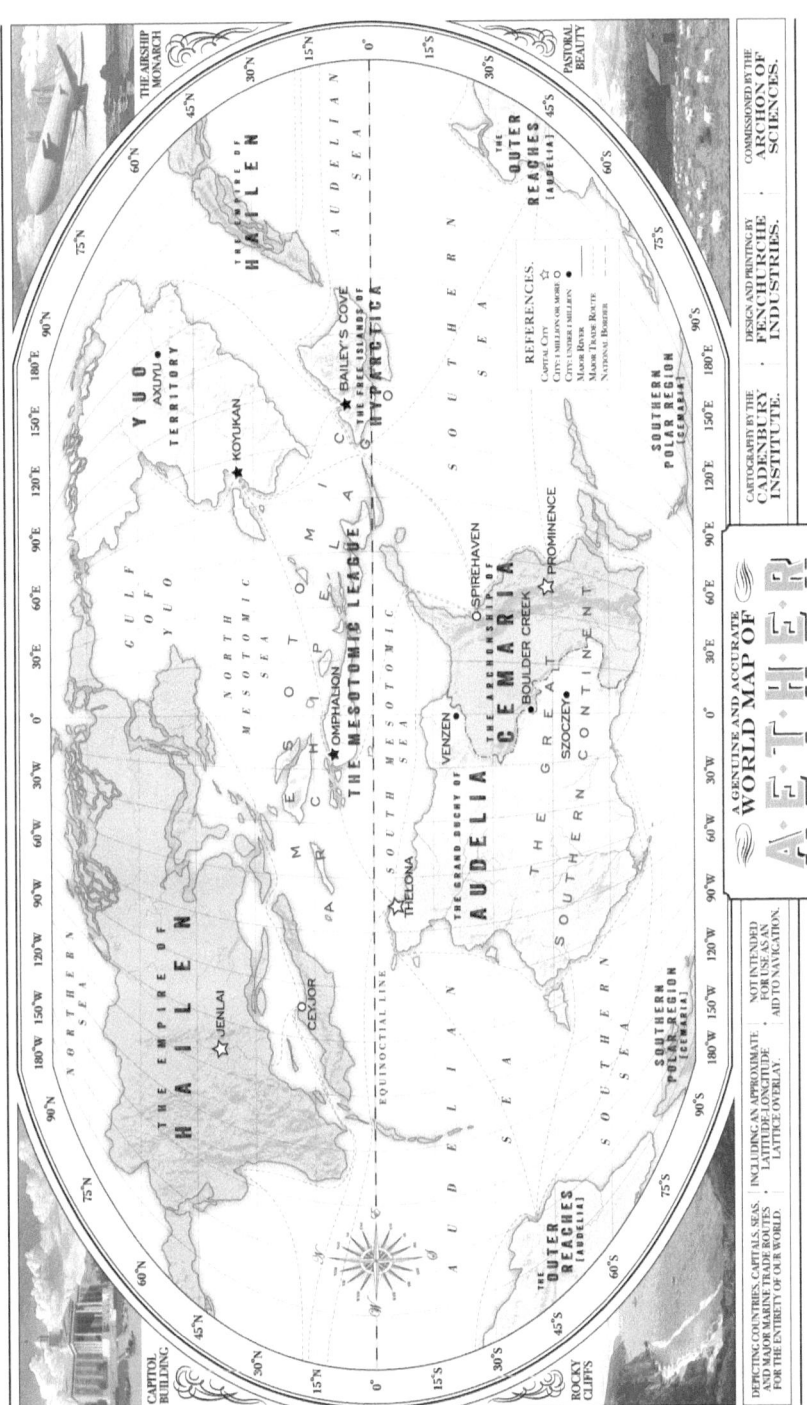

A GENUINE AND ACCURATE
WORLD MAP OF
AETHER

THE AIRSHIP
MONARCH

CAPITOL
BUILDING.

ROCKY
CLIFFS

PASTORAL
BEAUTY

THE EMPIRE OF HAILEN

JENLAI

CEXJOR

NORTHERN SEA

MESOTOMIC ARCHIPELAGO

MESOTOMIC SEA

GULF OF YUO

NORTH MESOTOMIC SEA

SOUTH MESOTOMIC SEA

YUO TERRITORY

AXUYU

KOYUKAN

THE MESOTOMIC LEAGUE

OMPHALION

BAILEY'S COVE

THE FREE ISLANDS OF HYPNOTICA

AUDELIAN SEA

SOUTHERN SEA

THE GRAND DUCHY OF AUDELIA

THELONA

VENZEN

THE ARCHENEMY OF CEMARIA

SPIREHAVEN

BOULDER CREEK

SZOCZEY

PROMINENCE

THE GREAT SOUTHERN CONTINENT

AUDELIAN SEA

SOUTHERN POLAR REGION [CEMARIA]

THE OUTER REACHES [AUDELIA]

THE OUTER REACHES [AUDELIA]

SOUTHERN POLAR REGION [CEMARIA]

REFERENCES.
CAPITAL CITY
CITY 1 MILLION OR MORE
CITY UNDER 1 MILLION
MAJOR RIVER
MAJOR TRADE ROUTE
NATIONAL BORDER

THE EMPIRE OF HAILEN

90°N 75°N 60°N 45°N 30°N 15°N 0° 15°S 30°S 45°S 60°S 75°S 90°S

180°E 150°E 120°E 90°E 60°E 30°E 0° 30°W 60°W 90°W 120°W 150°W 180°W

EQUINOCTIAL LINE

DEPICTING COUNTRIES, CAPITALS, SEAS,
AND MAJOR MARINE TRADE ROUTES
FOR THE ENTIRETY OF OUR WORLD.

INCLUDING AN APPROXIMATE
LATITUDE-LONGITUDE
LATITICE OVERLAY.

NOT INTENDED
FOR USE AS AN
AID TO NAVIGATION.

CARTOGRAPHY BY THE
CADENBURY
INSTITUTE.

DESIGN AND PRINTING BY
FENCHURCHE
INDUSTRIES.

COMMISSIONED BY THE
ARCHON OF
SCIENCES.

Chapter One

WILD CREATURES

I vey Thornton was six years old the first time she died. Born with an insatiable sense of curiosity, the daring girl had ventured alone into Thornhall Pond one summer day. As always, she'd made a solemn bargain with herself: if she merely waded along the pond's mossy banks, she wouldn't be breaking her parents' rule about not swimming unattended.

The youngest Thornton girl had always felt more at home in the primeval waters of the pool hidden behind her family's estate than she did within the old stone mansion. Thornhall Manor usually bustled with her mother's endless chores and the social obligations of her three older sisters. In contrast, the pond was peaceful and private—yet for Ivey, it was teeming with excitement just below the surface.

That day, she paddled gently along the water's edge, letting her hands and feet brush across the smooth surface of stones and reeds. As the sun climbed higher into the sky, a column of light pierced through the canopy of trees that circled the pond, illuminating the depths of a small cove at its far end.

That mysterious corner of her pond was forbidden. Even Ivey's father never took her swimming in the cove. His refusal to explain why only made Ivey's inquisitive fascination stronger. She liked to imagine that something special must be hidden there; perhaps a monster was lurking in its depths.

The sunbeam reached deeply into the shadowy water, and a small reflection from under the pool's surface caught her eye. Ivey's vow to remain safely by the pond's edge gave way to an intense desire to discover what was below.

She swam closer until the ring of warm sunlight spilled all around her. Looking down, she saw what looked like the remains of a sunken tree. The branches beneath her swayed in the current of her kicks like withered arms reaching up to snatch at her legs.

The glimmer of light she'd seen was coming from a mark on the underwater tree's gnarled trunk. The mark resembled a symbol made of lines and curves, like the letters in the books her father was teaching her to read.

Ivey had a strange feeling that the old tree was part of the cove's secret.

It was dangerous to linger near its tangled branches, but the little girl couldn't bring herself to return to the shore. She swam in circles like an insect around a flame, while the shaft of daylight crept along the bottom of the cove. The angle of the sun grew shallower, and soon the mysterious mark had all but disappeared into the darkness. Desperate for one last glimpse, Ivey dove under the water.

She pushed through the twisted limbs and swam toward the mysterious symbol. The sharp branches snatched at her bathing clothes and dug into her skin. Before she could reach it, the light faded, and the water grew frightfully dark.

Ivey tried to turn and make her way back to the surface, but the limbs tightened around her. The harder she struggled to escape, the more hopelessly she became entangled within the tree's clutches. It felt as if a lifetime had passed before her panic gave way to surrender.

She had no recollection of what followed.

Just before evening, Ivey's shoes were discovered at the pond's edge. Her mother's screams reached the estate's gardens.

Ivey's father sprinted down the path and plunged into the water. He instinctively made for the branches of the sunken tree and wrestled his child free.

Ivey's mother collapsed when he carried the girl's limp body from the water and laid it on the mossy bank.

To their astonishment, Ivey opened her eyes and coughed up water. Her parents wept with joy to discover their fourth daughter had survived unharmed.

Neither one suspected how long Ivey had been trapped below the pond's still surface.

❧

Years had passed since that incident, and Ivey was once again trapped beneath the water. Her heart pounded, and her lungs begged to exhale, but even a single bubble might give away her hiding place.

Suddenly, the ripples in the water changed.

The attack was coming from behind. She turned and pressed herself against a sunken log as a dark form streaked toward her. It veered at the last moment to avoid crashing against the solid wood at her back.

Ivey seized the moment to propel herself from the pond's bottom to the fractured light above. She broke the surface and gasped for air, her head immediately followed by an enormous pair of jaws. She surged backward to evade the nightmarish creature's teeth, then dove forward and gave the thing a heavy smack between its bulging eyes.

"Easy, Beast! You've gotten too big for this game. If you bite off my leg, you'll end up in a cage with all the other brutes at the Curiosity Exchange."

The creature responded by drawing its head back into the water and braying a sound of regret.

"Oh, you old pup." Ivey scratched the thing's rubbery head. "I know you'd never hurt me."

She could hardly believe how much the beast had grown since her father had brought him back from an expedition into the wilderness of Aether's northern hemisphere.

The little beast had caused a stir when Arvel Thornton presented it at the Cadenbury Institute of Sciences. No one, not even the experts, had known how to classify the bizarre specimen.

Ivey ran her hand down the side of his scaly body. Even though he had the long, fat tail of a reptile, his oddly shaped head, with its stubby ears and rounded snout, looked more like that of a mammal.

At the time of his capture, her father had classified the creature alongside a variety of large salamanders he called waterdogs. Some at Cadenbury claimed the beast was a mutated walking fish, while others proposed he was a descendent of the ancient creatures that had inspired the legends of dragons. The only thing the review panel agreed on was that the little devil should be kept under close observation in the Institute's Curiosity Exchange.

Ivey felt it was too cruel to lock the tiny beast away in a glass tank, so the night before he was to be removed from the aquarium in her father's study, she'd slipped him out and released him into her sanctuary—Thornhall Pond.

Ivey suspected her father had purposely overlooked her role in the disappearance, and since the beast had such a talent for hiding, she'd mostly managed to keep his residence on the estate a secret.

The bond between girl and beast had grown quickly. Although Ivey did not agree with the keeping of pets, this particular creature seemed as happy to have her as she was to have him. As far as she was concerned, he was a better companion than any of the simpering lap dogs her sisters paraded around in front of visitors to the estate.

Eagerly inciting their underwater duels, the creature was every bit as rambunctious as Ivey was. Her mother would have been horrified at the vicious battles that raged between the two, but Ivey never worried that her companion would hurt her—at least not intentionally.

"What are you two doing?"

Ivey looked up. Her little sister Iris was standing at the bank of the pond, wearing a worried frown.

"What does it look like we're doing, silly?"

"Hiding." Iris crossed her arms. "Mother sent me to find you. She says it's time."

"Well, it can wait until I'm good and ready."

Ivey gave the beast a pat and whispered, "Don't worry, my friend. She's not getting away with this. One way or another . . . we're staying together."

Her reassurance prompted the waterdog to make his happy sound, something of a cross between a foghorn and a rusted axle.

She clasped her hands across his gaping jaws. "Shhh! You'll give us away."

With a soft grunt of apology, the beast sank back into the water's depths and vanished.

It was too late. Ivey heard her mother's voice calling from Thornhall's veranda.

"Ivey . . . Ivey Thornton! Are you down there?"

The pond was at the bottom of a meandering path behind the manor. The water's surface was mostly hidden from view by the surrounding timber and a tall stand of reeds, but Winora Thornton's hearing was exceptional.

"Remember, Iris, no matter what happens, not a word about Beast," Ivey whispered.

The child put a finger to her lips and nodded seriously.

A moment later, their mother rounded a bend in the path. Her hands were on her hips, and her cheeks were flushed with annoyance.

"Have you taken leave of your senses, Ivey Thornton? Today of all days?"

Winora's tone was harsh. Ivey's penchant for disappearing when her presence was required had always been a source of contention between the two. "What in Aether are you doing in that filthy pond?"

"Oh . . . I was . . . just singing."

Iris stifled a giggle.

"That was hardly singing. You would have a lovely voice if you bothered to use it properly. I don't know what you're up to, but I want you out of that water and in the house immediately. You barely have time to get dressed for your engagement party, so hustle your bustle, miss."

"Yes, Mother," Ivey sighed as she and Iris followed their mother up the flower-lined path. There was no escaping it now.

Her mother was a fiend when it came to schedules. Despite her soft blue eyes, fair hair, and serene features, Winora was relentless in her pursuit of domestic perfection. It seemed to Ivey that her mother's only purpose in life was to serve and adore her husband. She rarely argued with Arvel, and they never let the sun go down on their anger.

According to Winora, when men gave orders and women accepted them gracefully, the balance of marital bliss was achieved. In Ivey's mind, her parents' happiness had more to do with her father's generous nature than her mother's obsession for obedience. For a Cemarian man, Arvel was quite happy to let his wife run the household, especially while he was away for work or on one of his expeditions.

Having achieved such perfect balance in her own marriage, Winora was now compelled to turn her five daughters into dutiful wives in their own right. For the most part, her efforts had succeeded. With the exception of one, the Thornton girls were well known in Cemaria's capital city of Prominence for possessing great charm and gracious manners.

Ivey didn't care that she was angular and socially awkward. She believed her curiosity about the world of natural science and her knowledge of its workings made her perfectly suited to follow in her father's footsteps.

Winora impatiently tapped her foot as Ivey made her way to the veranda. "Hurry your pace, or you will not be presentable when the Fenchurches arrive. How many times have I told you that first impressions do not get second chances?"

Ivey rolled her eyes. "Mother, they won't be here for hours, and frankly, I don't care what some la-di-da Fenchurche thinks of me."

Winora gasped. "I beg your pardon. This is the most important day of your life, Ivey Thornton. If you cross me, there will be consequences. Your father expects you to make every effort to be ladylike and compliant."

It was aggravating to hear her mother put words into her father's mouth, but Ivey rarely challenged the woman on such matters. Today she had little to lose.

"Oh, really?" Ivey jutted out her defiant chin. "We'll see about that. Where is Arvel?" She knew that her habit of using her father's given name greatly irritated her mother.

"Are you referring to your father?"

"I need to speak with him."

A strange, concerned expression crossed her mother's face. "He's in the lower garden."

"Thank you." Ivey grabbed her robe from the wrought iron railing and covered the immodesty of her wet bathing clothes. She resented the changes her body had undergone when she "blossomed into womanhood," as her mother would say.

Thankfully, her frame was still too boyish and lean to be considered desirable by Cemarian standards. Ivey intended to depend on her wits and strength to survive in the world. To her, being handed over as a pretty gift to some strange man seemed like a fate worse than death.

"And, Ivey . . ." Winora said.

"Yes, Mother."

"After your chat, you need to come directly inside. No dallying. Your sisters have arrived to prepare you for the evening."

"Oh, joy," Ivey growled under her breath as she walked away.

Ivey considered her three older sisters to be little more than beautiful accessories on the arms of the self-satisfied men they'd married. She wouldn't mind that they willingly submitted to such a stifling lifestyle, but it was hardly fair that they were now trying to force it on her by claiming that Iris' future was at stake as well.

Ivey glanced at the forest where she'd spent many nights roving with the beast. Although they both enjoyed learning to track and capture their small prey, Ivey graciously left the spoils to her companion. After her mother announced the engagement plans, Ivey had briefly entertained the notion of disappearing into the woods until the whole affair had blown over, but running away was not in her nature.

Her father had schooled her in many arts for defending oneself from danger, and one thing they'd discovered over the years was that when faced with a chance to fight or flee, Ivey would always stand and fight.

On this day, the battle would be against her dear father. He alone held the key to the gilded cage that her mother called a suitable marriage. Ivey would have to convince him to set her free before things got out of hand.

At the garden gate, Ivey paused to gather her courage.

❧

Arvel Thornton spent a great deal of time in the estate's lower garden, observing and cataloging the extensive collection of plants he'd acquired on his many scientific expeditions. He was foremost among the researchers in Cemaria's academic community who discovered and classified unknown species of flora and fauna.

This type of work had been considered odd when Arvel was younger, but over the years, the demand for scientists able to collect, capture, and classify potentially dangerous new organisms from across the world had increased, making him a valued member of the Cadenbury Institute. Arvel and his colleagues were responsible for restoring Cadenbury's old Curiosity Exchange from little more than an antiquated museum to a modern facility with an ever-growing collection of worrisome living things.

Hearing soft footsteps on the path, Arvel turned, steeling himself as Ivey approached.

"There you are," he said lightly. "I was wanting to speak with you."

It was no one's fault but his own that this child was struggling to find her purpose in life. From the moment of her birth, he'd cultivated the differences he saw in Ivey. Although Winora firmly believed that naming her daughters after flowers would make them desirable picks for future suitors, Arvel had refused to let the poor little soul to go through life stuck with a moniker like Daffodil. Primrose, Camelia, and Lilac were all lovely names that shortened to Prim, Meli, and Lill for convenience . . . but Daffodil? What would her friends call her? Daffy? Dill? Arvel had insisted she be named Ivey after her delicate fingers had intertwined with his when he first held her.

Now he offered his hand, and she clung to it as she had on that first day of her life. Her expression was so worried and miserable that Arvel struggled to conceal his emotions.

"Have a seat." He gestured to the garden bench where they'd enjoyed many long conversations about his hair-raising exploits and adventures. As she settled herself, Arvel felt a sharp pang of regret for the choices he'd made.

From the wide-set turquoise eyes, to the deep, plum-colored hair framing her sharp features, Ivey was his child through and through. Her slim frame concealed the strength and stamina of an athlete, and she shared many of the inexplicable traits that had made Arvel a misfit as a boy.

As she grew, Arvel tested her potential in everything from academics to combat, and the girl never failed to amaze him with her ability to succeed and survive. He had done it knowing his wife would disapprove. Now it was his daughter who would pay the price.

Before he could speak, Ivey began her appeal.

"I have a plan, Arvel. Please hear me out before you respond."

He sighed, and Ivey plunged in.

"First, we both know perfectly well that I have no business getting married. I would make a miserable wife, and I promise you, any man who treats me like his property will soon become even more miserable. If I'm not allowed to make my own decisions, I will suffocate. I honestly believe that my destiny is to follow yours and explore the world. So make the arrangements, and I'll study at Cadenbury. You taught me about science and nature—and I'm not ashamed to say that I'm intelligent. Plus, I have your constitution and more endurance than twenty boys my age. You said so yourself, and you always tell the truth. With your help, I believe the board of trustees would make an exception for me. I'll pass every test and make you proud, Father. I promise."

Arvel looked away. He reached into the pocket of his jacket and withdrew a letter.

"Everything you said is true, darling, except you couldn't make me any prouder than I already am. I knew this day was coming, so I made an inquiry to the Institute on your behalf." Arvel gently placed the letter in Ivey's hands. "We have an answer, and it will not change."

Ivey's face fell as she read the terse reply to the request.

The Cadenbury Institute of Sciences is not in the practice of educating women. There will be no exceptions.

Never one to accept defeat, Ivey had come armed with a better plan, ready to present it to her father.

"Very well. Let me work for you directly. I can classify plants and animals and track anything that leaves a trail. I have your instincts, and I can take care of myself. You know I'm not afraid to fight anything that poses a risk. After all, you are the one who taught me."

Arvel's face grew serious. "That was my selfish mistake, Ivey. I enabled you, encouraged you to act like a son. It was self-indulgent and unnatural, and if I could take it back, by my heart, I would. I regret the pain it's causing you now, more than I could ever say."

Ivey took in a short breath. "But it's all I've ever wanted. Please—"

"My world is no place for a young lady. I cannot allow you to choose a path that leads to disaster. Someday you'll understand why I have to say no."

She shook her head in disbelief. "No?"

"That is my final answer. You must accept it."

His harsh tone brought tears to her eyes. Arvel gathered her into his arms.

"Why do I have to be so unnatural?" she sobbed against his shoulder.

Patting her on the back, Arvel whispered softly, "Because I'm the king of all things peculiar. You come by it naturally."

His odd combination of humor and bluntness usually disarmed his daughter's anxieties, and this time was no exception.

She snickered against his chest and looked up with a glimmer of hope.

"Father, you can't let Mother send me away. Who but me would laugh at your silly jokes?"

He gently brushed a clump of wet hair away from her cheek. "There is something else you need to know, Ivey. I was the one who arranged this marriage."

His revelation left Ivey speechless, and Arvel pressed on. "I want you to experience the kind of love I found with your mother. You think you'd be happy doing my work, but darling, I won't be here forever. Someday, you'd wake up and find yourself alone in the world, and that is worse than anything you might imagine. Trust me. Maddox Fenchurche was my dearest friend until the day he died. I think his son has many of the same qualities that made Maddox so likable. His estate is beyond belief, and you will be safe there, Ivey. You might even be happy if you give it a chance. That's all I'm asking of you."

Ivey's expression went from confusion to curiosity, finally settling on defiance.

"Nowhere is safer than here—with you."

"Won't you even try? For me?"

Ivey thought for a moment. "Explain what you mean by giving it a chance."

Arvel spoke carefully. "The wedding will not take place immediately. Take some months to visit the estate and make the acquaintance of Miles before you set that pertinacious mind of yours. Then, if you are certain that life at Ferndale is unbearable, I will bring you home."

Ivey jumped to her feet and clapped her hands with joy. "Oh, Arvel! Thank you, thank you, thank you! I knew you wouldn't desert me."

Arvel held up his hand. "Not so fast. First, you must promise to keep our conversation private. And you must make me believe that you will give Miles a chance."

Ivey solemnly held out her hand, and Arvel took it.

"I give you my word, and like my father, I always tell the truth. Even if others don't care to hear it," she added with a touch of bravado as she shook on the deal.

"Especially if others don't care to hear it," Arvel responded with resignation. "So, we have a suitable arrangement. Now, would you be so kind as to let your sisters prepare you to meet your betrothed?"

Ivey's nose wrinkled. "Honestly, Arvel, do you have to use that ridiculous word?"

"No." He gave her a sly smile. "I think fiancé has a much better ring. And just this once, can you try to be cooperative for your mother's sake?"

Ivey gave her father a delicate curtsey. "It would be my pleasure, sir."

Before leaving, she threw a little challenge over her shoulder.

"I know how you capture those wild creatures you bring home. You make the cage look inviting, comfortable, and then you sit back and wait . . . and in the end, they trap themselves. I'm sorry, Father. I may be a little too clever to fall for that kind of trick." With that, she skipped up the path, reminding Arvel that, in many ways, she was still his little girl.

Once she was out of sight, he quietly confessed, "I'm sorry too, Ivey."

He looked around for the piece of paper on which he had forged the rejection letter, but it seemed to have vanished. Arvel searched the surrounding grounds and flower beds, but unable to find it, he left empty-handed.

Behind him, Ivey's beast, with the letter crumpled in his mouth, crept out of the flowers to bury his stolen prize in the woods. The creature's hide changed into an inky silhouette that hushed into the shade while Ivey's father strode up the path toward the manor.

These were troubling times, and now that Arvel's plan had been set into motion, other serious work required his attention.

Chapter Two

THE FENCHURCHE MISFORTUNE

Minnette Fenchurche sat in the parlor of the Imperial Hotel's finest suite. In her hand, she clutched a letter that proved her son was looking to escape his responsibilities once again.

The door opened, and Miles entered with a folded newspaper under his arm. He laid it on a side table. "If you're feeling better, I'll have them send up a breakfast tray. Doctor Brendel says you should eat before taking your medicine."

"Your concern is touching."

He looked into her eyes. "Is something wrong?"

"Why don't you tell me? I had your black tailcoat cleaned for the engagement party. They found this in the pocket." She held out the letter. "Would you care to explain?"

Miles' face flushed. He ran a hand through his hair and looked around the room.

"Well, I'm waiting."

"What do you want me to say, Mother?"

"Explain why a young man who's about to marry and settle down needs confirmation for a journey to the other side of the globe, to a place so savage that traveling there is unwise at best and life threatening at worst."

"Such visits can result in trade negotiations and sharing of information."

Minnette nearly laughed. "Are you trying to paint this as a business excursion?"

"No." Miles' expression hardened. "Mr. Belden is experienced in traversing the Empire of Hailen. He's been leading these tours for years without incident, and I've always wanted to see that part of the world for myself. I'm curious about the way they live."

"And die?" Minnette rose from her chair. "We have no trade negotiations with the Empire of Hailen because the people are barbaric, and their technology is crude. Hailen has nothing to offer Fenchurche Industries."

"Mother, I was speaking about myself. For once, I'd like to go to a place where my name means nothing. I don't need a host of tutors and managers planning and protecting my every move. I want to live like a person, not the figurehead of a corporation."

"When your father died, you became Fenchurche Industries, Miles. It all rests on you. Will you ever understand that? This company was built with your great-grandfather's sweat and blood. When your grandfather took over, he made it the biggest enterprise in Cemaria. Your father's inventions changed the world. And now it's your turn. What will your contribution be? You can't leave a mark if you never take aim. Stop dreaming about being a man, Miles, and start acting like one."

Miles slammed his fist against the tabletop.

"How can I do that, when every minute of my life you've treated me like a frail child?" He walked over and snatched the letter from her hand, ripping it in half.

"Miles, mind your behavior."

"No. Not this time, Mother. I have no desire to marry, and if I ever do, I will damn well choose the woman for myself."

Miles turned and went to the door.

"Where do you think you're going?"

"To Hailen," he called over his shoulder as he stormed out.

Minnette shouted after him. "Do that, and it will be the death of me—and the Fenchurche legacy."

The door slammed shut.

Minnette took a faltering step forward.

"Miles?"

ॐ

The governing district of Prominence was an excellent place to take a calming walk. Miles strolled aimlessly below the heavy marble facades that lined the lazy bends of the Naiadan River until he came upon a stone bench at the water's edge. There he sat for a long time, thinking about his future.

His plans had never included marriage. Aside from money, Miles had nothing of significance to offer a wife. He could only imagine what the Thornton girl had been promised.

He wasn't a dashing figure. His skin had a pallor that came from the many hours spent in dimly lit libraries and laboratories, and his shoulders sloped from hunching over his work. The bevy of young socialites that fluttered around his family estate often complimented his looks, but he knew their eyes were dazzled by his wealth.

If given a voice in the matter, Miles would choose a solitary life, one in which he could pursue ventures that enriched the mind, not the family coffers. After so many years of isolation, he saw no point in trying to force an emotional bond with a strange woman. Even if he did, such a relationship would bring endless opportunities for conflict with his mother.

In his whole life, he'd only known one individual whom he might consider a friend, but out of fear of Minnette's retaliation, neither of them dared acknowledge the fact.

As the sunlight cooled, Miles wadded up what was left of his confirmation letter and threw it into the river. He rose to his feet and started back.

His mother had not been well for some time, and her perpetual stress was taking a toll on her heart. Whether Miles liked it or not, Minnette was all he had, and without her guidance, he could destroy the family's legacy.

∿

Minnette had nearly worn a path across the hand-knotted rug in the suite's parlor. Her assistant had been out half the day looking for her son. It wasn't unusual for Miles to retreat in the face of conflict, but as the afternoon dragged on, she worried that this time he might not return. The hour of the engagement party at Thornhall was drawing near, and if Miles refused to play his part, Minnette stood to lose much more than her dignity.

She pressed the heel of her hand against her forehead, trying to erase the jagged thoughts that tormented her existence.

Her late husband's empire rested on the shoulders of a callow heir and sickly widow. If the Fenchurche name came to an ignoble end, the blame would be hers alone.

From the time of her youth, Minnette had been groomed toward an arranged marriage designed to bind her father's shipping company to Fenchurche Industries. She and Maddox had barely returned from their long honeymoon when Alistair Fenchurche succumbed to an illness, leaving the family's fortune in her new husband's hands. Maddox accepted the responsibility willingly, but because he was an only child, it was Minnette's duty to replenish the family estate with many hardy heirs.

Though she was petite, Minnette held a fierce desire to excel in her role as mistress of Ferndale Manor. As a girl, she'd learned to use her dark beauty and cunning intelligence to impress those who mattered and command respect from those who didn't. The one thing she hadn't been prepared for was Maddox's simple desire for her to be happy and carefree.

Minnette stopped pacing as the bittersweet memories of those early days washed over her. Maddox had been blessed with fair hair, fine features, and sea-green eyes that were impossible to resist. It hadn't taken long for her to give in to his unorthodox way of thinking. When he invited her to accompany him to the workshop and try her hand at engineering, she had resisted, but Maddox believed they were destined to work side by side. Under his gentle tutelage, Minnette discovered that she was a natural architect, and soon her ideas were as practical as they were beautiful.

They settled into a cheery routine at Ferndale and awaited the arrival of their first child. Tragically, complications during the birth nearly ended Minnette's life—and her son's. There wasn't a healer in all of Aether who could help Minnette escape the heart-wrenching outcome: her first baby would also be her last. All hopes of a large family were shattered, and it was more than Minnette's pride could bear.

Her guilt quickly evolved into bitter resentment. Ashamed of the scars on her body and driven by the scars in her heart, she'd started to lock her bedroom door at night. She began to lash out at her servants for any infraction of her ever-multiplying rules.

As the years passed, Maddox gave up on their marriage and turned his attention to Miles. When he tried to take the boy out to see the world, Minnette responded by locking Miles away in his nursery. She knew it was unreasonable, but she couldn't escape a dark foreboding that her son would suffer the curse of an untimely death, as had so many young Fenchurche heirs before him. That sense of dread bordered on madness after her husband had been killed in a horrible mining accident.

A sob escaped Minnette's throat. Her hand flew across her mouth to stifle the sound of her relentless pain.

"Ma'am? Did you need something?"

A stout woman peeked out from behind one of the suite's bedroom doors.

"Yes, Lucey Sue," Minnette replied hoarsely. "I'm going out. Prepare my son's black tailcoat and trousers. If Dolan returns with him, do not let either of them leave this suite before my return. Is that clear?"

"Yes, ma'am." The maid curtsied. "I'm sure all will be set right soon."

"We will accept nothing less." Minnette gathered her skirt and swept out of the room.

Inside the lobby, Miles hesitated. The thought of meeting Ivey Thornton on the eve of their betrothal was nothing short of terrifying. A drinking man might have made a straight line to the lounge, but Miles had never been able to find courage in a bottle.

He walked toward the music parlor. The musicians had not arrived for the evening, so he took a seat at the grand piano and began to play. Starting with a simple warm-up etude required by his music tutors, he soon lost himself in an odd tune that had haunted him since it first entered his mind. The theme was dreamy and sad with undercurrents of danger. He'd come to sense a promise of adventure in its climbing melody and faulty harmonic intervals. Each time he played it, he imagined the same setting.

Hailen.

∾

Minnette pulled a lever to call the hotel's elevator. Compressed gas churned in and out of a series of cylinders and valves, sending a colorful stained-glass car floating up the narrow shaft. The elevator's glazed doors quietly slid open. The metal casing surrounding the passenger compartment bore a distinctive filigree in floral patterns.

She swallowed hard. This design had been one of her final collaborations with Maddox.

After stepping inside, she carefully arranged her long skirt around her. The doors closed and the car glided down the shaft, pausing for the guests who came and went. One or two greeted her, but Minnette's mind was on her son.

It was too late in the day for an appointment at Cadenbury. She wondered if he'd gone to oversee the Zephyr Project at Honeycutt Mechanical. More than likely, her son could be found moping about in some library or museum.

Miles' suppressed emotions used to make managing his affairs easier, but now his woeful lack of spirit could thwart Minnette's determination to restock the family's bloodline. He had no interest in finding a proper wife, especially not among the pedigreed young ladies Minnette had proffered.

Minnette disembarked on the ground floor and walked without any particular destination until she heard a familiar tune echoing through the bustling lobby. She clutched her chest and followed the sound.

∾

Miles didn't have to look up from the piano to recognize the staccato clicking of his mother's boot heels crossing the parquet floor.

"Why do you insist on playing that pathetic music?" Her voice cut through his melody like a knife.

Without missing a note, Miles answered, "It suits the occasion, don't you think?"

She laid a hand on his shoulder. "Let's see how far you can test my patience today, Miles."

Miles stopped playing. "That was not my intention, Mother." He set his hand atop hers.

Minnette sighed. "You're agreeable with the arrangements then?"

As a young boy, Miles had learned that his mother's sanity hung on his responses to her demands. When he was old enough, he'd escaped this torturous relationship by convincing his tutors to send him away to study everything from music to medicine to metallurgy. But no matter how far he roamed, he was doomed to return to Minnette.

"If it is what you wish, Mother," he replied flatly.

"Tell me, Miles, what do you wish? I make no more efforts to guess."

"Honestly, it doesn't matter. I am Fenchurche Industries." Seeing his mother's struggle to retain her composure, Miles rose from the piano and offered his arm.

"You look tired. Let me take you back to the room so you can rest. Primrose is planning an elaborate dinner, and she's promised an evening we shall not soon forget."

∾

Chapter Three

First Impressions

"Prim, are you are trying to kill me?" Ivey whined as her sister jabbed a hairpin into the back of her scalp.

"Please sit still," Prim replied through tightly clenched teeth.

Primrose was the eldest Thornton sister, and behind her angelic expression lurked a temperament every bit as stubborn as Ivey's. In spite of the fact that she was growing heavy with child, Ivey knew that Prim would single-handedly drag her through the evening's formalities if need be.

"If you hadn't run around with wet hair flying to and fro, this wouldn't be so difficult. Another minute and we'll be ready for your gown," Prim said. "Wait until you see it, Ivey . . . it is a dream come true."

"Who dreams of such things?" Ivey muttered.

"Oh, dear," Prim doubled over, clutching at her side

"Is something wrong?" Ivey jumped up and turned to her sister.

Prim's eyes were shining. "Not at all. I've never had a baby kick this hard. I just know we're finally getting a boy."

Ivey seized the opportunity. "Oh, you poor thing. Why don't you lie down, and let me finish this myself?"

Prim's eyes narrowed. "Ha. Don't even think about it, Ivey Thornton. I'm not resting a finger until you are properly engaged. And if everything goes well, it won't be long before you finally accept your true purpose in life." She patted her rounded belly and gave Ivey a crooked smile.

Ivey shuddered at the thought. This would be her sister's fourth child in six years of marriage. If things continued at this rate, Prim and her husband would spawn a veritable army of squalling brats.

There wasn't a mothering bone in Ivey's body. When her little nieces and nephews came to visit, she avoided their sticky hands and drooling mouths. She'd much rather wrestle with the beast than with her sisters' little monsters.

As if reading her mind, Prim teased. "Trust me, there are things about marriage you'll learn to enjoy, Ivey. How many children do you want?"

Ivey's earnest attempt to be patient was beginning to slip.

"If anyone cared about what I want, I wouldn't be forced to take part in this ridiculous engagement."

Prim threw down the hairbrush in exasperation. "Ivey Thornton, you are the most selfish person I have ever known. Have some consideration for your sister. If you become a spinster, what will happen to poor little Iris?"

Ivey stamped her foot. "I'd be doing poor little Iris a big favor. There's more to life than marriage, Prim."

The notion that her younger sister couldn't marry unless she did was absurd. Since the older girls left home, Iris had begun developing her own independent spirit. She'd met the beast one day when he'd come leaping out of the water, pretending to attack. The poor little girl had nearly fainted, but after Ivey explained that the formidable monster was nothing more than an overgrown puppy who needed protecting, Iris had taken quite a liking to him and had sworn to keep him a secret. At least Ivey had the comfort of knowing that her sister would look after the beast while she was away.

Prim rattled on while Ivey did her best to ignore her.

"It's bad enough that you roam around dressed in men's clothes like some kind of wild savage, but now you mean to ruin Iris' reputation, too. People talk, Ivey. You don't know how many times I've had to make excuses for your behavior. If it were not for me, I sincerely doubt Minnette Fenchurche would have thought twice about letting her son marry someone like you."

Ivey's cheeks flushed. "Someone like me? I guess it's a shame she can't have you for a daughter-in-law then, isn't it? Is it possible that you've finally grown tired of your husband's bloviating?"

Prim's face flushed in return. "Do not be insulting, Ivey. I. Absolutely. Adore. My. Husband." She emphasized each word with a tug, and Ivey grimaced as her sister wrenched her hair into an ornate arrangement of pins, curls, and braids.

"And since you brought it up, my husband is involved in a critical project with Fenchurche Industries, so I have every right to be concerned about our social standing with the family. Stanley suggested that I put my best foot forward to assure Minnette Fenchurche that bringing a Thornton girl into her family would be a sound investment. Now she expects you to meet the standards I have set. Disappoint her, and Honeycutt Mechanical might suffer the consequences."

Ivey had precious little regard for Stanley Honeycutt or his consequences. Some years older than her sister, he was paunchy and balding. Ivey was annoyed by his obnoxious habit of patting his wife's waist to ensure that everyone knew that she was his property. In Ivey's opinion, wealth and connections were no compensation for his lack of substance, but Prim doted on every word that fell from his porcine lips.

"Don't you have any idea how ridiculous your life is?" Ivey asked.

"You may not care about Stanley, but Minnette Fenchurche is a board member at the Cadenbury Institute of Sciences. She could make things difficult for Father as well." Prim crossed her arms with a self-satisfied smirk. "Do you really want to drag his good name through the dirt?"

Using Arvel as a weapon against her was the last straw. Ivey's eyes glittered, and hot blood raced through her veins. Her skin prickled as if lightning were about to strike.

Prim took a step backward.

In times like these, Ivey feared that deep inside, she was every bit as dangerous as the beast. She took several long, deep breaths to calm herself, and the urge to strike slowly ebbed, leaving the two women in an uncomfortable silence. The tension was broken when the door to Ivey's room flew open, and the remaining Thornton sisters hurried in with the gown.

Lill carried the dress on an elaborate hanger while Meli and Iris kept its long train from dragging across the floor. Ivey could tell that the gown's iridescent fabric was a shade of turquoise meant to match her eyes. A laced corset with pearls and crystals accented a daring neckline and slim waist. The sleeves were full at the top, and they tapered to narrow, buttoned cuffs at the wrists. Lace overlays and heavy glass beading covered the train.

Ivey marveled at how quickly Prim recovered her ladylike mask of composure. "Isn't this delightful?" she sighed. "It came all the way from Spirehaven and was fashioned by the most sensational designer in Cemaria."

"A Fitzroy?" Meli asked.

While Meli and Lill responded with "oohs" and "ahs," Iris gave Ivey a wry shrug.

"Indeed," Prim said. "He only dresses the best, but Minnette Fenchurche asked him to make room in his schedule for our Ivey."

Ivey mocked her older sister's declaration with a sugary tone. "Oh, Prim, it is a dream. Why . . . it's so beautiful, I think I might swoon. Do catch me, Iris, or I will surely fall and bruise my delicate bottom."

Iris snickered, but Prim took her taunt and returned it with a vengeance. "Oh, Ivey, I knew you would adore this dress. I gave the designer one of your old dresses so he could fit your size, and he suggested that we add extra padding to the bosom and hips to make a good impression on your future husband. Hopefully, Miles won't be too disappointed on your wedding night."

"I don't give a precious damn what he—" Before Ivey could finish the string of curses coiled on her tongue, the older girls pulled the gown over her head. "Hey—watch it—easy—" Her complaints were stifled by a mouthful of crinoline.

After Meli and Lill forced her arms into the sleeves, Prim laced up the back of the corset.

Ivey tugged at the front neckline, trying to cover herself.

Meli playfully slapped her hand away. "Oh, Ivey, don't be so shy. This dress really gives you a figure."

"And it's high time you put some feminine assets on display," Prim goaded her.

"That hardly seems ladylike," Ivey retorted.

"Hush." Prim grabbed the laces and cinched the corset so tightly that Ivey groaned in pain. "Give me a hand with this bodice, Lill. The laces at the bottom aren't meeting properly."

They struggled and tugged so hard that Ivey had to grab Iris to keep from being pulled over backward.

"Good heavens, this is complicated," Prim complained.

"Are you sure that's the way it's meant to be laced?" Lill asked.

The buttoned cuffs were already digging into Ivey's wrists, and now her torso was so constricted that she could hardly speak. "Prim—too tight—can't breathe," she gasped.

"Really? Then don't waste your breath complaining," Prim replied flippantly. "Oh, it is perfection," she purred as she finished securing the laces. She turned Ivey around so she could admire her reflection in the full-length mirror by her vanity. "What do you say?"

Ivey barely recognized herself. "Grotesque," she wheezed.

"It is not," said Meli.

Iris giggled. "I think you look silly."

"Pay her no mind, Ivey. You've finally found your hourglass," Meli said.

"Remember when we looked like that, Prim?" Lill, who'd recently welcomed her second baby boy, laughed. "It will be some time before my corsets regain that degree of perfection."

In the mirror, Ivey saw her mother enter the room. Winora's hands flew to her cheeks.

"I would not have believed this possible. The gangly cygnet has become a swan." Winora rushed over and gave her daughter a robust hug. Ivey yipped as a sharp pain tore through her side, but her mother didn't seem to notice.

"The Fenchurche carriage is coming up the drive, so everyone take her place. Prim, you and I will make the introductions. Meli, I want you to serve the refreshments. Lill and Iris can provide musical entertainment to set the stage for bride's grand entrance." Winora turned to Ivey. "Remember, dear, you only get one chance to make a first impression on your groom. Please make it memorable."

As Winora hustled everyone out of the room, Prim lingered to give Ivey a last instruction: "Wait here 'til I come for you."

"Please . . . get this off me," Ivey's voice rasped. The constriction of the corset seemed to be worsening with every breath.

Prim reached into a small pocket hidden in the seam of her gown and withdrew the key to Ivey's bedroom door. She held it up before whisking out of the room and pulling the door shut behind her. As the lock clicked, Prim called through the door, "Mother put me in charge of you for a good reason, sister dear. I will be back when the timing is perfect, and if you muss your hair or wrinkle that dress, you will be sorry."

Ivey felt the walls closing in on her. "Prim," she gasped, "it's my life. Don't—"

"Ivey!" Prim shouted through the locked door. "When will you learn? Life is not about getting your way. We all say and do whatever it takes to survive. And by the way, you might like to know that your intended is just as miserable about this marriage as you are. I heard he ran away from the Imperial Hotel earlier today. Luckily for you, Miles Fenchurche can always be counted on to do whatever it takes to satisfy that abominable mother of his. Now grow up and act like a lady or so help me..." Her voice trailed off as she walked away.

Ivey kicked the door and rattled the knob. "Prim? Come back!" As soon as the words left her lips, the corset tightened like a snake around her ribcage. She leaned her forehead against the door and considered her options. There was another way out of her room, but it would be risky.

✺

Miles saw his mother's nose wrinkle as she took stock of Thornhall's decor. He knew what she was thinking, and as usual, he disagreed. The furnishings were simple and elegant, nothing like the outlandish ornamentation at Ferndale. Instead of sprawling wings, the Thornton's manor house had a long series of parlors, drawing rooms, and dining areas bisected by a large foyer with a winding marble staircase to the second floor.

Winora Thornton was gracious, and her golden-haired daughters were more than socially acceptable. When Primrose boasted about the nursery upstairs overflowing with their collective little ones, he saw the first glimmer of approval on his mother's face.

While the ladies engaged in parlor talk, Miles hung back, carefully avoiding eye contact. Women like Prim and their idea of polite conversation left him dazed. In situations like these, he'd found the best thing to do was to blend in with the furniture and wait the evening out.

When Prim's husband, Stanley Honeycutt, entered the room, Miles knew that would not be possible.

In their few business dealings, Stanley had come across as overbearing, always on the verge of the next great discovery. The one nice thing about having a conversation with Stanley was that it could be completely one sided, and the man either didn't notice or didn't care.

Miles was relieved to catch sight of a little girl waving him over as she entered the drawing room. He assumed she was the youngest Thornton daughter, as she had Winora's fair hair and icy blue eyes. Something in this girl's smile was different, though—it seemed to radiate from within, unlike Prim's, which was meticulously posed as if she were continually sitting for a portrait. He went to the child immediately.

"Hello, Miles," she said. "I'm Iris. Oh bother, I was supposed to call you Mr. Fenchurche."

He found her youthful candor refreshing. "How about this? You can call me Miles if I may call you Iris," he spoke softly.

"Please do." Iris stared into his eyes with an odd expression. It appeared she'd lost her train of thought.

Miles finally spoke, "Was there something—?"

Iris blushed. "Oh, yes . . . I, uh . . . forgot. My father asked me to show you to his study." Iris leaned forward and spoke with great seriousness. "He wants to have *the talk*."

"Oh, I see." He bent toward her. "Sounds serious."

Miles had temporarily forgotten the reason for his visit. His stomach lurched at the prospect of having "the talk" with the father of a girl he was being forced to wed.

He'd met Arvel Thornton on a few occasions, and thankfully, there was something reassuring about the man. Miles didn't hold many memories of his own father, but somehow, he'd imagined that Maddox and Arvel would have had much in common.

Miles had a small amount of hope that Arvel's fourth daughter would be more like Iris than like Prim. He took a deep breath and offered her an arm. "I guess I'm as ready as I will ever be. Please, lead the way."

As they left the drawing room, Iris said, "At least you're ready. Prim had to lock Ivey in her room to keep her from running away."

Miles stopped walking. The poor girl was being dragged to the altar as well. "Really?" He tried to sound casual. "How interesting."

"Well, that's what Prim said, but she was just being mean," Iris stammered. "Oh, bother . . . Prim isn't mean, she just thinks Ivey will ruin the night."

There was much more going on in this household than Miles had anticipated.

They arrived at the study door, where Iris took one last stab at explaining the situation.

"Ivey has to be the bravest girl in the whole world. My sister never runs away from anything. So, maybe you could just pretend you didn't hear what I said. All right?"

The worried look in the girl's eyes touched Miles. He took her hand and gave her a slight bow. "Iris, it just so happens that I'm an expert at that."

She giggled in relief and gestured for him to enter the study. "Good. I like you. Maybe Ivey will too."

Miles almost smiled. "I certainly hope so."

As he stepped into the room, he felt a strange sensation, as if a small portion of the weight he'd been carrying had lifted.

"Mr. Thornton, you wished to speak with me?" Miles tried to sound confident as he entered the room and approached the handsome desk where the man of the house sat jotting notes into a leather-bound book in front of him. When Arvel looked up, his expression of concern turned into disbelief.

"Was there a misunderstanding?" Miles asked, uncomfortable in the piercing gaze.

Arvel sighed and snapped the book shut. "My apologies. For a moment, you looked like someone else."

Miles had heard this many times before. He offered a slight smile as he extended his hand. "Did you know him well, sir?"

Arvel nodded as he rose to take it. "Your father was my one true friend. I look forward to getting to know his son now. I haven't seen you in years, Miles. You have really grown up."

Miles stepped back, glancing at his feet. He feared it wouldn't take long for Arvel Thornton to discover that the son could not measure up to the father.

"Please have a seat and let's talk about the arrangements," Arvel said. "I'm going to ask you to swear an oath, and there are things you need to know about my daughter and her secrets, but first I'd like to discuss the real reason you're here."

Miles sat straight, his heart beating faster. This was not at all what he'd expected.

"You see, I need your help," Arvel said.

Miles leaned forward. "Go on."

"I understand you met Stanley Honeycutt and Nicolai Slate while working on the Zephyr Project at the Fenchurche plant in Spirehaven."

"Yes, but I spent most of my time with the Fenchurche fabrication team."

"Well, there's an offshoot of the project in the works at Honeycutt Mechanical in Prominence. Have you heard anything about the *Boreas*?"

Miles shook his head. "No."

"It's highly confidential," Arvel explained. "Stanley has been appealing to your mother for the funding needed to accelerate this project, but it seems that her business manager wants to wait and see how your Zephyrs sell before taking the next step. I have to convince her otherwise."

"Oh. Changing my mother's mind is no easy task."

"I know, and I wouldn't involve you in this, but it's a matter of life and death. The success of this project could help me on a dangerous venture that I've been asked to undertake."

"What kind of venture is that?"

"I'm not at liberty to say more, but the request came from the Chief Archon's office."

Miles found himself holding his breath.

"While I'm away on this mission, I need you to protect my daughter. And Miles," Arvel paused, "there is a possibility that I might never return."

Arvel folded his hands and stared directly into Miles' eyes.

"So, is there anything a man could do to help get the funding needed to start the work at Fenchurche Industries?"

Quite unexpectedly, Miles found himself saying, "Yes. I will personally take charge of this project, Mr. Thornton."

"And your mother will agree to that?"

"There's no need to involve her. I think it's time I made my mark. After all," he set his jaw, "I am Fenchurche Industries."

∽

Since her younger years, Ivey had been adept at escaping from her bedroom to shorten punishments or join the beast for moonlit adventures. Her window overlooked the veranda's roof, and from there, she could leap onto the branch of a nearby tree and climb down the ropes of a swing hanging from its limb.

There was no time to lose. With every breath, her corset was becoming tighter, and the lack of air was making her dizzy. She made her way to the window, the train of the dress dragging behind her like a beaded anchor.

She raised the window, sat on the sill, and gathered the flowing skirt into a thick bunch. She crawled out and held the fabric tightly as she picked her way across the stone tiles. When she neared the edge, she gathered herself and took a running leap, releasing the fabric to grab a tree branch as she landed on the limb.

Not bad, considering this poor excuse for clothing.

As if responding to her unspoken insult, the train of the dress went taut. A section of the hem had wedged between the tiles at the edge of the roof, tethering Ivey to the house. She tried to pull it free, but the train wouldn't budge.

The corset's deathly grip had her head swimming. Ivey jerked as hard as her failing strength would allow, trying to tear the fabric. Unfortunately, this was a finely made garment designed to withstand the perilous environs of civilized society.

~

In Arvel's study, the conversation had turned to his daughter's unique personality when Miles noticed something odd through the window facing the back garden. For a moment, it looked as if a peacock were perched high on a limb in one of the trees. Miles blinked and looked again, realizing that it was a girl in a blue gown.

"Forgive me, Mr. Thornton," he interrupted. "There's a lady in your tree."

Arvel turned to look where Miles was pointing. "My word, that's Ivey. What is she—?"

They both came to their feet and watched as Ivey gave the dress a fierce yank. A tile broke away from the roof, releasing the train. The weight of the beaded fabric pulled Ivey so far backward that the branch she was holding snapped.

She pitched headlong out of sight.

"Miles. Have my wife send for the doctor." Arvel raced from the room and disappeared down the hallway.

Miles ran back toward the parlor. The first person he met was Iris. He did his best to explain the situation without frightening the little girl.

"Will Ivey be all right?" Iris' lower lip quivered.

Miles took her by the shoulders and looked into her frightened eyes.

"I've studied medicine. I can take care of her until the doctor arrives. Now go tell your mother. And hurry."

Iris dashed off, and Miles fled back down the hallway until he came to the open door that led to the rear of the property. He sprinted around the corner of the house and stopped short, his mouth agape.

In front of him, a terrifying monster with blood-red eyes and sizable talons was holding Arvel at bay while his daughter lay facedown in a low wooden trough filled with mud.

The thing snarled and gnashed its long teeth at Miles.

"Hey you!" Miles waved his arms, hoping to distract it while Arvel crept forward.

The beast sensed Arvel's movements, and a ridge of sharp spikes rose along its long, sinewy spine. The creature hissed and slowly flicked its tail as it turned and advanced.

"What should I do?" Miles could barely speak.

"Stay still. I think it's protecting her." Arvel's voice was soft and low. "I'll get my gun."

Arvel backed away until it was safe for him to turn and run.

Meanwhile, the girl was sinking into the muck inside the trough. If left unattended, she would asphyxiate.

Miles held his hands out and crept closer.

"It's all right . . . easy . . . that's a good . . . thing." He thought it was working, until the thing sprang forward, knocking him onto his back. Its sharp claws pinned his shoulders down while the monster sniffed at his face. Miles held his breath.

Apparently it didn't care for his scent. The creature threw back its head and roared.

"No!"

The youngest Thornton had appeared on the veranda. "Bad, Beast! Don't hurt him," she screamed.

"Iris! Stay away!" Miles warned, but the girl ran right up to the monster and gave it a shove.

"Get off."

Like a guilty dog, the beast hung its head and stepped back.

"She needs him. You go hide. Now," Iris commanded.

It whimpered, then turned and vanished into the trees while Miles scrambled to his feet and ran to the trough. He'd been taught never to move victims of serious accidents, but the girl would smother if he didn't get her out. He rolled her over and scooped her out of the sticky mess, then laid her on the grass.

"Miss Thornton?" Miles frantically scraped the tarry substance away from her nose, and wiped it on the side of his jacket. "Iris, help me clean off her face so she can breathe."

Iris grabbed the hem of her skirt and furiously scrubbed her sister's face.

As Ivey's pale skin and sharp features emerged, Miles experienced a fleeting sense of recognition. She reminded him of an old doll the gardeners had dug up when he was a boy. He'd rescued it from the dustbin and painstakingly restored the figurine, intrigued by the untold story of a little girl's toy that had been lost in the soil behind Ferndale.

Miles patted her cheek.

"Miss Thornton, can you hear me?" He leaned over and put his ear close to her face and listened. "I don't think she's breathing." He felt her neck, searching for a pulse.

"Is she dead?" Iris choked.

Miles shook his head. "Not if I can help it."

He tilted Ivey's head back, opened her mouth, and pinched her nostrils shut between his fingers. After inhaling deeply, Miles placed his lips over hers, laying his other hand across her ribcage. He expected to feel her abdomen rise when he emptied his lungs into hers, but it didn't. He blew into her mouth again with greater force, and then again with the same results. He sat back on his heels to think.

"Why did you stop?" Tears welled in Iris' eyes.

"If her lungs ruptured . . ." Miles paused. He didn't have the heart to tell Iris that her sister might be beyond hope.

She searched his eyes. "Miles, you are supposed to save her."

Miles looked down. "I'm not sure what's happening. The air isn't going into her lungs."

Iris grabbed his sleeve. "It's the corset. They tied it too tight. Ivey said she couldn't breathe."

Miles grabbed the neckline of the gown, and tried to rip it open. The structure of the bodice contained many layers and a good deal of boning. It may as well have been armor. He rolled her onto her side, hoping to undo the back laces, but the tight and muddy knots were too much for his trembling hands.

Arvel ran up, tossing aside the gun he was carrying while dropping to his knees. "What are you doing?"

"This dress is suffocating her. Do you know how to remove a corset?"

"Put her on her back," Arvel said as he grabbed a curved knife from an inner coat pocket. He flipped the knife open and sliced through the front of the dress without so much as nicking the silk camisole underneath. Iris helped pull the boned fabric apart while Miles leaned over and forced several deep breaths into Ivey's parted lips. This time he felt the rise and fall of her chest. He stopped to see if she was breathing. There was nothing. After many long attempts, Miles finally looked up at Arvel.

"I'm afraid she went too long without air."

"Ivey, please . . . don't leave us. Not like this." Arvel gripped his daughter's hand tightly and bowed his head. "I'm so sorry."

Ivey wasn't sure where she was, but she no longer felt the panicked urge to breathe. She'd never been so peaceful.

A light flickered somewhere below her. A familiar voice called her name.

Ivey let herself be drawn closer. The light danced around her, inviting her into a hidden world. She opened her arms, ready to remember.

"No. She can't die." Iris sobbed over her sister's body. "Do something."

Miles felt an overwhelming sense of guilt. Ivey must have been desperate to escape their engagement. Iris said that her sister had never run away from anything. Would he be the first and only item on such a list?

He'd always known his life was a curse. Bringing him into the world had cost his parents everything. He hadn't even met his prospective wife, and now she was lying on the ground, muddied and lifeless. It had to stop.

"Damn it, Ivey Thornton. You will not die because of me." Miles leaned over and caressed her face. With a passion he had never before possessed, he breathed his determination into her still body.

He laid his head against Ivey's chest, listening for her heart's response. There was nothing but a cold silence.

He sat up, looking down at her pallid face.

"Give me a chance to know you, Ivey. Please!"

Ivey awoke with a strangled gasp. Miles watched as Ivey's eyes blinked down at her ravaged gown and then moved from her sister's tear-streaked face to her father's. Finally, her gaze met his own.

He had never seen anything as glorious as the spark of life in her turquoise eyes. His thoughts were completely scrambled, but his manners remained intact.

"Hello, Miss Thornton. I am Miles Fenchurche. It's a pleasure to finally make your acquaintance."

Her eyes burned into his. For the second time, he had the strange feeling that he'd seen her before.

She started to speak, but then—without warning—she sneezed, and every bit of the muck that had seeped into her nose was blown onto Miles' face.

The stunned silence was broken when Iris snorted rudely. Miles did something he hadn't done in years—he laughed. And then, with a girlish sigh, Ivey fainted.

Arvel grinned and gave Miles a pat on the shoulder. "Now that's how you make a lasting first impression."

Chapter Four

SISTERS AND WATERDOGS

Ivey awoke late the next afternoon, with Iris perched on the side of her bed, staring at her intently. When she tried to sit up, Ivey's body ached from head to toe.

She groaned. "What have I done now?"

"Not much," Iris said. "You just fell out of the swinging tree and—died. Then Beast tried to eat your fiancé, but I saved him, which was lucky for you because just like the prince in a fairy tale, Miles Fenchurche kissed you and brought you back to life."

Ivey was horrified. "Iris, stop making things up."

"I'd say she's got this one right."

Ivey saw her father leaning against the frame of her open doorway.

"Though she did leave out the part where you blew black slime all over the boy's face before you fainted like a perfect damsel in distress. It was quite the ruckus, Ivey, even for you." He chuckled. "How do you feel?"

"Everything hurts." She struggled to piece together her fragmented thoughts. "And my head is full of stuffing."

"Iris, go get your sister something to eat. She hasn't had a meal since all this began."

"What began?" Ivey rubbed her eyes.

"I'll be happy to refresh your memory, dear child." Arvel shooed Iris away. "This may take some time."

"Enjoy your talk, Ivey," Iris called over her shoulder as she bounced from the room.

Arvel pulled a chair to the bedside and sat down, reaching for Ivey's hand. "Where would you like to begin? Perhaps with the part where you attempted to flee and ended up diving backward out of a tree? Or we could discuss the vicious creature that appeared out of thin air to stand guard over you. Or maybe the fact that your engagement party ended with a distraught Minnette Fenchurche dragging her son off for a good disinfecting after we told her that he'd stumbled and fallen into a trough of fertilizer.

"And, you might also like to hear how your escapade nearly sent Prim into an early labor."

Slowly, things were starting to come back. "Father, Prim locked my door and I couldn't breathe. I had to escape from the dress. I swear I wasn't running away."

"I know. Prim accepts her blame in the matter," Arvel said. "She was horrified to hear that the gown was responsible for your accident. The doctor thinks that between the fall and the corset, you might have cracked a rib or two. At the very least, you took a good bruising."

Ivey touched her side, making sense of the racking pain. "I have no doubt that miserable garment was trying to kill me."

Arvel nodded sympathetically. "Luckily, you landed in my compost, because otherwise it may have succeeded." His voice grew serious. "However, that does not explain the presence of that enormous and vaguely familiar-looking lizard. According to Iris, he nearly killed Miles Fenchurche. Do you understand what a dire mistake it was to harbor a creature like that at our home?"

Ivey nodded soberly. "Is he all right?"

"Iris said he was very brave," Arvel answered. "I told Miles to wait while I got a gun, but he jumped to your aid empty-handed."

Ivey gasped in horror. "I meant the beast. Oh, Father. Did you shoot him? Is he—?"

Arvel shook his head. "Your little sister saved them both. It seems I have two rambunctious daughters and a monster roaming my property."

Ivey covered her face. "Beast isn't a monster. He just didn't know what was happening. What will happen to him?"

"We will deal with that later," Arvel said. "My concern is with you, Ivey. You nearly did it this time."

Ivey crossed her arms. "For pity's sake, Arvel, we've been through this before. If something can't manage to kill me, it only schools me in the art of survival."

Arvel gently stroked her cheek. "I know you're convinced that you have lives to spare, my dear, but this was different. You were about to leave us."

Ivey reassured him. "Father, you know I'm too stubborn to go anywhere until I'm ready, and I've got things to do." Ivey's mind was clearing, yet something nagged at the corners of her memory. "But there was something strange. A place I wanted to see. It almost felt like home."

Arvel hung his head. "You were at the brink of death. If it wasn't for Miles—"

"Good grief!" Ivey suddenly remembered the pale green eyes and serious face hovering above her exposed camisole. "Did that man tear off my clothes?" She clasped her chest in mortification.

Arvel shifted uncomfortably. "No, I did. But that's beside the point, Ivey. That man saved your life."

"By kissing me?" Ivey shuddered at the thought.

"He used a medical technique whereby one person can breathe for another. You should ask him demonstrate it when you get to Ferndale."

"Ferndale? After everything that happened?" Ivey pulled the covers close. "I would rather die than go there now."

Arvel crossed his arms. "The party may have ended abruptly, but your engagement is still on."

"Prim told me that Miles tried to run off yesterday, and his mother sounds hateful. How can I give him a chance if he doesn't want one?"

Arvel's face softened. "Miles gave me his word that you will be treated with kindness and respect while you're under his care. He isn't too keen on the idea of marriage, but things may have changed last night. Something lit up inside that boy. I believe his heart brought you back."

"Father, we're perfect strangers."

"Trust me, Ivey, love doesn't need an invitation. It happens in the blink of an eye."

"I don't see that as part of my future, and according to Prim neither does Miles."

"That remains to be seen, but saving you was a defining moment in his life. He finally has a chance to break free of his mother's misery, but he can't do that on his own. He needs you to show him how to live."

"I'm sure there are plenty of girls who'd be happy to show Mr. Fenchurche how to live."

"But there's only one like you," Arvel laughed. "According to ancient wisdom, when someone saves the life of another, that life becomes the rescuer's responsibility. So you and Miles are bound to each other now."

"I don't need any man to take care of me."

"Maybe in this case, Miles needs you. You are a clever girl, and he's a thoughtful boy. You'll teach each other things you never thought possible. In any case, we struck a deal, and I do expect you to honor it." Arvel's tone of voice indicated that the discussion was over.

"Fine. How about this? I'll agree to save his life, and then we can go our own ways."

"That would be wonderful, darling. Now get some rest. As soon as you are recovered, Miles has a little surprise for you."

"Surprise?" Ivey's left eyebrow shot up.

"He's decided to take you to Ferndale on his airship."

Ivey's eyes opened wide, and a smile stretched across her face. She'd been fixated on the possibility of taking flight since she was a moppet. Her favorite childhood game was pretending to soar through the air as Arvel swept her around the grounds, holding her high in his arms.

"Arvel, is that true?"

"Yes. The *Monarch*'s schedule is being arranged even as we speak."

Ivey squealed in delight. "The *Monarch*? I'm going to fly on the *Monarch*?"

"Indeed. You'll have six days aboard the ship of kings."

"Six? Isn't the flight to Spirehaven only two days?"

Arvel's eyes flashed with mischief.

"Somehow, word of your adoration of the *Monarch* reached Miles, so he's asked the captain to set a leisurely course that will afford the most astonishing views Cemaria's northern climes have to offer."

Ivey shook her head in disbelief. "Can he do that?"

"I suppose being a Fenchurche isn't all bad," Arvel mused.

Venturing aboard an airship was one of the greatest desires in Ivey's life. She'd dreamed of flying a small vessel of her own someday, but the

Monarch was no ordinary airship. It was the most glorious airship Aether had ever known: the jewel of the Fenchurche Cosmopolitan Fleet.

When the airship's plans were first presented, critics had claimed that Fenchurche Industries was sure to suffer a monumental failure. A ship of such excess would never get off the ground, the naysayers had crowed. The *Disreputable Times* had even run an exposé, calling it an outright fraud against the wealthy enthusiasts who were prepurchasing exorbitantly priced reservations. After months of wild speculation, the mechanical wizards at Fenchurche Industries had proved the doubters wrong.

Following the *Monarch's* maiden voyage, her passengers disembarked with rave reviews of the top-notch accommodations and service. Before long, anyone wishing to book a passage aboard the airship could expect to be added to the end of a year-long waiting list.

Now the legendary vessel was setting a course to Prominence, just for Ivey. She rubbed her hands against her cheeks to ensure she wasn't lost in a fantastic dream.

In spite of herself, Ivey sighed in anticipation. "How soon do I leave?"

Receiving no answer, Ivey glanced over at her father's face. His lips were smiling, but the expression in his eyes was distant and worried.

"What's wrong?"

He blinked, and chuckled. "I'm somewhat jealous. I think you're going to have a real adventure on that airship." Arvel leaned over and gently kissed Ivey's forehead. "Now, get to work on healing, and stay out of that tree." He rose to leave.

Ivey gave him an impish salute and then settled into her pillows as Iris entered with a tray of food.

It was dark outside by the time Ivey finished her meal. The two sisters chatted about the excitement of flying aboard the *Monarch* until Winora came to shoo Iris off to bed. Ivey tried to sleep, but her racing thoughts would not permit it.

The idea of lying unconscious with some strange man's lips pressed against hers was humiliating. Miles Fenchurche could not be responsible for saving her life.

Her memory of that moment was hazy, but she had felt a sense of peaceful acceptance unlike anything she'd never known.

Could he really have saved me?

Ivey dispelled the thought. She couldn't explain how it happened, but she was certain that she would have made it back on her own. She was no damsel in distress, waiting to fall into the safety of a man's arms. The sooner Miles Fenchurche learned about her true nature, the sooner he'd be happy to part ways.

She closed her eyes and concentrated on restoring her constitution. The next time they met, she would be back on her feet, standing strong and ready to make the right impression on Mr. Fenchurche and his mother.

∾

Two days later, Ivey crawled from her bed with a plan to convince Arvel that her oversized waterdog belonged at Thornhall. Because the doctor had forbidden her to engage in any physical activities, she'd extended an invitation to her little sister to perform with the beast. Iris was thrilled, and she changed into her bathing clothes right away.

Despite the girls' high praise of the creature's obedience and talents, Arvel's expression was one of skepticism as the three walked down the path to the pond. When they arrived at the water's edge, he held up his hands.

"Enough talking. Let's see what he can do. Call him, Ivey."

Ivey crossed her arms confidently. "No need. He's already here."

Arvel cast a wary glance around the area. He had a well-trained eye that easily spotted minute details others might overlook. Ivey smirked as he went from looking for the creature to listening intently. When that failed too, he inhaled deeply through his nose.

Arvel closed his eyes, loosened his shoulders, and stood quietly for some time.

Iris cocked her head and looked up at Ivey. "What's he doing?"

"It's one of those peculiar talents that Father and I have. If I tell you about it, will you keep our secret?"

Iris nodded. "I like keeping secrets."

"Very well." Ivey laid a hand against her chest. "All living things have something special inside. We call it our soul, the core element of life. Our ancient ancestors called it the pneuma biou."

"Pneu...ma...biou," Iris repeated softly. "I know what that is. It's the light inside us."

"Yes, in a way. All creatures' souls have their own essence—and if you know how, you can feel it radiating from their bodies into yours. That's how Arvel and I find creatures that don't want to be found. Watch."

They waited quietly until Arvel opened his eyes and walked toward a nearby tree.

"He's here—somewhere."

"You wouldn't know that if you hadn't cheated," Ivey teased.

Arvel gave her a pained look. "When you are tracking a dangerous beast, Ivey, the last thing you want to do is to be fair."

"The beast isn't dangerous, Father." Iris was the picture of girlish innocence as she stepped forward. "He's our friend. He would never hurt anyone in our family."

"We shall see." Without warning, Arvel grabbed his youngest daughter and threw her over his shoulder, the way he had when she was a toddler. Iris squealed and wiggled in response.

With a menacing hiss, the waterdog seemingly appeared out of nothingness, clinging to the trunk of the tree. He dropped to the ground in front Arvel, who jumped back so quickly it made Iris scream.

Ivey didn't move. To earn her father's trust, she knew the beast would have to pass this test on his own.

Arvel set Iris down and stood in front of her.

The beast's spines rose up from his back. A low growl warned of his intentions.

Arvel took another step forward and assumed an aggressive stance of his own. In a single, swift movement, he pulled the folding knife from his pocket and held it open in his steady hand.

"No—" Iris started to cry.

"Shhh." Arvel gestured for her to stay behind him.

Ivey held her breath, and Iris covered her face.

The creature let out another hostile rumble.

Arvel's eyes locked on the beast's. He moved forward with knife raised. "Back off before I strike."

The creature's tail twitched. Arvel's hand tightened.

"Please don't." Iris sobbed from behind him.

The beast looked to Ivey, who couldn't resist throwing him a clue by submissively dipping her head.

With a grunt, he plopped down at Arvel's feet, setting his blunt snout on the ground.

In spite of her injuries, Ivey ran to him and dropped to her knees.

"Well done, old pup." She hugged his thick neck and then grinned up at her father. "See? He's smart enough to know who's the master here. Aren't you impressed?"

Arvel broke into a grin of his own. "Very."

Iris peeked out from behind her father.

"Can I come out now?" she asked meekly.

Arvel pulled the shaking girl into his arms. "I'm sorry, darling. I didn't mean to frighten you."

"I wasn't scared," Iris softly replied. "I just don't want anyone to get hurt."

Arvel patted her back. "I know. You're a very brave girl," he said proudly. "Just like my big sister."

Ivey tried to rise, but the pain in her ribs made her stagger.

Iris rushed to help. "Poor Ivey. Do you want to go back to your room?"

"Not until you show Father more of your adventurous side," Ivey said.

"How?" Iris giggled.

Ivey gestured to the stand of reeds by the pond's edge.

"Go lie down over there." Once Iris was in place, Ivey pointed at the creature. "Hide her."

The waterdog tromped over and laid himself down in front of Iris. In an instant, his hide emulated the surrounding vegetation, causing the two to vanish from sight.

Arvel walked over and bent down to take a closer look. "I've never

seen anything like this before," he said thoughtfully. "His skin is mim-
icking the light from his surroundings."

"There's more," Ivey boasted. "Beast, show yourself." The waterdog
returned to his natural inky color, and Iris popped up from behind
him. "Now take her for a swim," Ivey commanded.

The waterdog obediently stretched out. He relaxed his spines so
they were flat against his hide, but Arvel was concerned. "Iris, are you
sure you're ready for something like this?"

Iris hopped onto the creature and wrapped her arms around his
neck with an exaggerated air of bravado.

"Just watch me," she giggled as the beast marched into the water and
began to swim away with her clinging to his back.

Arvel shook his head and gave Ivey a sideways glance. "Your mother
is right. Iris is spending too much time around you."

"Is that why you want to get rid of me?" Ivey was teasing, but her
father's face looked sad. She took his arm and laid her head against his
shoulder. "I don't have to leave."

Arvel sighed. "My mind is set. You need to discover life outside
Thornhall, but your creature may stay. We'll have to keep his existence
a secret until I'm convinced that he poses no threat to the community."

Ivey smiled. "Beast is wild like us, Arvel. He would die in a cage.
Now that you've met, he really is a part of our family."

Arvel nodded. "I could use his help."

Ivey's left brow went up. "Help with what?"

Arvel casually crossed his arms. "Research expeditions. Field tracking. The usual things."

Ivey studied his face. "If I didn't know better, I'd say you're keeping a
secret from me." She would have pressed for more information, but her
sharp ears heard footsteps.

"Beast, hide," she called out softly. The creature's skin transformed even
as he dove beneath the water—taking an unsuspecting Iris down with him.

Before anyone could move, Winora rounded the corner on the
path. "Ivey Thornton? What in mercy's name are you doing down
here again?"

She quickly joined them at the water's edge, casting an accusing glance at her husband. "Arvel, the *Monarch* arrives this week, and we can't have Miles delay the flight because Ivey made herself ill. Minnette Fenchurche needs no more reasons to suspect her son's fiancée in anything less than perfect condition. You said you would have her follow the doctor's orders."

"Yes . . ." Arvel nervously glanced at the pond. "And the doctor advised her to get plenty of fresh air . . . to aid the healing process. I assure you everything is under control, my darling."

Just then Iris sputtered back to the surface of the water.

"I touched the bottom!" Seeing her mother's shocked face, she tried to explain herself. "Oh, I was . . . just . . . exercising."

Arvel sighed with relief as Iris made her way out of the water.

"What's going on here?" Winora asked suspiciously.

"Arvel's just making sure that we both get plenty of fresh air and exercise. Isn't that right?" Ivey snickered.

Winora turned to her husband. "Is it?"

Arvel grinned like a boy caught stealing from a candy jar.

"I do what I can, my love."

As usual, the twinkle in his eyes melted Winora's worried frown into a smile.

"Yes, well, as long as you have things under control, *my love*."

She started to leave then turned back. "Oh, I nearly forgot. Stanley Honeycutt is in your study. He has news about something. I believe he called it the Zephyr Project."

Arvel started up the path. "Winora, if you would, please see Ivey back to her room. I shouldn't keep Stanley waiting." He hurried away.

Ivey couldn't believe anyone would be so eager to talk to Prim's husband. She would have asked him about the Zephyr Project, but Arvel was halfway to the house before she could open her mouth.

Winora turned to Ivey, "And you have a visitor, too."

Ivey cringed.

"No, it is not your young man," Winora chided. "Prim is waiting for you on the veranda."

Ivey's face clouded with doubt, but Winora gave her a gentle push. "Go on. And play nicely, Ivey." She took Iris by the arm. "And you, little miss, have some explaining to do."

As she followed her mother and sister up the path, Ivey chewed on her bottom lip. The last thing she wanted was to provoke Prim. Her baby wasn't due for a few more months, and Ivey was worried about what had happened the night of the party. Apparently she'd put the child in some danger. As she walked up the path, Ivey wondered where this feeling of concern came from. She'd never worried about the safety of Prim's girls, Meli's son and daughter, or Lill's two little boys, especially not before they were born. Now she had a small nagging in the pit of her stomach, the kind she felt when something wasn't right.

The afternoon's light sifted through a wisteria along the far side of the veranda where Prim was waiting. The woman never had anything less than a perfect smile on her face, and yet even she looked disquieted. Ivey cleared her throat as she approached. Prim jumped to her feet and rushed to give Ivey a hug so tight it made her grit her teeth in pain.

"Ivey, I'm so sorry. I never meant any harm," Prim declared as she held her close.

"It's all right," Ivey whispered, "but could you let go?"

Prim stepped back remorsefully. "Oh dear. It seems I'm having a hard time controlling myself these days."

"So you know how I feel."

Prim took Ivey's hand and led her to the table and chairs where a tall glass of tea was waiting.

"I will never understand you, Ivey, but it's no excuse. Dear sister, you have been nothing but mischief since the day you were born. Even as a small child, you did not care if something scratched, bit, stung, or burned. You had no fear of pain, punishment, or death itself, and you will never know how hard the rest of us worked just to keep you alive. But all the same, we adored you. Especially Father. When Iris told me how close you were to death, and I realized that it would have been my fault . . ." Tears fell from Prim's eyes as she hung her head.

"Prim. You know how Iris exaggerates things. I just knocked myself silly. Besides, I'm the one who should apologize. I would never forgive myself if anything happened to your baby."

Prim wiped her eyes and leaned forward with a conspiratorial air. "Between us, that was something of an exaggeration as well. After Iris told us about your accident, we had to act quickly to keep Minnette Fenchurche from finding out. I was the most likely to be in need of the doctor, so I pretended to have pains. Poor Stanley—before mother could tell him what we were up to, he feared the baby and I were in grave danger. He said he would do whatever it took to keep us safe. It was so sweet and romantic." Prim blushed.

Ivey could not imagine Stanley as anyone's hero, but she was relieved to hear that her sister's brush with disaster was as overrated as her own. It was beginning to look as if everyone in her family was keeping secrets these days.

"Oh, Prim, speaking of Stanley, do you know anything about the Zephyr Project that he came to discuss with Father?" She tried to sound nonchalant.

Prim set her glass down so suddenly that it clanked against the metal tabletop. "I can't say I know a thing. That is Stanley's business. What I can say, Ivey, is that it seems your brief encounter with Miles has already had a positive effect."

Ivey was stunned. "Tell me, Prim. How could anything good have come from that travesty of an engagement party?"

"Well, Miles has finally taken an interest in my husband's work. I don't mean to speak out of turn, but according to Stanley, Miles has never cared much about the management of Fenchurche Industries. Stanley says that Minnette is quite forceful in their meetings, but you would hardly know her son is in the room."

"He doesn't sound very thrilling," Ivey muttered.

"Ivey, please do not misunderstand. Stanley and I have attended many social functions with the Fenchurches. Minnette dominates every conversation, and while he is quite shy, I believe Miles could be charming if he ever got away from his mother. She keeps him on a leash so tight that no one can approach him."

Ivey blinked. "Then why in Aether would she force him to marry me?"

Prim leaned forward and spoke with a quiet ferocity. "Minnette is constantly complaining that there are no heirs for the family business, so Miles will have to get married and give her grandchildren whether he likes it or not. In truth, I think she will not be happy until he's as miserable as she is."

Ivey grimaced. "So I'm his punishment?"

"Dear sister, you may be his only hope. Father really believes that you are the one to put that woman in her place once and for all. To that end, I will teach you everything you need to know to impress her so you can help Miles without hurting Father's career. Or Stanley's."

Ivey had never heard Prim talk like this before. It was surprising and exciting. "Good grief, Prim. What has she ever done to you?"

"That woman has bullied my husband for years, and it drives me mad. I would love to see her knocked down a notch or two."

Ivey laughed. "Prim, have you always had this side to you?"

Prim's expression softened when she laughed. "I hardly know what's come over me lately." She rubbed her expectant stomach. "I think it's this baby. Something tells me that he will love to fight, just like his Aunt Ivey. Here, feel him kick."

Ivey was squeamish about touching her sisters' pregnant bellies to feel the thumps and bumps of the little creatures inside, but this time, she was curious. She timidly laid her hand beside Prim's and waited. There was nothing. She closed her eyes and let her hand slide down, pulled along by a peculiar awareness of the precious life within.

Hello, little one. What's it like in there?

The baby gave her hand a healthy kick. Ivey jumped.

"Prim, your baby, it's—" she stopped herself. "It's so strong." She knew it wasn't her place to say any more than that.

The sun was setting by the time Ivey returned to her room. She was tired, and her ribs ached from the day's activities, but her mind still raced with past few days' events. For better or worse, her life had taken a turn she'd never imagined. It was some time before she was able to relax. While drifting off to sleep, Ivey remembered the beautiful light she'd longed to embrace after her fall from the tree. She'd been floating so peacefully, while something had invited her to slip into a secret world.

Ivey might have remembered more, but a vivid dream carried the strange memories away. She was soaring through the clouds, the captain of a great airship making its way into the twilight sky.

∽

Arvel was preparing for a dangerous campaign. On his desk lay a new set of plans delivered by Stanley Honeycutt, along with the news that Arvel had been hoping for. Funding for the *Boreas* would be provided by a new division of Fenchurche Industries. Until the *Monarch* arrived in Prominence, Miles Fenchurche himself would be working with Arvel and the team at Honeycutt Mechanical to produce an amazing new type of flying machine.

∽

Chapter Five

THE ENGAGEMENT SATCHEL

With only one day left before the *Monarch's* arrival, Ivey could hardly wait to take flight. Prim had invested much time in coaching her to win Minnette's favor. With any luck, Ivey would be able to help Miles gain his freedom. She suspected the lessons were also meant to keep her from worrying too much about her engagement to the young man.

She had nearly finished packing her things when she heard a familiar knock on the bedroom door. She quickly buried in her trunk the trousers she had been folding. Her mother detested her daughter's penchant for dressing in Arvel's old clothes, and Ivey wanted to appear as cooperative as possible.

"Come in," Ivey said, busily arranging one of the more feminine dresses she was taking to Ferndale.

"Do you need any help?" Winora's voice was cheerful yet oddly strained.

"I think I'm ready."

"I think that you are, too." Winora looked down at her hands before she continued. "Ivey, please trust your father to know what is right for you. He would be greatly obliged if you would try to make the best of this situation."

"I am going to try, but from what I've heard, the Fenchurche family is most peculiar."

Winora laughed. "Peculiar can be delightful, you know."

Ivey set her hand on her hip. "And when did you ever believe in such a thing?"

Winora replied, "When I first arrived in Prominence, all the proper ladies warned me that Thornhall was a haunted place, inhabited by a deranged hermit who mucked around in the occult."

Ivey laughed. "Isn't that what they would say about me these days?

It's why I avoid 'proper ladies' who have nothing better to do than gossip about things they don't understand."

"Sometimes you have to make an effort to help them discover who you are, Ivey. Since I didn't know a soul in Prominence, I decided to listen politely and hope for the best."

"That's horrible. Why didn't your family come with you?"

"My parents knew that I would be in good hands. My father used to visit Thornhall when Arvel was a boy. In fact, your grandfathers were very close when your father and I were young, and it seems that somewhere along the way, they decided that Arvel and I were destined to be together."

"They decided? But how could they possibly know? Mother, what if it turned out that Father really was a deranged hermit? Things might not have ended so well."

Winora sighed as she sat on the edge of Ivey's bed. "Darling, things wouldn't have ended so well if I had chosen not to come here. Arvel was an only child and a misfit among his peers. After his mother's death, his father died of a broken heart. Arvel had no close friends to help him with his grief, so he shunned society and buried himself in his work. He truly was becoming a hermit, but my father intended to keep his promise to the Thorntons. When I turned sixteen, he brought me here to have a talk with Arvel."

Ivey knew where her mother's story was going. "Let me guess. Arvel didn't want to get married."

Winora smiled. "Well, that's what he said until we met face to face. It happened in the blink of an eye. I saw the man of my dreams, and he saw a woman who would fill his life with happiness. Giving him a family to love was my duty and my honor. It has made me happier than I ever could have hoped. I wouldn't want to go on living in this world without your father, and I know he feels the same way."

Ivey saw tears in her mother's eyes, but her mind was busily racing ahead. Before leaving, Ivey leaned down and gave her mother an usually tight hug.

"Thank you," Ivey said, finally releasing her.

"For what, dear?"

"For ignoring those busybodies and being brave enough to take a risk." With that, Ivey trotted off to find Arvel.

∾

Winora wiped her tears away and rose from the bed to leave. Something caught her eye. A familiar tuft of rough wool fabric peeked out from under the top layer of clothes in Ivey's trunk. She carefully slid the garment out, leaving no trace that the trunk's contents had been disturbed.

"Oh, Ivey," she sighed. "If a lady is going to charm the likes of Minnette Fenchurche and her son, a gentleman's trousers cannot be part of her wardrobe."

∾

Arvel looked up from his desk to discover Ivey standing a few feet away, watching him. She had his talent for entering a room unnoticed.

"I was expecting you," he said as he straightened up the papers in front of him. "Come sit down. Let's enjoy our last afternoon together."

Ivey sank into the chair near his desk with a dramatic sigh. "That sounds so final."

"You aren't being sent into exile. Think of this as the adventure of a lifetime. After all, you'll be flying first class aboard the *Monarch*. Even I haven't done that."

"I didn't come here to argue with you, Arvel. I'll keep my end of the bargain, but I have to know. Why me?"

Arvel knew Ivey's question went deeper than the details of the trip. "Of all my daughters, it was your destiny to become a Fenchurche."

"And when did you come that realization?"

Arvel had to look away from her keen eyes. He sat back in his chair, fully aware that she would leave his study with more information than he'd intended. "When you were just learning to walk." A memory from those early days flashed through his mind, causing him to chuckle softly. "Actually you never bothered with walking, my dear. You just got up and ran."

"How charming." Ivey leaned forward. "And still, I have to ask. Why me? You had two other daughters who were closer in age to Miles. Why not choose Lill or Meli?"

Arvel sighed. "You were so full of spirit. Maddox was quite taken with you."

"I met Maddox Fenchurche?"

"In fact, I remember you sitting in his lap, in that very chair, flirting with him. You nearly coaxed him into giving you his pocket watch. It was extraordinary."

"Arvel. I have never flirted in my life."

"So you say," Arvel laughed. "But you trailed him around the house like a little puppy for days. You adored him."

Ivey sat quietly for a moment. "Was his family here?"

Arvel's smile faded at the thought. "No. Minnette refused to let Miles travel in those days. Maddox was always alone."

Ivey cringed. "So why was he here?"

"He had to settle some things before he left on an important mission," Arvel's voice choked.

"Oh. The mine." Ivey's eyes lowered. "I'm sorry you lost a friend."

Her father looked away with a pained expression. "It was the last time I ever saw Maddox. Perhaps if I'd gone along, things might not have ended that way."

"From what I've read, no one could have survived that disaster. You would have died with him, and then I would have grown up without a father."

Arvel quickly changed the subject. "Maddox didn't come here to discuss that. He was concerned about his son. The boy was almost seven, and he had never been away from Ferndale. Not even to visit a friend, as Minnette strictly forbid him from having friends. She barely let him step outside to take a breath of air."

"What could you do about that?"

"Upon his return, Maddox planned to take the child away from Minnette. It would have been very difficult, and we were to provide Miles a safe place to stay until the matter was settled."

Ivey's eyes softened for a brief moment. "So how did I come to be mixed up in all of this?"

"That last night, before Maddox left, we sat up late and talked. He said he'd dreamed of having a little girl like you. I told him that I would have been thrilled to have a son like Miles. And then we realized it was destiny. Miles could be my son, and you would be the daughter Maddox longed for."

Ivey leaned back and folded her arms. "How perfect for the two of you. But I know my own mind. My destiny is to explore the world, performing thrilling deeds."

Arvel shrugged. "And what better way to do so than beside the man who owns the biggest transportation company in all of Aether? You could go anywhere your heart desires, and with great style. I daresay that travel aboard a ship like the *Monarch* could become routine."

Ivey blinked and sat straighter, then chewed her lip as she thought it over.

"Well, I've gathered that Miles Fenchurche is not the adventuring type. And if he were, I am sure his mother would put a quick stop to it."

Arvel smiled. "When a man loves a woman, he will move the heavens to make her happy, and he would trade his life for hers, trust me on that."

Ivey squirmed in her seat.

"Father, I will do what I can to make Miles less miserable, but falling in love is not part of our bargain. I'm not like Mother. I don't need a family to make me happy. All I've ever wanted is to take care of myself."

"That sounds familiar, my dear." Arvel set aside his papers. "However, I have no desire to argue with you. So tell me, how are you feeling? Are you ready for Minnette?"

"I shall pass inspection."

"Good. Then I have a going-away present for you." Arvel reached behind his desk and retrieved a leather satchel with a long strap. Ivey inched forward in her seat.

"This gift is for the adventures you will have in your new life."

Arvel opened the bag and withdrew its contents. First, he produced a spring-loaded dart gun. Its polished metal and glass design resembled the gun he himself carried, but this one was smaller—a perfect fit for Ivey's hand. Alongside it, he laid out a bundle of sedative cartridges.

Ivey laughed. "Those are for Madame Fenchurche, I take it?"

"Only in an emergency," Arvel smirked. "These are potent. They will make sleepy friends of sizeable animals."

Ivey gave him a quizzical look. "You said the Fenchurche estate was a haven of safety. Do they have a problem with wild bears, or does something wicked roam the grounds of Ferndale?"

Arvel looked at her sternly. "As far as I know, the only things roaming the grounds of Ferndale are the peacocks—at least until you arrive."

"Me?" Ivey asked innocently.

"I know how you slip away for nocturnal mischief. And I also know that if there is a dangerous thing within fifty leagues, it tends to find you, when you don't manage to find it first. I won't be there to watch your back, Ivey. You must be prepared for anything."

Arvel could see that his daughter was becoming intrigued. He hoped it would be enough to get her all the way to Ferndale.

"What else have you got in there?"

Arvel resumed pulling items from the satchel. "The usual effects: a compass, a rope. The rope is strong, light, and impossible to chew through."

Ivey grinned. "Most fathers give their daughters expensive jewelry or a parcel of land at a time like this."

"You are not like most daughters." Arvel emptied the rest of the contents onto his desk. "And we also have a tourniquet, healing balm, bandages, flint, chalk—"

"Chalk?"

"Luminous chalk, to mark a path when you enter a cave or deep woods. If you don't leave a trail, you'll be lost. Didn't I teach you that?" Arvel drummed his fingers on the desk to make his point.

"Of course," she replied humbly.

"Now, I've saved the best for last," Arvel said as he placed a folded knife in her open palm.

"I can't take it. It's yours."

"Look closely."

Ivy inspected the knife's handle, turning it over in her hands until she finally caught on.

"Ah, the luster is pristine. No nicks. It's never been used. Did you have a copy made?"

"No. It's a sister to the one I carry. I was asked to hold it until the time came. It's an engagement present."

"Really? Other than you, who would think to give a girl a knife as a wedding gift?"

Arvel quietly answered, "Maddox. He made the original for himself. Its performance was so perfect that he made me one as well. This knife was meant for Miles, but once Maddox met you, he decided that it was intended for your hand."

"So I was right in liking him," Ivey mused. "He sounds every bit as peculiar as you."

"Doesn't that make you wonder what his son is capable of?"

Ivey took the knife from her father's hand and flipped it open. "If anyone can find out, I suppose I can." Her eyes twinkled as she tested the point of the blade on her fingertip. She flinched as it pierced her skin, drawing a small bead of blood. "It's sharp." She closed it and flipped it open again, slicing through the air. "I like how it fits my hand."

Arvel leaned forward. "Promise me now that you will never use that weapon against someone unless it is absolutely unavoidable."

"Are you afraid I'll attack Mr. Fenchurche?" Ivey teased.

"No." Arvel sternly replied. "But if there comes a moment when life and death are held in a balance, you cannot hesitate. You must trust your instincts, Ivey."

Ivey's brow drew tight. "I don't plan on letting down my guard, if that's what you're worried about."

Ivey closed the knife and began packing the items scattered across the desk back into the satchel. When she finished, she stood up, slinging the main strap across her shoulder and fastening the smaller strap that held it securely across her back.

Arvel smiled. If only Maddox had lived to see the impish baby who stole his heart bloom into the graceful heroine standing before him.

Ivey patted her satchel.

"All in all, a good fit. Thank you, Arvel. I promise to use this gift wisely. Now, what do you say we go for a long walk to see if any vile thing out there is foolish enough to confront a pair of Thorntons armed with Fenchurche blades?"

∾

MONARCH
THE FENCHURCHE LINE

YOU ARE CORDIALLY INVITED
TO BOOK PASSAGE
ON BOARD THE

AIRSHIP MONARCH

DEPARTING FROM THE DOCKS OF

PROMINENCE

ON THE 21ST DAY OF THE 8TH MONTH

FOR A ONCE-IN-A-LIFETIME VOYAGE HOSTED BY

THE FAMILY FENCHURCHE.

THE VOYAGE INCLUDES THE FINEST DINING, INSPIRATIONAL VIEWS,
AND A GRAND BALL TO BE HELD ON THE 25TH,
THE PENULTIMATE EVENING OF OUR JOURNEY TO

SPIREHAVEN.

SOUTHERN
SEA

SPIREHAVEN

PROMINENCE

THE
ARCHONSHIP
OF
CEMARIA

THE PREEMINENT AIRSHIP

MONARCH

OF AETHER'S FAIR SKIES.

THE FENCHURCHE LINE

Fig. 1. EXTERIOR VIEWS OF THE GREAT SHIP IN FLIGHT CONFIGURATIONS.

Fig. 1b. BOW VIEW: WINGS DEPLOYED.

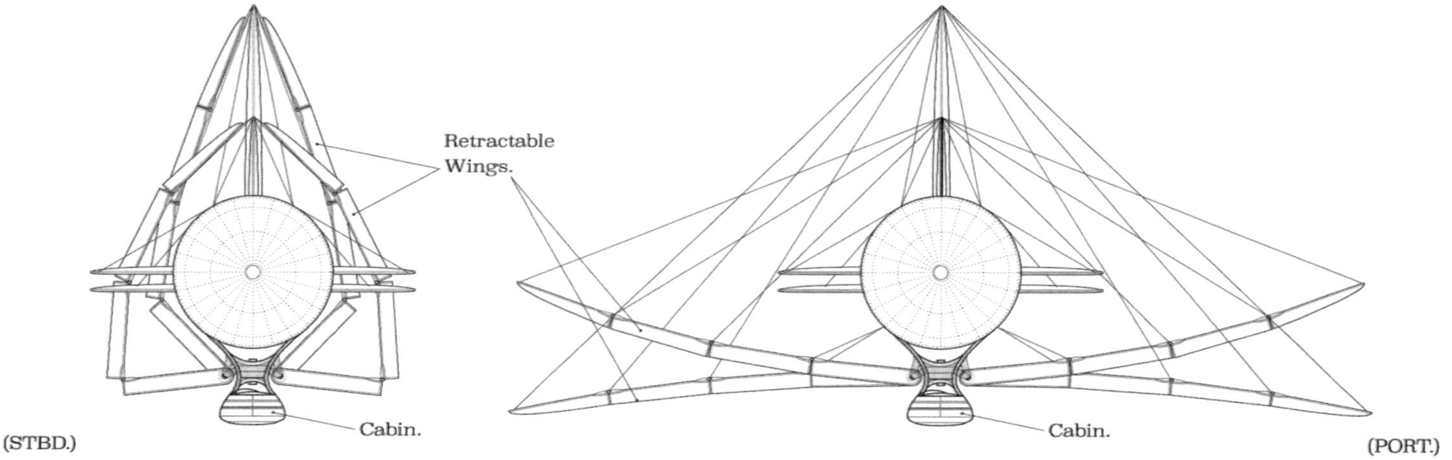

Cabin.

(PORT.)

Fig. 1a. BOW VIEW: WINGS RETRACTED

Retractable Wings.

Cabin.

(STBD.)

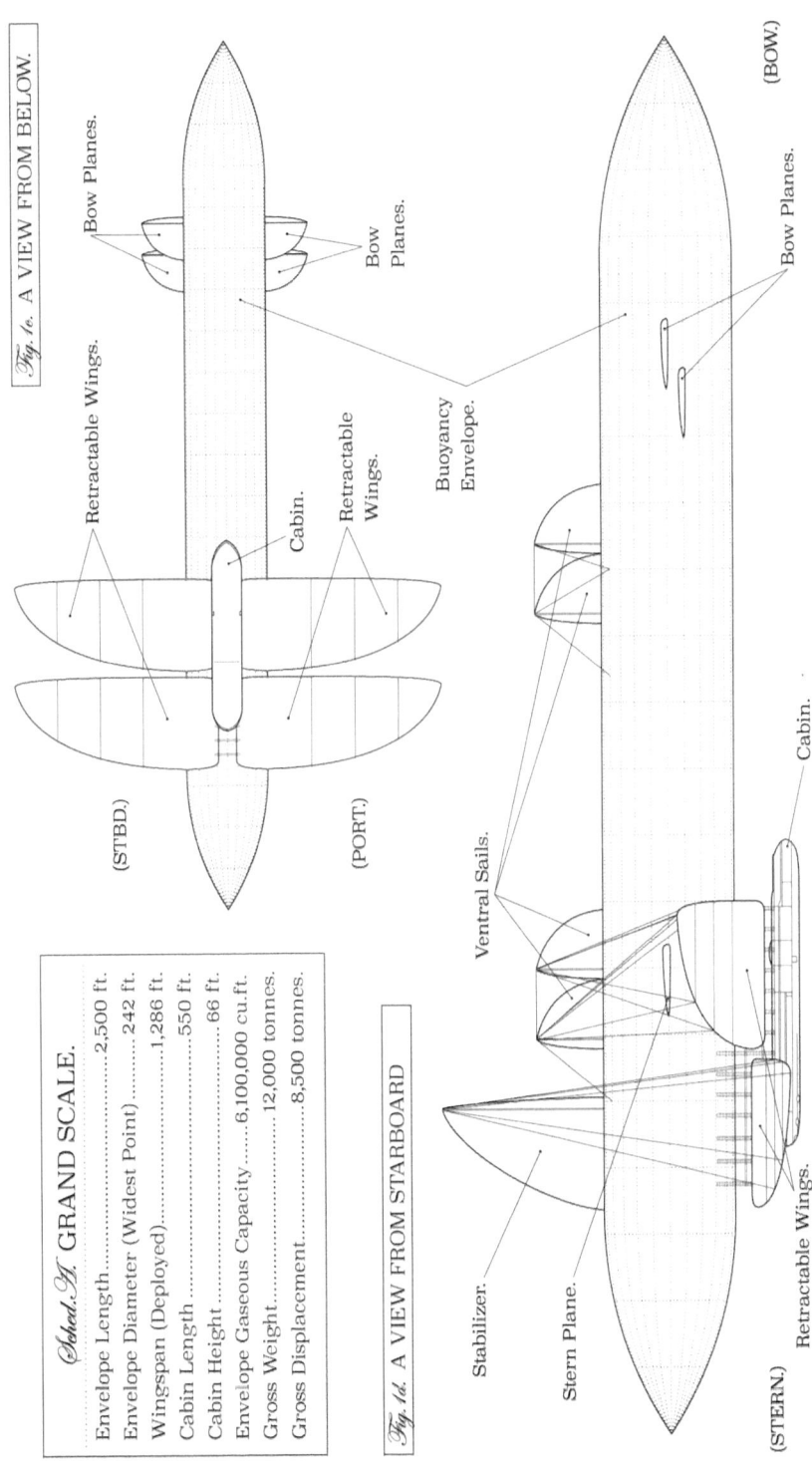

Fig. 1c. A VIEW FROM BELOW.

Bow Planes.

Bow
Planes.

Retractable Wings.

Cabin.

Retractable
Wings.

(STBD.)

(PORT.)

Buoyancy
Envelope.

Bow Planes.

(BOW.)

Sched. A. GRAND SCALE.

Envelope Length...................................2,500 ft.
Envelope Diameter (Widest Point).........242 ft.
Wingspan (Deployed)..........................1,286 ft.
Cabin Length...550 ft.
Cabin Height..66 ft.
Envelope Gaseous Capacity......6,100,000 cu.ft.
Gross Weight..................................12,000 tonnes.
Gross Displacement.........................8,500 tonnes.

Fig. 1d. A VIEW FROM STARBOARD

Ventral Sails.

Stabilizer.

Stern Plane.

Cabin.

Retractable Wings.

(STERN.)

THE PREEMINENT AIRSHIP

MONARCH

THE FENCHURCHE LINE

OF AETHER'S FAIR SKIES.

Fig. 2. A MAP OF AND GUIDE TO THE GREAT SHIP'S RICHLY-APPOINTED CABIN INTERIOR.

Fig. 2a. DECK 3.

Stairway Down to Captain's Lounge.

Wardroom. (below loft)

Elevator. (below loft)

The Bridge.

Wind Screen.

(FORE.)

Mechanical.

Stairway to Observation Deck.

Map Room. (below loft)

Bridge Loft.

Boatswain's Suite.

Officers' Quarters Hallway.

Flight Crew's Quarters.

First Mate's Suite.

Captain's Suite.

Housekeeping Closet.

Private Suite of Mrs. Minnette Fenchurche.

Garden Overhead Space.

Private Stairway to Ballroom.

Stairway to Deck 2.

Private Suite of Mr. Miles Fenchurche.

Fenchurche Private Parlor.

Fenchurche Private Elevator.

Service Hallway.

Housekeeping & Elevators.

Fenchurche Guest of Honor Suite.

Passengers' Quarters.

Passengers' Quarters.

Stowage.

KEEL LINE

(AFT.)

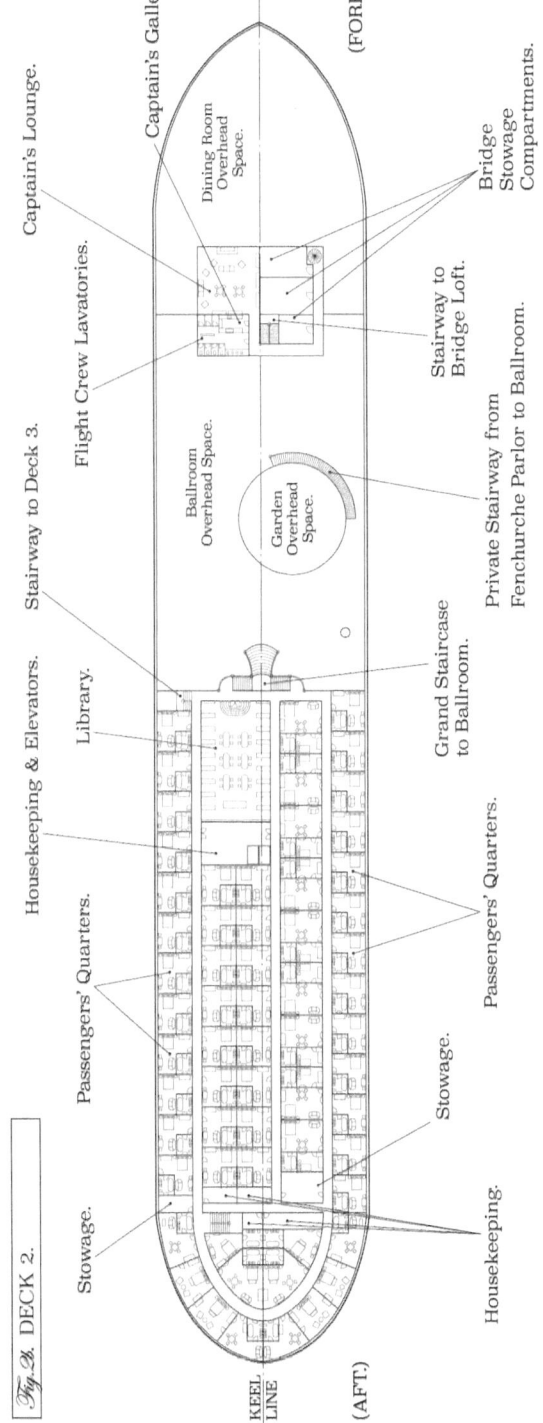

Sched. B. THE GREAT SHIP'S CAPACITY AND PERFORMANCE SPECIFICATIONS.

Passenger Berths: 250 • Crew and Service Staff: 150 • Guest Capacity While Docked: 500
Average Cruising Altitude: 1,900 ft. • Service Ceiling: 7,300 ft. • Rate of climb: 220 ft./min.
Maximum Airspeed: 648 Leagues Per Day • Range: 9,072 Leagues • Maximum Cruise Length: 14 Days

Fig. A. DECK 2.

Captain's Lounge.

Captain's Galley.

Dining Room Overhead Space.

(FORE.)

Bridge Stowage Compartments.

Flight Crew Lavatories.

Stairway to Bridge Loft.

Stairway to Deck 3.

Ballroom Overhead Space.

Garden Overhead Space.

Private Stairway from Fenchurche Parlor to Ballroom.

Housekeeping & Elevators.

Library.

Grand Staircase to Ballroom.

Passengers' Quarters.

Passengers' Quarters.

Stowage.

Stowage.

Housekeeping.

KEEL LINE

(AFT.)

THE PREEMINENT AIRSHIP MONARCH OF AETHER'S FAIR SKIES.

THE FENCHURCHE LINE

Fig. 2. A MAP OF AND GUIDE TO THE GREAT SHIP'S RICHLY-APPOINTED CABIN INTERIOR.

Fig. 2. MAIN DECK.

Dining Room Waiting Area.

Dining Room.

Diningware Storage.

Fenchurche Family Private Dining Room.

Service Corridor.

Elevators.

Gents' Lav.

Ladies' Lav.

(FORE.)

Main Entry Sliding Doors.

Glass Garden.

Glass Garden Airlock.

Private Stairway from Ballroom to Fenchurche Parlor.

Lounge Lavs.

Ballroom (Lobby).

Gentlemen's Smoking Lounge.

Fenchurche Private Elevator.

Auxilliary Entryway.

Grand Staircase to Deck 2.

Auxilliary Entryway.

Passengers' Quarters.

Kitchen Storage.

Elevators.

Crew Uniform Cabinets.

Main Kitchen.

Servants' and Crew's Quarters.

Servants' and Crew's Water Closets.

Crew Showers: Female, Male.

Passengers' Quarters.

Infirmary.

Nursery.

Gymnasium.

Crew Lounge.

Crew Mess Hall.

Tea Room.

KEEL LINE.

Business Offices.

(AFT.)

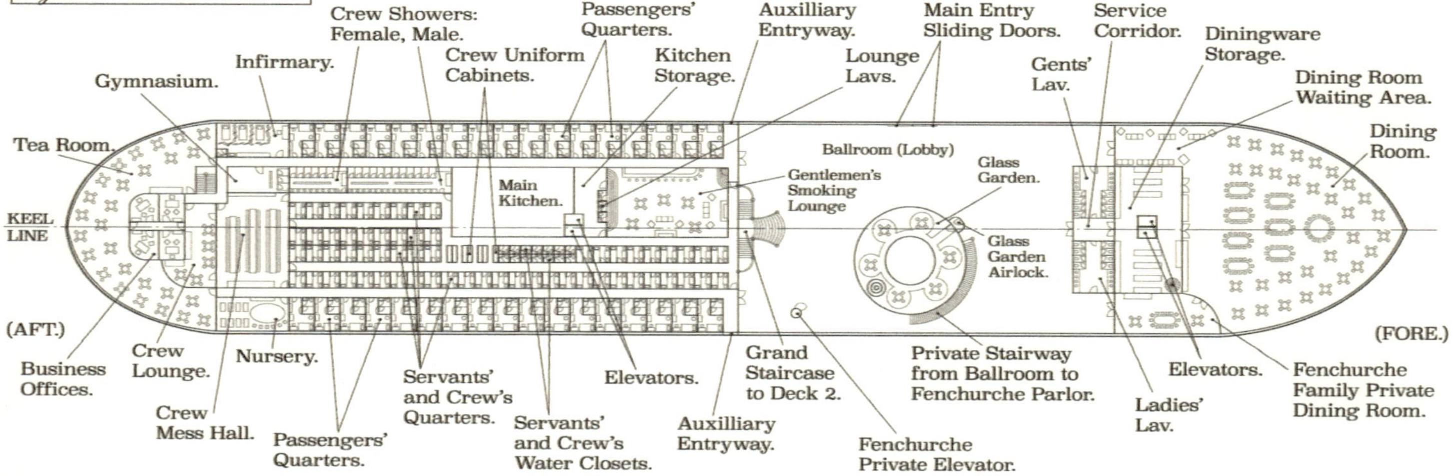

Fig. 1. UPPER DECK. (Topmost.)

Captain's Observation Deck.

KEEL LINE

(FORE.)

Skylights.

Cabin Roof.

Cabin Roof.

Garden Glass Dome.

Cabin Roof.

Stairway to Bridge.

Sched. C. PROVISIONING & HOSPITALITY, WEEKLY.

Beef Served..700 lbs.
Domestic and Game Fowl Served.................................500 lbs.
Eggs Served..3,800, Extra-Large
Wine & Spirits Served to Passengers.................925 Bottles
Fruits and Vegetables Served......................................900 lbs.
Caviar Served..53 lbs.
Drinking Water Consumed.......................................1,000 gal.
Sweets Consumed..125 lbs.
Fresh Flowers Placed...2,400 Stems
Cigars Provided..675
Bedding Sets Laundered and Applied...........................2,800
Gentlemen's Suits Cleaned, Pressed and Mended...........390
Ladies' Dresses Cleaned and Mended.............................360
Gentlemen's Hats Brushed and Blocked............................40
Violin, Cello and Contrabass Strings Replaced..................12

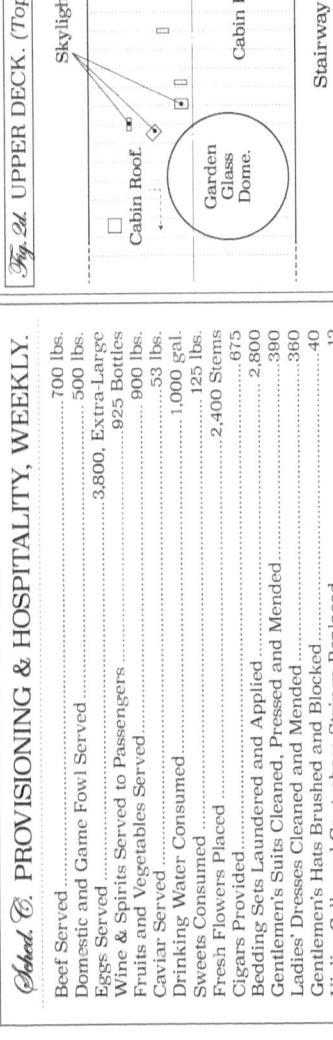

Fig. 2. SERVICE DECK. (Bottom-Most.)

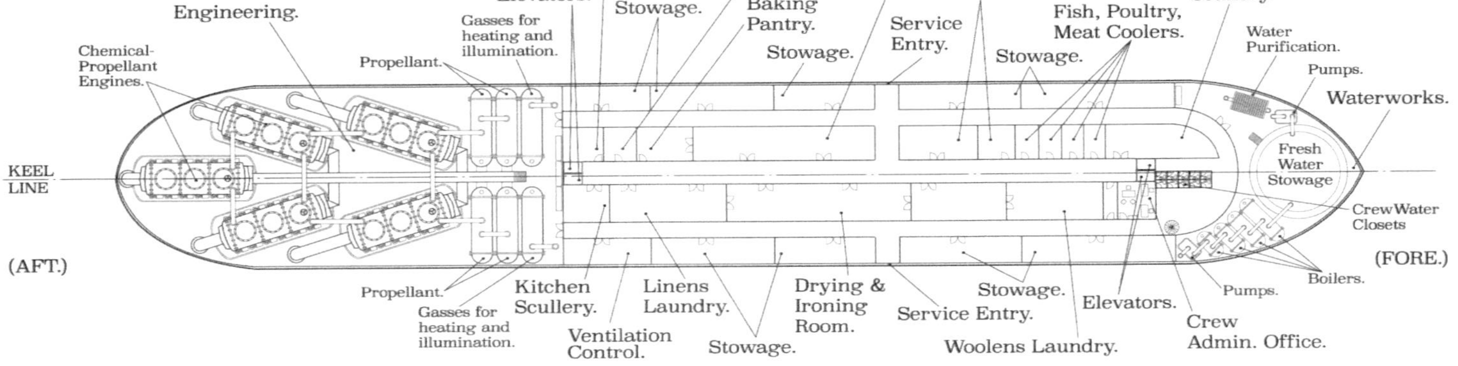

Dining Scullery.

Waterworks.

Water Purification.

Pumps.

Fresh Water Stowage.

Crew Water Closets

Boilers.

Pumps.

(FORE.)

Coolers: Vegetables & Fruit, Dairy.

Fish, Poultry, Meat Coolers.

Stowage.

Crew Admin. Office.

Elevators.

Service Entry.

Bakery & Patisserie.

Baking Pantry.

Stowage.

Woolens Laundry.

Stowage.

Service Entry.

Potato Room.

Can Pantry.

Stowage.

Drying & Ironing Room.

Linens Laundry.

Stowage.

Elevators.

Gasses for heating and illumination.

Propellant.

Kitchen Scullery.

Ventilation Control.

Propellant.

Gasses for heating and illumination.

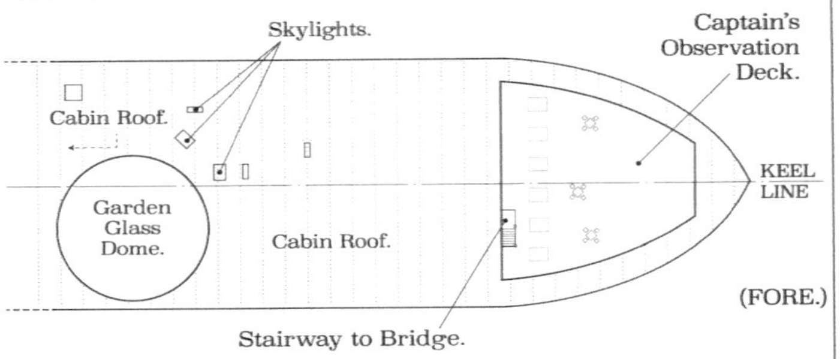

Engineering.

Chemical-Propellant Engines

KEEL LINE

(AFT.)

Chapter Six

A Royal Introduction

The docking platform at Prominence was bathed in the heavy amber light of a late summer's afternoon. Ivey had arrived early with her sisters and mother to watch the *Monarch* crest the mountains north of the capital city.

The bustling crowd around them fell silent when the dirigible came into view, its sleek cabin and expansive balloon perfectly framed against the golden sky. The majestic proportions of the ship were surreal, and yet, Ivey felt a strange sense of belonging.

Iris gave a disappointed little sigh. "I thought it had fairy wings."

"Just you wait," Ivey said. "They fold the wings up whenever they cross tall mountains to keep the rough winds from damaging the riggings."

Winora looked at Ivey in wonder. "How would a young lady know such a thing?"

Ivey rolled her eyes. "By reading everything that has been written on the subject."

Iris squealed. "Here they come."

Two sets of wings hugging the envelope unfurled as the ship crossed the foothills outlying the city. Ivey's heart nearly stopped at the sight. With its enormous wings gleaming in the sunlight, the airship transformed into a mystical entity from another world.

In the large lecture hall at the Cadenbury Institute of Sciences, Arvel Thornton stole a quick glance at his timepiece. He'd promised his daughter a proper farewell, and fearing that it might be his last, he wanted her to remember a joyous parting.

A voice cut through his thoughts. "We're waiting."

The terse words came from Silas Harp, commander of Cadenbury's resident division of the Promacheon, Cemaria's bureau of war. The Promacheon's task under Harp was to promote scientific advancement in the interests of national defense and foreign conquest. Silas had called the afternoon meeting in spite of Arvel's conflict of time, or perhaps because of it. He was around Arvel's age and held similar social standing, but they differed in every other way possible.

Arvel rose from his seat and walked to the lectern. "Thank you, Silas." He tipped his head and turned to the large assembly of university rectors, industry chiefs, and Cemarian officials.

"My esteemed colleagues, I've been asked to report on recent developments concerning the Zephyr Project. As you know, we are at the dawn of a new age, one in which roads, locomotives, ships, and dirigibles are no longer the only way to travel across land and sea. Before I present the prototype for the newest class of self-propelled flying machines, allow me to introduce an executive member of the design party. I give you Stanley Honeycutt."

Arvel gestured to his son-in-law, who pushed himself into a standing position from a sturdy wooden chair. Stanley's cheeks were red, and fat beads of sweat dotted his forehead. Stanley's paternal uncle held one of the five archonships on Cemaria's executive council. As the Archon of Industry, Albert Honeycutt had asked his nephew to address the assembly regarding the risks of exploiting the nation's scientific achievements for war.

Arvel gave Stanley a firm pat on the back and leaned close to his ear. "I have every confidence in your ability to make the case, son."

"Thank you, Arvel," Stanley's voice rasped. He stepped up to the lectern, cleared his throat, and began.

"At the turn of this century, a remarkable event forever changed our understanding of the world. While surveying for veins of commercial ores in a mine deep beneath the Rosman Mountains, a Fenchurche Industries engineer detected a new species of energy that had an alarming effect on his test equipment. After an initial assessment was made, the Cemarian government felt it prudent to study this phenomenon thoroughly before announcing its existence to the rest of the world.

"During those efforts, Maddox Fenchurche and his party were lost in a devastating explosive event that collapsed Whiterock Mountain and forever sealed the mine. This caused great concern about the potential of such a destructive force. The Cadenbury Institute sent teams of geologists to conduct tunneling operations at a number of sites around the world with the hope of uncovering another instance of this strange energy. The results were quite startling. This new species of energy was found at great depths below every single land mass tested.

"Excuse me, Mr. Honeycutt," Silas Harp interrupted. "This meeting was called to discuss the Boreas and its military applications, not for you to lecture us on well-known history."

Arvel rose. "If we hope to avoid the tragedies of the past, sir, we must be mindful of that history, and Mr. Honeycutt is an authority in that regard."

"Very well. It's your time to waste, sir," Silas said. He waved a dismissive hand at Stanley. "Proceed."

Stanley gave Silas a curt nod.

"The consensus was indisputable: the energy was not isolated in pockets. It was uninterrupted, proving that in Aether's heart lies a cosmocrene. Gentlemen, the surface of our world is not set on solid matter, but atop a singular core of energy."

While he paused to let the words sink in, one of the newer council members rose to his feet.

"Mr. Honeycutt, please do make your point. My schedule is quite busy."

Stanley cast an eye toward the speaker.

"Councilor Weyland, our entire existence rests above a field of energy that some are eager to tap. Many distinguished men of science are concerned that hastily pursuing commercial interests of this kind could trigger an event like the one that annihilated the Fenchurche party. If such an event were to occur on a large enough scale, it could obliterate this world in a heartbeat. That is why our attempts to harness the power of the cosmocrene must proceed with caution and discipline."

Some in the audience grumbled and muttered while others softly clapped their hands in agreement. Stanley glanced at a sheet of paper in his hands before continuing.

"When Honeycutt Mechanical initiated the Zephyr Project, our intention was to develop industrial machinery that harnessed the strength of the cosmocrene. It took thirteen years of tedious study to discover that two materials could safely interact with Aether's core of energy," he said. "The mineral element lunial is attracted to the source of the energy, while gelthinium is repelled."

Stanley placed his documents beneath a small glass globe mounted to the lectern, causing a series of lighted diagrams to be projected on the blank wall behind him.

"A year after we learned of these interactions, Honeycutt Mechanical successfully levitated small weighted ballasts by generating a coupled force between arrays of these materials and the gravity of Aether. That gave rise to the first generation of the Zephyr Project's flying machines. We had achieved levitation, but the force was insufficient to lift a manned vehicle.

"Then a young engineer came to me with a brilliant invention."

A dark-haired man with a long face appeared on the screen. He held an odd looking contraption with a circular disc flanked by coils of metallic wire and precision gears mounted on a wooden base.

"This is Nicolai Slate with the device he calls an otheophainer. It generates energy in the form of charged particles channeled through ductile metal to deliver a great deal of excited power. That power, when directed through gelthinium, dramatically strengthens its repulsion from cosmocrene energy."

The next image depicted a refined version of the device, this time encased in metal cladding.

"When this model of otheophainer was integrated into the Honeycutt levitating panels, it excited the lunial–gelthinium lattice and increased the lifting force by more than a hundredfold. A stable and tunable field of resistance to gravity was created, one that could command the craft's lift, orientation, and elevation with extreme precision."

"And how long before these machines make good on our investment?" a man in the audience shouted.

The hall resounded with murmured comments and resonances of agreement.

"At present, the only hindrance to the mass production of Zephyrs has been the rarity of lunial and gelthinium ores. These minerals have yet to be discovered within Cemaria's borders, so we have no choice but to deal with foreign territories," Stanley replied.

He called up an image of people dressed in layers of rough wool garments, toiling with sieves and rakes in a riverbed as neatly dressed Cemarians looked on.

"Commerce in regions like Yuo is complicated and tedious, but Cadenbury's mineralogists are increasingly efficient at extracting lunial and gelthinium from the raw ore.

"With both simplicity of design and easy availability of high quality glass and components produced by Fenchurche Industries, the Zephyr flight machines are being manufactured quickly and at reasonable costs.

"The time has come. In a matter of days, we will be ready to introduce them for public purchase."

A hushed excitement swept over the hall, quickly growing in volume and intensity.

Stanley raised his voice to be heard. "And so, without further ado, the Zephyr."

A peculiar-looking vessel appeared on the projection wall. The small craft had dark brass tracery encasing an iridescent glass sphere. The frame was fashioned with two large wings, a rudder, landing rails, and a long and pointed, stabilizing nosepiece. A pair of cylindrical fuel-powered turbine engines like those that propelled airships were mounted to the back of the passenger compartment to provide the vehicle's directional thrust.

"The glass cabin is feather light yet exceptionally resilient. Inside, a finely leathered bench seats a passenger on the right and a pilot on the left. Before long, anyone with the means to purchase the vessel and master its controls will have independent air travel at his disposal. Gentlemen, we have finally arrived at the threshold of an era in which Zephyrs will carry us skyward into the new millennium."

The hall burst into applause and cheers.

Silas rose and banged a paperweight on the lectern to quiet the assembly.

"May we discuss the strategic capabilities of your ship now, Mr. Thornton?"

Arvel stood and shook Stanley's hand before taking his place behind the lectern. He had a sense of what Silas wanted, but he wouldn't let the man impose his heavy-handed tactics on a scientific mission. A representation of a different ship lit up the wall.

"Gentlemen. This is the Boreas, the prototype for a much larger, self-propelled craft operating on the same principles as the Zephyr. It provides greater power and a larger freight capacity to serve Cemaria's industrial needs.

"As many of you know, I've been tasked with a mission that will put my hunting skills and this marvelous technology to the test. The Boreas will rapidly transport me to the target area in Boulder Creek. There, the ship will provide shelter against the elements while I track the predator responsible for the carnage that has cost so many lives.

"The ship's hold is large enough to carry everything I'll need to capture or kill—and then retrieve—the creature carrying out these deadly attacks. If successful, I'll deliver it to the containment center at the Curiosity Exchange, where we can determine whether the perpetrator is an unknown beast of prey or something more sinister. Thank you and good day."

Arvel started to walk away, hoping to avoid questions. He checked his watch and saw that it was nearly time for the *Monarch*'s arrival.

Silas Harp took Arvel's vacated position in front of the men and brought the crowd to order. "Gentlemen, if the Boreas is as powerful and capacious as Mr. Thornton claims, I suggest we put a team of my men on board in the interest of national safety."

Arvel turned back.

"Silas, how many of your agents have been sent to Boulder Creek now?"

"The exact number evades me but that is neither here—"

"Then answer this," Arvel cut him off. "How many of your men have returned safely?"

Silas folded his arms, and answered quietly. "None."

"So," Arvel spoke slowly and clearly. "Your highly trained and heavily armed combatants have proven themselves no match for whatever they went up against. We should assume that conventional means are ineffective. Success will ride on my ability to move quickly and without detection."

The sound of voices escalated as members of the audience began arguing among themselves.

"Gentlemen," Stanley shouted. "These are important issues. I suggest we take a recess before any course is decided upon."

A gaunt man sitting at a desk beside the lectern rose to his feet. Phineas Langley was Cemaria's Archon of Sciences and Cadenbury's chief administrator.

"Come to order," he said with great authority, banging a gavel against his desk.

The room fell silent.

"Thank you, Mr. Honeycutt," Phineas said. "We will meet here in the morning, once everyone has had time to carefully consider the matter. This meeting is adjourned."

Arvel clapped Stanley on the shoulder.

"Well then, Stanley, you really are coming into your own."

Stanley checked his watch. "We'll have to hurry if we wish to make it to the station before the *Monarch* departs." He grinned sheepishly. "If we don't, I'll be answering to my wife."

Arvel laughed. "And I'll be answering to her mother."

They rushed from the lecture room and down the passageway that led to the front entrance.

❧

While the crowd on the platform held their breath, the *Monarch* withdrew its mighty wings before softly coming to rest in its dock. The massive doors of the grand lobby slid open, and a boarding walkway was put in place as uniformed attendants welcomed the passengers and their visitors on board. As the crowd thinned, Ivey's unease grew.

Her father was nowhere to be seen, but she noticed a tall, thin man in a dark suit heading her direction.

"That's Minnette's executive assistant, Dolan," Prim whispered in her ear. "Everything he sees and hears is made known to her in great detail, so mind yourself around that one."

"Mrs. Honeycutt." He bowed slightly upon approach. "My pleasure, as always."

"Allow me to introduce my family," Prim cooed in return. "My mother, Mrs. Thornton."

Winora offered her hand, and Dolan shook it.

"And my youngest sister, Iris."

Iris curtsied.

"And I am proud to present my sister Ivey," Prim said sweetly.

Dolan turned to Ivey. "I am humbled by your rare beauty, Miss Thornton."

Although she wanted to laugh at his forced compliment, Ivey extended her hand, just as Prim had coached. "The honor is mine, sir. I do look forward to enjoying the hospitality of your magnificent airship."

Dolan offered his arm. "Mrs. Fenchurche asked that I escort you and your party to the secure entrance on the far side. There's a lift that will take you directly to the family's private quarters on the upper level."

Ivey was curious to see what Fenchurche private quarters would be like, but she was determined not to leave the platform on anyone's arm but her father's.

"Thank you, sir. It is a lovely afternoon, and the view is sensational. I should like to linger here for a bit longer." Ivey did her best to sound like a gracious female.

Dolan's expression showed that he was not at all accustomed to anyone refusing the suggestions of his mistress. "Mrs. Fenchurche wishes for you to come aboard now," he stated flatly.

"I think not." Ivey turned away from his extended arm.

Winora jumped forward and grasped the man's arm, flashing a dazzling smile.

"My husband means to have a word with Mr. Fenchurche before the ship departs. Would you be so kind as to give Iris and me a tour while the girls wait here for their father? I would love to see the airship's furnishings."

Winora nodded at Iris, who quickly scampered around to reach for Dolan's other arm.

"You're the tallest man I've ever seen," Iris giggled.

Minnette's right-hand man appeared flustered as he was led away by Winora and her exuberant little girl.

Prim laughed. "Poor Dolan—he's hardly a match for the Thornton girls. Wouldn't you say?"

Ivey couldn't concentrate on her sister's words. Her ears rang, and her instincts warned of approaching danger.

"What is it, Ivey? You look like you've seen a ghost."

As they descended the stairs of Cadenbury's main entrance, Arvel saw a familiar figure tinkering with the controls of a gleaming Zephyr sitting at the edge of the lawn.

"Ah, Nicolai, you're spot on time," Stanley called out.

The young man turned to greet them. "Good day, sirs." He tucked a measuring gauge into one of the many pockets of his carrot-colored waistcoat before pulling a polishing cloth from another. He wiped his fingerprints from the glass door as he spoke. "She's fresh from the factory and certified for flight. I tested her myself."

Nicolai stepped back and gestured toward the craft. "This one's all yours, Mr. Thornton."

Stanley invited Arvel to take the pilot's seat. "Today, we're flying in style."

Having cut his teeth as a test pilot in the early days of the project—a time when Zephyrs still had the nasty habit of flipping themselves over—Arvel couldn't wait to feel how the latest design handled.

Once he and Stanley were seated inside, the young engineer leaned in. "Enjoy the ride, gentlemen."

"Thank you, Nicolai," Arvel smiled. "When do we begin testing the *Boreas*?"

"In a few more days. I want to have things working perfectly before the ship enters the field."

Stanley held up his watch.

"Yes, we're in a hurry, but we need to talk as soon as possible," Arvel said.

Nicolai Slate nodded as he closed the door, which sealed neatly for the safety and comfort of the passengers inside.

Arvel depressed an ivory plunger to activate the exciter panels on the underbelly of the craft. They came to life with a distinctive pulsating sound that swelled in volume and frequency as they energized. He rotated a large metal wheel at his feet one half-turn, allowing the panels to revolve away from the shielded housing that kept them in an inert state. As soon as the gelthinium panel turned to face the ground below, the Zephyr began to rise.

Arvel let it climb to a safe height before engaging the engines that gave the vessel forward thrust. They departed, cruising at a speed that would deliver them to their destination across the city within minutes. Arvel was amused by the stunned expressions of the people below who looked up to see the mechanized bird and its two passengers whizzing over their heads.

∾

A wave of apprehension washed across Ivey, completely drowning out the pleasant surroundings and her sister's voice.

"Don't fret, honey." Prim wrapped her arm around Ivey and squeezed. "He'll be here any minute."

Despite the warm sunlight on the platform, Ivey's blood ran cold. Her ears ached, and a dull ringing that had been lurking in the back of her head was growing louder by the moment.

She felt Prim shaking her arm, but all Ivey could focus on was an odd-looking shadow racing toward them across the platform. Something about it was terrifying. Ivey wanted to grab Prim and run, but she was unable to move or speak.

The blackness fell across them, completely engulfing the two.

In its darkness, Ivey felt the presence of a life force unlike anything she'd ever encountered. Its energy was overpowering. As it enveloped her, she felt it taking control of her mind and body.

A cold, wet sensation crept up her legs.

Ivey broke free of her stupor long enough to stagger forward a step, but the paralyzing energy snatched her back in its grip, rendering her helpless.

Ivey's gaze went to Prim's skirt, where a dark form was seeping up the hemline. Prim seemed to be unaware of its presence, but Ivey sensed her sister's unborn baby in deep distress.

There was no fear in Prim's eyes as the gelatinous mass slid up her neck and completely covered her face. With every breath Prim took, the vile presence sank deeper into her body, until it disappeared down her throat.

Chapter Seven

SHIP OF DREAMS

From across the docking platform, Miles Fenchurche heard a woman scream.

"Someone help us, please!"

Seeing Primrose Honeycutt struggle to support the sagging weight of her sister, Ivey, he dashed across the platform and caught the two before they fell.

Prim clung to his arm. "We need a doctor."

"Is it the baby?" he asked.

"No. Something's wrong with Ivey."

Miles made sure that Prim was steady on her feet before lowering Ivey to the ground. He leaned in close and listened. She was breathing, but her face had turned a dull bluish gray, and her open eyes were fixed and glazed.

"Miss Thornton? Can you speak?"

He touched her cheek. It was icy cold; a sign that blood wasn't flowing to her brain.

"I think she's fainted. Perhaps this dress is too tight."

Just as Miles began to unbutton the high collar, Ivey blinked and her face flushed as her eyes widened with mortified recognition. Miles had to suppress the urge to smile at the girl's comical expression.

"Sir," her voice rasped. "This dress is fine—and so am I. Now, kindly get your hands off me." She pushed him away.

Prim laughed nervously. "Ivey, please. Miles was only trying to help. You fainted on us."

"I have never fainted in my life," Ivey declared.

"Actually, you fainted the night of the . . ." Miles started to correct her, but the girl's scowl made him stumble. "I mean it appeared that you . . . um, yes." He thought it best to stop. Clearly Miss Thornton did not care to be reminded of those events.

"You can be on your way now, Mr. Fenchurche."

When Ivey attempted to rise, Miles laid a hand on her shoulder. "I think you should give your body time to recover."

"I can think for myself, sir." She sat herself upright in one swift move.

Miles offered his hand, but the girl jumped up on her own, straightening her dress and hair, looking anywhere but at him.

While he searched his mind for something appropriate to say, Arvel and Stanley ran to join the disheveled group.

"Another ruckus, Ivey?" Arvel grabbed his daughter by the shoulders and peered into her eyes. "What happened?"

"Nothing. I'm perfectly fine, and I most certainly did not faint." Ivey fired a look of annoyance at Miles.

Stanley wrapped an arm around Prim's waist and held her close.

"And what of you, darling? It looked as though you had some kind of mishap."

"Oh Stanley, the baby was kicking so hard I stumbled and twisted my ankle." Prim looked at Miles. "I nearly knocked Ivey down in the process, but thanks to our Mr. Fenchurche, no harm was done to either of us.

"Isn't that so, Miles?" Prim pleadingly batted her eyelashes. "We are all perfectly fine, so let's not make a fuss that might delay Ivey's departure. She is so excited about her journey."

Miles had no idea what he was expected to say. Before he could work it out, Stanley scooped Prim up into his arms.

"Well then, you must stay off your feet until we're certain you're not injured. It's time to say your good-byes, my darling."

Prim quietly wrapped her arms around his neck, letting her head rest against Stanley's shoulder. Her perfect smile faded as if a sudden fatigue had come upon her. Her husband gently kissed the top of her head.

"Do you see this? The fact that my wife's not insisting that I put her down so she can manage the introductions means we need to go right away."

Arvel stroked Prim's cheek. "Take care of yourself, dearie, and perhaps you should consider a form of practical footwear, like those buckled shoes you girls loved when you were little."

Prim sighed. "You loved those shoes, Father. We only tolerated them to make you happy."

Arvel gave a shrug of resignation. "Good luck raising girls," he said to Stanley.

Prim lifted her head and gave her sister a look that once again begged for cooperation.

"I'm sorry I made such a scene, Ivey. Please don't let anything spoil your voyage and all of our plans for your nuptials."

Ivey rolled her eyes. "Oh, there's hardly a threat of that. I'm more worried about you, Prim."

She leaned close to her sister's ear, but Miles heard her whisper.

"Stay on your guard, Prim. Something's not right here." With a mock frown, Ivey leaned down to have a word with her sister's belly. "And you in there, stop kicking my sister, or you'll answer to me."

When Ivey straightened, she turned to Stanley.

"I trust you to do whatever it takes to keep my sister and the baby safe."

Stanley gaped at Arvel. "Is something the matter with her? She doesn't sound like herself."

"She's growing up, Stanley," Arvel replied. "Be careful not to blink; it will happen to your girls before you know it."

Prim beckoned to Miles. He slowly stepped forward, mystified by the complex social interactions of the Thornton family.

"Miles, thank you again for that impeccable timing of yours. You always seem to be there just when a Thornton girl needs you."

Ivey looked away, obviously embarrassed, as her sister continued.

"Ivey is very dear to our hearts, so I will leave with the comfort of knowing that you'll always be there to offer aid and companionship when she needs it."

Now Miles had to look away. It was painfully clear that the young lady had no intention of allowing him to do either of those things.

Prim gave him a weak smile before her head drooped again. "Darling, can we go now? I should like to lie down."

"Arvel, I hope you won't mind if I use the Zephyr to fly Prim home." Stanley hurried off toward the flight engine that had been landed at the end of the docking platform.

"That's a Zephyr? Did he say it flies? Why didn't anyone tell me about this?" Ivey's eyes sparkled with excitement.

"Give Stanley a hand getting Prim inside and you can have a look at it." Arvel shooed his daughter away with a grin.

Ivey peppered Stanley with more questions as she dashed after him.

Arvel took Miles by the arm and walked him the opposite direction. "So, tell me what really happened to Ivey."

"I can't say. She was unconscious, but her eyes were open, as if she were caught in a moment. Then she blinked and it was over." Miles slowed his pace. "I hope you don't mind my asking: has your daughter suffered any type of seizures before? Perhaps she should see a doctor before we depart."

"No. We don't have time for that. I'm confident that this has nothing to do with an ailment, so there's no need to be alarmed or cancel your trip. My daughter is unique in a variety of ways. Once you come to know her, this will all begin to make sense. Trust me, your time together will be unparalleled."

Miles sighed. "I'm not so sure. It seems she finds me annoying."

Arvel chuckled and gave him a reassuring pat on the shoulder. "Ivey is easily annoyed. Ask Stanley. She has yet to discover who you really are, Miles. You must earn her trust and she will have to earn yours as well. Once you have her respect, she will be the most steadfast person you have ever known. Given a chance, something wonderful can happen between the two of you."

Miles shook his head. "Sir, I know what you need, and I will do my best to keep her safely occupied. I never promised anything beyond that."

"Trust me. I intend to stand by our agreement," Arvel said as they approached the *Monarch*'s entrance. "If the two of you are not happy with this arrangement by the time I return, I will release you from your pledge, and Ivey will return to Thornhall. I just need you to keep her occupied at Ferndale while I'm away. I am sorry to admit that it will be no easy task."

Miles crossed his arms and lifted his chin. "I'm prepared to do whatever it takes."

"That's good to hear." Arvel stopped walking and turned to face him. "There's something else that has been weighing on my mind, Miles. In the event I don't return from my assignment, Ivey will need a champion to guard her honor and, if necessary, her life. I would like for you to become that man, even if the two of you are not meant to marry. Are you willing?"

Without hesitation, Miles' eyes met Arvel's. "I give you my word. As long as I am able to prevent it, no harm will come to Ivey Thornton." He offered his hand to seal the promise, and Arvel accepted it.

Miles found himself wanting to please Arvel, even if it meant dealing with his prickly daughter.

"Now, I have another wee favor to ask," Arvel said blithely. "After what just happened, I need to spend a moment with Ivey. If we conform to your mother's schedule, there will be no time for our family farewells, and I want to leave on a good note. Would there be anything a man could do that might ground the *Monarch* temporarily?"

A fleeting smile crossed Miles' face. "A man could have it arranged. I warn you, though, my mother will not be pleased."

"Then a man would be very wise to make it look like a malfunction . . . and whatever you do, dear boy, don't get caught."

Miles struck a hand across his heart. "Take your time, Mr. Thornton. This ship won't take flight until I say so."

Ivey watched as the Zephyr rose from the *Monarch*'s docking platform. She paced forward to stare up at the shimmering panels that lined the small flying machine's underbelly, feeling wonder that such a thing existed.

As she neared the craft, she began to feel the distinct pulse of the ship's engine radiate through her body. The sensation was exhilarating and intoxicating. She moved closer until she was directly below the ship. Even though her feet were firmly on the platform, she felt herself rising into a blinding light.

The next thing she knew, Arvel was shaking her by the shoulders. "Come out of it. Focus on me."

"What?"

"You slipped into another trance."

"Father, what in the world is happening to me?"

"I'm not sure. Tell me how it began with you and Prim."

Ivey shuddered. "I had an awful feeling that something bad was coming, and then it attacked us."

"How?"

"In my mind. I couldn't stop it. Prim didn't even know it was there, but her baby did. And then—Miles Fenchurche was leaning over me."

Arvel pulled Ivey into his arms. "It's as I thought. You were having a vision."

Ivey looked up at her father. "But I don't have visions. This was real."

"It is and it isn't." Arvel took her shoulders and leaned close. The sadness in his eyes was alarming.

"I started having visions after my parents died. I saw things that weren't there, heard voices, felt presences—good and bad. It was quite frightening until I realized that they were nothing more than my own phantom thoughts and feelings. They could not hurt me, and they will not hurt you, Ivey."

"Father, something dark came across this platform. I felt its coldness against my skin."

Arvel looked around the platform. "Could it have been the Zephyr's shadow as I flew over?"

"I don't know." Ivey thought about the direction it had been moving. "But how—"

"Sometimes elements of reality become entangled in such visions."

Ivey blinked. "Then it was an omen. Death is coming for one of us."

Something frightening passed through Arvel's eyes, but his voice was soft and reassuring. "Visions needn't tell the future. They are often nothing more than unconscious reflections of our anxiety. Do you feel as though leaving Thornhall is the end of a life you love?"

"Perhaps. But I have no doubt that Prim's baby felt it as much as I did."

"Well, maybe you're not the only one with the ability to sense another's distress. Something tells me that she's going to be a lot like us."

"Arvel? You know she's a girl, too?"

Arvel smiled. "I didn't mean to let that slip. Such perception is a gift that must be used wisely. I'm glad to know you didn't want to spoil the surprise for your sister or anyone else. Now that you have a better perspective, can you set this unpleasantness aside and allow me to escort you aboard the ship of your dreams?"

"No." Ivey's brow wrinkled. "I've just had two of these disturbing spells, and I haven't even made it off the docking platform. What if I go into a trance in front of Minnette? She'll be rid of me before we can get off the ground."

"That is a good point," Arvel acknowledged. "So you've never experienced anything like this before?"

"Never."

"Then something here could be acting as a trigger."

Ivey caught her breath. "The Zephyr. I was standing beneath it when the second one began."

"And the first episode started as I flew over your head. I think you're right, Ivey."

"But how would such a machine cause me to have visions?"

"It's possible that your body is affected by the energy of the vessel's otheophainer."

"Otheophainer?"

"It's a device that generates a field of force between a Zephyr and Aether's core. This force is powerful enough to lift the ship and its passengers; there's no telling what it might do to someone like you. I will discuss this with the engineer who invented the contraption. In the meantime, it would be wise to stay away from the force field generated by a Zephyr."

"Does that mean I can never ride in one?" Ivey asked in dismay.

"No. The cabin is specially shielded from the vessel's dynamic fields. While you're at Ferndale, Miles can take you for as many rides as you like. You know, if you try being nice to him, he might even teach you how to fly one yourself."

Ivey's eyes lit up. "Really? He could do that?"

Arvel threw his arms up in exasperation. "Dear girl, on how many occasions will I have to remind you that the man is the Fenchurche in Fenchurche Industries? By the time you arrive, he'll have an entire fleet of Zephyrs at Ferndale."

Ivey had always known she was destined to fly. Suddenly, being sent away to Ferndale didn't seem quite as distressing. She grabbed her father's arm.

"Then what are we waiting for? We're late, and I have an airship to catch. I don't want to aggravate Mrs. Fenchurche just yet."

Arvel feigned a grimace. "Oh well, I may have already done that."

Ivey's eyebrow went up as she replied in her refined ladylike character. "Why, Mr. Thornton, what are you up to? Please, I really must hear all about this." She tossed her head back with a carefree laugh as they swept across the platform toward the *Monarch*'s entrance.

∾

On a catwalk high above the docking platform, Miles disengaged one of the airship's wing control cables with a twist and a tug. It was a malfunction that would prove difficult to pinpoint but serious enough to delay takeoff when the prelaunch rigging checks were performed.

Miles looked down just as Ivey smiled up at her father, a look of pure joy evident on her face. Such a happy and lively scene made his act of sabotage well worth every bit of irritation the delay would no doubt cause his mother and her unfortunate staff. As Miles left the catwalk, he wondered whether the headstrong young lady boarding his ship would ever feel so inclined to smile at him that way.

∾

Entering the *Monarch*'s portside doors, Ivey and her father were rendered speechless. The lobby occupied two levels of the ship's interior, with a decor more palatial than anything they'd ever seen, even at their high station in society.

Softly diffused gas lighting radiated from crystal lamps and chandeliers fashioned in the shapes and colors of exotic flowers. The parquet floor boasted inlays of every type of imported wood imaginable, and the recessed paneling of the interior walls was meticulously carved with botanical themes. Between the panels hung tapestries made from silk threads and jeweled metallic fibers woven into the filigreed Fenchurche coat of arms.

The outboard walls were floor-to-ceiling windows formed by Fenchurche Industries' signature curved glass, affording passengers an unobstructed view of the world below when the ship was in flight. On the starboard side of the lobby, a circular garden room—filled with a living colony of flowering plants, slender trees, butterflies, and fancy birds—towered straight through the lofty ceiling and into the ship above.

Beside the garden, a string quartet played while handsome young porters in smart uniforms offered beverages and delectable pastries to the milling passengers in the cavernous lobby.

Arvel softly whistled. "How do they get this thing off the ground?"

Remembering Prim's advice to take everything in stride, Ivey nudged her father in the ribs.

"Stop staring, Arvel. Prim says it's bad form."

Arvel's jaw dropped open. "What has your sister done to you?"

Ivey lowered her eyelashes demurely. "Turned me into a lady . . . or at least that's what we want Mrs. Fenchurche to think."

Minnette's lanky assistant was approaching, so Ivey took the opportunity to show off more of her rehearsed pomp.

"Dolan, please allow me to introduce Arvel Thornton. Father, Dolan is Mrs. Fenchurche's personal assistant, and to hear Prim tell it, he is well worth his weight in gold."

Dolan gave Arvel a curt nod. "How do you do, Mr. Thornton? I'm sorry, but it's time for all visitors to disembark. The *Monarch* is in danger of falling behind schedule."

Ivey's expression clouded over, and she tightened her grip on her father's arm.

Arvel gave her a sly smile before replying. "I understand completely. We wouldn't want to inconvenience the other passengers, would we, Ivey?"

Ivey recognized the look in her father's eyes, so she bit her tongue and let him handle the matter.

"If you would be so kind as to help me locate my wife and youngest daughter, we will depart at once," Arvel said.

"They are waiting in Miss Ivey's quarters. Come with me."

They followed Dolan to a wide staircase that wound around the back of the garden. He nodded as they passed a pair of sturdy porters standing by to make sure the "private" sign at the bottom of the stairs was properly heeded.

As they climbed up and around the glass vault, Ivey marveled at the beautiful oasis on the other side. The Fenchurche family certainly had a flair for capturing nature's beauty. Looking up, she saw that the garden soared all the way to the top of the cabin, where it ended in a beautiful dome.

The stairway continued without exit until they reached the third floor. Dolan sternly explained that this was the family's private parlor, and no passengers were allowed to visit without an invitation from the Fenchurches. Ivey hid a smirk at the implication that she might be inclined to bring strangers into such a delightfully private place.

As they topped the stairs, Ivey drew in a long breath. The parlor was more beautiful than she'd expected. To her right, the curved glass that encased the garden filled the room with light and offered a splendid view of the vegetation's lush canopy.

An impressive collection of artwork adorned the parlor's walls, but in Ivey's estimation, it paled in comparison to the view through the windows on the starboard side of the cabin.

From this vantage point, one could clearly see the network of riggings that controlled the *Monarch*'s retractable wings. Ivey's father paused to stare out the window, but Dolan impatiently motioned for them to follow him to a door across from the landing of the staircase.

"This is your suite, Miss Ivey. I will wait here to escort your family members to the dock by way of the elevator." He gestured to a glass tube situated between her door and the window.

"Thank you." Ivey grabbed her father's hand and dragged him along, closing the suite's door firmly behind them. "Arvel. Tell me you have a plan to stay on board for a while," she whispered.

He grinned. "I don't need a plan. I have an ally."

"An ally? Who? How?" Ivey asked. Arvel took her to the sitting room window and pulled back the drapery. Outside, several officers in red flight uniforms were directing men in work tunics as they darted this way and that on the rigging's catwalks, checking each of the wing's control cables.

"What is this?" Ivey asked.

"Looks as though there may have been a mechanical difficulty."

Ivey gasped and covered her mouth. "Father, what have you done?"

He smiled. "Nothing permanent, but those wings will not take flight until you are ready."

Ivey threw herself into her father's arms. "I love you, Arvel."

The door to the suite's bedroom opened, and Iris cried out with delight. "Father is here! I told you he would make it in time. Ivey, wait until you see your bed, and the bathtub is made of glass!"

Winora followed her giggling daughter into the sitting room and welcomed Arvel with a kiss. "You cut it very close, my dear."

"You would hardly believe," Arvel sighed. "So, now that we are all accounted for, it's time to go."

Winora and Iris stared in disbelief upon hearing her father's abrupt announcement, but Ivey grinned.

"You're not going anywhere. Father has a strategy."

Winora glanced sideways at her husband. "I am sure he does," she laughed.

When the Thorntons exited Ivey's suite, they walked into the middle of a tense discussion going on in front a fireplace at the far end of the parlor.

"This is completely unacceptable, Captain LeClere. Why was I not informed earlier?" A petite woman Ivey presumed was Minnette Fenchurche stood with arms crossed in aggravation.

Although the man she was addressing was nearly twice her size, he appeared to be in the unfortunate position of answering to his displeased employer.

"The problem wasn't discovered until we began the preflight inspections, madam. The wings operated perfectly after crossing the mountains. We've got every available man working on it."

Minnette spoke through clenched teeth. "Then have them make the repairs after we are underway, Captain. I will keep my schedule."

The captain's voice raised a few degrees. "This is not a problem that can be resolved in the air, madam. If we depart as scheduled, the wings may be inoperable for the duration of the flight. You understand what that means."

Miles Fenchurche appeared at the top of the winding stairway. "Of course we do, Captain," he said with great seriousness. "The *Monarch's* passengers are expecting a show. It is important that we keep to our schedule, but the welfare and enjoyment of our passengers is always of first concern. Wouldn't you agree, Mother?"

When Miles glanced in Arvel's direction, his mother's gaze followed and finally fell upon Ivey. The woman's expression soured even more as she scrutinized Ivey's appearance from head to toe.

"I see Miss Thornton had to make her own way onto the ship, Miles. Why didn't you escort her to the guest suite as I requested?"

Miles faltered. Seeing that he was in trouble, Ivey made an excuse for him.

"Mrs. Fenchurche, please allow me to explain. My sister suffered a slight accident on the docking platform, but thankfully your son saved her from taking a nasty fall. He then volunteered to stay with Prim until her husband arrived. Therefore, my father escorted me onto the ship. I am safely on board, and it is with great pleasure that I make your acquaintance."

Arvel gave her a self-satisfied grin and a pat on the back. "It's a joy to have the two of you finally meet."

Minnette turned her steely gaze back to Ivey. "Really. Come, let me get a look at you."

Ivey walked forward, making sure to keep her eyes respectfully lowered. Minnette lifted Ivey's chin with her hand and stared at her face. Ivey didn't relish being inspected like a show animal, but she played her part and submitted without so much as a flinch.

That seemed to please Minnette. Her face softened.

"Is Primrose all right?" she asked. "I hope she is not having a difficult time with her condition."

Ivey smiled sweetly. "Thank you for asking, but she and the baby are fine. It was merely a twisted ankle."

Minnette seemed satisfied, even relieved. "Very well. Since there will be an unavoidable delay, I would like your family to join us for dinner this evening. I have decided that the *Monarch* will depart in the morning. Dolan, inform the master of the captain's table that we will be entertaining additional guests."

As Dolan started off down the staircase, Ivey winked at her parents. If this kept up, she might have a little bit of fun on this trip. Feeling generous and hoping to lay the groundwork for her future flying lessons, she turned to Miles.

"I never had the chance to thank you for helping my sister, Mr. Fenchurche. It was wonderful to make your acquaintance. I very much appreciate your assistance, and your impeccable timing." Ivey flashed the ladylike smile she'd learned from Prim.

"Now that we're staying on for dinner, how would you like to give Ivey and me a grand tour of your ship?" Arvel asked.

Miles' face brightened. "It would be my privilege, sir."

Minnette scowled. "I apologize, Miles, but considering your concern for the welfare and enjoyment of our passengers, your expertise on the wing assembly would be greatly appreciated by Captain LeClere's crew."

Miles' face fell as he dutifully accepted his mother's suggestion. "Of course. I would be happy to offer my assistance, Captain."

The captain nodded and made a hasty exit to tend to his ship.

Iris rushed forward. "Don't worry, Miles. Mother and I took a tour of the ship. We'll show them around and save you a place at dinner."

She tried to give him a hug, but Miles jumped back stiffly. "Thank you, Miss Thornton, I have important matters to tend to."

Minnette stared triumphantly at Arvel. "Well, I shall see you at dinner. Please excuse my exit."

As Minnette stalked off after the captain, Iris muttered softly, "What a mean old biddy."

Ivey tapped her sister's shoulder. "Iris! That is no way for a proper young lady to speak about our hostess. She has many responsibilities. It is not easy running a company as important as Fenchurche Industries. I can't even imagine having to think about all of those serious matters."

Luckily, Iris was left speechless by Ivey's statement; Dolan had reappeared on the stairs behind them.

"Excuse me, Miss Ivey. I meant to tell you that Mrs. Fenchurche expects her guests to take their dinner seats promptly at one quarter to the hour. The entrance to the dining hall is on the port side of the lobby."

"Thank you, Dolan," Ivey replied. "I will see to it that our party is squarely on time."

A satisfied Dolan nodded and disappeared down the stairway.

Ivey grinned at her father. "If he intends to sneak up on me, he'd better find some less fragrant toiletries."

Arvel took his wife by the arm with a wide grin.

"Iris, make good on that tour you promised me. The Thorntons are going to have a grand time tonight."

Chapter Eight

The Monarch Head-Throe

The next morning, Ivey awoke to a gentle tap on her shoulder.

"We're leaving now," her mother whispered softly.

Because Arvel had an early meeting at Cadenbury, Ivey had convinced her parents to spend the night on her bed while she and Iris slept under blankets on the pillowy sofas in her sitting room.

Ivey rubbed her eyes. Her sleep had been usually sound.

"I'll get up." She reached for the dress she'd left draped across the arm of the couch.

"There's no need," Winora said. "We must hurry if the ship intends to leave on its new schedule." She smiled at her husband. "Isn't it amazing that the wing malfunction was discovered and repaired just in time for an early morning departure?"

"Wonders never cease, my dear." Arvel leaned down and kissed Ivey's brow. "It's time to say our goodbyes."

"No. I can't bear to." She clung to him.

He patted her softly on the back. "Then don't. Our hearts will always be together. Nothing in the world is stronger than love, Ivey. Never forget that."

"I wish I were flying away on the *Monarch*," Iris piped up. "You're going to have so much fun. And be nice to Miles, Ivey. He really is a handsome prince when his mother isn't making him cross. But, if you don't want him, tell him to wait for me."

Ivey squeezed her little sister tightly.

"Oh, Iris. Girls don't need handsome princes to make them happy. By the way," Ivey leaned in close, "I'm counting on you to take good care of our friend in the pond until I return. Tell him that I love him, all right?"

Unfortunately, Ivey hadn't spoken softly enough to elude her mother's sharp sense of hearing.

"What does that mean? Really, Arvel, not another secret."

Arvel put his arm around his wife. "You know, I was meaning to tell you about that, but it will have to wait. We need to go, before Dolan comes looking for us." Arvel gave Ivey a guilty wink as he opened the door for his wife and youngest daughter and ushered them out.

The door closed. For the first time in her life, Ivey was on her own in the world.

She fell back onto the couch, feeling small and weak, which wasn't at all her nature. Refusing to waste her time being pitiful, she jumped up and went to the window to watch the ship's departure.

She pulled back the drapes and looked up at the *Monarch*'s silvery body glistening in the morning light, with its mighty wings folded high around the envelope. Ivey set her jaw, promising to make every minute of her voyage an adventure. At the end of her journey, something even more fantastic would be waiting: her first flight in a Zephyr.

Oh no, I forgot to tell Father something!

Ivey turned and ran for the door.

❧

Arvel was nearly across the ship's boarding walkway when he heard his daughter's voice.

"Wait! Come back!"

He spun around and saw Ivey racing across the lobby, heedless of the passengers who'd gathered to celebrate the airship's launching. A hush fell across the revelers as she streaked past them.

The color drained from Winora's face. "Oh, Arvel, do something."

He ran back to meet Ivey. "Dear girl, what in Aether's name are you doing?"

"This is important," Ivey said, pulling him close and lowering her voice. "Prim's baby was kicking because she felt the Zephyr passing overhead, too. Tell Stanley that neither of them should be exposed to that much energy."

"You may be right. I'll tell him to take every precaution." Arvel leaned even closer to his daughter's ear. "Ivey, your concern is much appreciated, but wouldn't it be wise to go back to your room and put some clothes on before you join the party?"

Ivey blinked and looked down. Too tired to unpack her trunk, she'd gone to sleep in nothing more than a camisole and ruffled pettipants. Her feet were bare, and her hair was frightfully tangled. Ivey's face turned a bright red as she saw the throng of gaping passengers around her. She tried to cover the exposed skin of her shoulders with her hands.

"Oh, mercy."

She spun to beat a retreat, but ran straight into Miles Fenchurche, who was looking down at some papers in his hand as he walked. Their collision sent his documents flying.

"Oh, good morning. I'm—um, oh you're looking . . . oh."

Arvel had to laugh at the array of expressions flashing across the young man's face.

With eyes averted, Miles peeled off his jacket and held it out to the panic-stricken girl. "Please."

"Thank you." Ivey snatched the jacket from his hand and wrapped it around herself, shooting an exasperated look in Arvel's direction before fleeing the scene.

"Your timing really is impeccable, Mr. Fenchurche," Arvel said, smirking.

"Yes, well, I was trying to catch you, and I didn't see her. I mean, I saw her after we, well." Miles cleared his throat and started again. "Because I was unable to join you for dinner, I wanted to have a word with you before we departed. It is most important."

"Certainly." Arvel turned as his wife joined them. "I've arranged to have a carriage waiting by the dock to take you and Iris to Thornhall. I'll be home after things are settled at Cadenbury," he said.

Winora stepped forward and offered her hand to Miles, acting as if nothing out of the ordinary had happened. "Miles, may your journey be safe and joyful."

Iris had gathered the scattered papers from the floor. She timidly held them out.

Miles dropped to his knees to accept them. "Iris, I hope you will forgive my rude behavior last night. It would have been an honor to dine beside the brave young lady who saved my life. I hope that we will always be friends."

He looked up at Arvel. "Perhaps she can visit Ferndale soon, to keep Ivey from becoming homesick."

Arvel grinned. "That's a fine idea. Would you like that, Iris?"

"Oh, yes!" Iris wrapped her arms around Miles' neck and gave him a tight hug. "Please marry my sister. You were meant to be my brother."

Miles quickly jumped to his feet and brushed off his trouser legs.

Winora held out her hand. "Come along now, Iris. The men need to talk." Iris took her mother's hand and they disembarked.

"So, is there a problem, aside from my daughter's choice of travel attire?" Arvel asked, trying to make light of the situation.

"No, sir." Miles put his papers in order while he spoke. "Last night, while I was out inspecting the *Monarch*'s wings, I got to thinking about a conversation we had while working on the *Boreas* the other day. I was struck by your description of Ivey's creature and the role he could play on your mission."

Arvel nodded intently. "Beast has many useful qualities. Go on."

"Well, I was considering the ability he has to mask himself—when it struck me. What if the exterior of a flying machine were also fashioned to adapt to its surroundings?"

"Certainly an intriguing idea, but how would such a thing be possible?"

"Fenchurche Industries recently developed a glazing technique used in the private quarters of the *Monarch* that allows passengers to see from the inside out. The other side of the glass reflects light almost as well as a mirror does. We discovered that by using this technique in conjunction with an otheophainer, such as in the wing panels and undercarriage of a Zephyr, reflected light can be conducted through one point in this glass to another. If the image of something visible on one side of the ship could be transferred through a glass shield so that it appears precisely on the opposite side, one would create an illusion that nothing exists to obstruct the light. That would render the ship nearly invisible."

He offered a portfolio of diagrams. Arvel opened the folder and looked through the documents as Miles continued.

"These are the preliminary notes and sketches that I drew up last night. They outline the principle. Please share them with Stanley and Nicolai after your meeting. When I return to Ferndale, I will dedicate myself to building a shield that will give your ship the ability to disappear into its surroundings, in the air or on ground."

Arvel was stunned.

"Miles, have I heard you correctly? You can actually build a shield that will make the *Boreas* invisible?"

"I believe so. My calculations show that it is physically possible."

"Well, if it is, I'd say you are about to make your mark on the world of science, Mr. Fenchurche. Such a thing could be life altering. I don't know what to say."

Miles stepped back and looked away.

"It is imperative to everyone in your family that you return safely, Mr. Thornton."

It pained Arvel to see the unfortunate position in which he'd placed the boy.

He patted him on the shoulder. "As long as I have the likes of you and Stanley by my side, I will be a force to reckon with. I can promise you that."

The ship's doors began to close.

"You'd better hurry," Miles warned.

"Yes, but there's one more thing. Make sure Ivey tells you about her reactions to the Zephyr."

"I'll try." Miles added softly, "If she'll even speak to me."

"I have every confidence that you'll find a way to win her over. Now, try to enjoy your trip, Miles, but do keep an eye on that daughter of mine. She has a tendency to leap before she looks."

"Oh, dear, we never told her about the bath. I have to go. Goodbye, Mr. Thornton."

The flustered young man rushed off, leaving a trail of curious looks and whispers swirling in his wake.

༄

Ivey's face was still burning with embarrassment as she topped the staircase and entered the parlor. She looked toward a large door carved with the Fenchurche coat of arms. Iris had said it was the master suite, designed for the man who owned the ship.

Ivey considered sneaking inside Miles' quarters to leave his jacket, thus avoiding the humiliation of returning it in person. She wanted to pretend the frightful episode had never happened, and she hoped he would prove bright enough to do the same.

She tested the door handle. It opened. She took one step inside and stopped. With her luck, Miles would probably run smack into her on her way out. She pulled the door shut and turned to find Minnette's assistant watching her from the staircase.

Dolan stared at the jacket draped across her bare shoulders, but his voice remained casual.

"Good morning, Miss Thornton. Might I be of assistance?"

Without a word, Ivey ducked her head and ran to her suite, knowing her antics would be reported to Minnette Fenchurche in great detail. She had no choice now but to give the jacket back to Miles herself and beg him to explain the unusual circumstances of the morning to his mother.

Once inside her quarters, Ivey decided to put all unpleasantness out of her mind with a steaming bath before venturing out to explore the ship.

According to the articles she'd read, one of the *Monarch*'s most luxurious charms was a network of conduits that delivered heated air and medicinal water to the large crystal tubs in the passenger's quarters. A brass lever controlled by the bather allowed the compressed air to pass through thousands of tiny pores that lined the inside of the tub, giving the water a relaxing effervescence.

While the water ran, Ivey inspected an excessive assortment of bath oils and salts on a silver stand beside the tub. Unable to make up her mind, she finally elected to concoct a fragrant stew from all of them. It didn't take long for the tub to fill with delightfully scented water topped with a cloud of bubbles.

Ivey dropped her clothes on the floor and stepped into the warm water. She reached down and turned the brass lever. The water began to dance as a swarm of bubbles raced to the surface.

She lowered herself into the water and rested her back against the gentle slope of the slipper-shaped tub. Above her head, a skylight window offered a breathtaking look up at the airship's envelope as it passed gently through low-lying clouds.

The ascent had been so effortless that she hadn't even noticed the ship's departure.

A few minutes later, she heard a low, pulsing sound. The ship had engaged all of its forward engines to navigate the stronger air currents when it crossed the mountains.

I could stay here forever.

Ivey closed her eyes, letting the past week's difficulties melt away as the vessel's soft heartbeat lulled her into a peaceful sleep.

When Ivey awoke, the bath had lost its bubbles, but the heated air had kept the water delightfully warm. She yawned and stretched, so relaxed that she barely had the strength to move. She glanced at the floor. Her clothes were gone.

Ivey sat up with a start, looking around the room.

To her bewilderment, a pretty young woman was standing beside the tub offering her a large towel.

"What are you doing?"

"I'm here to help you out of the tub, miss. You've been in for over an hour now." The woman's voice seemed even kinder than her smiling face, but Ivey didn't appreciate such an invasion of her privacy.

"I don't need help. Please get out." Ivey snatched the towel from the woman's hand and wrapped it around herself as she stood. The room began to spin.

"Whoa," Ivey groaned as she stumbled out of the tub.

The young woman grabbed her by the arms to keep her from falling over.

"That's what we call a *Monarch* head-throe, miss."

"A what?" The spinning was making Ivey queasy.

"A sickish feeling brought on by the ship's slow rocking motion. It takes a few days to adjust. We've had many a passenger faint after a hot bath—especially when they stay in for too long. Mr. Miles said you're a swooner, so he sent me to make sure you didn't take a nasty fall."

"I do not swoon." Ivey moaned and sank to her knees. "But I might be sick."

The woman helped Ivey lie on her back before retrieving a large pillow from the bedroom to put under her legs.

"We've got to get the blood back to your head," she said. The woman went to the silver stand beside the tub and selected a vial. She removed the stopper and knelt beside Ivey, holding it close to her nose. "Now, take a deep breath."

Ivey inhaled. The brisk scent instantly calmed her churning stomach. She closed her eyes and took long, slow breaths. "Much better."

Her nausea passed, leaving Ivey with a pleasant sense of weakness. The woman replaced the vial and pulled the lever to stop the airflow into the water. There was a long silence.

"Please tell me, how did you know I was in the bath?" Ivey was almost expecting to hear that Miles Fenchurche had managed to walk in on her as she slept.

"Mr. Fenchurche meant to warn you last night, miss. Since he didn't get the chance, he had the engineers in the pipeworks ring me when your bath was in use."

Ivey sighed with relief. "Just so you know, I am not and have never been the fainting type. It's just that I haven't eaten a bite today, and it's been a bad week. I'm not at my best, but I do appreciate your help. What is your name?"

"Sylvia," the woman replied.

"Are you and Mr. Fenchurche friends?"

"Oh, heavens no, miss." The young woman looked down and tugged at the small black apron cinched around the waist of her full figure. "I'm just a servant. Mr. Miles asked me to be your personal chambermaid."

Ivey sat up. She hadn't noticed the servant's apron against the woman's dark blue dress.

This was something Prim hadn't prepared her for. Although her mother cherished her role in genteel society, she'd never kept servants in her home. She expected the girls to assist with the housework themselves. In her opinion, a good wife was happy to make the home comfortable for the family by her own efforts.

Ivey offered her hand.

"Delighted to meet you, Sylvia."

Sylvia took her hand with a slight curtsy. "Thank you, Miss Thornton. It's my honor."

Ivey giggled. "Don't be so formal; please call me Ivey."

Sylvia's hazel eyes sparkled. "Actually, miss, there are rules that must be obeyed. Many, many rules."

Ivey nodded coyly. "Of course there are, Sylvia, but between the two of us, some rules are quite good to break." She quickly added, "As long as you do it properly, of course."

Sylvia looked down, letting her dusky blond hair fall across her eyes, but Ivey sensed the maid's amusement.

"Are you feeling well enough to get up now, Miss Ivey?"

"Yes, I'm fine. There is something I have to ask you, though."

"Yes?"

"I left a jacket on the floor earlier. Did you see it?"

"Yes, miss. It's put up in the wardrobe, along with the things from your trunk."

"Good. And thank you for doing that," Ivey added. "You see, I had a bit of a misstep this morning, and Mr. Fenchurche offered his jacket. Could you return it and ask him to explain things to Dolan, so there are no misunderstandings about the matter?"

Sylvia's widening smile gave her away.

"You already know," Ivey sighed. "What did you hear?"

"Well, there's more than one rumor floating about," Sylvia shrugged apologetically. "Don't you fret. Some passengers have nothing better to do than tittle-tattle."

Prim had warned of this. She said that gossip would spread like wildfire among the elite passengers on the *Monarch*, who rarely found anything more intriguing than speculations on the sensational comings and goings of their peers.

"Just know the servants never discuss the family or their guests, miss."

"Thank you," Ivey said. "So you'll return the jacket?"

"I'll see to it as soon as I have you dressed and on your schedule, miss."

"My schedule?"

"Mrs. Fenchurche has arranged a full social calendar for your voyage, and I'm afraid that we've already missed the first two appointments of the day."

Ivey sighed. She wanted to explore the ship on her own, and there was no telling how oppressive a social calendar would be. Sylvia seemed nice, but her duties might include reporting back to the mistress, so Ivey gritted her teeth behind a genteel smile and rose to her feet.

"Well, let's find something pretty for me to wear. I cannot wait to discover what she has planned for me."

∽

After helping Ivey into a nice dress and fixing her hair, Sylvia offered to show her the way to Minnette's luncheon in the *Monarch*'s tearoom.

"I was there with my family last night. I should have no problem finding it on my own."

"Are you sure? Most passengers stay lost for days," Sylvia said.

Ivey gave her a satisfied smile. "Well, I am not one of them. Before we arrive in Spirehaven, I intend to know everything there is to know about this glorious vessel." She exited the suite, Sylvia close behind her.

Ivey walked over to inspect the family's private elevator. She didn't see any familiar-looking controls. "How does this work?"

"Oh, miss, you need a key to use that lift. Mr. Dolan, Mr. Miles, and the captain all carry one."

"I prefer the stairs anyway," Ivey said. "I don't need anything else, if you've got other things to do."

"Thank you, miss. Have a nice time, and feel free to ring for me when you get back."

"I'm looking forward to meeting the ladies Mrs. Fenchurche has invited. I'm sure I'll have much to talk about," Ivey said with a smile. She turned away before rolling her eyes.

On her way down the stairs, Ivey tried not imagine what she must have looked like chasing after her father wearing nothing but undergarments.

Half-lidded eyes were cast in her direction, and hushed whispers followed her around the side of the glass garden. Ivey held her head high and walked toward the back of the lobby, where a grand staircase rose to the *Monarch*'s second level. On either side of the staircase, large double doorways opened into long corridors that ended at the tearoom, which was situated at the very back of the *Monarch*'s cabin. Ivey made for the corridor closest to the garden.

As she entered the passageway, she admired the beautifully finished doors engraved with botanically inspired motifs and room numbers. All the doors were to her left, meaning that every passenger's room had an outward-facing window. The opposite wall of the corridor contained an expanse of wooden paneling.

Ivey wondered whether the ship's kitchens might lie behind this wall. She was eager to learn more about the location and layout of facilities large enough to provide food and service for 250 passengers and nearly as many crew members.

At dinner the previous night, an endless stream of waiters with plated meals had passed through the swinging doors of a wide room at the back of the grand dining hall. Thinking those doors might lead to the kitchen, Ivey had excused herself from the captain's table long enough to take a peek inside. All she'd seen was a shallow space filled with rows of china cabinets and crowded with rolling carts of empty food trays.

The large dining hall occupied the entire the bow of the ship. Its two-story outer walls were made of the same curved glass panels as those in the lobby. The only way into the dining hall was through the passengers' reception entrance on the portside of the lobby or via a small private dining room on the starboard. Neither of these entrances showed any sign of waiters bringing service carts, yet the food delivered to the captain's table had been piping hot.

Ivey was eager to discover where the food was prepared and how it got into that service room. She would have loved to bring up that topic during her father's dinner discussion with the captain and his senior crew, but one of Prim's etiquette lessons had come to mind.

It's important not to be too inquisitive around Minnette and her staff. Young ladies valued by high society do not care about pedestrian matters.

Ivey cared. As soon as she could break free of her social engagements, she intended to snoop about the ship to her heart's content.

Near the end of the long corridor, she passed by the window of the *Monarch's* nursery, a feature of the ship that held little interest for Ivey. During the family tour with Iris, her mother had stepped inside to chat with the neatly uniformed attendants about the accommodations for parents traveling with small children, while the others continued on to the tearoom.

The round tables in the darkened tearoom had already been set for the next day's service. Iris had been enchanted by the delicate china and unusual floral arrangements, but Ivey wasn't impressed.

Now that the ship was in flight, Ivey realized that the tearoom had been nestled in the *Monarch's* stern for a good reason. It was only one story high, but through its V-shaped wall of windows, it offered a fabulous panoramic view of the countryside in the ship's wake.

Minnette and a few other pinch-faced women were seated at a table in the tip of the stern. Seeing Ivey, she nodded for a waiter to show her to a seat while the rest of the women turned to stare.

"Good day, ladies." Ivey sat and delicately arranged the linen napkin from her place setting across her lap while she recalled Prim's advice about such situations.

A polite lady lets others steer the conversation. It makes them feel appreciated, and you'll learn a lot more about their true intentions when you let them do the talking.

Ivey smiled and nodded attentively as Minnette made the introductions. She fought the urge to stare out the window at the beautiful landscape passing below. Having missed breakfast, Ivey was especially regretful that she would have to be satisfied with the dainty portions sure to be presented when the waiter returned.

The food arrived, and Ivey was enjoying an immodestly long drink of tea when Miles Fenchurche entered the tearoom and approached her table. He avoided looking at her as blatantly as she avoided looking at him.

"You needed to speak with me, Mother?"

Minnette meticulously folded her napkin. "Yes, Miles. I heard that your suit jacket was missing this morning. I hope you haven't lost anything important."

The ladies at the table cackled like hens, but Ivey gasped at her implication, inhaling a mouthful of tea. She began to choke, spraying tea from her nose onto the beautiful food sitting in front of her.

Minnette didn't bat an eye, but the ladies at the table tittered into their napkins while pretending to be concerned.

Miles moved toward Ivey with an overly anxious expression that rankled her nerves.

For pity's sake, I'm not going to swoon, sir.

She held up her hand and vehemently shook her head.

He kept coming. "Please, Miss Thornton, just raise your left arm, and let me pat you on the back."

Ivey jumped to her feet to escape the man, somehow turning her chair over backward in the process. Her nose was running, and tears streaked her face.

"Please excuse me," she sobbed into her napkin, before fleeing the tearoom.

Ivey was confident that she would never cry over anything as silly as spilt tea, but the tears brought on by her choking presented the perfect excuse to hide in her suite for the rest of the day.

It was irksome, though, that both of the Fenchurches now held equally wrong assessments of her everyday conduct. While Minnette was surely questioning Ivey's prudence, Miles seemed to have decided that she was a fragile flower in need of constant protection. The sooner she could put that ridiculous notion out of his head, the better.

☙

Miles set Ivey's chair back on its feet and faced his mother. Sylvia had returned his borrowed jacket with a warning that rumors about the character of his fiancée were spreading throughout the ship. His pledge to protect Ivey's honor still rang in his ears. For once, Miles was willing to put up a fight, and he didn't care who overheard it.

"You were curious about my jacket, Mother, so let me make this clear. Mr. and Mrs. Thornton stayed the night with their daughter, in her suite. This morning, when Miss Thornton discovered that her father had left something of great importance behind, she ran to catch him before he left the ship, forgetting her improper state of dress. I happened to pass by and offered my jacket so that she could return to her room with dignity." Miles cast a stern look around the table. "The only thing I am in danger of losing is my temper. I should let you all remember that Miss Thornton is my honored guest, and I suggest she be treated with respect."

The ladies at the table looked properly rebuked. Minnette simply nodded and gestured for the waiter to remove Ivey's dishes.

"That will be all, Miles," she said, and casually dismissed him.

Miles left the tearoom, marveling at how easily he had found the words to defend Ivey's innocence. In truth, he had no idea what she was doing in the lobby wearing only her undergarments, but now it was his duty to respond to these situations on Arvel's behalf. He only wished that the girl would let him help her out of her habitual predicaments without being so easily offended.

If she knew how seriously he took his pledge to keep her out of harm's way, she might learn to trust him. It would be nice to come to an understanding, though he doubted a girl as high-spirited as Ivey would ever enjoy spending time with someone like him.

Miles shook his head, trying to clear his thoughts. The endlessly complicated interactions of people made Miles prefer to spend his time alone. He readily retreated to his study, where he continued to work out plans for a sheath of invisibility to conceal the *Boreas*.

Ivey stayed by the window in her sitting room for hours. She marveled at the *Monarch*'s titanic wings and the scenery passing far below them. As they passed over blue lakes and rich forests, Ivey was reminded of the colorful charts in Arvel's book of Cemarian maps.

Late in the afternoon, she'd sent word with Sylvia that she was suffering from a headache and would be unable to appear at dinner. It was a ploy that Prim had advised her to use on occasions when she needed time alone, as Minnette was frequently confined by her own ailments.

Sylvia appeared at her door that evening with a heavily laden tray of food bearing samples of everything the *Monarch*'s kitchens had to offer. Ivey considered eating every last bit of it herself, but she wanted to spend more time getting to know her thoughtful maid.

"Sylvia, this is far too much food for one lady alone, and my mother frowns upon waste. Won't you stay and enjoy it with me?"

"Oh, no, miss. Servants never share meals with the Fenchurche family," Sylvia protested.

"Well, I'm not family yet," Ivey corrected her. "And remember what Miles said about my delicate nature? What if I should choke on a piece of meat, or swoon into my bread pudding with no one here to save me?"

Sylvia couldn't stifle her giggle. "A terrible shame, miss, and I suppose it would be my fault. Maybe I'll just sit over here and watch you eat."

Ivey handed her a silver fork from the tray. "Not so fast. Some dastardly enemy of the Fenchurche family may be trying to poison me. I insist that you taste it first, for my safety's sake."

Sylvia gave in with a shrug. "Well, Mr. Miles asked me to look out for you."

Ivey and Sylvia had a fine time polishing off the meal and telling their histories. Sylvia talked about growing up on a farm outside of Spirehaven. She'd left home at the age of fourteen to work at Ferndale. Despite Minnette's rules, Sylvia found her work rewarding and had no plans to leave. She shared Ivey's love for animals and often assisted her brother with his chores at the Ferndale stables.

Ivey would have liked to share more of her childhood stories from Thornhall in return, but many of her most memorable experiences were best kept solely between her and her father. Even Arvel didn't know all of her secrets. Some things were so unsettling that Ivey denied their existence, sometimes to herself.

A knock at the door interrupted their conversation.

"Miss Ivey, may I have a word?"

It was Dolan.

The two quickly made it appear as if Ivey had been resting on the settee with a cool cloth on her head. After admitting Dolan to the suite, Sylvia hurried to the bedroom to busy herself arranging Ivey's wardrobe.

"Good evening, Dolan. To what do I owe the honor of this visit?" Ivey asked with a tragic hint of pain in her voice.

"Mrs. Fenchurche has offered to have her personal physician see to your headache," Dolan said. "He carries medicines that can ease the pain and invite sleep, if you are in need."

"Thank you for your kindness. I believe the worst of it has passed. Sylvia brought food, and I managed to eat some, which helped. I must have been overcome by the past week's excitement. A good night's sleep is the best medicine now." Ivey looked toward the door of the bedroom. "Sylvia, have you reorganized my wardrobe as I requested?"

Sylvia answered from the bedroom doorway, "Yes, miss. Just finishing. I will try to remember where you wish to keep everything in the future."

Ivey gave Dolan a prim smile. "I prefer to do things a certain way. Sylvia has been very cooperative, and I appreciate the quality of her service. I hope that I did not keep her too long."

"Mrs. Fenchurche will be pleased that you've taken a firm hand." He bowed slightly. "Sylvia is at your disposal, day or night."

"In that case, I would like her to get me ready for bed. After she clears the dinner tray, I will dismiss her."

Dolan nodded approvingly. "And feel free to alert me if you have any issues with the services offered on board the *Monarch*."

"Yes, I will. Oh, and what time am I expected for breakfast in the morning? I wish to start my day off on a better footing tomorrow." Ivey locked eyes with Dolan. She hoped that he'd appreciate her firm hand with him as well.

"The captain's table is served at the seventh hour of the morning. Will you require someone to wake you?"

"No, thank you. I am an early riser."

"Very well. Good evening, Miss Ivey."

Dolan closed the door. Ivey held up one finger, warning Sylvia to remain silent. She sensed him lingering on the other side. Sylvia nodded and went back to the bedroom.

"Sylvia." Ivey spoke just loudly enough to ensure her voice could be heard. "Lay out my nightgown, I am ready to retire."

Ivey joined Sylvia in the bedroom and closed the door. "You don't know how happy I am that you stayed with me tonight."

"Well, truth be told, miss, Mr. Miles asked me to spend extra time with you. You know, in case you were missing your friends," Sylvia confessed.

Ivey recoiled. "He really doesn't know the first thing about me. I don't have friends."

Sylvia looked shocked. "Someone like you? I thought you would have friends by the basketful."

"No. I've never had a need for them."

Sylvia sighed. "How sad. You and Mr. Miles look like you have so much, but when it comes to things that matter—"

Ivey interrupted her. "Please don't compare my life to his. I had a wonderful childhood. I have the greatest father in the world, my mother is extremely good at mothering, my sisters are delightful, and I suppose I do have one very dear friend, although he lives in a pond."

"In a pond? I will want to hear more about him. But now, you should have your rest."

Sylvia began to leave, but Ivey stopped her. "Wait."

"Yes, miss?"

"I'm being untruthful. I do regret not having friends. It's just that I haven't met anyone, who lives outside of a pond, who suits me. I find myself liking you very much, and if you are willing, I would like to be your friend."

"I would, too, but my job is to serve Mr. Miles by serving you, and that is my first duty."

Ivey offered her hand. "Agreed. And about Miles—I'd like to keep our conversations private. It is best that he discovers who I really am for himself."

"Yes, indeed. And you should do the same, miss. I think you'll both be surprised, in the nicest way. He's a curious person, much like you."

"What do you mean by curious?"

"Oh, you'll have to find that out for yourself, miss."

Ivey's left eyebrow arched at the thought. She didn't know a thing about Miles Fenchurche. They'd said no more than a few words to each other, and those had been uttered under the most unpleasant circumstances.

Sylvia had cleared the tray and was on her way out of the room before Ivey noticed.

"Goodnight, miss. Have sweet dreams."

"Goodnight, Sylvia."

The door closed, and Ivey fell back onto her bed. Looking up, she gasped in wonder. The tall posts of her bed were connected by a railing festooned with ornamental drapery that had hidden the large expanse of glass above her head.

From where she lay, the sharp edge of the *Monarch*'s balloon was silhouetted against night sky, where a million stars shined down upon her.

Chapter Nine

DARK OMENS

Prim looked in on her daughters, worried that the approaching storm may have frightened them. The three girls were sleeping like cherubs in the Honeycutt mansion's nursery.

A clap of thunder rattled the window as if something were trying to get in. Prim looked out as a flash of lightning briefly illuminated the treetops.

Unlike Thornhall, which was nestled in a wooded area on the outskirts of Prominence, Stanley and Prim's estate was in the heart of the city. It was situated within walking distance of the headquarters of Honeycutt Mechanical and the Cadenbury Institute. Despite its central location in the busiest part of town, the expansive park-like grounds surrounding the large residence offered a sense of seclusion. The sprawling gardens and groves were a vestige of the house's history as one of the oldest manors from the capital's early days.

Prim softly closed the nursery door and checked the time on the pendulum clock in the hallway.

"Oh, Stanley, when will you be home?"

While Prim was pleased that Stanley had been working so hard on a project that involved her father, something about this night felt wrong, and she wanted her husband at her side. He had been spending long hours at the Institute's laboratories ever since construction of the *Boreas* had ramped up. Many nights, he didn't return until after she'd gone to bed.

Prim hurried down the staircase to make sure the front door was securely bolted. The torrential rain pounding against the building's copper roof matched the racing of her heart.

An odd sound echoed in the front solarium. She listened intently.

What is that?

It sounded like water dripping into a deep well.

Prim carefully made her way down the tile steps into the room. It was too dark to discern whether the atrium's glass roof had developed a leak. She slowly crossed the floor, following the haunting sound.

A flash of lightning lit the room.

Prim froze. The entire floor was covered in dark water—and yet her feet felt perfectly dry.

It's here again.

"No! You can't have my baby," Prim screamed.

There was no escape as a misshapen form loomed in front of her, attaching itself to her waist and forcing her down.

ॐ

For a second night, Stanley awoke to Prim's terrified screams. After he roused her from the nightmare, she wept in his arms.

Prim had always been the most practical of the Thornton girls. Foolishness like premonitions and omens had no place in her material world, but this particular dream was now haunting her night and day. She was convinced that it warned of an impending tragedy.

"Oh, Stanley," she sobbed. "I am going to lose this child."

"No, my dear," he tenderly replied. "It was only a dream. I promise that you and our baby are safe."

"Something is wrong," she whispered.

Stanley held her close and stroked her hair, trying to comfort her.

"The doctor said everything was fine, darling. If you like, I'll have him return tomorrow and check again."

Prim looked up with a tear-streaked face. "Yes, please. I am sorry to be so much trouble, but I cannot rest until everything is right."

Stanley kissed the bridge of her nose. "You are the most precious thing in my life, Primrose. You've given me so much. I'd do anything for you, anything. Would you like me to rub your shoulders?"

Prim nodded. Stanley massaged her knotted muscles for a long time. Finally, her body began to relax. As he eased her back into her pillows, she clung to her husband. "Promise me, if the storm comes, you won't let it take us."

Stanley held her close. "Of course. I will protect you."

He began to stroke her hair. When she finally drifted back into sleep, he heard her mumble.

"We should warn them."

"Warn who, darling?" Stanley asked. There was no answer.

Arvel paced the wooden floor of his study. After hearing Stanley's description of his oldest daughter's agitation since the incident on the *Monarch*'s docking platform, he had a growing concern that it was still too early to introduce Zephyr technology to the public.

Throughout the craft's development and testing phases, no one involved had experienced anything notably out of the ordinary, but the device's energetic principles were still a fundamental mystery of science. Maddox Fenchurche's death in the mine explosion served as a solemn reminder of how quickly things could go wrong when one started poking around the unknown.

In spite of his concerns, Arvel's need for the *Boreas* was greater than ever. Phineas Langley had approved his proposal to track the murderous predator in Boulder Creek without the escort of Silas Harp's Promacheon detachment. During a private meeting, Archon Langley had directed Silas to share some details of a highly confidential report that painted an even bleaker picture. Near Cemaria's eastern border, the small village of Boulder Creek and its surrounding farmlands continued to suffer grisly attacks. As the number of victims grew, so did the range of the attacks. Whatever was killing those people was on the move.

The Promacheon report offered little in the way of useful leads. Most victims simply disappeared. On the rare occasion that a body was discovered, the condition of the corpse spoke of a violent and horrific death. Even among those present during the attacks, no one claimed to have gotten so much as a glimpse of the creature responsible.

Arvel had no idea what he would be hunting or how to avoid becoming its prey. If Miles' plan to cloak the *Boreas* with a glass shield was successful, he hoped to be able to stalk the thing long enough to discover a weakness.

He'd asked Silas to procure patches of the victims' clothing before he left. Arvel had used a game of hide and seek with Iris to test Ivey's waterdog, and his unique stalking talents included a keen sense of smell. Along with helping him locate the predator, the formidable waterdog could prove a valuable ally in any potential confrontation. He hoped his daughter would forgive him for taking that risk.

Arvel sighed. Thinking of Ivey brought on a tremendous sense of loss. He'd known he would miss her, but since her departure, he felt as though a bright light had been dimmed at Thornhall. He wondered whether she was suffering any more ill effects from her exposure to the otheophainer, and he wished he could know how her trip aboard the *Monarch* was progressing.

Arvel rubbed his eyes and sank into Ivey's favorite leather chair. His heart ached. The world was quickly changing, and there was little he could do to stop it.

"Time for a break?"

He looked up and saw Winora offering him a bundle of dried sage incense and her beautiful smile, two things that never failed to brighten his mood.

"I can feel your sadness from across the house," she said, caressing his cheek with her hand.

Arvel kissed her fingers. "There's no room for sadness in my heart when you are here. Would you sit and talk a while, my love?"

She set the sage on a side table and gazed into his eyes. "I've been wondering when you would finally tell me what's going on at Cadenbury and why you are making preparations for the worst."

Arvel sighed, "You know everything there is to know about me, don't you?"

"There's been a strange feeling of tension in the air at Thornhall for some time."

Arvel pulled Winora into his lap and held her tight. "We must get Prim and the girls under our roof as soon as possible. She needs her mother's loving touch, and Stanley and I have much to do. In the morning, I will tell you everything you need to know about my next expedition. Oh, and there is a friend of Ivey's you need to meet as well."

Winora leaned back in his arms. "Do you mean that hideous monster she keeps in the pond?"

Arvel's obvious astonishment sent Winora into a fit of girlish giggles. "You've seen him?" he asked.

"Who do you think you're dealing with?" she teased. "You may have a talent for tracking, but all mothers have the uncanny ability to see what's happening behind their backs and hear a child's guilty footsteps from across the grounds."

Arvel set Winora on her feet as he rose from the chair. "You'll always be a step ahead of me. What do you say we call this a night, my love?"

"Poor dear, are you tired?"

"No. Life is fleeting." Arvel took her hand and led her from the study. "I cannot afford to waste a single night that I am allowed to spend in the arms of my beautiful wife."

A bright flash woke Ivey. Through the glass above her bed, streaks of lightning illuminated the *Monarch*'s envelope as it was buffeted by the winds of a raging gale.

Ivey sat up. She was well aware of the threat that storms posed to airships, but a part of her was thrilled by the prospect of watching such an event from the big window in the family parlor. She threw on a green dress from her wardrobe and tied back her hair with a matching ribbon, lest she be caught out and about in her undergarments again.

She opened her door and peered out. The parlor was empty. She ran to the great window by the landing of the staircase. The rocking of the ship was so violent that Ivey had to crouch on the floor to keep from falling over. Roiling clouds engulfed the dirigible. The scene outside the window hardly seemed real. The *Monarch*'s wings had been retracted, but the cables of the riggings were whipping up and down as the ship bowed in the grip of the storm.

Ivey heard voices approaching. She instinctively ducked behind one of the couches in the darkened parlor before Miles and Sylvia emerged from the glass car of the private elevator.

"Should I wake her, Mr. Miles?"

"Yes. If we cannot outrun the turbulence, the captain will make an emergency landing. Take her to the library and wait."

"Yes, sir," Sylvia answered. "And your mother?"

"Dolan will see to her. I'm needed on the bridge." Miles set a steady hand on Sylvia's shoulder. "You know I count on you to keep Miss Thornton safe." He leaned close. "We may have a rough landing, but the library is fortified. Once it's over, I will come for the two of you."

The maid reached up and clutched his hand with a brave smile. "We'll be fine, Miles."

"I'll make sure of that." He ran off toward the back of the parlor. Sylvia rushed to Ivey's door and began to knock.

"I'm here." Ivey rose to her feet. The ship pitched, throwing Ivey against the window and Sylvia to the floor.

"C'mon, miss," Sylvia cried as she struggled to her feet. "We've got to get to the library."

Ivey heard a high-pitched creaking from outside. She turned to see one of the rigging cables being stretched to its breaking point.

"Get down," Ivey screamed.

She dove to the floor just as the cable gave way—sending one length of the heavy steel flying straight toward the window. It cut through the glass above her head like a scythe through new grass, smashing every piece of heavy furniture in its path. A section of window ruptured around the gash, and broken glass blew into the room.

"Hang on," Ivey yelled above the roar of rushing air that pulled glass shards and bits of furniture through the hole and into the wild night sky.

Sylvia screamed. The frayed end of the severed cable had caught upon the skirt of her uniform and was dragging her toward the broken window as it retracted. Ivey threw herself forward, just managing to grab Sylvia by the arms. She dug her legs against the rug as she wrestled to free her maid from the cable's hooked grasp. When they reached the edge, Ivey grabbed ahold of of the broken glass with her left hand and held on as Sylvia's legs disappeared through the hole.

"I need help," Ivey screamed as she clung to the girl's arm. "Anyone? Please!"

In the howling of the wind Ivey heard a monstrous voice reply, "No one can help you. Let go."

Ivey shrieked as Sylvia fell from her grasp. When her left hand slipped from the glass, Ivey followed her into the swirling black clouds.

She woke with a start, the sound of her terrified cries still ringing in her ears.

Sylvia was standing over her, screaming.

"What's happened?" Ivey asked. "Did we crash?"

It took a moment for the maid to form words. "No, miss," she sobbed. "I couldn't wake you. There's blood everywhere, and you were stone cold. I thought you were killed in your sleep."

Ivey raised her head.

The coverlet on her bed was stained red. She looked down. Blood was running from the palm of her left hand.

The broken glass.

Ivey slowly rose to a sitting position.

The storm had seemed real, but now she felt a strange disconnection from her body. There was no pain from the wound on her hand, and her brain was in a fog. "What should I do?"

"Come with me." Sylvia gently eased Ivey out of bed and led her to the bathroom. She filled the washbasin with cool water and lowered Ivey's bloody hand into the bowl.

"I may need to fetch Mr. Miles or the doctor. It looks like a deep cut."

"But I was sleeping. How did that happen?"

"I don't know, miss. Maybe there's a sharp edge on the bed."

Sylvia gently rubbed Ivey's palm as the water turned dark with blood.

"Let's see how bad it is." She raised Ivey's hand and turned it over. The two leaned closer. A jagged red scratch spanned the heel of Ivey's palm, but it was hardly the kind of wound that could have produced such an alarming amount of blood. Ivey trembled in relief.

"I suppose we won't need the doctor then," Sylvia whispered with wide eyes.

Ivey took a deep breath. "Strange things tend to happen around me. I can't explain how or why. I'll understand if you'd rather not be my friend."

Sylvia sighed and laid a comforting arm around Ivey's shoulders. "Mr. Miles told me you were special. I've seen an odd thing or two in my day, and I'm not easily frightened—well, except for when I thought you'd been murdered."

A loud knocking made both of them jump.

"Oh me," Sylvia said, "they'll be breaking down your door after the way I was screaming and carrying on. What should I tell them?"

Ivey still couldn't compose her thoughts.

"All right, then, you sit here." Sylvia helped Ivey to the dressing table in her bathroom.

The forceful knocking at the suite's outer door had become furious by the time Sylvia arrived to open it.

"What is going on?" It was Dolan's voice.

Ivey listened as her clever maid explained how she'd overreacted upon finding her mistress's face and bedding stained from a nosebleed. Ivey appreciated that Sylvia's wits were quicker than hers.

When Dolan insisted on speaking to Ivey directly, Sylvia politely informed him that her mistress did not intend to start another day aboard the *Monarch* being ogled in her sleeping clothes.

"I'm certain Mr. Miles would want you to wait until his fiancée has had her breakfast and is ready to receive visitors."

"Very well. Tell her that I will be entering her quarters to look into this matter after she is properly dressed."

The door closed and Sylvia returned.

Ivey stared at her reflection in the dressing table's mirror.

"What's wrong, miss?"

Ivey looked up. "I don't know how, but the cut on my hand came from broken glass."

"You broke a glass?" Sylvia asked.

"No. It happened in a dream."

"What?"

Ivey told her every detail of the nightmare, from Miles' words of encouragement to the disembodied voice in the storm clouds. When she finished, Sylvia lifted Ivey's scratched hand and looked closely at it.

"So, you did this to save me?"

Ivey's head drooped. "I don't think either of us were saved."

"Sweet girl, you tried. Dreams are tricky things, but I promise you that we are more than safe. You'll feel much better when you've had something to eat."

Ivey groaned. "I cannot face Minnette and her harpies right now."

"Oh, you won't. Mr. Miles has asked you to join him for breakfast in the garden room this morning."

Ivey perked up. "The garden room?"

"Yes, indeed. That is what I came to tell you before all the fuss."

"So what does Mr. Fenchurche want?"

Sylvia looked off. "Well, you are his fiancée. Maybe he'd like to spend time with you. May I help you get dressed now?"

"Yes, please."

Ivey's senses were returning to normal, and she'd been meaning to get a closer look at the glass garden.

When Sylvia opened the wardrobe, Ivey noticed that the green dress she'd worn in her dream wasn't there. She couldn't recall whether she'd even packed it, so she dismissed the thought and chose a posh frock her mother had given her for special occasions. The fabric was a deep shade of blue that Winora claimed would give an impression of cool regality.

For some reason, Ivey felt the need to look her best now that she finally had the opportunity to meet Miles Fenchurche during something other than a medical emergency.

❧

As Ivey made her way down the stairs and into the main lobby, she was approached by two girls she recognized from Prominence.

"Ivey Thornton, is that you? We heard you were flying in a first-class suite, but it seemed so unlikely," Chenille Foxton said with a toss of her head.

"That is, until you went running through the lobby in your unmentionables. Then we knew it had to be you," Amelia Buxhill giggled into her glove. "Dear Ivey, will you ever learn how to dress like a lady?"

In her early days at domestic school, Ivey had successfully defended herself against such teasing with hearty shoves and smacks. As the girls in her class grew older and their abuse more subtle, the tables had turned against Ivey. The genteel social interactions of finishing school made it easier for her classmates' taunts to go unnoticed by the adults in charge. When the girls successfully goaded her into an act of retaliation, Ivey's tormentors suddenly acted like innocent victims, tearfully recounting her bizarre outbursts and savage behavior.

Ivey took a long breath and braced herself. If they were inviting her to make another scene, she was determined to give them no such satisfaction.

"And then there's that ridiculous rumor floating around that the purpose of this sightseeing excursion is to announce your engagement to Miles Fenchurche," Chenille added.

"Why would a man who could have any woman in Cemaria settle for a cloddish, misfit freak in men's clothing?" Amelia asked.

"Well, we all know his mother wears the trousers in his family; maybe he prefers things that way," Chenille added.

Ivey's temper was about to get the better of her. She tried to walk away, but Amelia caught her sleeve.

"If you're going to stand a chance with Miles Fenchurche, you'd better learn how to make conversation like a lady."

Ivey was a heartbeat away from slapping the girl's face when Miles Fenchurche stepped forward and extended his arm.

"I am sorry to be late, Miss Thornton. I hope these vulgar young ladies aren't annoying my fiancée."

The girls' stunned expressions tickled Ivey. She gratefully took the arm that Miles offered and let him walk her to the garden room, feeling a rare sense of social victory as the two girls sputtered off.

Miles opened the outer door of a small vestibule that buffered the inside of the garden from the lobby, and they stepped inside. After the outer door was closed, a waiter opened the inner door. Ivey entered the garden and looked up. High overhead, the bright light outside the dome filtered down through the garden's canopy. The tree branches were alive with colorful flowers, birds, and butterflies.

Miles waited quietly while Ivey took a moment to enjoy the beautiful environs. He finally gestured for the waiter to lead them down the curving, flower-lined path to the polished stone fountain at the garden's far side. Ivey was far more impressed with the garden's botanical collection than with the ornate silver settings and intricately painted bone china waiting on their table.

She would have preferred to spend more time wandering about the garden, but Miles offered her a chair, and she felt compelled to let him go through the ridiculous ritual of helping her into the seat and then pushing it up to the table.

Her attitude lightened when a bright green butterfly grazed by her cheek before landing on the corner of the table. She smiled, and as her gaze passed over Miles, she saw that he'd been watching her.

What is he staring at?

Her smile faded and she looked away, making sure to keep her eyes on the surroundings until a waiter set a plate of sumptuous-looking fruit and crepes in front of her.

Ivey was ravenously hungry, but Prim had instructed her to only take a few bites of the small portions when eating in front of Miles or his mother. Worsening her trepidation was the memory of snorting tea out of her nose during her last attempt at fine dining in the tearoom.

Miles sat silently, waiting for her to begin. The two of them remained stuck in an uncomfortable silence until Ivey finally caved in.

"I'm actually very hungry. Would you mind if I eat everything that is on my plate?"

"Please do, and I will eat what is on mine, too, if you do not mind," Miles smiled shyly.

"That's fair," Ivey answered.

They spent several minutes cautiously trying to enjoy their food without making eye contact or doing anything to embarrass themselves.

When the main course arrived, Miles finally spoke up. "So, your father wanted me to talk to you about something."

Ivey blushed. "I can only imagine what that would be."

Miles blushed, too. "Oh, it's nothing too personal. He wanted you to tell me about your reaction to the Zephyr."

"Yes, of course," Ivey spoke confidently. "Father said that you could teach me how to fly one."

"I don't think that's what—"

Ivey continued. "The fact that I am female doesn't mean I won't make a good student. I can assure you of that."

Miles persisted. "Well, of course not. I only meant to say, I don't think that's what your father was talking about."

Ivey pushed a piece of garnish around her plate before relenting. "Alright. There was something else. It concerns a device on the Zephyr—the otheophainer."

"You know of otheophainers?"

"Yes. I'm quite good with scientific terminology, Mr. Fenchurche."

Ivey saw the corners of Miles' mouth turn up slightly, but his gaze remained serious. "I will make note of that, Miss Thornton. Please, go on."

"Well, he thinks I might have had a reaction to the energy field generated by a Zephyr, so Father warned me to stay away from them until he knows more. However, he also said that it would be perfectly safe for me to fly one. In fact, he thinks that you should teach me."

"What exactly do you think the otheophainer did to you?"

Ivey looked away. "Do you remember when you *thought* I fainted?"

"I do. That appeared to be a serious reaction."

"Yes, and when Stanley took off, it happened again, only that time it was exhilarating, as if I were weightless."

Miles studied her for a moment. "Have you noticed any other ill effects since then?"

"Yes," she blurted out, compelled to show him the phantom wound. "It happened last night. Look at this." She extended her hand.

He studied her palm, then looked up in confusion. Ivey pulled her hand back and examined it for herself. The scratch had vanished. She rubbed her hand, looking for some evidence of the injury, but there was nothing, not even a mark. Ivey frowned.

"Maybe you should ask Sylvia to tell you what she witnessed, and please tell her she has my permission to share everything with you."

"I will do that," he said.

"Now, I have a question for you, Mr. Fenchurche. What would happen if the *Monarch* were caught in a thunderstorm?"

"We do everything possible to stay out of a storm's path."

"What if it were impossible?"

"Then, I suppose we'd have no choice but to set the ship down in an open space."

Ivey leaned forward intently. "And how would that work?"

"Without a dock and in a storm, it would be a very risky maneuver."

"Where would your passengers go if such a thing were to happen?"

"The library on the second level is the designated shelter in the event of an emergency landing."

Ivey finished the thought. "Because it's located in the middle of the cabin, where there is no exposed glass."

"Exactly," Miles agreed. "I'm curious, how did you know that?"

Ivey glanced away. "I dreamed about it."

"Oh. I see." Miles smiled. "There is no need for you to worry about storms, Miss Thornton. The captain is too skilled to see us caught in a dangerous situation."

Ivey felt her blood rising. "Mr. Fenchurche, please do not assume that I am a weak or fearful person. In honesty, I find that irritating."

"I never meant to imply you were. Please forgive me."

Ivey ignored his apology. "And furthermore, I am not afraid of storms. I promise you that if this ship were in distress, I'd easily outrun the likes of you to help Captain LeClere and his men save the *Monarch* from destruction."

Miles held his hands up in surrender. Fortunately, the waiter had appeared with the final course. They returned to their food, enduring another uncomfortable silence.

By the time their dessert plates were empty, Ivey was ready to escape the tension that had settled over their table like a wet blanket. For some reason, Miles agitated her in a way she'd never experienced before. Ivey wondered how she could make his life any happier, if all he ever did was oblige her to prove him wrong. She also feared that he might become less inclined to teach her how to fly a Zephyr if she continued to speak so sharply toward him.

Miles laid his napkin on the plate. Before he could rise from the table, Ivey reached out and grabbed his arm. "Mr. Fenchurche, wait."

He sat back in his chair with a small sigh, as if bracing himself for another scolding.

"I wish to apologize. I didn't mean to be ungrateful. My father and Iris swore that you brought me back from the dead, and Prim might have been seriously injured if you hadn't arrived in time to catch her. It's just my nature to reject unneeded assistance, especially when it comes from a stranger. So far, you've only seen me at my worst. If you'll give me a chance to show you what I am made of, you will discover that I am not like any of the other girls you know, and honestly, I cannot stand to be treated like one."

Miles appeared hesitant to speak. The expression in his eyes made Ivey feel even more guilty.

"I appreciate your feelings, and I don't want to make you uncomfortable, Miss Thornton," he said. "It seems I have a gift for saying and doing the wrong things where you're concerned."

"That's not completely true." Ivey smiled. "I'm quite pleased with your choice for my companion. Sylvia is wonderful. I find her to be extremely trustworthy, and I will enjoy having her as a friend." Ivey suddenly realized the carelessness of those words. "Oh. Please do not repeat that to your mother."

A sadness filled Miles' eyes. "I understand. I'd hoped that you would find Sylvia's personality agreeable, and I would never stand in the way of your friendship. She is a wonderful girl, and I'm sure it is gratifying to enjoy her company."

At that moment, Ivey's heart sank for Miles. His childhood must have been unbearably lonely. She reached across the table and squeezed his arm. "Who knows, Mr. Fenchurche. Some day we might find ourselves becoming friends, too."

"We can only wait and see what happens, Miss Thornton." As he held her in a steady gaze, Ivey noticed what a cool shade of green Miles' eyes had taken on in the verdant surroundings of the garden. After a long pause, he rose to help her out of her chair.

"May I escort you back to your suite?"

"You may."

They made their way out of the garden and back up the stairway toward the family's parlor. They didn't speak, but Ivey felt a sense of peace in their silence. She was beginning to feel hopeful that they could find some common ground.

Minnette spied her son and the Thornton girl leaving the garden from across the lobby and decided to trail them as they ascended the stairs. She'd seen no sign of attraction between the two thus far. Things were off to a rough start with the young lady, and Minnette was not confident that the arrangement would end in a marriage. Perhaps she was also beginning to fear that it might.

As desperately as she needed Miles to take a bride, the thought of another woman demanding her son's attention was quite troubling. The girls Minnette had previously introduced may have left Miles unmoved, but in marriage, those young ladies would have been easily kept out of her way.

Following her son's impassioned speech in Miss Thornton's defense, Minnette had become concerned that this particular girl might offer more of a problem than a solution. Dolan's reports about the young lady's determined temperament were also worrying.

At the top of the stairs, she paused and laid a hand against her forehead. One of her sickening headaches had come on without the usual warning signs. Her ears rang and her head ached so badly that she had to close her eyes and wait for a tremor of nausea to pass.

❧

At the door to her suite, Ivey turned to thank Miles for the breakfast.

"What is it?" he asked, startled.

Her eyes followed his downward gaze to where both of her hands were tightly wrapped around his wrist. She didn't remember taking his arm.

Against her will, Ivey's grip tightened until her fingers were digging deep into his skin.

Miles winced in pain. He tried to pry himself free, but her fingers were like stone.

"Ivey, what's wrong with you?" Now he looked frightened.

Ivey's eyes blurred, and her ears were on fire. She blinked, trying to clear her vision. She felt her lips move in time with a low, dry voice.

"Miles."

A blinding flash of pain tore through her head. With it, she felt another's presence . . . a person in unbearable agony.

Whoever it was, Ivey sensed that the other soul was in great danger. She could feel the pounding of a heart and the flash of terror that ran through the other person as they started to lose their balance.

The voice spoke again, forcing her lips to move with it.

"Miles, help! I'm going to fall!"

This time she recognized the voice.

Minnette.

In a rush of jumbled sensations, Ivey's vision returned, and her fingers released their grip on Miles' arm.

"Catch her!" she screamed.

"Who?"

"Your mother!"

She shoved him toward the landing of the staircase, where Minnette stood swaying with eyes closed, about to tip backward.

Miles raced for the stairs and grabbed her by the waist, pulling her back from the edge. Minnette collapsed into her son's arms.

Ivey stumbled back and sank into the nearest chair, grasping her temples.

Miles carried his mother across the parlor to her suite. He called to Ivey over his shoulder as he reached for the door handle.

"We need the doctor. Hurry!"

Miles disappeared inside, and the pain in Ivey's head ended as quickly as it had come on.

She was shaken, but she jumped up to go for help. She had no idea where to find a doctor, but remembered that Sylvia had shown her the call button in her suite. She glanced around and spotted a similar button above a parlor table. She ran to it and jammed the switch repeatedly before hurrying to the stairs to wait for help.

"Is there a problem?" Somehow, Dolan had appeared in the parlor behind her.

Ivey explained Minnette's urgent need for a doctor, and Dolan rushed off through a hidden panel that swung open from the wall near the door to her suite.

Ivey wasn't sure what to do next. She was too upset to go back to her room, but she couldn't risk having another bizarre episode in front of strangers. She realized that the effects of the Zephyr's otheophainer had been far more drastic than she or Arvel imagined. That realization was followed by a frightening thought.

When Ivey was little, a part of her nature had occasionally become wild and violent. Much more than just a child's tantrums, her fits of destructive anger were vicious and spastic, rooted deep in the same strangeness that set her apart from her sisters and peers. The occurrences could have become uncontrollable if not for her father's strength and calming influence.

Now, confined to an unfamiliar environment and cognizant of the menacing forces flowing through her body, Ivey feared what might happen if she were to become a danger to herself or others.

A rush of homesickness caught her off guard.

"Oh, Father," she choked. "What will I do without you?"

She wanted to cry, but her stubborn nature fought back the tears. After lecturing Miles Fenchurche to respect her unusual capabilities, she couldn't afford to fall to pieces at the first trial. Something malevolent had attacked her on the docking platform, awakening her instinct for survival. She had to act.

Ivey went to the window that had shattered in her dream. She slowly ran her hand along its surface, searching for a drop of blood or a crack in the glass—any sign that the dream had been more than a figment of her untethered imagination.

The glass was flawless. Nevertheless, the dreadful anxiety in her stomach told her to take that dream as a warning of impending disaster. Ivey could no longer doubt that something dire was going to take place aboard the *Monarch*.

The sound of knocking caught her attention.

Sylvia was standing in front of the door to her suite, looking exactly as she had in the dream.

"I'm over here," Ivey called out.

Sylvia joined her at the window. "Mr. Miles is terribly sorry for leaving you. He sent me to see if you needed any help."

"Yes, I believe I do. I want you to tell me everything about this ship.

Start with how I may find you in an emergency, and then show me the way to the library and the captain's bridge."

Ivey had made up her mind. If the *Monarch*'s voyage was headed for disaster, she would not go down without a fight.

Chapter Ten

MASTERING THE BATTLEFIELD

Sylvia led Ivey across the airship's lobby and into the corridor of passenger cabins to the left of the grand staircase. She stopped and set her hand upon one of the wooden panels of the solid wall to their right. She pushed firmly, and with a heavy click, the panel unlocked and swung open.

Just like the one Dolan had emerged from in the family's private parlor, this hidden door had no frame or handle, only a hinge that allowed it to swing inward. The maid stepped through the opening and Ivey followed, taking a moment to inspect the edges of the panel where it met the wall. A sturdy, spring-loaded latch held the door tightly closed but released when enough pressure was applied in the correct spot along its edge. As she pushed it shut, Ivey saw a handle on the back, allowing the hidden door to be opened from the inside.

"Very clever," Ivey said. "I see the wizards of Fenchurche Industries put a lot of thought into making their servants invisible."

"Or protecting us from the passengers," Sylvia joked. "Follow me. Hopefully we won't attract too much attention."

Sylvia led her down a narrow hallway lined on both sides by servants' quarters. They passed by dozens of doors until the hall widened. There, Ivey saw banks of cabinets with tall, slim doors.

"What are these for?" Ivey asked.

"They hold our uniforms." Sylvia opened a cabinet full of dark blue dresses with black aprons identical to the one she was wearing. She picked out a hanger. A tag inside the uniform's neckline was marked *S. Feather*.

"This one's mine. Each night, housekeeping cleans the day's garments and leaves them here so we always looks our best."

"The *Monarch* has a laundry?"

"It has three, miss. One for linens, one for woolens, and a room for drying and ironing."

"Where are they?" Ivey asked, looking around.

"Just below us. In the belly of the ship."

"Oh, that's right," Ivey said. "I remember reading that the engine room and waterworks were on a service level at the bottom of the ship. Funny, the article never said a word about laundries."

"Well, I suppose people don't care about dirty linens, miss."

"They'll care, but only when they're out of clean ones. What else is down there?"

"There's the bakery, vegetable stores, a can pantry, the coolers for fresh dairy and meats, and storerooms for maintenance. Oh, and there's a scullery under the dining room."

"Everything needed to make the ship self-sufficient. How fascinating. I think the lower level might be my favorite. Could you take me there some time?"

"I can take you to the service rooms, but if you're wanting to see the waterworks or engine room, you'll have to ask Mr. Miles. I'm sure he'd be willing to satisfy your curiosity about his ship."

"He would?" Ivey's left eyebrow arched at the thought. "Maybe I'll do just that, once his mother is better."

Sylvia continued through the passageway between the rows of cabinets to a parallel hall that was lined with more crew cabins.

"These rooms are for the senior staff." She pointed. "That's Mr. Dolan's room." Sylvia walked a ways further.

"And here's my room. I'm together with the mistress's maid." Sylvia opened the door. "Have a look-see. Lucey Sue will be out for some time. When Mrs. Fenchurche has her spells, Lucey and Mr. Dolan stay in her quarters round the clock to help her through the pain."

Having shared mere seconds of Minnette's suffering, Ivey shuddered. "It must be horrible."

"The doctor says it puts a strain on her heart. He's got special tonics to keep her calm."

"How long has she been afflicted?"

Sylvia bit her lip. "We're not to speak of such things, but since you'll soon be a Fenchurche—I've heard the first attack came not long after she birthed Mr. Miles. They've grown worse as the years passed. It's why he went off to study healing. He hoped to find her a cure, or at least a better way to relieve the pain."

Ivey found it odd that a maid would know so much about his intentions, but she listened quietly.

"Nothing works anymore. It is a terrible burden on the both of them."

"Thank you for telling me," Ivey said softly.

Ivey would walk through fire to help her father, so she could understand Miles' devotion to his ailing mother.

"Enough of that talk," Sylvia said cheerfully. "This is where you'll find me when I'm not tending to you."

Ivey looked around the small, simply furnished room. A wooden table folded down against the wall when not in use. A pair of small chairs stacked and stored against the back wall. Two narrow beds were placed atop each other to make the most of the space.

"Who sleeps up there?" Ivey inquired, gesturing toward the top bunk.

"That would be me, and yes, you may."

Sylvia pointed out the climbing rungs on the foot of the bed, but Ivey couldn't resist showing off. She backed away, and with a few nimble steps and hardly any effort, she launched herself up, twisting in midair to land on her back. Sylvia's mouth dropped open.

"How'd you do that one?"

Ivey leaned over the edge, grinning mischievously. "I like to pretend I can fly."

"Are you sure that was pretending?"

"It takes practice, but anyone can do it," Ivey laughed.

"Do what, exactly?"

Ivey's face grew reverent. "Put the mind before the body. If one truly believes she can fly, her body will follow. Of course, you have to know your limits. A body can only follow so far."

Sylvia looked dubious. "Well, my mind knows this body was never meant to fly."

Ivey smiled. "Don't be so sure, Miss *Feather*. When we arrive at Ferndale, I will teach you all sorts of amazing things."

Sylvia shrugged. "You can try. Now, if you would like to fly back down here, I'll show you to the library."

As they stepped back into the senior staff's hallway, Ivey noticed the wide swinging doors of the main kitchen to their right.

"Would they mind if I have a peek?" Ivey asked.

"Not a bit. After all, you may be planning their menus one day as the new Mrs. Fenchurche. Isn't that right?"

Sylvia gave her a hopeful grin, but Ivey intended to avoid the complications of that subject.

She hurried over and pushed open one of the swinging doors. Her intrusion was hardly noticed by the chefs and their assistants who were hard at work preparing the day's lunch offerings. The kitchen was quite large and fully equipped, but her attention was drawn to a pair of elevators side by side in the back corner.

Instead of a single car that traveled up and down, these contraptions had a procession of square boxes with no doors that arrived and departed at regular intervals, and always in the same direction.

A stream of waiters pushed large trolleys loaded with trays of appetizers into the cars of the lifts, and soon disappeared through an opening in the floor.

So that's how they do it.

Ivey imagined that the carts were taken down and rolled through a passage in the ship's belly before being brought back up on another elevator in the dining hall's service room.

"Sylvia, do you know how those elevators work?" Ivey asked.

"It's something, isn't it, miss? Those boxes move on a big metal loop that goes from the top to the bottom of the ship. One side goes up and the other goes down. The servants use them to haul food, linens, and luggage, and to provide room service. You've got to mind your step getting on and off, though."

"Brilliant." Ivey smiled. She felt a strange sense of pride in the clever contraption. The *Monarch* really was the ship she had always dreamed of.

At the other end of the senior staff's hallway, they walked through a door and into the crew mess hall. Unlike the finely placed seats that passengers enjoyed while dining at the front of the ship's cabin, the *Monarch*'s workers ate at three long tables with fixed benches.

"And here's the lounge where we relax when off duty, miss," Sylvia said as they entered a connecting room with couches and chairs.

Curious glances followed Ivey as she passed through these areas. She resisted the urge to ask questions about the crew's various duties and kept her attention on memorizing the path from her room to Sylvia's room to the library.

From the lounge, they went through a set of doors that opened into the tearoom. Sylvia started up a staircase just to their right.

"We'll go up one floor, but the library actually sits between the first and second levels of the ship."

They climbed to the second story and traveled down a long hallway back toward the front of the ship. This corridor opened out onto the top landing of the lobby's grand staircase. Across from the landing, a short set of stairs descended into the library.

As they entered, Ivey could see that the library had no windows. The walls consisted of bookshelves filled with a vast collection of leather-bound volumes. Sturdy metal grates were pulled across the shelves to keep the books securely in place, even when the ship rocked from side to side. Several rows of stout reading tables were secured to the floor in the center of the room.

Ivey turned to Sylvia. "What must be done to borrow a book?"

"You're free to take as many as you like. Just leave them on a table in the family's parlor when you're finished, and the staff will return them to the shelves."

Ivey smiled with satisfaction. "Very, very good. Now, how do I get from here to the bridge? I need to see—"

Sylvia held up one hand. "I'm sorry, but my tour ends here, miss. For safety's sake, the bridge is strictly off limits to everyone except the flight crew and the family. You'll have to ask Mr. Miles to take you there."

Ivey sighed. "He has too much on his mind. I'll work that out later."

To make sure everything was straight in her head, Ivey led the way back to the stairs, down to the tearoom, and through the servants' lounge and mess. She stopped at Sylvia's door. From there, she retraced their steps to the hidden door, and then back to her quarters.

"Very good, miss. You're right as can be now." Sylvia pointed at a door to the left of the fireplace in the family's private parlor. "That one's the hallway to the bridge, just so you know. If you require nothing else, I'm going to help Lucey Sue tend to Mrs. Fenchurche."

"Thank you, Sylvia. I should be fine on my own. I think I'll go back to the library to pick out some books, and then I'll treat myself to a bath." Ivey grinned sheepishly. "I promise to be more careful getting out of the tub."

Sylvia gave Ivey a slight hug. "Please do. You've already given me a gray hair today."

"I am sorry to have frightened you like that. You were very kind to stay and help me through it."

"It's no bother at all taking care of you, miss. And know that I carried your bedding straight to the laundry and put it in a stain soak, so there won't be any questions from the housekeepers."

"Thank you again. It wouldn't take long for any more rumors to start." Ivey rolled her eyes.

"Oh, but you will have to speak to Dolan. My apologies; I couldn't convince him to let things drop."

"Sylvia, I am very lucky to have made a friend like you. If you are ever in need, I promise not let you down."

"I have no doubt of that, miss."

Once Sylvia left, Ivey made her way back to the library. Paying no regard to the stock of serial romance novels intended for the female passengers who read, Ivey selected a heavy volume on the history of flight and another about the dynamics of airships—subjects in which mastery would be vital for the successful operation of a Zephyr.

As she passed a collection of books prominently displayed in a wooden case near the front of the room, a familiar face caught her eye. Miles' portrait was painted on the cover of a leather-bound collection of scientific essays. She picked the book up, surprised to discover it had been written by Miles' father, Maddox. The resemblance was uncanny.

With the same features and green eyes, Maddox's face differed from Miles' only in its impish sense of confidence.

She had no doubt that he and her father had been kindred spirits. She tucked the book under her arm, eager to learn what Maddox Fenchurche had written about the world.

As she climbed the steps out of the library, Ivey met a sharply dressed man with slick black hair and a curled mustache. They nodded politely as they passed one another. The man's walking stick caught the journal that Ivey was carrying under her arm, sending it tumbling down the stairs.

"Goodness, that was entirely my fault." The gentleman's voice had a distinct drawl. He sauntered down the steps to retrieve the book. As he climbed back up to where Ivey was standing, he looked at the cover, and then rested his eyes upon her.

"Boning up on the in-laws, eh?" he laughed.

Ivey stepped back, taking offense at the tasteless joke.

"I am sorry. Where are my manners?" His silky voice barely masked an attitude of conceit. "You and I haven't been properly introduced. I am Paisley Fitzroy, and you must be Ivey Thornton."

Ivey continued to glower.

"I'm an acquaintance of your sister Primrose, and like you, I'm traveling as an honored guest of the Fenchurche family. There's no harm in making nice with me, darling girl."

"May I please have my book, Mr. Fitzroy?" She extended her hand.

"Only if you call me Paise . . . all my friends do." The gentleman shot forward to give Ivey's hand an unwelcome kiss. She jerked her arm away.

He laughed, his breath carrying the distinct smell of liquor. "Well, I've heard you're not too keen on manners."

"I need to be on my way. Give me the book, now."

"Oh, dear me, I hope I haven't upset you. You see, we're going to spend a lot of time together, and before I'm finished, I'll know every last detail of that sturdy figure of yours."

"How dare you!" Ivey glared, ready to deliver a swift kick to the weakest part of his anatomy.

"Oh please, do you live under a rock? You really haven't a clue who I am? Paisley Fitzroy? Everyone who's anyone will tell you that I am the most sought-after dressmaker in all of Aether, and it just so happens I fashioned that crafty number Primrose commissioned for your engagement party."

He leaned forward with a sneer. "I hope you appreciated the enhancements."

Ivey's face went bright red.

He grinned and continued. "As a favor to Minnette, I'll be working at Ferndale to make you a gown worthy of a Fenchurche bride. And please relax, dear girl. You're not at all my type."

With a flamboyant bow, Paisley handed the book back to Ivey and disappeared down the staircase into the library. Their meeting explained much about the cruel dress that had nearly crushed her to death.

Ivey turned and ran down the grand library staircase toward the safety of her room. Sylvia's passing comment about needing protection from the passengers had taken on a whole new light, and Ivey intended to avoid all contact with strange travelers for the rest of the day.

ॐ

Ivey curled up on the couch in her sitting room with Maddox's essays and began to read. She learned about the processes Fenchurche Crystalworks had developed to fabricate every variety of marvelous, indestructible glass used in buildings, machinery, and vehicles. She was fascinated by Maddox's accounts of the early chemical experiments in which seemingly endless combinations of natural materials were coaxed into yielding light, heat, and power. This research had set the stage for many of Aether's greatest technological advancements.

Late that afternoon, Ivey reached an essay that expounded upon Maddox's theories of physics. She was captivated by his contemplations on how time and dimension must intertwine to give rise to the various states of existence in the world.

A great deal of the terminology and concepts he alluded to were foreign to her, but she wondered if this might explain the bond that had sprung up between herself and Maddox when she was just a baby. Maybe he'd sensed that the fabric of her being was woven in an unusual manner. She longed to know whether Arvel had ever confided in Maddox about his own odd capabilities.

A soft knock at the door startled her. She laid the book down and cautiously called, "Who's there?"

She was relieved to hear a familiar voice. "It's Miles Fenchurche. May I have a word with you, Miss Thornton?"

Ivey got up and opened the door. "Miles, how is your mother?"

"She's resting at the moment, thank you. May we talk about what happened this morning?"

Ivey stepped to the side, inviting him into her sitting room. "By all means."

Miles hesitated. "You might be more comfortable in the parlor."

Ivey appreciated his attention to propriety. "Oh, yes. Of course." She followed him to a sofa by the fireplace, where they took a seat.

"I cannot thank you enough for what you did for my mother, though I am not exactly sure how it transpired."

"Didn't you hear her calling you?"

"Ivey, yours was the only voice I heard. If you hadn't warned me, there's no telling what might have happened."

Ivey frowned. If Miles hadn't heard his mother's voice, it must have been only been in her head. Ivey always had a knack for sensing another's thoughts, but she'd never heard them as if they were being spoken aloud.

Miles continued, "I hope you'll accept my apology for leaving you alone like that. If not for the urgency of my mother's situation, I would have stayed to make sure that you were alright."

"You really needn't worry about me, Mr. Fenchurche. As you can see, I am perfectly fine."

"Yes, well I spoke to Sylvia about the incident in your room this morning. She was convinced that something terrible had happened to you, and she is not prone to panic." A crease appeared on Miles' brow.

"I'm quite concerned, Miss Thornton. It's hardly been more than a week since you nearly fell to your death. Now, it appears that your exposure to the otheophainer is causing severe effects."

Ivey shifted uncomfortably. "What is your point, Mr. Fenchurch?"

"I am responsible for your well-being, so I've asked Doctor Brendel to see you for a thorough examination in the morning."

Ivey stood. "Do I look like I need a doctor, Mr. Fenchurche?"

"Miss Thornton, I am not implying that you are frail. You have been through more in one week than most could survive in a lifetime, but it is clear that you're suffering a medical disorder."

Ivey sighed. "No, I'm not. Your doctor will find nothing wrong with me."

"Then where's the harm in merely having him examine you?"

"If you call attention to these oddities of mine, there will be consequences."

"Such as?" Miles frowned.

"First come the strange looks, then whispers and rumors, and it won't be long until the people of the town are at my door with their torches in hand, ready to have me burned, or at the very least, sent home in disgrace."

"That's quite an exaggeration, isn't it?"

"Is it?" Ivey held out her left hand. "Would you tell your mother that I awoke in a bed soaked with blood from a wound that has vanished?"

"May I?" Miles took Ivey's hand and ran his fingertip across her palm. He palpated the tissue, feeling for anything unusual below the surface.

He stared for some time, until Ivey quietly asked, "Mr. Fenchurche?"

"Yes?" He looked up.

"Are you finished?"

Miles released her hand and rose to his feet. "This may be inexplicable, but it cannot be ignored. What if Sylvia hadn't come to your room when she did?"

Ivey looked at the floor. "I hardly think I would have bled to death."

"Well, I only want to make sure nothing like that happens."

"At least we can agree on that." Ivey crossed her arms.

Miles sighed. "I am at a loss. If you have any suggestions, I'm willing to hear them."

Ivey was pleased by the invitation. "Yes I do, thank you. To begin, excepting Sylvia, no one should know about this, especially not Dolan or your mother. For the remainder of the voyage, Sylvia may check on me first thing every morning. If she discovers anything unsettling, I will allow you to decide whether I require a doctor's attention. I suspect that whatever the otheophainer did to me is neither observable nor explainable. To that point, I came across a book in your library that may hold some answers. Would you be willing to look over it with me?"

"Yes. In fact, I'm quite curious to see what you found. We could begin at once, if you like."

Ivey's face brightened. "Yes, thank you. I'll go and fetch it."

Ivey dashed to her room, relieved that her relationship with Miles might take a pleasant turn. She grabbed the journal from her couch, pausing momentarily as she wondered how Miles would react when he learned that they were his own father's theories.

She emerged from her suite to find Dolan informing Miles that his mother had called for him. Miles looked at her apologetically, but Ivey nodded.

"Please, do what you can for her. We will continue this later."

"Yes, let's do."

As Miles turned to leave, Dolan addressed Ivey. "It is my role to report any strange disturbances on this ship, Miss Ivey. I have known Sylvia Feather long enough to say that she is not easily frightened. I must wonder if something more serious than a bloody nose took place in your room this morning. Was she being truthful?"

Ivey cringed. She could think of nothing more cunning than Sylvia's story to offer.

Miles returned to her side.

"I have already spoken to Miss Thornton. There is no need for you to bother yourself with this matter."

"Thank you, sir, but I must answer to your mother, and she expects a full account of such matters," Dolan said dismissively.

It was clear the man would sooner cross Miles than disappoint Minnette.

"I will give her a report when I feel it is appropriate," Miles argued. "Now is not the time to burden her with trivial matters."

"She would want—"

"I assure you, I will take full responsibility for this." Miles set a firm hand on Dolan's arm. "Have I made myself clear?"

Dolan nodded silently, but the muscles of his jaw twitched in aggravation.

Miles looked kindly at Ivey and hurried off.

"Do you require anything else before I leave, Miss Ivey?" Dolan asked with a forced smile.

Ivey answered just as pleasantly. "Yes. Could you have a dinner tray sent to my room? It's been a trying day, and I'd like to dine in peace tonight."

"Of course." Dolan gave her a polite bow and left.

Ivey hoped that the matter had been put to rest. Though she was determined to return to Thornhall, she did not wish to be sent home any time soon. Her unexpected friendship with Sylvia was heartening, and she had no intention of abandoning her flying lessons with Miles, who appeared to possess some commendable qualities after all.

Most importantly, she'd discovered that her special connection with Maddox Fenchurche may have run deeper than either he or Arvel had realized. From what she'd read of his journal, Ivey was sure that Maddox had formed the type of inquiries which could yield answers to her deepest questions about her strange talents and physical oddities.

The rays of the setting sun glancing off the undersides of the *Monarch*'s wings filled the parlor with a warm color that drew Ivey back to the window. She laid her hands and cheek against the glass and felt the steady hum of the engines as they propelled the ship into the twilight sky waiting beyond the horizon.

She gazed up at the wings and their vast expanse of cabling, hoping never to see them torn apart in a real storm. Her eyes spotted the cable that had been severed in her dream. She followed its line back to the pulley where it had snapped.

A gentle fluttering captured her attention. Something appeared to be caught on the cable where it crossed over one of the metal service walkways. She strained her eyes in the fading light. Just before the cable disappeared for the night, a last bit of sunlight caught the object long enough to send Ivey's heart racing.

A length of green ribbon was lashed around the cable—the very same ribbon she'd used to tie back her hair in the dream.

Chapter Eleven

THE RIBBON

E arly the next morning, Sylvia took a deep breath and braced herself for whatever might be waiting on the other side of Ivey's
bedroom door. She crept forward and laid her hand across the
girl's warm arm, taking care not to wake her. Ivey mumbled and rolled
over, snuggling deeper into her down quilts.

Sylvia backed silently out of the room, relieved that she would be
able to deliver an encouraging report to the exhausted Mr. Miles. He'd
been attending to his mother without sleep for two days, and Sylvia
hoped to convince him to return to his suite for a nap of his own.

∽

As soon as she heard the soft thud of the suite's front door, Ivey's head
popped up from her pillow. It had taken every scrap of patience she
could muster to wait for Sylvia to make the first of her early morning
visits. Ivey threw back the covers and jumped out of bed. She had a
plan, but it would only work before the ship became busy.

Long after midnight, Ivey had snuck into the servants' quarters to
raid the uniform cabinets. After a haphazard search, she located a cabinet filled with the red uniforms worn by the flight crew and engineers.
She took one—tagged *R. James*—that didn't look too terribly large.

Having returned to her suite undetected, she had spent the rest of
the night rereading Maddox Fenchurche's essay about the dimensional nature of space. His theory posited that Aether's familiar plane of
existence was comprised of only a single aspect of a larger multifac-
eted world. As such, the flow of time could be progressing in parallel
through a number of universes that continuously splintered off from
themselves. At every fracture, even the tiniest of differences between

one reality and its sisters held the potential to drive them all toward very different outcomes.

If it were possible to peek from the perspective of one world into another, the accumulation of differences between them might reveal a strange, alien landscape. The idea seemed absurd in its scope, but Ivey was haunted by its simple and lonely assertion that she existed in only a tiny sliver of space and time.

She couldn't understand the long equations filled with unfamiliar symbols that Maddox referred to in support of his ideas, but she wondered if her exposure to the otheophainer was breaking down the boundaries between her existence and these other branches of reality.

First, there was the injury to her hand that had followed her back from her dream. Her bloodstained bedding proved its reality beyond any doubt, but the wound had vanished almost immediately, as if its presence didn't belong within her body.

Now, the green ribbon had also crossed the threshold into her world. For Ivey, that ribbon was proof that what she'd experienced was more than a dream—she'd actually leapt from one plane of existence to another. If that was the case, and if the stream of reality she'd visited in her sleep was at all closely linked with her own, then her premonition of the *Monarch*'s terrible fate should be heeded.

She couldn't wait for Miles to return from his mother's bedside to discuss what she had found. Before it vanished or was blown free from the riggings, she had to retrieve the ribbon and convince Miles to help her safeguard the ship. In the process, he might finally break free from the shackles of his life's duties and take up the work his father had left unfinished. If he could enjoy such a noble destiny, she would be free to pursue her own, with Arvel's blessing.

When the sun finally broke over the horizon, Ivey was at her bedroom window, watching.

A green ribbon danced in the morning breeze, daring her to come and claim it.

It does exist.

The cable on which the ribbon was entangled ran close to one of the catwalks the crewmen had used to inspect the wings after she'd boarded the *Monarch*. She was envious of the thrilling view they must have had from such a perspective.

Ivey had always been an excellent climber, and she had little fear of heights. It would be easy enough to retrieve the ribbon and return the flight uniform before anyone discovered it was missing.

She dressed herself in the red uniform jacket and black trousers. Having underestimated its size, Ivey rolled up the extra material at the cuffs of the sleeves and turned the pant legs under. She stuffed her hair beneath a red wool cap. The effect was less than ideal, but she hoped it would provide enough disguise to get her into the restricted passage that led to the ship's bridge.

The first part of her plan would be exiting the family's quarters without incident. If the door were locked or if she were seen dressed as a crewman in the private parlor, she'd certainly be stopped.

She cracked open the front door of her sitting room. No one was in the vicinity at this early hour. She darted past the entrance to Miles' suite and reached the door that Sylvia said led to the bridge. Minnette's suite was just on the other side of the fireplace, so she had to be quiet.

She held her breath and tested the door handle. It opened.

She slipped through and pulled it shut silently behind herself. At the end of a short hall, she encountered a sign with large red letters warning that the area was restricted.

She turned to her right and started toward the front of the ship, looking for a way outside the hull. The wide corridor was lined on one side with windows but no hatches.

Ivey's heart skipped when she finally spotted a glass portal with a hatch lever. It opened out onto a small deck nestled against the side of the cabin. At the far end of the outer deck was a steep stairway with rails. *That's it.*

Ivey pulled the lever and stepped through. She had to struggle against the difference in air pressure to push the hatch back into place.

She lingered for a moment, letting the crisp morning air flow across her face as she watched the sun rise over the countryside below.

They were approaching the Rosmans, a range of rugged peaks that ran along the coast of Northern Cemaria. Ivey had heard at the captain's table that Miles' scenic route would venture out over the sea for a hundred leagues before turning and heading northwest toward the docks at the port city of Spirehaven.

From the corner of her eye she saw movement in the corridor behind her. She dropped and flattened herself below the windows' line of sight.

A man paused on the other side of the hatch.

Oh please, just go away.

As if on command, the man continued moving toward the bridge. Ivey breathed a sigh of relief and peeked into the corridor. Once he was gone, she rose to a crouching position and crept up the stairs.

At the top, Ivey stepped onto the railed service walkway that ran along the entire length of the cabin. Up ahead, a tall metal ladder on the outside of the hull rose from the walkway to the first level of catwalks, which were little more than wooden planks suspended from cables of their own.

She started up the ladder. It was a thrilling climb, but the higher from the body of the cabin she went, the more turbulent the flow of air became. By the time Ivey reached the catwalk, the riggings around her were bobbing in the gusty winds coming over the mountains.

She stayed low, keeping a firm grip on the handrails as she made her way across the cabin and toward the cable that held the mystical ribbon.

She came to the point where the catwalk extended away from the side of the ship. Looking down, she saw the ground hundreds of feet below. The farther she ventured out into the riggings, the more the catwalk pitched and lurched in the wind.

When she finally came alongside the cable with the ribbon, she discovered that it was just out of her reach. Gripping the handrail tightly, she leaned over its edge and stretched her arm out far as she could. The cable was still beyond her grasp. Ivey threw her weight from side to side, rocking the catwalk until it finally swung far enough for her to catch ahold of the cable with her left hand. She clutched it tightly, pulling the catwalk as close as possible.

"Hey, you! We're in mountain currents. What in blazes are you doing up there?" An angry voice rang out from below.

She looked down. Miles Fenchurche and his impeccable timing had struck again.

"You'll get yourself killed!"

Ivey held tightly to the cable and let go of the catwalk's handrail long enough to make a grab for the ribbon with her right hand. A wicked gust of wind jerked her body from the catwalk. If not for her left hand's desperate grip on the cable, she would have plunged to the ground below.

The red cap was swept backward from her head, releasing a torrent of plum-colored hair across her eyes.

"Ivey? What in Aether? Don't panic! I'll come help you down!" Miles cried out as he ran toward the ladder on the side of the cabin.

"No!" Ivey shouted. "It's too windy! You'll fall!"

He fumbled with the leather belt that tethered climbers to the ladder while Ivey hoisted herself up and caught the cable with her right hand. She held tight as she swung her legs up and around the cable.

"See? I can do this!" Ivey started to shimmy her way back to the point where the cable ran over the service walkway. It would be a long drop, but she knew how to tumble and roll upon landing.

Miles abandoned his safety harness at the ladder and ran ahead to wait for her.

The wind whipped Ivey's hair into her eyes and tangled it against the cable. She paused, hanging only by her legs, while she pulled her hair back and tied it into a knot.

A warning bell sounded.

"Keep moving!" Miles shouted. "When the wings retract, that cable feeds into a pulley!"

He didn't have to explain what would happen if she were still holding on.

Ivey concentrated on coordinating her arms and legs to speed her progress. Once she was over the walkway, Miles raised his arms.

"I'll catch you!"

"Get out of the way so I can jump!" she screamed in frustration.

"It's too far!"

"Not for me!"

"Let go!"

The winch rotors emitted a piercing whine as they came to life. Ivey's heart froze. The very same sound had been in her dream, right before the cable snapped.

When the cable jerked into motion, she lost her grip and fell.

∾

Slowly, Ivey regained her wits.

Was it only a dream?

Something felt soft and warm against her face. She lifted her head and discovered that her cheek had been resting against Miles Fenchurche's.

Not a very good catch.

She would have been annoyed by his clumsy intervention, but he was awfully still. She rolled off his body and knelt beside him on the walkway. His eyes were closed. She tapped his shoulder.

"Mr. Fenchurche?"

There was no answer. She cupped his head between her hands and leaned close. "Mr. Fenchurche? Say something!"

Ivey felt something warm and sticky on her hands. She looked down and saw blood dripping through the walkway's metal grate beneath his head.

Ivey gasped in horror. "What have I done?"

She looked around, but saw no one to call to for help. She put her ear against his mouth, but the roar of wind and winches made it was impossible to tell if he were breathing.

Have I killed him?

Ivey felt a terrible sense of despair. Her tears fell on his face as she began to weep.

"Wake up! Please, wake up, Mr. Fenchurche!"

His eyes flickered and opened. He reached into a coat pocket and pulled out a handkerchief, which he offered with a dazed smile.

Ivey clutched his hand between hers. "Listen. You're badly injured. Please don't move. I'll get help." She started to rise, but Miles gripped her hands tightly.

"No, no. The only thing that's injured is my pride."

"Sometimes it takes a while to feel the pain. You need a doctor."

Miles reached back with his other hand and rubbed his scalp. "It's only a bump."

Ivey spoke slowly. "You're losing so much blood."

A red stain spread across the handkerchief trapped between their hands. Miles sat up and pulled the cloth away, revealing a deep, jagged gash across the heel of Ivey's left hand.

"It's not my blood," Miles said.

Ivey's hand started to ache as a cold darkness sank over her.

The next thing Ivey knew, she was in her bed, and Sylvia was holding a cool cloth to her head. Ivey blinked a few times.

"Did we crash?" she asked. Her tongue was thick, but her head felt light.

"She's waking up, Mr. Miles."

Miles joined Sylvia beside the bed.

Ivey's heart jumped when she saw his face. "Oh, thank you for not being dead, Mr. Fenchurche."

Miles sat on the edge of the bed. "I am fine, but you had quite an accident. How are you feeling?"

Ivey smiled. "Like I'm floating away."

"Mr. Miles gave you a dose of his mother's pain reliever," Sylvia explained.

"But I'm not in pain at all. I'm too happy."

"Sylvia, please tell Doctor Brendel to hurry," Miles said. "We wouldn't want the injection to wear off and take this rare pleasant mood with it."

Ivey pointed at Miles in surprise and giggled. "I didn't know you could be funny."

"Nor did I, miss," Sylvia teased. "I'll fetch the doctor."

"No. I detest doctors." Ivey's smile melted into a frown.

"The cable was frayed. It cut your hand quite deeply. You'll need stitches," Miles replied firmly.

Ivey lifted her bandaged hand from the pillow where it was resting. "My father said you know about healing. Can you sew hands?"

Miles nodded.

"Then you do it."

Miles looked at Sylvia. "Would you be willing to assist me?"

"I would."

Miles went to cleanse his hands while Sylvia laid out the suture needle and thread from his canvas surgical bag. She opened a bottle of a sterilizing liquid and wiped the needle clean. After feeding the thread through the eye of the needle, she laid it down on a clean cloth.

Miles returned and sat on the edge of the bed. He unwound the blood-soaked bandage from Ivey's hand. Once the bandage was off, Miles poured sterilizing solution on a cloth and prepared to clean the wound.

"This will hurt, so take a deep breath and hold Sylvia's hand."

Sylvia came around to the other side of the bed, taking Ivey's right hand in her own. Miles nodded encouragingly at Sylvia.

"Are we ready?" he asked Ivey.

"I need a moment." Ivey closed her eyes and let herself go, employing another exceptional trick she'd learned from her father. He reasoned that pain existed to protect his body from illness and injury, but he could choose to disassociate to escape unnecessary suffering. Fortunately, the effects of Miles' medicine made separating the body and mind effortless, and soon Ivey nodded that she was ready.

Miles softly touched the cloth to Ivey's palm. She stayed perfectly still, letting her mind go to a different place. He did a thorough job cleaning the wound and was soon ready to begin stitching.

"All right, Ivey, you will feel the needle and thread now. It will be uncomfortable. Tell me if it becomes too much, and I will stop."

Her eyes opened. "I want to watch."

Miles shifted uneasily. "It might be better if you just keep doing what you were doing."

Ivey struggled to sit up. "I never liked Mother's sewing lessons, but stitching a severe injury is something I should know how to do."

Sylvia looked at Miles with incredulous eyes while she arranged the pillows behind Ivey's back. As he began to work, Miles explained that the frayed strands of metal had cut so far that he would have to stitch the deepest layer of her flesh first. He showed her how the needle should pierce the tissue and why it was necessary to use a weaving stitch. Ivey's curiosity outweighed the pain she felt, and she was full of questions.

When Miles was satisfied with the first course of stitches, he used a different angle of the needle to penetrate the upper layers of skin, and he placed stitches that looked something like railroad tracks.

At one point, Ivey decided that she'd like to try making a stitch. Sylvia looked away as Ivey carefully drew the needle through her own skin, replicating Miles' artful seams. With the last stitch finished, Miles tied a knot to keep everything in place as the wound healed.

"You're an excellent patient," Miles said with a wide smile.

Sylvia patted Ivey on the arm before rising to clear away the blood-soaked bandages and cloths. "You were braver than any man on this ship, miss."

"The stitches look good, but I'm afraid this will leave you with a nasty scar," Miles warned as he cut the thread and cleaned the skin around the wound one last time.

"I don't scar," Ivey replied. "I never have."

"Well, I hope you won't be angry with me if you end up with one this time."

"Angry? With you?" Ivey felt a sudden twinge of guilt. The euphoria of the pain reliever was wearing off. "I could have killed you. I wouldn't blame you if sent me back to Thornhall tomorrow."

Miles' face became stern.

"Yes, about that. I was returning to my suite when I caught sight of a deranged crewman through the parlor window. The *Monarch*'s engineers know better than to go out on the riggings while crossing mountains. Would you care to explain what *this one* was thinking?"

Ivey knew that her head wasn't clear enough to discuss Maddox's theories, so she did her best to relate, simply and honestly, everything she'd done since seeing the ribbon on the cable the night before.

When she'd finished, Miles shook his head.

"I'm having a hard time understanding how a nightmare gave you justification to go out onto a highly restricted part of the ship and climb the riggings."

"I wanted to prove that what I experienced in the dream was physically connected to our reality. I believed the ribbon was a warning that something bad will happen to the *Monarch*."

Ivey stopped to look down at her bandaged hand. "You said the cable was frayed, so maybe there was a risk to the wings."

Miles stared at her a long time before he spoke.

"I thought we'd reached an understanding last night. Why didn't you at least talk to me before risking your life—and mine?"

Ivey looked down in shame. "I often have a hard time telling the difference between instinct and impulse."

"Indeed. Your father did warn me that you leap before you look."

Ivey's chin lifted as her temper flared. She was shocked to learn that such a patronizing conversation had taken place behind her back.

"That may be true, but I know how to land on my feet, Mr. Fenchurche."

Miles leaned forward. "Not from what I have seen, Miss Thornton. Do you know what would have happened if you had come to me first?"

He reached into a pocket of his jacket and pulled out the green ribbon. "I would have shown you this."

Ivey's eyes grew wide. Her hand trembled as she reached out to take it from Miles, half expecting it to disappear into thin air when her fingers touched it.

"That's impossible. Did you go back for it?"

"I didn't need to. It's a maintenance flag. I typically have one or two stuck in a pocket somewhere, and when I don't, there is a whole box full of them in the ship's engineering bay. I tied that ribbon to the cable while inspecting the wings the day you came aboard the *Monarch*. The metal was worn, so I flagged it for repair when we dock at Spirehaven. You must have seen it before you even had the dream."

Ivey's mind was spinning. "I did?"

"I'm certain of it. So, you risked your life to tell me something that I already knew. And at any rate, one broken cable will not bring down my ship. I can promise you that."

Ivey hid her face. "I've been a perfect fool. Will you ever forgive me?"

Miles' voice rose. "Only if you swear never to take these matters into your own hands again. And the next time I try to help you, listen to me and cooperate."

"Yes, sir." Ivey nodded humbly.

"In addition, you will tell me of any new symptoms that might have been caused by the Zephyr's otheophainer, regardless of how trivial they seem to you. There is a logical reason for the appearance of the ribbon in your dream, but it does not explain how you experienced that injury to your hand before it happened. I have growing concerns about your health."

"Yes sir. Is that all, Mr. Fenchurche?"

Miles' expression softened into a half smile. "No, I'd like you to stop calling me sir . . . and admit that you have a tendency to faint."

"That's not—"

Miles raised his hand and stopped her. "It's happened three times now since I've met you. Ivey Thornton, you are a fainter."

Ivey crossed her arms accusingly. "Well, perhaps that is your fault."

"How so?"

"I never fainted once in my whole life until you came along. It seems I only swoon when you meddle in my affairs."

"Oh really? And every time I snatch you from the jaws of death, I seem to get knocked flat on my bum."

Sylvia added under her breath, "It seems this may be a match made in the heavens."

"What was that?" Ivey suddenly felt self-conscious about her playful teasing. Her lighthearted mood was probably an adverse effect of the powerful medicine, but she didn't want to give him the wrong impression.

Sylvia grinned. "It's nice to see some color back in your cheeks, miss." She smoothed the covers. "Now, you've been up since last night, Miss Ivey. And Mr. Miles, you haven't slept in two days. Why don't you both take a nice rest?"

Miles shook his head. "Not until she gets some nourishment."

"Then I'll fetch a dinner tray for her," Sylvia said.

Ivey hadn't eaten since the night before, but the thought of food made her stomach churn. "I'm sorry, but something's off. I don't think I can."

Miles frowned. "May I see your good hand?"

Ivey held it out. He pinched the skin on the back of her hand between his fingers and released it. It took a few seconds for the skin to smooth itself out.

Ivey's curiosity was instantly aroused. "What does that mean?"

"Your body is in distress. Without care, you could become ill. Please take in plenty of water, and try to eat something as a favor to me."

As he spoke, Ivey's queasiness became worse. She pushed back against the pillows and took a deep breath.

"Sylvia, could you fetch the vial that helped settle my stomach?"

"Of course." Sylvia dashed off.

Ivey turned away and stiffened as she struggled to control another wave of nausea. "You should leave."

Miles stroked her arm lightly. "Getting some food into you will help absorb the medicine. I promise."

His touch gave her a small amount of comfort until Sylvia returned. She handed the vial to Miles. He opened it and held it beneath Ivey's nose, allowing her to take several deep breaths of the pungent salts. Soon, the tension in her body eased, and Ivey's head relaxed back into her pillows.

She closed her eyes and visualized herself in a high mountain forest, lying on a bed of moss beside a pond. All the stresses in her body evaporated as she imagined lowering herself into the deep, cold water.

"Ivey?"

She felt a warm hand against her cheek.

"Should I be worried?" Miles asked.

Ivey softly sighed. "I didn't faint. I'm just swimming."

"Swimming?"

She opened her eyes.

Miles leaned close. "Could you try some food now?"

Ivey sat up and waited a moment. The queasiness was gone, but her head still felt light.

"I'll eat if you take me to the glass garden."

"I think you need to rest."

"I'm sure the surroundings will greatly improve my appetite."

Miles stood. "Well then, I'll go arrange things. Sylvia, could you please have her dressed when I return?"

After he left the room, Ivey stared down at her nightgown in embarrassment. "What happened to the uniform?"

"I had you changed and tucked in before Mr. Miles even returned with his surgeon's kit."

Ivey grinned gratefully. "What can I do to deserve a friend like you?"

Sylvia sat on the side of the bed. "You don't have to do a thing, Ivey Thornton, but something tells me that someday you will."

Chapter Twelve

A Taste of Freedom

Miles entered his mother's sitting room, which was littered with members of her personal staff, exhausted from caring for her day and night. Lucey Sue snored on the fainting couch, Doctor Brendel dozed on a settee, and Dolan sat in a wingback chair, sleeping upright with his arms folded neatly across his chest. Miles had yet to see the man approaching a state of relaxation.

He quietly slipped past them and into the bedroom. His mother's eyes were open, but Miles wasn't sure whether she was aware of his presence. The effects of the medicines her doctor administered during these episodes were overpowering, and Miles worried that they would exacerbate his mother's attacks. His occasional suggestions of botanical remedies from abroad were met with such resistance from his mother's doctors that he had given up trying.

"Where were you?" Minnette weakly lifted her hand.

Miles knelt by the bed. "There was business to attend to. Why aren't you resting?"

"I can only sleep when I know you're here. Will you stay?" Minnette's eyelids drooped.

Miles hesitated. He didn't want to leave his mother, but Ivey also needed his attention now. Miles laid his hand on his mother's forehead.

"I will be here when you wake. Sleep."

Once the sound of her breathing changed, he rose to his feet and rubbed his eyes. He'd been nursing a headache of his own since hitting his head against the *Monarch*'s walkway, and his need for sleep was becoming increasingly hard to ignore.

When he returned to Ivey's sitting room, Miles found her resting on a couch, awaiting his return. She looked remarkably lively considering everything she had suffered. Miles made a quick inspection of her bandages.

"How's your pain?"

"Nothing I can't endure."

"Has the nausea worn off?"

"I'm ready to eat."

"Then I'm sorry to have kept you waiting."

"Are sure your mother doesn't need you?" Ivey smiled. "This ship has become something of a flying hospital. You haven't even had the time to tend to your own injury."

Miles absentmindedly rubbed his aching forehead. "How did you know that?"

"I could sense your pain."

Miles cocked his head. "Really? Has that ever happened before?"

"Yes. I've always been this way. It's not due to the otheophainer."

Miles offered his arm. "Would you care to tell me more about it over lunch?"

Ivey accepted it. "Certainly."

"Please have her back before long, Mr. Miles. You both need rest," Sylvia called out as Miles ushered Ivey from the suite.

When they reached the staircase, his grip around her arm tightened.

"Just so you know, I'm not prone to falling," she said sternly.

"Good. Then I can count on you to keep me steady," Miles replied softly.

"In that case, I won't let you be knocked on your bum again, sir—" she caught herself, "—Miles."

❧

When Ivey and Miles entered the garden room, Paisley Fitzroy was holding court at a table with Amelia Buxhill and Chenille Foxton. The threesome halted their conversation to stare as Ivey and Miles approached.

Ivey looked away as they walked past Paisley's table. Somehow, the awful man managed to slide his walking stick in front of Miles' leg, causing him to stumble. Good to her word, Ivey held Miles' arm tightly to keep him from tumbling face first to the floor.

"My deepest apologies. That was entirely my fault," Paisley drawled. His glance toward the girls sent them into a fit of laughter.

"I should have watched my step," Miles muttered.

Ivey longed to put the scoundrel in his place, but she held her tongue in an act of perfect restraint that would have made Prim proud.

"Good day, Mr. Fitzroy. If you'll excuse us, our table is waiting."

Paisley leaned toward his companions and spoke from the side of his mouth. "It would look as though the little lady already has her Mr. Fenchurche on a short lead. That poor boy never did learn to act like a man."

Miles didn't seem to notice, but the way the girls fawned over Paisley's taunt made Ivey blush. She was ashamed to remember how recently she had also felt that Miles lacked nerve. In only a few days' time, she'd come to realize that the way he negotiated the difficult relationships in his life demonstrated a real strength of character. Even when her foolhardy exploits threatened both of their lives, he'd been calm in the face of her temper and gentle while caring for her injury. In fact, his gracious mannerisms might actually become endearing if he would ever stop fussing over her unnecessarily.

As if on cue, Miles leaned forward to touch Ivey's reddened face. She recoiled in embarrassed confusion.

"I'm sorry," Miles apologized. "I only meant to feel your forehead. It looks like you may be starting a fever."

Ivey's skin blushed even more.

"Oh, that's not a fever is it?"

Ivey looked down, afraid her eyes would give away her racing heart. She hadn't expected Miles to be at all appealing, but she couldn't allow him to think that she was interested in a romantic future of any kind.

They sat quietly for a few moments.

"Ivey, you have me at a great disadvantage," he finally spoke. "It seems that you can read my mind, but I haven't a clue what goes on in yours."

"No one does." Ivey confessed. "Not even me. I still can't believe how wrong I was this morning. I was convinced that ribbon was a sign of bad things to come."

"And now you know it wasn't."

"But what if—"

"Let's not worry about such matters." Miles gestured for the waiter. "I'd like to see that appetite you promised."

When the meal was delivered to their table, their conversation turned to the operation of the *Monarch*. Miles responded enthusiastically to Ivey's plentiful questions ranging from how the ship's engines helped maintain elevation to the chemical composition of the glass windows installed throughout the cabin.

"Father believed the best way to learn about our world was by knowing how to ask the right questions, and then by conducting experiments to determine their answers."

Miles smiled. "I would agree."

"My mother didn't. One time, he showed me what would happen when he mixed droplets of two new chemicals that reacted to release a burst of light and pressure. I stole the vials from his bag that night and tried to recreate the effect by myself. Would you believe I blew the roof off the stable?"

"As chance would have it, the *Monarch*'s engines are powered by that very same type of reaction."

"Isn't it amazing? I would love to see how it works on such a grand scale."

Miles laughed. "I can show you the engine room, but only if you promise not to blow my ship to pieces."

Ivey folded her napkin and placed it on her empty plate. "I love everything about this ship, Miles. That's why I went out into the riggings this morning. I wanted to believe that I was destined to protect her. I would never let anything happen to the *Monarch*."

"Trust me, Ivey. This airship may appear to be cumbersome and fragile, but there's more to her than meets the eye."

"Don't you think the same could be true about me?"

"I think it could," he replied. "So I'm hoping that we can forget your dream now. The *Monarch* is fine, and I'd like you to enjoy the rest of your voyage."

"That would be nice," Ivey lied.

Dread lurked in her heart. Something was not right on board the ship, but until she discovered what that was, Ivey would keep her premonitions to herself.

"We still need to discuss the otheophainer, and what I've been reading," she said.

"I would be delighted to, but it can wait until after you've gotten some rest." Miles rose from his seat.

"I'd like to stay a little longer. Please go on if you need to see your mother," Ivey protested.

Miles offered his hand. "I'm afraid I can't."

"Why not?"

"I've escorted a lady out, and I am bound to see her safely back to her quarters."

Ivey rolled her eyes. "I'm perfectly capable of seeing myself back to the room. What could possibly go wrong?"

Before Miles could answer, there was a loud thud followed by the screams of the girls at Paisley Fitzroy's table.

A yellow songbird had flown into the glass wall and fallen onto Amelia Buxhill's blue porcelain plate. The little bird flapped its wings and writhed on its back.

"How revolting! I cannot bear to see it!" Chenille covered her eyes.

"Oh, Paisley, make it stop!" Amelia begged.

Paisley leaned close and inspected the bird for a few seconds.

"I'll be sure to put it out of its misery," he said. "Look away, ladies."

The girls clung to each other in horror as Paisley raised his walking stick to crush the injured creature on the plate.

Ivey leapt over an adjacent table and caught the end of his cane before he could strike. She twisted the stick, wrenching his arm behind his back.

"What the devil?" Paisley cried.

"My deepest apologies," Ivey spat into his ear. "That was entirely my fault."

She jerked the cane away from him and stepped back. He spun around with one hand raised. Ivey raised the walking stick, assuming a defensive stance.

"I say, I do like a girl who plays rough."

"Is there a problem, Mr. Fitzroy?" Miles had appeared at Ivey's side.

"You'd better be watchful, Miles. It seems your fiancée cannot keep her hands off me."

Miles ignored him. "Are you all right?" he asked Ivey.

"Yes. Mr. Fitzroy seems to have a problem controlling his stick." She glared at Paisley. "I hope you can learn to manage it, sir."

When Paisley reached for his cane Ivey handed it back.

"Come along, girls. I think these love birds want to be alone."

As they walked off, Ivey turned her attention to the wounded bird. She gently scooped it into her hands. A spot of blood from its beak sank into the bandage on Ivey's palm. Its head drooped to the side, and its chest heaved with every labored breath.

The bird was dying.

Ivey looked up. "She's too young to die, Miles. Can you help her, like you did me?" She offered the tiny body.

"I'm sorry, Ivey, but that is beyond my capabilities. Would you like me to take it from you?"

"No." Ivey held it close. "She needs the warmth of my hands." She cradled the bird to her chest as a tear rolled down her cheek. "She was only trying to escape. Wild creatures can't be kept in cages, you know."

Miles took her arm. "Maybe I can help you ease its suffering. Will you come with me?"

He led her out of the vestibule to the private elevator tucked behind the garden. They ascended to the private parlor and followed the restricted bridge hallway to where it ended at a sturdy metal door. Miles opened it for Ivey.

She stepped through and found herself inside the *Monarch*'s bridge. It was much more expansive than she'd expected, filled with banks of wooden consoles that housed precise navigational instruments and control apparatuses manned by the flight crew. Like the ship's main dining room directly below, the bridge offered an unobstructed view through the curved window at the bow of the *Monarch*'s cabin. Against the back wall was a large, lofted gallery that rose several feet above the rest of the room.

Ivey didn't see the captain, but they passed by a few crewmen on their way to a small, steep stairway at the far side of the bridge. Miles indicated that she should go first. Unable to hold onto the rails with the bird in her hands, she leaned back against him, letting Miles keep the skirt of her dress from tripping her.

At the top of the stairs, he reached around her to open a small hatch door.

"This is the captain's private observation deck. No one will disturb you here."

He held the door open as she passed through.

Ivey felt a surge of fresh air sweep around her body as she emerged onto a large wooden terrace. The observation deck, enclosed by brass railings dotted with spyglasses at its front and sides, sat atop the prow of the cabin.

Looking up, she saw the *Monarch*'s envelope reaching into an endless expanse of blue sky; ahead, the ocean sparkled on the horizon.

Miles waited by the hatch, his head bowed in respect, as Ivey moved to the middle of the platform. She dropped to her knees and held her hands out to share the warm, salty air with the dying bird. She bowed her head over the wounded creature, whispering the words of an old Cemarian blessing for the dying.

May your spirit soar if the body is unwilling.

Ivey remained in that position for a long time as the flow of the sea breeze sent strands of her dark auburn hair licking like flames around her. The energy of the setting flowed into her body. For a moment, she was one with the air around her, the sea ahead of her, the ground below her, and the spark of life that flowed through her veins.

Live.

She raised her arms and threw the bird into the air.

To her amazement, the creature lifted on the wind. It extended its wings and began to fly. Her arms lifted in unison with the yellow bird as it disappeared high into the ship's riggings and out into the sky.

Ivey's heart soared with the bird's.

She turned to Miles with a joyful smile. "Thank you."

When he started toward her, the vitality surging through her body ebbed and her knees gave way. She nearly fell, but Miles caught her and carried her to one of the hooded chairs against the back wall of the observation deck. He laid her on the cushion and brushed the tousled hair back from her face.

"That may be the most incredible thing I've ever seen." Miles took a deep breath. "What did you do?"

Ivey trembled. "*We* did it. Giving the bird a taste of freedom helped it find the will to live."

"Ivey, you look spent. Let me take you back to your room."

Ivey closed her eyes. "Could I rest here? I need fresh air, too."

He made her promise to lie quietly on the reclined chair, and then he disappeared down the stairs back into the *Monarch*'s bridge.

Miles returned with a flask of hot tea and a blanket to ensure Ivey would not take a chill if the air temperature dropped when they ventured out over the sea. He inspected the bandages on her injured hand once more and carefully tucked the blanket around her.

He sat back on another of the covered chairs and watched as Ivey sank into a deep sleep. It calmed him to see how happy she looked, even in her slumber.

Thinking back to the smile she'd given him after saving the bird, a realization dawned on him: he felt happy. He closed his eyes, wanting to savor his awareness of the feeling, but Sylvia would be awaiting their return. Miles decided to rest for a moment longer before fetching her to sit with Ivey while he returned to his mother. Before he knew it, he was sound asleep.

Chapter Thirteen

Starry Night

Ivey didn't move a muscle until sundown. A slight rustling from her chair as she rolled over woke Miles.

He sat up with a start, and a moment passed before he remembered what had happened.

He stood up to check on Ivey. The evening air had already grown brisk, and he recalled the deep chill of her body during her strange episodes.

When he placed his hand to her cheek, Ivey threw off the blanket and leapt out of her chair with a ferocity that made Miles step back and throw his hands up in defense.

"Ivey, it's only me. We're on the observation deck, so please mind your step."

The wild look faded from her eyes as she took in the beauty of her surroundings.

"Oh, thank you for letting me sleep out here. I feel much better."

"You're not angry?"

"Why would you think that?"

"The look on your face when I woke you. I thought I'd done something to offend you again."

Ivey smiled. "That was just a reflex. I can't afford to let anything dangerous sneak up on me when sleeping outdoors."

Miles studied her face. "Are you afraid that I am dangerous?"

Ivey laughed. "I'm afraid there isn't a dangerous bone in your body, Mr. Fenchurche."

"Am I to take that as a compliment?"

"After everything that's happened, I have no desire to insult you, Miles."

He frowned and tried to take on his mother's authoritative tone. "Well, I hope you continue to remember the promises you made this morning. If you ever put yourself at risk like that again, you might find out just how dangerous I can be."

Ivey looked away, failing to hide her bemused smile.

"If you are steady on your feet, we should go back inside," Miles said. "Sylvia must be wondering what became of us."

Ivey gestured toward the end of the observation deck, where the horizon blazed as the sun disappeared into the glittering sea.

"Have you ever seen anything as beautiful as this? It feels like a dream. Can't we stay awhile longer?" she begged.

"We've been out all day, and your bandage needs changing."

"Arvel says never to waste a sunset. There will only be one scene exactly like this in our entire lives, Miles."

"All right, for a minute longer, but only if you stay in your chair," Miles conceded.

Ivey's expression grew troubled as she sat down and wrapped herself in the blanket.

"Is your hand hurting?"

"No. It's just that I wish my father were here to see this."

He winced. If anything happened to her father, Miles could not imagine how someone as sensitive as Ivey would handle her grief. As fond as he'd grown of Arvel since the engagement, Miles didn't want to think of how he would handle that loss himself.

He quickly changed the subject. "Let me get you something to drink."

He poured a cup from the flask of tea he'd prepared in the captain's private galley beneath the bridge. "Please have as much as you can."

"I'm not in the habit of being spoiled like this." Ivey cheerfully sipped the fragrant brew. She wrinkled her nose at his expression. "What does that look mean?"

"What look?"

"You think I'm spoiled?"

Miles hesitated. Such a thought had just crossed his mind.

She is perceptive.

For some odd reason, Miles found himself enjoying the prospect of pitting his wits against this girl.

"It's not that you're spoiled, but you are, without a doubt, one of the most stubborn people I've ever encountered."

Ivey's eyes brightened. "I'm not stubborn, Mr. Fenchurche. I simply have strength of purpose. When I believe in something, I'm not afraid to stand my ground."

"Even if you fall flat on your face?" Miles had to ask.

"You've only seen me at my worst," Ivey sighed. "By the time we arrive at Ferndale, you'll know who I really am."

Miles looked up at the evening sky. "It could take a lifetime to know someone like you, Ivey Thornton."

Ivey followed his gaze. They sat quietly as the sunset faded and the sky above began to light up with stars.

"We really must go in now." Miles started to rise.

"Why?" Ivey caught his arm.

"Because passengers aren't allowed outside the cabin after sundown. Captain's rules," Miles said firmly, determined to be taken seriously.

"Miles, the stars are so beautiful, and you own this ship. Aren't you the one who makes the rules?"

He shook his head. "You never stop trying to get your way, do you?"

Ivey looked at him out of the corner of her eye. "If you sit down, I'll tell you a secret."

"Your father said you keep many secrets."

"I do. But this is the deepest and darkest of them all."

Ivey's smile contained an element of such mystery that Miles settled back onto his chair, completely captivated. "Please, go on."

Ivey scanned the night sky. "First, there's a constellation I want to show you. Just below the Firedog, and above the Dark Star. There! Do you see those five stars arranged in a pentacle?"

Miles located the conspicuous shape of the Firedog constellation and searched the sky below. "Yes, I can see them, but I don't believe that is a constellation."

"It was in an ancient legend, one that's lost and forgotten in this world," Ivey explained.

"Then how do you know about it?"

Ivey smiled slyly. "Because I'm a part of it." She took a long drink of tea for effect.

"So, tell me the legend of Ivey Thornton."

"I don't know, it's a rather long story," Ivey teased, "and if the ship's rules say all passengers should be in by sundown . . ."

Miles sighed. "Very well. I hereby amend the captain's rules. We must stay here until you tell me this legend. And your secret."

"Thank you." Ivey made herself comfortable in the chair and took another sip of tea. "That constellation is the Five Sisters. Its story has been passed down in the Thornton family since the beginning of time, or at least that's what Arvel says.

"According to the legend, at the dawn of our world, Aether was an enchanted place full of many wondrous beings who lived peacefully under the rule of a magical queen. All living things prospered until an ancient demon escaped from the underworld and began to sow discontent. The queen's subjects soon became angry and jealous, and they were determined to make war among themselves."

"What did she do?" Miles asked.

"The queen went to the demon and offered to grant him a wish if he would stop leading her subjects into darkness. The demon admired the queen's courage and was intrigued by the purity of her heart. He vowed to leave her world if she would surrender the light of her spirit to brighten his own dark world for the rest of eternity."

Miles reached for the flask and poured Ivey more tea. "Did she accept the bargain?"

"No, not completely. The queen's subjects had acquired a thirst for war, and even if the demon was driven out, she knew her realm would be cast into turmoil."

"What could she do to stop that?"

"She performed a solemn ritual that gave each of her five daughters a piece of her soul so they might save her realm once she had gone."

"A piece of her soul?"

"Yes. The eldest daughter was given her mother's voice, so that the creatures of the world would never misunderstand one another. The second daughter received the queen's kindness, because only compassion can undermine violence. The third daughter was given inspiration, to motivate others to seek beauty and harmony."

Ivey leaned forward, fastening Miles in a steely gaze. "Now, the fourth daughter had a warrior's heart, so the queen gave her the gift of immortality. Her fate was to wage a great war to put the broken kingdom back in order."

"And what of the fifth daughter?" Miles asked.

"She received the queen's desire for peace; she was to heal the wounds of war and bring happiness back to the world."

"That sounds promising."

"It was, but before the queen could anoint the princess she'd chosen to take her crown, the demon appeared, angered by how much of her soul's light had been given away. He dragged the queen down into his world, where she perished."

"And then what happened?"

"With no clear successor, the princesses argued amongst themselves over which one was best suited to rule. Eventually, they turned against one another and split their mother's realm into five new worlds. As time passed, each princess forgot the existence of her sisters, and the queen's magic was lost. In the end, the five splintered lights of her soul drifted to the heavens until the day her daughters were reborn to fulfill their destinies."

Miles stared at the constellation for a while. "And how exactly do you figure into this legend?"

"Isn't it obvious?"

"What's obvious is that your father came up with a fantastic bedtime story about five daughters who sound a lot like his own. Somehow, I doubt that makes you the reincarnation of a warrior princess."

Ivey leaned back in her chair and sighed. "I might agree, but you haven't heard my secret." She took a deep breath and paused.

"I've never shared this with anyone, not even my father."

Her shift of mood left Miles feeling uneasy.

"You can trust me, Ivey."

"Very well. When I was very little, I drowned in Thornhall Pond. I broke my parents' rules and went into the water by myself. I was an excellent swimmer, but I became tangled in the branches of a sunken tree. Father thinks he pulled me out just in time, but I was underwater for so much longer than anyone knows. I cannot explain what happened, but this I know: no matter how close I come to the other side, I always find my way back, without so much as a scar to show for it."

"What does that mean?" Miles felt his pulse quicken.

"I was born with the queen's gift of eternal life. Death cannot claim me until I've fulfilled my destiny. That's why I take so many risks."

"Ivey? You can't possibly believe that you're immortal. You are only flesh and blood. If you had fallen from the riggings today, you would be gone forever."

"Yet, here I am."

"Only because you didn't fall. And what about the night of our engagement party? You nearly suffocated."

"Don't you see? Your fate is intertwined with mine. I believe you have the power to bring me back if I ever go too far. That is your destiny, Miles."

He put a hand across his eyes. "Destiny? Such a thing does not exist, Ivey. I don't believe in unseen forces that dictate life and death."

He felt her hand on his arm. "There's more, if you care to hear it."

"I do," he answered softly, although a part of him wanted her stop.

"Your father believed in fate."

Miles' head shot up. "What?"

"Maddox came to Thornhall when I was a baby. Our fathers wanted us to be together. I've been reading your father's essays, and I've come to believe that you and I are fated to carry on his work, to change our world."

Miles held up his hands. "I'm sorry, but this is too much. I don't know what you're hoping for me to say."

"I see. There's always been something wrong with me. I don't fit in this world. I thought you and your father could help me understand why, but I made a mistake. If you need to send me home, I won't blame you."

She threw the blankets from her lap and stood up. "I'm ready to go inside."

Miles was caught in a whirlwind of emotions. He leaned back in the chair, covering his face as he struggled to find the right words to apologize to her. He heard the hatch slam shut. Ivey had left the observation deck without him.

Miles jumped to his feet to stop her. "Ivey, please. Give me a chance—"

He entered the bridge, but Ivey had already passed through the metal door and disappeared into the corridor. Miles raced to catch her.

A movement outside the hatch caught his attention. Ivey had gone out onto the deck that led to the service walkway alongside the cabin. She turned and ripped the bandage from her wound, holding her hand against the glass.

There was no sign of the cut or stitches. A tear rolled down her cheek and fell on the railing. She pointed toward the sea. Her eyes met his. There was something almost hopeful in their expression.

"I'm sorry." Ivey grabbed the railing and flung herself over.

In an instant, she was gone.

"Ivey!" Miles screamed.

He had to turn the ship around and search for her in the water. Miles spun back toward the bridge.

Ivey was standing behind him, dripping wet. Her skin had the bluish pallor of a drowning victim. A cold terror swept over him.

"Don't be afraid, Miles," her voice echoed in the hallway. "You can still save me if you're willing to take a risk."

"I am." Miles' heart was pounding. "What should I do?" he whispered.

"Wake up."

Chapter Fourteen

DEADLY MEDICINE

M iles bolted upright.
It was a dream. Only a dream.
He was sitting in the deck chair. The heat of the late afternoon sun was still shining brightly onto the observation deck.

Ivey was asleep in the chair next to him, wrapped in the blanket, just as she had been when he dozed off. He took several deep breaths to gather his wits.

He had experienced a terrible nightmare, yet every detail was painfully vivid. In comparison, the world around him now felt less than real. Some time passed before Miles could leave his chair.

He reached for Ivey's cheek but stopped, afraid he might startle her again. He knelt beside the chair and spoke softly.

"Ivey. We have to go in now." She didn't respond. "It's time to wake up."

The hair around Ivey's face was damp, and it clung to her skin. "Ivey?" He touched her shoulder. Her dress felt soaked. The terrible image of Ivey flinging herself overboard flashed through his mind.

He reached for her face, expecting it to be cold and lifeless. She was burning hot.

Infection.

Miles drew back the covers and pulled the gauze away from Ivey's hand. Her wound was swollen, and streaks of red radiated from her palm.

"Ivey! Please wake up!" He took her face in his hands.

She mumbled. "Father. I'm here."

Miles raised his voice. "Ivey, it's Miles. Wake up. I need your help."

Her eyelids fluttered open, but her vision was unfocused. "I was lost."

"You have a fever. I need you to do that certain thing; I need you to go swimming again. Can you try to cool yourself down?"

Ivey's heavy eyelids closed.

"Ivey? Did you hear me?" Miles sat anxiously for a long while, until it appeared that the flush on her face had faded.

"Good. That's good. Just don't go back to sleep."

Ivey was drenched with sweat, and he knew her body must have become even more dehydrated. Her condition could deteriorate quickly if he weren't able to control the infection.

He laid his wrist against her forehead. "Sit up. You need to drink."

Ivey tried to comply, but her efforts ended in a painful moan. "I hurt all over. What have I done now?"

Miles slid his arm under her back and helped her up. "Nothing. You have a serious fever. I should have never allowed you to sleep in the sun, and underneath a blanket." Miles picked up the flask of tea and brought it to Ivey's lips. "Drink."

The effort of holding her head up seemed to exhaust her. "I don't get fevers."

Miles brought the vessel back to her lips and coaxed her to take another drink. "It was my mistake. I should have disinfected your wound and changed the bandage after you handled the bird."

"Mr. Fenchurche, I didn't know you made mistakes."

"Of course I do, and I'm quick to admit them."

"I'm too quick to make them."

A brisk wind blew across the platform, causing Ivey to shiver.

"We need to go inside. Put your arm around my neck. I'll carry you."

Ivey's face contorted. "I will manage, thank you."

"You can barely hold your head up. You'll need to save every bit of strength to fight this infection."

Ivey looked him in the eye. "That which does not kill me teaches me how to survive."

Miles sighed. "You are, without doubt, the most stubborn person I have ever met."

Ivey took a deep breath as she wobbled to her feet. "I am not stubborn, merely—"

"—strong in purpose," Miles finished the thought for her.

Ivey looked at him. "Can you read my thoughts now?"

"Only in dreams," he replied. "Now, you can either hold onto me or come crashing down again. I'll leave it up to you."

Ivey took a swaying step. She quickly relented, extending her right arm in his direction. Miles put his arm around her waist, and they made their way to the hatch.

Captain LeClere and the evening shift of the flight crew looked surprised as Miles helped his dazed companion down the stairs.

"Good to see you, Miles," the captain said. "They've turned this ship upside down looking for the two of you. I'm afraid your mother was beginning to think you'd fallen overboard."

Miles had forgotten about his promise to be at his mother's side when she awoke.

"I'm sorry, Captain. Miss Thornton needs immediate medical attention. Have Doctor Brendel meet us in her suite. Tell him to bring everything this ship has to treat an infected wound."

Ivey let out a small moan and set her head against Miles' shoulder.

"My head is splitting."

Her ears were a bright red.

"There's no time to waste," the captain said. "I'll take her to the suite. You go explain things to Doctor Brendel."

Ivey was barely conscious as the captain swept her into his arms and hurried from the bridge.

By the time they reached her suite, Ivey's breathing had grown ragged. The captain sent Dolan to let Minnette know that Miles was safe. Sylvia put Ivey into bed and draped a cool cloth across her neck. Before leaving, the captain gave Ivey's arm a reassuring pat.

"I hear you have a fascination with airships. Once you've recovered, I'd be more than happy to show you about the bridge."

Ivey's eyes slowly opened. "Will you teach me how to fly the ship?"

The captain chuckled. "No one's ever requested that. It would be my honor, young lady."

Ivey sighed and her eyes drifted shut.

Doctor Mathias Brendel's reputation as a shrewd practitioner of medicine had been formed over three decades of service to the Fenchurche family. The blustery man had been attending to Minnette's maladies for as long as Miles could remember. Any attempts the young master made to address his mother's ailments were always met with the good doctor's derision, and when an opportunity came along to point out Miles' medical shortcomings, Dr. Brendel was more than happy to do so.

Arriving at Ivey's bedroom door, Doctor Brendel took Miles by the arm. "Before we go in, I'll ask you to keep your opinions to yourself. I am the doctor, and Miss Thornton is my patient now."

"Of course." Miles opened the door and hurried to the bedside.

Sylvia had elevated Ivey's hand on a pillow. The wound was weeping and streaked, both signs of a serious infection.

"This is much worse than I expected, Miles," the doctor said. He sat his medical bag on a side table and opened it. "Why in Aether's name didn't you come to me before you tried to stitch her up?"

Miles looked down. "I thought things were under control."

"You only know enough to be dangerous. Wait outside."

Ivey stirred. "Don't go." She grabbed for Miles' hand.

Doctor Brendel glared at Miles.

"Ivey, you can trust our doctor," Miles said. "Sylvia is here, and I will be right outside." Miles loosened his hand from Ivey's and exited the room.

Sylvia removed Ivey's sopping clothes and dressed her in a sleeveless gown while Doctor Brendel arranged his instruments.

"Should I fetch fresh cloths for her head?" Sylvia asked.

"No, we need to let the fever do its work while I drain the wound. Hand me that jar."

Sylvia picked up a lidded glass jar filled with muddy contents. "This one, sir?"

☙

Miles paced the sitting room, blaming himself for Ivey's grave condition. He noticed a pile of books on the table, and his mind flashed back to the dream, when Ivey had talked about reading a book written by his father. He lifted the topmost books and uncovered one of the leather-bound journals his father had written before his death.

Had Ivey actually reached through the terrible dream and into his unconscious mind to ask for help? He opened the book and scanned its table of contents. There were headings for treatises covering many of the topics he'd discussed with Ivey in the garden room.

Farther down the page, a title jumped out: "At Aether's Edge: A Proposal of Existence as Manifold in Its Structure."

He flipped through the journal, searching for the first page of the essay, when a sudden bloodcurdling scream from the bedroom sent him rushing back inside.

Doctor Brendel had been knocked to the floor, and Ivey stood beside the bed, clinging to Sylvia in a state of terror.

"What happened?"

"The doctor was tending to her infection when Miss Ivey went wild. She is out of her mind with fever, Mr. Miles."

Ivey panted like a trapped animal while Miles pried her hands from Sylvia's arm. "You have to calm down," he said gently.

"No!" she cried. "They're evil . . . don't touch them!"

Miles looked at Sylvia. "What is she talking about?"

"The leeches, Mr. Miles. When the doctor tried to put one on her, she knocked him flat on his back."

Miles looked down at the rotund doctor who was struggling to sit up. "Are you hurt?"

Doctor Brendel rose and brushed himself off angrily before picking up the jar of leeches that Ivey had kicked from his hand. "Tell her to cooperate, or I will have her restrained."

The doctor's patient responded to his threat by making a dash for the bedroom door. Miles and Sylvia had to struggle to wrestle her back onto the bed and pin her down.

"Ivey, stop fighting us," Miles begged. "You're very sick."

She tried once more to break free, but her strength was ebbing. She looked up and sobbed, "Don't let them near me; they will kill us all."

Miles sat on the side of the bed and laid his hand on her forehead to calm her. "These leeches can help you heal."

"They will bring death. My father knows," Ivey whimpered. "Please believe me."

Miles leaned closer. "I promised him I would protect you. You can trust me."

Ivey shook her head. "I can't do it."

Miles was firm. "This is your fever talking. Iris said you aren't afraid of anything, and I believe her."

Miles lifted Ivey's arm and laid it across the pillows, then gestured for Doctor Brendel to approach. Ivey saw the jar in his hand and trembled violently, but Miles turned her face back toward his. "Just look at me. We're going to help you."

Ivey's body went limp and her eyelids grew droopy.

"Yes," whispered Miles. "Be calm. It will be over before you know it."

"Sylvia," she mumbled.

The trembling maid had tears in her eyes. "Yes?"

"In my satchel, the tin of balm . . ." Ivey's voice faded to a whisper as she sank into unconsciousness. "A storm is coming . . . don't give up."

"We won't, Miss Ivey."

Miles looked at Sylvia. "What is she talking about?"

"There's a satchel in the wardrobe. I'll fetch it for her."

"Miles." Doctor Brendel waved the jar of leeches. "Can you keep her under control, or do I need to get help?"

Ivey looked as though she was entering a meditative state. Once her body had completely relaxed, Miles nodded to the doctor, keeping a firm grip on both of her arms.

Doctor Brendel pulled a leech from the jar with a long pair of forceps while Sylvia laid the satchel on the bed and began to unpack an odd assortment of items. He carefully placed the creature's mouth parts against the inflamed flesh that bordered Ivey's wound. The creature immediately took hold, and its slimy body pulsated as it began to gorge on her blood.

Doctor Brendel applied a second and then a third leech.

Ivey hadn't moved, so Miles cautiously released her arms and picked up a metal tin Sylvia had just pulled from Ivey's bag.

Inside, he discovered a sticky golden substance with a pungent scent reminiscent of tree sap. That Ivey had called it a balm made sense. During his studies abroad, Miles had encountered many such medicinal concoctions. He dipped his hand into the ointment and rubbed it between his fingers, noting how quickly it grew warm and tacky against his skin.

He closed the tin and wiped the sap's residue onto his handkerchief.

"What demonry is this?" Doctor Brendel muttered.

Miles looked over. The skin of Ivey's forearm had turned a deathly shade of blue and taken on a strange, scaly texture.

"Could she be allergic to the leeches?" He leaned over to look closely.

The doctor shook his head, mystified. "I've never seen anything like this before."

Sylvia pointed at the parasitic worms. "Mr. Miles, should they be doing that?"

The leeches had more than tripled in size, acquiring a bluish-gray hue of their own.

A terrible apprehension was overtaking Miles. "Get them off," he demanded.

Doctor Brendel dismissed his plea. "It takes time. Leeches release when they are satisfied."

Miles jumped up. "Does anything about this look satisfying to you, doctor? Remove them now or I will."

Doctor Brendel glared at Miles, but he relented. "Fine, but one has to be careful. Forcing a leech off can cause its head to be left behind in the skin."

He rolled up his sleeve and prepared to separate the first of the swollen creatures from Ivey's arm. As his fingers closed around its slimy body, it lifted its head, making a hissing sound.

"Ouch! It has a stinger! The little son of a—" Before the doctor could even finish his curse, he fell forward and collapsed.

Miles was sure that the leech hissed defiantly at him before plunging its teeth back into a vein on the inside of Ivey's wrist.

"Get off of her, you devil!" Sylvia dove forward to help.

Miles barred her with his arm. "Sylvia! Don't touch it."

Miles ran to the other side of the bed, stepping over the doctor's body, to find the forceps. By the time he had them in hand, the leech was so swollen that the jaws of the device barely opened widely enough to grasp it.

When Miles squeezed down and began to pull, the body of the leech burst, spewing blood across the bed.

Sylvia shrieked, and Miles fought his urge to gag.

The leech's head was still attached to Ivey's hand. Blood pumped through the leech's ripped abdomen and onto the pillow. Miles grasped the head with the forceps and tried to wrestle it free, but it held tight, threatening to tear Ivey's skin and the vein itself.

Sterilizing solution.

Miles dropped the instrument and dashed to Doctor Brendel's bag. As he frantically rummaged through it, Sylvia ran to the bathroom. Miles found the bottle just as Sylvia reappeared at the bedside with a jar of bathing salts.

She dumped the contents over the leeches. They squealed and rolled themselves into tight balls to escape the burning of the salt.

Miles grabbed the jar the leeches had been stored in from the side table and quickly scooped them up. He filled the jar with sterilizing solution and screwed the lid down tightly.

Sylvia pressed the coverlet against Ivey's wrist to staunch the flow of blood rushing from her open vein.

"Mr. Miles, help me."

Miles knew that a leech's saliva contained chemicals that that thinned the blood. Simply bandaging her wounds would not be enough to stop the bleeding. He scrambled back around the bed and found the tin of balm he'd dropped. He dipped his finger into the ointment and rubbed it across the Y-shaped incisions left by the leeches, instructing Sylvia to pinch the skin together until the balm could seal each wound. The lacerations ceased to bleed.

"Sylvia, check Doctor Brendel." Miles felt for a pulse on Ivey's neck. He was relieved to detect a faint, slow heartbeat. He spoke urgently into her ear.

"I need you to be strong."

Sylvia rolled the fallen doctor onto his back and leaned over him. "He's breathing. What about Miss Ivey?"

"She's alive . . . barely."

Miles elevated Ivey's arms and legs with pillows before feeling her forehead. The fever was gone, but her body temperature had fallen drastically. She seemed to be in a state of shock.

"We need blankets."

The strange blue tinge in Ivey's skin had crept up her arm. Miles wasn't sure if it was caused by blood loss or the same venomous sting that had felled the doctor.

Sylvia returned with extra blankets from the linen chest in the bathroom.

"All of this blood. How could it be happening again?" Sylvia's voice quivered. "What should I do, Mr. Miles?"

"Have Dolan find any other doctors on board and send them here at once." As she started toward the bedroom door, Miles called out. "Wait! How many leeches were there in that jar?"

Her eyes widened as she realized what he suspected. Sylvia snatched her skirt up around her ankles and scanned the rug.

"I'm sorry, Mr. Miles. It all happened so quickly, I didn't see. The doctor would know, but he's . . ."

"Then tell Dolan to alert Captain LeClere. We need the crewmen to search this suite and guard the door. Warn them that these creatures may be lethal."

Sylvia ran to the bathroom to retrieve another jar of salts. "If you find any more of the bastards, you let 'em have it."

Miles set the jar on the nightstand beside the bed. "Good thinking. Now hurry."

Sylvia paused at the open door. "Will she die, Miles?"

"No. Ivey Thornton will not leave this world while under my care. I am sure of that."

Chapter Fifteen

THE TRANSFUSION

Miles answered a sharp rap at the bedroom door. Dolan entered, carrying a list of the ship's passengers and accompanied by several armed crewmen. Even he seemed shaken by the scene in Ivey's bedroom.

Doctor Brendel was unconscious on the floor beside the blood-splattered bed where Ivey lay, gray and motionless.

While the crewmen carried the doctor to a couch in the sitting room, Dolan approached Ivey to have a closer look. He reached out to touch her afflicted arm, quickly recoiling from the clammy flesh.

"Miles," Dolan hesitated, "I'm afraid she may have expired."

"Ivey is stronger than she looks," Miles replied tersely. "Did you locate a doctor on the ship?"

"No, but there is a chemist from Cadenbury aboard. He is willing to examine the leeches and offer any medicinal assistance he can."

"Give him access to anything he requires." Miles checked Ivey's pulse. The beat was steady, but the discoloration of her skin was continuing to spread up to her neck and face. She was taking on the uncanny appearance of a drowning victim that he'd envisioned in his dream.

He felt Dolan's hand on his shoulder.

"Perhaps we should prepare for the worst."

Miles jerked away. "Keep those comments to yourself. If you go back and upset my mother, you will have to deal with me. Doctor Brendel is fighting for his own life, and I will not leave Ivey's side."

"Please forgive me, sir," Dolan said. "I'll see that the chemist is situated, and I'll do my best to satisfy your mother's questions. She will be proud to know that you are taking charge of the situation."

After Dolan left, Miles faced his growing despair. Nothing in his studies had prepared him for a situation like this, and even if the chemist were able to identify the leeches' poison, the presence of an antidote or treatment on board the *Monarch* was unlikely. He would have gone to examine Doctor Brendel's state, but the crewmen had only begun their search of the bedroom. Until he was certain that no more of these creatures were on the loose, Miles could not leave Arvel's daughter unguarded.

Pulling a chair close to her bed, Miles sank into it and leaned forward to rest his head in his hands. The day's events replayed in his mind. The image of Ivey as she restored life to the dying bird haunted him the most. It was her own life at the tipping point now. Even if the leeches' venom proved not to be fatal, the extreme loss of blood might still cause her body's systems to fail.

Miles ground his fists against his temples, racking his mind for any way to save her. He remembered reading about a battlefield hospital procedure in which blood was transferred directly from a volunteer to a patient. The technique was deemed reckless and could possibly cause the death of both participants. If Ivey were able to hold on until the *Monarch* delivered her to a surgeon willing to attempt the operation, she might survive.

Sylvia returned with Captain LeClere.

Miles jumped to his feet and turned to the captain. "How quickly can you get us to Spirehaven?"

"I've got bad news. I've never seen a squall move from land to sea, but a storm is blowing in from the west. We've no choice but to head north along the coast and look for a break in the weather that will let us approach the shore."

"Damnation," Miles cursed under his breath. "I'll have to do it myself, then."

The leeches, the storm, the risk. One by one, Ivey's fearsome premonitions were coming to pass.

"Get us to land as quickly as possible." Miles picked up the jar of leeches beside the doctor's bag. "Give these specimens to the chemist that Dolan has approached. Use extreme caution in handling them, and have this suite guarded until we are certain that none of them escaped."

The captain checked the tightness of the lid before putting it into his pocket. "How is the doctor?"

"We are about to find out. Sylvia, do not take your eyes off her." Miles grabbed the medical bag and gestured for the captain to follow.

∾

The doctor's skin tone, temperature, and heart rate were all normal, but he was completely unresponsive. Using a magnifying glass from the medical bag, Miles scanned the fingers of the doctor's right hand.

"There. See those bristles?" He held the glass for the captain. "They must be the stingers." Miles produced a pair of short tweezers and an empty medicine jar from the bag. He handed the jar to the captain. "Hold this while I remove the stingers. With any luck, our chemist will be able to isolate their toxin." Miles carefully plucked the barbs from the doctor's fingers.

"And what of Miss Thornton? Is there anything that can be done for her?"

"Are you familiar with the blood transfers that have been performed in battlefield hospitals?"

The captain's brow creased. "Enough to know it's far too dangerous to attempt on a ship, let alone one heading into a squall."

Miles dropped the last stinger into the jar. "She's lost too much blood. It is the only way."

The captain sealed the jar and carefully placed it in another of his pockets. "I have a strong constitution. You may give her mine."

"No, Captain. Your place is at the helm, keeping us ahead of the storm. I will need you to have two small pipe clamps from engineering and a yard's length of pliable tubing boiled, wrapped in a clean towel, and brought to my study as quickly as possible."

"To your suite?"

"This room is contaminated."

"Of course. Should I find a crewman willing to give blood?"

"No. It has to come from me."

The captain looked dumbfounded. "Why is that?"

Miles answered tersely. "If the blood isn't compatible, it will kill her. I have no time to explain, but I am sure of it."

"Miles, you cannot perform such a dangerous procedure on yourself."

"Sylvia will help me."

"And you trust a maid with your life?" The captain shook his head in dismay, but Miles was steadfast.

"I could have no better assistant."

A flash of lightning lit the darkened sky outside the sitting room window.

"The winds are picking up, Captain. See to the chemist and return to the bridge. I need a steady ship."

Captain LeClere clapped Miles on the shoulder. "Very well. I trust you know what you're doing, Miles. Good luck."

"And you, Captain. Oh, there's something else. Have an engineer take the tension off that worn starboard cable we flagged before takeoff. Ivey discovered a serious fray that could come apart during the storm."

"How did she discover a frayed cable all the way up in those riggings?"

Miles shrugged and slowly drew his finger across the heel of his left palm. "With her hand, sir."

The captain opened his mouth as if to speak, but nothing came out. He left the suite, shaking his head.

Sylvia spoke from the bedroom doorway behind Miles.

"What if your blood does not match?"

"You overheard me."

Sylvia looked down. "If it might kill her, you have to know for sure."

"Our compatibility can be verified by mixing small samples to see how they react. If I'm wrong, I'll test volunteers until we find a suitable donor. But I have no doubt. I'm a match." He picked up the doctor's medical bag and rummaged through its contents. "None of these needles are large enough for the procedure. I'll have to go looking in the ship's infirmary."

"Should I get you something to eat before we start?"

Miles waved her off. "It's better if I don't think about food until this is over."

"Then at least make sure you've had plenty of water. You told Miss Ivey that she needed to drink fluids to recover from the loss of blood. Shouldn't you follow your own advice?"

Miles smiled wearily. "Yes, I should. Do you have any other suggestions?"

"Well, she's cold as ice and you are not. Does that matter?"

Miles paced as he mulled the question. Introducing overly warm blood could be a shock in Ivey's fragile state.

"You'd make a good doctor, Sylvia."

"I will do whatever you need."

"Thank you. Once everything is prepared in my quarters, I'll be back."

On his way out, Miles addressed the crewmen who were searching Ivey's bedroom.

"Gentlemen, the ladies need privacy. Please wait in the sitting room and stay on your guard. I am leaving Miss Feather in charge. Bring her whatever she needs." Turning back to Sylvia, Miles said, "Put clean bandages on Ivey's wounds."

❦

The cabin had begun to rock vigorously by the time Miles returned to his suite. He passed through the sitting room and went directly to the workbench in his study, where the rubber tubing and clamps were waiting for him.

He looked over the components, deciding how a hypodermic needle could best be attached to flexible tubing in a way that would not taint the blood. Miles decided that melted candle wax would create the best seal. After attaching the first needle, he held a flame close to the other end of the tubing to sterilize it and create a vacuum in the line before clamping both ends. He quickly affixed the second needle and wrapped the device in a clean towel. He carried it to his bedroom, along with a bottle of sterilizing liquid.

Back at Ivey's suite, Sylvia met him at the bedroom door.

"Something's happening. She's gone blue from head to toe, but look at her hand."

Sylvia pulled back the bandage from Ivey's hand. The signs of inflammation were gone, and the gash was hardly noticeable.

"She's healing?" The thrilling hope that Ivey may somehow recover on her own was dashed when Miles felt for a pulse. It was extremely faint, and he could not be sure that what he felt wasn't the pounding of his own heart in his fingertips.

"We're out of time."

He swept up Ivey's lifeless body and ran for his room. Dolan was standing in the parlor when Miles rushed past, followed by Sylvia. He stepped out of their way without a word.

Miles laid Ivey in the middle of his large canopy bed.

"Sylvia, make me a raised pallet out of bedding to Ivey's right on the mattress."

While Sylvia gathered the linens, Miles ran to his bath and turned the cold water faucet. He stripped off his clothes and struggled to lower himself into the frigid water.

He returned, shivering, in his sleeping trousers and set a bundle of damp towels beside the bed.

"Once the needles have been inserted, release the clamps to begin the blood flow," he explained while wiping Ivey's right arm with sterilizing solution.

"Mr. Miles, you haven't tested the blood," Sylvia warned.

"It is now or never, Sylvia. You must be strong. Do not turn back, no matter what happens. Are you with me?"

Sylvia took her place at the side of the bed.

The blue discoloration made it impossible for Miles to see where the vessel ran under the skin. "Watch how this is done," he told Sylvia. "If I miss the vein, my blood will collect under her skin when the transfer begins. Clamp the line and try again."

"You will not miss, Mr. Miles. Just do it." The rocking of the ship was becoming violent.

Letting his instincts guide him, Miles pierced the skin on the inside of Ivey's elbow and tied a strip of gauze around her arm to keep the needle and tubing secured. Miles laid his hand on Ivey's brow and whispered in her ear.

"Miss Thornton, I will not give up on you. Please don't give up on me."

Miles had no difficulty locating the large blood vessel on the inside of his own forearm. He inserted the other needle and lay back on the pallet.

"Now, put a cold towel on me, and wrap the rest around the tubing to help cool my blood."

As Sylvia draped a damp towel across his chest, Miles began to shiver. A deep chill was settling into his muscles. He took a long breath and nodded for Sylvia to release the clamp on his side of the device. The vacuum Miles had created in the tubing drew his blood into the line so violently that he cried out.

Sylvia grabbed his hand. "Should I stop it?"

Miles gritted his teeth. "No, it will pass." The agony eased when his blood completely filled the line. "Now, remove the clamp on Ivey's end and watch closely," Miles spoke through chattering teeth.

Sylvia held her breath and released the clamp, allowing Miles' blood to flow directly into Ivey's vein. The cabin pitched in the worsening storm, and Sylvia grabbed a bedpost to keep from being thrown off her feet. Miles had to close his eyes to control his nausea.

"Tell me everything that is happening," he pressed Sylvia.

"There's no blood around the needle." Sylvia sounded encouraged. After a minute passed, she placed her hand on Ivey's arm. "She's warming up. It's working, Mr. Miles."

Miles exhaled. "Good. Watch her closely, and don't stop the transfer until after I lose consciousness."

"Is that safe?"

"No, but she needs everything that I can spare."

"Mr. Miles, you could die."

"I will be fine," Miles mumbled as he fought the urge to drift away.

When his shivering turned into a violent shaking, he felt a hand on his arm. "Miles?" He opened his eyes. Sylvia was reaching for the needle.

"Not yet," he said.

"Please stop. I'm afraid."

"Don't be. It's beautiful," he whispered.

"What is?" Sylvia leaned closer.

"The sunset." Miles pointed at the glass panel above his bed. Sylvia looked up.

"It's black as pitch out there. I'm stopping this."

Miles grabbed her hand. "Not yet. She has to survive."

"But what if you don't?"

Miles' shaking calmed, and a peaceful glow filled his body. "Then I will die happy."

Sylvia squeezed his hand. "Hold on, Mr. Miles. Your love is a powerful force."

Before Miles could form the words to reply, he was gone.

To survive the venomous attack of the leeches, Ivey had tried to retreat into the secret waters that restored her strength, but her consciousness was lost along the way. When awareness returned, she was in a darkened catacomb, running through a maze of stone passageways. There was no time to think; something dangerous was on her trail.

If I cross my own path enough times, it might lose track of my scent.

"Only a fool runs in circles when there is no escape," a hideous voice—the voice from her nightmare!—rasped from somewhere in the pitch-black maze of tunnels.

Ivey stopped running. She held her breath and listened for movement. The silence was so oppressive it ached against her ears.

"Your sister's greatest fear is losing her child. What frightens you?"

Ivey gasped. It knew what was she was thinking. She tried to stop it, but her intense fear of tight spaces slipped through her mind. Immediately, the walls around her swelled, pinning her inside a tight cocoon of rock. She could hardly draw a breath.

"Where am I?" she panted. There was no answer. "What do you want with me?"

"Control."

"Of what?"

"Everything your soul possesses."

"Then try and take it," Ivey spat defiantly.

The rocks tightened around her until the pressure was unbearable. Her right arm gave way with a snap. Alongside her agony, Ivey felt a white hot rage.

"I'm not afraid of pain."

"Others will suffer for you. One will soon be dead."

At that moment, Arvel's words came back to her.

I saw things that weren't there, heard voices, felt presences—good and bad. They could not hurt me, and they will not hurt you, Ivey.

Ivey realized she was having a vision. If she could come back to consciousness, it would stop.

"I don't believe you, but if anything happens to my family, I'll find my way back here to destroy you."

"We will wait."

The rock faces came together, melting Ivey into a dark pool.

Chapter Sixteen

ACROSS THE ABYSS

Something touched Ivey's face. She leapt to her feet; ready to kill whatever had attacked her in the catacomb of tunnels.

"Ivey, it's only me."

She saw Miles standing in front of her, silhouetted against a setting sun.

"We are on the observation deck," he said, "so please mind your step."

"How did I get here?"

"We came up to set the bird free. Don't you remember?"

"Yes, but I shouldn't be here now."

Miles spoke gently. "But you were so happy. You asked to stay and see the stars."

"No I didn't." Ivey frowned. "What's the last thing you remember before this?"

A strange expression came over Miles' face.

"Tell me," she insisted. "What were you doing?"

"Saving you."

Ivey's heart sank. "Oh, Miles. What did you do?" She ran to the railing of the observation deck and looked down. Far below them, dark clouds were closing in around a familiar shape.

"The *Monarch*."

She spun around. "You have to go back!"

Miles squinted at her. "Back? To where?"

Ivey dragged him to the railing and pointed. "To your body. It's down there, on the *Monarch*."

"Ivey, we're on the *Monarch*." He moved away, shaking his head.

"This place isn't real, Miles. If you don't go back and wake up you'll be trapped here for an eternity."

"This is the happiest I've ever been. I could stay here with you forever."

"No! You deserve a better life. Please wake up before you die!"

"You're confused. Perhaps you knocked your head when you cut your hand and fell from the riggings."

Ivey held up her uninjured left hand. "How do you explain this?"

Miles drew in a sharp breath. "That can't be. The wound was infected. Doctor Brendel arrived . . . and then Sylvia and I were . . ." Miles stared at his own hands. "Is this death?"

"No, but we're at the threshold," Ivey whispered. "Our souls have separated from our bodies. The longer they remain apart, the harder it is to reunite them. We have to go back now."

The light on the observation deck dimmed. Ivey saw that Miles had begun to shake.

"Ivey, I've never been so cold. I think I'm dying."

Ivey held his arm to keep him from collapsing. "Don't give up. We can still make it."

"Go while you can."

Miles tried to pull away, but Ivey tightened her grip and dragged him back to the railing. "I can't leave without you, and if I don't go back, the *Monarch* will crash, and everyone on board will die with us."

Miles set a hand on the railing and steadied himself. "Then tell me what to do," he said.

Ivey's stomach dropped as the truth dawned on her. "I don't know. I never remember how it happens."

Miles peered down at the *Monarch*, which had nearly disappeared into the black clouds. "You were right. They're flying straight into the storm." He turned back. "Please try, Ivey. Someone has to warn them."

Ivey closed her eyes and tried to visualize her spirit reentering its body. She felt nothing, but a deathly chill creeping up her legs.

"I'm afraid we've both gone too far." Ivey hung her head in despair. If she was meant to save the *Monarch* from disaster, she had failed. As a tear fell from her cheek onto the railing, she whispered, "I'm sorry."

Miles stared at the rail, then looked up at her. "We have to jump."

Ivey looked over the railing toward the dizzying scene below. "Jump?"

Miles nodded emphatically. "I dreamed that you threw yourself overboard. I thought you'd fallen to your death, but you came back and made me wake up. It makes sense now."

Ivey frowned. "No it doesn't."

"That's how we save each other."

Ivey's frown softened. "I guess we have nothing to lose."

With a nod of determination, she reached for his hand.

They climbed over the railing and clung to it tightly, preparing to let go.

"If we survive, will we remember this?" Miles said.

"I don't think so."

The strange expression on Miles' face made Ivey ask, "What is it?"

"I was wondering . . ." He hesitated. "May I have a kiss?"

Ivey blinked in surprise. "I don't know how to do such a thing. How could I start now?"

"I've never kissed anyone either, but if my life ends here, I'd be happy to have shared my first kiss with you, Ivey."

Miles' wistful eyes made it impossible for Ivey to deny his request.

"Very well," she said seriously. "If I kiss you, you must promise not to die."

He placed a hand across his heart. "I promise."

"Then we have a deal."

Ivey lifted her chin in his direction, bracing herself.

Letting go of the railing with one hand, Miles cupped the side of Ivey's face and leaned forward.

Her eyes closed as he drew near.

She felt his lips gently press against hers. They were soft and warm, and his breath was sweet.

They lingered in the kiss for some time before Miles retreated.

Ivey opened her eyes.

The kiss had been surprisingly pleasant, but something about it felt unfinished.

Without thinking, she let go of the railing and leapt onto Miles, throwing her arms around his neck. He wrapped his arms around her, and they tumbled off of the cabin, plummeting into the darkness below.

Ivey squeezed her eyes shut tightly as a glass panel on the roof of the *Monarch*'s cabin rushed toward her.

∾

Ivey awoke to the sound of a woman's mournful screams.

Her eyes cracked open. Everything was white.

She stared blankly until she realized that a piece of fabric was lying across her face. It took some time and effort to move her arms and push the cloth away.

Looking up, Ivey saw the top of a canopy bed. She lifted her head and gazed around the unfamiliar room until she discovered the source of the screaming.

Minnette Fenchurche was standing at the foot of the bed, wailing uncontrollably, while Dolan stood by, wringing his hands.

Ivey turned her head to see what had them so distraught.

Miles was lying next to her in the bed. His shirtless body was sprawled atop a pile of blankets. Sylvia was bent over his body, giving him a long kiss on the lips.

"Well, that's nothing to cry about," Ivey moaned as her head dropped back to the pillow.

Sylvia's tear-streaked face shot up. "Miss Ivey? You're alive?"

Minnette lifted her head and screamed, "You! How dare you draw a breath when my son is dead!"

"Dead?" Ivey looked back at Sylvia.

"His heart stopped," she sobbed. "I'm trying to make him breathe again, but it won't work."

Sylvia's statement brought another round of heartbroken wails from Minnette until she mercifully collapsed in a dead faint.

Ivey summoned the strength to sit up. The room was pitching back and forth as a violent storm raged outside.

It's happening!

"We're going the wrong way," Ivey shouted at Dolan, whose only care was to rouse Minnette. "Dolan!" she screamed. "Go to the bridge and tell the captain to turn our ship around. The *Monarch* is flying into the heart of the storm!"

Dolan gaped at Ivey as if she were speaking gibberish. He went back to patting his mistress's cheek.

"Listen to me, or this ship will go down at sea, taking every soul on board with her. Get off your skinny bum and do what I say!"

Dolan shuddered, then straightened his jacket and ran from the room.

Ivey collapsed back onto the bed. "How did this happen?"

"Those horrid leeches drained you dry, so Mr. Miles gave you his blood." Sylvia rubbed her eyes with her sleeve. "I begged him to stop, and then he was stone cold, like you."

"Keep breathing for him, Sylvia. He's still with us."

Ivey closed her eyes and loosened her shoulders. She could sense his presence in the room, but it was drifting away. Ivey rolled over and took Miles' hand in hers.

"Miles! You need to come back right now. Follow my voice until you can feel my hand."

Sylvia stopped to check for a pulse. Fresh tears spilled from her eyes. "The last thing he said," she sobbed, "was that if he saved you, he would die happy."

Ivey's cheeks burned, and a searing current flowed through her veins.

"Miles, you promised to stay with me!" She raised up and pounded her fists against his chest. "Fight for your life. Fight for me!"

Sylvia sat back with a horrified expression. "Miss Ivey, don't."

"He's not getting away with this, Sylvia. I'll follow him to the underworld and drag him back. Don't stop!" she cried.

Sylvia resumed her efforts as Ivey threw herself across Miles' bare chest and focused her energy on his still heart, willing it to match the beating of her own.

"Our engagement does not end like this. Please?"

Ivey's heart skipped a beat as an overwhelming sense of loneliness passed through her.

Sylvia was breathing into Miles' parted lips when she jumped back in shock. "He kissed me."

As if he were waking from a wonderful dream, Miles sighed. "I never knew how much you cared."

"Mr. Miles!" Sylvia simultaneously laughed and cried.

A moment later, Miles' eyelids opened. He stared up at Ivey and Sylvia in wonder, his eyes brimming with tears.

"The blessed sprites . . . look how they guide our souls into the heavens."

"Don't be insulting, Mr. Fenchurche," Ivey said through tears of her own. "You are still among the living, and I am no sprite."

Chapter Seventeen

Terror at Thornhall

Arvel arrived at the pond to find Iris adjusting a pink bow she'd tied around the beast's stocky neck. His jaws stretched into a wide grin, seemingly delighted with her enhancement to his appearance.

"Iris, what have you done to the poor thing?"

"He wanted to look his best for Prim. Mother said I'm in charge of cheering her up." Iris smiled sweetly.

Arvel crossed his arms. "Your mother may have been kind enough to let the beast stay at Thornhall, but he is not to go anywhere near our guests."

Iris scowled and stamped her foot impertinently.

"Prim is family, and so is Caven."

"Caven?"

"He wants to be called by his real name." Iris patted the creature's back.

Arvel cocked his head. "And how did you come by that information, dear girl?"

Iris hesitated, looking at the waterdog as if seeking his permission to answer the question.

"Iris? Have you been talking to one of your special friends again?"

Iris looked down at her feet, her usual sign that she was being secretive.

"Young lady?" Before Arvel could pry an answer from his daughter, Winora rounded the bend in the path.

"What is this?" She pointed at the pink bow adorning the monster. "Oh, no. No, no, no! Arvel Thornton?"

Arvel held his hands up. "It isn't my doing."

Winora clapped her hands at the cowering waterdog. "Scat, shoo, go to your hiding place and stay there!"

Beast bolted, his pink ribbon bobbing up and down as he loped off into the timber.

"Arvel, if that thing comes anywhere near Prim or her girls, he will find himself in a cage at Cadenbury faster than he can change his spots, or whatever it is that he does."

"I'm sorry, Mother," Iris said quickly. "This was my idea. I promise Caven won't go near them. Please don't be angry at him."

Winora looked at her daughter in exasperation. "Iris, Prim is not well. She needs peace and quiet. I was counting on you to help with the little ones. You want to set a good example for them, don't you?"

Iris straightened her posture and curtsied precisely. "It would be my honor, Mother."

Arvel tapped Iris on the shoulder. "Then go watch for Prim's carriage. Your sister will need to rest after the ride, and you can help settle the little ones into the nursery." He watched for a moment as Iris strolled up the path toward the house, then turned back to his wife.

"Winora, I saw Stanley this morning. He wants us to be prepared."

"For what?"

"The doctors cannot find one thing wrong with Prim or the baby, but her condition is worsening."

"Then what is it?"

"It's as if the nightmares are haunting her waking hours now. Stanley is afraid she's losing her sense of reality. He's asked that you keep a close eye on her."

"Arvel, Prim has always been so sure of herself. How could such a thing happen?"

He hadn't wanted to burden his wife with his concerns about the Zephyr's otheophainer, but it seemed that he no longer had a choice.

"It is possible that this is related to an incident that took place on the dock before Ivey boarded the *Monarch*. Something happened when the craft I was in flew over the girls. It knocked Ivey off her feet."

Winora's hand flew to her mouth.

"She wasn't hurt," Arvel reassured her, "but she was under the impression that some unseen force had attacked the two of them. Now that Prim is experiencing ill effects as well, I'm beginning to fear that both of our daughters are suffering from adverse reactions to the power generated by the Zephyr's machinery."

"Can the damage be undone?"

"We're not sure. Stanley has proposed that he and Nicolai Slate, the inventor of this technology, fly to Ferndale."

Winora's face fell. "If they bring Ivey home, what will become of her engagement, and your mission? Arvel, you know she will follow you into harm's way."

Arvel took his wife's hand. "I will not let her return to Thornhall. Nicolai is taking the equipment needed to conduct tests on Ivey at Ferndale. With Miles' help, they will try to fathom what effect the device had on her. If they do, Stanley and Nicolai may be able to return with a therapy for Prim."

Winora was hesitant. "It sounds so dangerous. You should go with them, Arvel. I can manage things here."

"Miles understands this technology better than I ever will. I trust him to take every precaution our daughter will allow. The more time I spend around that young man, the more I realize what a remarkable match he is for Ivey. If she comes to that realization before rejecting the engagement, she may find herself happily married."

Winora gave him a sideways glance. "Is she under the impression that she has a choice in the matter?"

"Darling, I've done everything in my power, but I cannot make Ivey fall in love. If her heart says no, we will have to accept that."

Arvel realized that Winora was staring past his shoulder. "What is it?"

She pointed at the pond. "Something flashed out there, in the cove."

Arvel turned. The water's surface was as smooth as glass, but the hairs on the back of his neck were rising. "I should go take a look."

Winora reached for his arm. "It was probably that waterdog skulking around. You said he can disappear."

"That's true," Arvel agreed, but he knew the beast could not completely vanish with a bow around his neck. "Why don't you go wait with Iris? I'll make sure he doesn't frighten Prim or the girls."

As Winora walked away, Arvel started to pace along the pond's mossy bank.

A child's scream split the stillness of the morning air.

Arvel dashed past Winora up the path to the manor.

As he neared the front of the property, he saw the Honeycutt carriage lurching forward on the drive while Stanley fought to calm his panicked horses.

Prim's daughters had made their way out of the carriage, and her oldest daughter Neveah was leading her younger sisters, Seren and Celeste, to safety.

Iris lay crumpled on the ground, dreadfully close to the churning wheels and dashing hooves.

Arvel sprang forward and pulled her to safety. She seemed to be uninjured except for several deep scratches beading with blood across her face.

"Something's spooked the horses!" Stanley shouted as he wrestled with the reins. "Get Prim out of the carriage!"

When Winora arrived at his side, Arvel handed her their dazed daughter.

"Take Iris and the little ones into the house!"

The horses were becoming increasingly agitated. Out of the corner of his eye, Arvel saw a dash of pink moving through the tree line.

"Stay back, Beast," he shouted, afraid the waterdog's intervention would only worsen things.

Arvel leapt into the carriage. The curtains were closed, making it difficult to see inside.

"Prim?"

Arvel spotted her fair hair in the opposite corner of the darkened interior.

"Prim, give me your hand."

Her face turned in his direction, but there was no recognition in her eyes.

Her lips moved. "Father, I'm here."

The voice was not Prim's.

Something rushed toward him, knocking Arvel backward through the door, and causing the horses to rear violently.

Stanley fell from the driver's seat, and the crazed team bolted around the side of the manor and down the path toward the pond.

"Beast!" Arvel struggled to his feet. "Stop them!"

A pink blur flew past him, quickly gaining on the rear of the carriage. Arvel watched as the ribbon sailed up and over, landing on the path in front of the horses.

The waterdog revealed himself, fangs bared and spikes bristling. He threw his head back and let loose a howl that echoed from one end of the estate to the other. His hide reflected the sun's rays in a blinding flash of light.

The horses reared and stopped. Whatever had driven them toward catastrophe was instantly forgotten. They nervously snorted and pawed the ground while the waterdog held his position.

Arvel drew his knife and stealthily approached the carriage.

"Stay, Beast."

He peered inside. The darkness had subsided. Prim was slumped over, breathing heavily. He flipped the blade back into its handle and climbed into the carriage.

"Prim, can you hear me?" Arvel gently rubbed her cheek.

She turned her face to look at him. "Father?" Prim struggled to sit up. "I was at the *Monarch*. Something's happened to Ivey."

Arvel gently eased her into a sitting position. "That was days ago, darling. Do you know where you are?"

Prim rubbed her temples. "No, I couldn't find a way out." Prim's eyes grew wide. "Did it take my baby?"

Arvel put his arm around Prim. "Your baby is fine. Stanley brought you to Thornhall. Your mother is with the girls, and everyone is safe."

Prim shook her head. "It's still coming."

"What's coming?"

They were interrupted by a commotion outside the carriage.

"Egads, what is that?" Stanley shouted.

Arvel looked out the window to see Prim's husband making his way down the path where the agitated waterdog was standing guard.

"Stay with Prim, Arvel! I'll get a gun," Stanley shouted.

Arvel leaned Prim against the side of the carriage and jumped out. "Stanley, come back. That is Ivey's creature. He's tame."

"Are you sure?" he asked. "Ivey's barely tame herself."

"He stopped the horses from running your carriage into the water. Now he's protecting Prim." Arvel gestured to the wary beast. "Stand down, boy."

Stanley gingerly approached.

Beast drew in his spikes and plopped down with a satisfied grunt. Stanley quickly rushed past the creature and climbed into the carriage.

"Stanley, darling, I've been so lost." Prim reached for him with tears in her eyes.

Stanley wrapped his arms around her. He looked to Arvel. "This is the first she's spoken since yesterday morning." Stanley hugged his wife tightly. "You're back now, Prim."

"I'll lead the horses back to the house." Arvel started to close the carriage door. "Once we have Prim inside, Winora can send for the doctor."

❧

In the nursery, Winora cleaned the deep scratches on her daughter's face.

"Iris, please. Why won't you tell me who did this?"

The little girl stood unresponsive, staring straight ahead.

Neveah looked up from where she was playing with her younger siblings.

"It hurts Mommy, too."

Winora's brow creased. She went to her oldest grandchild and knelt down. Taking Neveah's hand, she gently asked, "Tell Mimi. What is hurting your mother?"

The small child shrugged. "It talks in the dark."

Winora didn't want to frighten her, so she smiled and spoke comfortingly. "Is that so? Does your father know about this?"

"No one hears it but me and Mommy." Neveah pointed at Iris. "And her."

Winora felt her spine tighten with apprehension. It did look as though her daughter was listening intently to something.

She went back to Iris and took her by the shoulders.

Her body felt strange and lifeless.

"Stop it, Iris!" She shook her firmly. "Stop whatever you are doing right now and tell me. What do you hear?"

Neveah pointed at a spot on the floor where a dark smoke had started to seep up between the floorboards.

"It's coming again."

The room grew dank and cold as the haze thickened. It crept along the floor, coming to rest at the edge of Iris' skirt, where it rose, curling around the little girl's legs.

Winora tried to lift Iris out of the cloud, but a great force pulled both of them to their knees.

"Neveah! Go get Papi. Take your sisters and run!" she cried.

Neveah grabbed Celeste and Seren by their hands and dragged them out of the room.

"Don't be afraid, Iris." Winora held her tightly. "Your father will know what to do."

Iris smiled up at her. "Hello."

Winora's grip loosened. "What?"

"I want one."

Winora let go and sat back on her heels.

The expression in her daughter's blue eyes was not a little girl's.

"What's happening?" she whispered.

"Which one will I take?" Iris' voice lilted as if she was reciting a nursery rhyme. "The mother, the misfit, or the little one?"

Winora was frozen by terror, unable to move or utter a sound.

"I'll have them all."

As the floorboards began to splinter around Iris, she could only watch.

"Say goodbye."

The child fell into the swirling pool of black mist.

The force holding Winora back suddenly released, and she felt herself pitching forward into the hole.

❧

Arvel knelt beside his fallen wife.

"Winora! Are you all right?"

She drew a raspy breath. "Help Iris!"

"Iris is fine. I'm worried about you." Arvel lifted her shoulders from the floor. "Are you hurt?"

"No! She's falling! Save her!" Winora dug her fingers into his arms, trembling violently.

"Sweetheart, please calm down. Nothing has happened to Iris."

She shook him by the shoulders and screamed. "Listen to me, or she will die!"

Arvel pointed toward the doorway, where Iris was watching in disbelief.

"Look, there she is."

Winora burst into tears. "Iris! Is it really you?"

Iris looked at her father in distress. "Why is she saying that?"

Arvel tried to sound reassuring. "She just needs a moment. Go find Uncle Stanley and the girls. Stay with them while I check things out."

Iris hesitated. "Please don't let anything bad to happen to Mother."

"I won't. I'll take care of her," Arvel said. "Now run."

After she left, Winora clutched his arm. "I'm afraid that's not our Iris. What if it's a trick?"

Arvel laid a hand on his wife's forehead. "Iris said you barely made it into the nursery before fainting. Do you remember that?"

Winora recoiled in fear. "Arvel, listen! Something abominable was in here. It said it's going kill our children. Look at what it did to the floor!"

Arvel looked around. "I don't see anything out of order."

Winora touched her face. "It tore a hole in the boards. Iris fell in, and then I did."

"Iris said you were acting strange coming up the stairs," Arvel said. "Were you feeling dizzy?"

"No!" Winora gasped for air. "It's not me. Something was in this nursery. It took Iris. If you won't believe it's real, she will die."

Arvel held her closely. "I believe you saw something that made you faint, but I don't think it was real."

"I'm not like you, Arvel. I never see things that aren't there."

"Neither did Prim or Ivey before this started. Something isn't right here."

"What can it be?"

Arvel gently rocked her, stroking her hair. "I wonder if Prim's condition may be affecting those around her. We've had more than one disturbing incident since her carriage arrived."

"Prim wouldn't harm a soul."

"Of course not. Not purposely. Perhaps she's imparting her fear of losing a child, and that affected you."

"Oh, Arvel, I felt Iris die. If this is what Prim has suffered, something dreadful will happen."

"I won't let it. Whatever this is, you must trust that I will find a way to stop it."

Winora laid her head against Arvel's chest. "I do. I trust you with everything I have."

At that instant, Arvel was aware that they were not alone in the nursery. Another life force had attached itself to his wife . . strange and new, yet with a familiar resonance.

"We'll talk after you get some rest, my dear."

He swept his wife into his arms and carried her to their bedroom. Shortly after she was tucked under the covers, Winora fell sound asleep.

Arvel leaned over to kiss her forehead. "You have given me the greatest gifts in the world. I will protect every last one of them with my life."

He would have stayed at her side longer, but through the open window, he heard the sound of another horse approaching.

Moments later, there was an urgent pounding from the front entry-way. Arvel hurried downstairs and threw open the door.

Silas Harp rushed past him into the manor's foyer.

"What is it? Another attack?"

Silas turned with a sigh. "Arvel. The *Monarch* has gone down at sea."

Chapter Eighteen

MISTER CURIO

S omething dangerous—a stranger—had entered the room.
Ivey's head shot up, and she threw her arm across Miles in a
protective reflex.

"Who are you? What are you doing here?"

A distinguished-looking man with dark, wavy hair took a step back.
"I didn't mean to disturb you."

"Then you should have knocked," Ivey stated coldly.

The man gave a shrug. "I did. You and your husband were fast asleep."

"He is not my husband," Ivey declared.

He smirked. "How unfortunate."

"I beg your pardon, sir. What do you want?"

"Do forgive me. You've caught me off guard. May we start again?"

"No." Ivey had been on board the *Monarch* long enough to know
that no one would be permitted to let themselves into a Fenchurche
family suite.

"State your business, or I will remove you from my presence."

The man bowed. "My name is Ildwick Curio. I am a chemist at the
Cadenbury Institute of Sciences, sought to help with a medical emergency on board the ship. Captain LeClere wished me to share my
findings with Mr. Fenchurche, who is in desperate need of answers regarding a nasty variety of leeches that attacked the family doctor and a
female passenger."

Ivey sat up. "Very well then. What did you learn?"

The man hesitated. "My report is for Mr. Fenchurche."

"Does he look at all inclined to hear your report?" Ivey nudged the
unconscious man lying next to her. Miles stirred and reached out for
her. "Your kiss saved me."

Ivey hastily tucked his hand back under the covers. "Miles! I never
kissed you. That was Sylvia."

The chemist backed away, reaching for the door handle behind him. "It seems Mr. Fenchurche's attention lies elsewhere. I will return later."

Ivey's cheeks burned with embarrassment.

"Stay where you are, sir. Mr. Fenchurche is not distracted—he's barely alive. I am the female passenger who was attacked by those leeches. To save my life, he gave me a great deal of his own blood, which nearly killed him. Sylvia is my maid, and the two of us have been fighting to keep his body warm and his heart beating. She's gone to refill our hot water bottles and will be back at any moment. If you have anything to tell me about those leeches, Mr. Curio, I suggest you do it now."

The man looked taken aback. "You cannot be the victim. She would be very ill if not dead."

"I assure you, I am the victim."

"That is impossible. My analysis showed that venom is lethal."

"Then perhaps you do not know as much about chemistry as you think, sir." Ivey cocked her head. "Maybe you should go back and analyze things more carefully."

The man started forward, then hesitated. "May I approach?"

"Only if you intend to tell me everything you know." Ivey's eyes narrowed as she looked him over.

The man gasped as he drew closer. Ivey followed his shocked gaze as it traveled up her bare arm. With everything that had happened in the dimly lit room, she hadn't noticed anything strange about her appearance. Now, with the predawn light coming through the portside window, she saw that the skin of her left arm was a dull blue.

"What in damnation?" she muttered.

"May I?" Ildwick crept forward.

Ivey nodded, completely at a loss. The man slowly drew a pair of spectacles from inside his jacket and placed them on his aquiline nose. He inspected her extended arm for a long while.

"Well?" Ivey demanded.

A pair of striking gray eyes stared at her over the rim of his glasses. "You appear to be somewhat blue."

Ivey jerked her arm away. "Do not toy with me. I can see that. Explain how this is possible. Was it caused by the leeches?"

The expression that flashed across his face made Ivey uneasy.

"This is altogether unexpected. I am not sure what to make of it." He looked away evasively.

"What about my face?" Ivey touched her cheek.

The man nodded. Ivey threw back the comforter and pulled up her nightgown to inspect her legs. They were blue as well.

"You have very fine muscle tone for a girl," he chuckled.

"Sir, are you a stranger to decency?" Ivey snatched the bedding up to her chin.

"If there is indecency in stating a mere fact, then I am quite guilty."

Ivey considered his blunt answer for a moment. "Just tell me what else you know, then go."

Ildwick removed his spectacles, meticulously wiping them with his handkerchief before returning them to a pocket inside his jacket. "Yes, and I heed orders from you because—?"

Ivey took a moment to recall the gracious character that she had portrayed upon boarding the *Monarch*. Flashing a brilliant smile, she offered a dainty blue hand from underneath the comforter.

"Do forgive me, Mr. Curio. My nerves have gone to pieces. I am Ivey Thornton, a personal friend of Mr. Fenchurche's. Actually, I'm his fiancée. As a future member of the family, it is my duty to act in the best interests of this ship and of Fenchurche Industries."

The chemist bowed to give her hand a respectful kiss. "My pleasure, Miss Thornton. My full name is Ildwick Curio the Second. Please, call me Ildwick."

Ivey withdrew her hand. "So, Ildwick, now that we're properly acquainted, I will hear your report."

"That will have to wait." Ildwick straightened, pulling an empty hypodermic syringe from one of his pockets. "I must have a sample of your blood."

Ivey's eyes narrowed. "That will not be possible." Having no intention of letting someone with his skills snoop about her unique chemistry, Ivey continued in a soft voice. "You see, I have a great fear of needles . . .

and I am famous for my fainting. Surely, you will understand. After everything that I have been through, I am far too frail for that." She looked up at him innocently and batted her eyelashes.

Ildwick appeared unmoved. "How unfortunate. I suppose the doctor will die after all."

"Are you serious?" Ivey leaned forward.

"Deathly. He is paralyzed, possibly aware of his predicament, but unable to move, speak, or swallow a sip of water."

"That is horrible!"

"And it's getting worse. His muscles are becoming rigid, almost as if they are petrified. I have no doubt that the whole thing is very painful. Considering his age and heft, he will be dead in two days. One if he is lucky."

Ivey shuddered at the thought. "Can anything be done to help him?"

"His only hope is that I will be able to produce an antivenin." Ildwick shrugged. "You survived the leeches' poison. A quantity of your blood may do the trick."

Ivey hesitated. "But my blood has been diluted by Mr. Fenchurche's transfer. It may not be effective."

"Yet, but it is the doctor's only hope, and perhaps the dilution will spare him from suffering your colorful affliction."

"Very well," Ivey relented. "Make your serum. But I expect you to hold to a doctor's oath. Mr. Fenchurche is extremely protective of his friends and family. If you speak about our private matters, I can't be responsible for what he might do to you." Ivey did her best to sound convincing.

"Consider me warned."

Ivey drew back the comforter and held out her right arm. Ildwick pulled a sterile swab from a waxed envelope in another of his many pockets and cleaned the area thoroughly. He removed the sheath from the syringe and carefully inserted the needle. While the syringe filled with blood, he offered to send a medicine to the suite that would aid Miles' recovery. He also cautioned Ivey to keep Miles flat on his back, with pillows beneath his legs to assist his heart in supplying enough blood to his vital organs.

Moments later, the needle was withdrawn, and a piece of gauze protected the small wound it left behind. Ivey suspected that the man was more than a simple chemist.

Ildwick placed the cover back on the needle and stood silently, staring at her.

"I thought you were in a hurry," she said.

"I thought you were a fainter. I will not leave if you are about to suffer a vaporous attack."

The man's smirk was increasingly annoying.

"Do not patronize me, sir."

Ildwick nodded and briskly crossed to the bedroom door. "I would never underestimate the likes of you, Miss Thornton. You embody the element of surprise."

With that, he was gone. If the chemist's intent was to stir Ivey's curiosity, he'd been successful.

Miles moaned in pain. Ivey could see that he was taking another chill. She quickly removed the pillows from under his head and placed them beneath his calves. After she rearranged the bedding, Ivey crawled in next to him.

His teeth were chattering. She wrapped her arms around him and closed her eyes, enveloping the two of them in a healing warmth. Eventually, Miles' shivering ceased, and his breathing became slow and steady. As Ivey drifted off to sleep, she heard him whisper.

"There it is."

"What?" she whispered back.

"The light that saved me . . . your heart."

"Shhh," Ivey murmured. "Go to sleep."

"Wake up! You have to wake up."

Ivey felt someone shaking her shoulder.

"The ship is going down, miss."

"Oh, Sylvia." Ivey stretched, not ready to open her eyes. "I'm getting tired of this dream."

Sylvia shook her harder. "Miss Ivey, please! They'll be coming to take Mr. Miles to the library before the *Monarch* crashes into the sea."

Ivey's eyes flew open. "What?" She bolted upright and looked out the window. Rays of morning sunlight were glancing off the sea's horizon. "The storm is over."

"There's a hole in the envelope's mixing chamber. We've been losing gas all night, and the captain has nearly used up the reserve supplies. They say we're going to hit the water."

"I must go help." Miles struggled to raise himself.

Ivey easily held him down. "Stay still. If you try to get up, your heart could stop. We don't have time for that."

"It is my duty . . ." he mumbled.

Ivey jumped out of bed and tucked the covers back around him.

"Sylvia, run to my suite and bring me my satchel. Make sure that my knife and rope are inside."

"What?"

"Do it. This ship isn't meant to crash while I'm on it."

"Miss Ivey, you nearly died, too. Please don't."

Ivey had forgotten all about that. She ripped the bandage off her left hand and inspected the wound. The stitches were still there, embedded in the perfectly healed silvery flesh. Ivey's gaze met Sylvia's.

"How curious," Ivey said. "I guess the little devils do make you heal. Now, go get what I need, and hurry!"

Sylvia left with eyes the size of saucers.

Ivey rummaged about in Miles' wardrobe until she found a shirt, belt, and trousers that would suffice. She pulled them on, rolling up the sleeves and pant legs to fit her smaller stature. All of Miles' shoes were far too big, but Ivey preferred to climb with bare feet anyway. She had to do something about her hair as well.

She thought for several moments before noticing that the jacket Miles had lent her in the *Monarch*'s lobby was hanging in his wardrobe.

She reached into the breast pocket and found a green engineering ribbon, just as Miles had promised.

"Hello again. Fancy helping me this time?"

She tied her hair back with the ribbon, then wrapped the ponytail into a tight bun, tucking the tip under the green fabric.

When Sylvia returned with the satchel, she helped Ivey find the large suture needles in Miles' medical bag and thread them with workable lengths of surgical filament.

Ivey stuck the threaded needles into lining fabric at the top of the satchel and put the spool of thread in her trouser pocket before slinging the bag over her head and fastening it beneath her shoulder.

"What should I do now?" Sylvia asked.

"Get in the bed and keep Miles warm. Moving him could be fatal. It will be up to you to convince the others to wait for my return, all right?"

Sylvia nodded. Ivey paused before she left.

"It's vital to keep Miles in a prone position. If I don't make it back, tell them to use a cot to carry him to the library."

Sylvia laid a hand across her heart. "Miss Ivey, I believe that you were sent to save the *Monarch,* to save us all."

"I owe you, don't I?" Ivey smiled.

"Ivey . . . wait . . ." Miles mumbled.

She paused. "Miles, please. I have to save the ship."

"But there's something you need to know . . ."

Ivey returned to the bed and leaned over him. "What?" Miles' eyes were open, but he didn't respond. Ivey gave him a little shake. "Miles, focus. What do I need to know?"

"Don't breathe the gasses . . ."

Ivey impulsively caressed his cheek. "I appreciate the warning. But let me assure you, I can hold my breath longer than anyone in this world, and my days of fainting are over, Mr. Fenchurche."

Chapter Nineteen

THE CLIMB

The storm's damage to the *Monarch* was worse than Ivey had anticipated. Much of the sitting room furniture was overturned, and unsecured items littered the floor of the master suite.

Upon entering the family's private parlor, Ivey went to check the section of window that had been smashed in her dream. The wall of glass was intact, but it was spread with fine cracks.

The vases and statuaries hadn't fared as well. Broken shards of porcelain and alabaster were everywhere. She considered getting a pair of boots from her wardrobe, but Sylvia had warned her that Doctor Brendel was under watch in the guest suite, and there was no time for explanations.

Ivey picked her way across the debris on the parlor floor and stepped around one of the side tables that had fallen over. A leg had come off the table, exposing the joinery. She knelt down to take a closer look.

"Well, I'll be."

She reached into her satchel and withdrew her knife. Flipping it open, Ivey scraped the blade against the table leg, peeling away the thick layer of dark paint that covered a milky looking surface. She thought for a moment, then went to the wall and scratched through a piece of the wooden paneling, yielding the same result. She ran to the fireplace and peeled back a strip of marble-patterned paper from the mantle.

"That's how they got you off the ground," she said looking around the parlor.

Ivey had uncovered one of the ship's greatest secrets. All the fine wooden and stone surfaces that made the luxurious cabin impossibly heavy were in fact made from a molded form of glass that Ivey had read about. The highly porous material lacked all the crystalline beauty of Fenchurche windows and lift carriages, but it was strong, lightweight, and cheap to produce.

While some might have been disappointed by the forgery of the expensive decor, Ivey was impressed with the *Monarch*'s practicality. Miles had told her the ship was not as cumbersome as she seemed, and now she knew what he meant.

Ivey hurried through the door to the bridge. She'd almost reached the hatch when an enormous man came storming her way. He wore the dark blue uniform of Cemaria's national investigative agency, the Dicæon.

"This area is restricted. Go back." The Dicæon officer gestured for her to turn around. "Take the stairs down to the library."

Ivey ducked her head in an attempt to hide her odd appearance. "Oh, sorry." She turned around and took several steps, hoping the man would rush past her. She slowed down, and so did he. Ivey stopped and bent over, pretending to have stepped on something sharp with her bare foot. She felt the man approaching and tried to wave him on.

"I'm fine. I can make it to the library on my—Hey!" He picked her up, tossing her over his shoulder like a sack of potatoes, without even breaking stride. She struggled, and he tightened his unbelievably strong grip. "Put me down! I can walk."

The brute offered no response to her demand.

"Please. Set me down and tell the captain that Ivey Thornton needs to see him. It is urgent."

Nothing but silence.

"Can you hear me?"

He was clearly not one for polite conversation.

"Hey, you big ox! I was sent by my fiancé, Miles Fenchurche. Have you heard of him? You're on his ship!" Ivey couldn't waste any more time. "This is your last warning. Let me go or I will put you down."

She finally got a response. The brute laughed.

"Fine!" Ivey screamed and flailed wildly, then went completely limp, waiting for him to adjust his hold on her. The second he did, she reared back and struck the base of his neck with the sides of her hands. The unexpected blow sent him stumbling face first toward the carpet. She pushed away from his chest and dropped to the floor just in time to catch his head before it hit the rug.

"Sorry, but sturdy and slow is no match for small and sharp."

Ivey turned and ran.

She made it to back to the open hatch and ducked through. Hurrying to the top of the stairs, she peeked over the edge of the landing. The walkway was teeming with crewmen carrying tools. She couldn't fight them all. She spotted a tall figure watching their efforts with hands clasped behind his back. Before anyone could stop her, Ivey dashed over and spun him around.

"Dolan, I need your help."

He didn't seem particularly surprised to see her. "Miss Ivey, you are looking . . . well. How is Mr. Fenchurche?"

Ivey tugged on the strap of her satchel. "He's still very ill, so he sent me." She couldn't read Dolan's expression. Even amidst disaster, his dispassionate poise was impeccable.

"Go on."

"I've come to repair the envelope. Miles approved of it, I swear on his life."

Dolan's face remained unmoved. "Who am I to argue with a girl that comes back from the dead just in time to lead us out of a storm. That being said, I'm afraid a repair is impossible, even for you."

Ivey gazed up at the *Monarch*'s massive balloon. The envelope had developed a dip near the middle, and its surface was pocked with tears and gashes.

"Oh. I thought it was just one hole."

"This ship is more than capable of surviving any number of leaks, but the envelope's structure has been compromised in the worst possible location. The wall of the central mixing chamber has been punctured."

Dolan pointed to a particular perforation toward the front of the cabin. The hole was situated at the bottom of the band of fabric around which the envelope had begun to crease.

"We're losing the concentrated mixture of gas through that hole before it can flow into the rest of the envelope's cells. As those cells lose pressure, the entire envelope becomes unstable and loses its shape."

"Why haven't we lowered the wings to gain elevation?"

"The masts atop the envelope that support the armature of the wings have sagged out of place. Putting any tension on the cables to open them now will only cause the body of the ship to deform and expel more gas."

Ivey lifted the flap of the leather bag and showed Dolan her threaded needles. "Then let me fix it."

"If it were simply a matter of patching up the leak, Miss Ivey, we would have done so." He pointed past Ivey as he continued, "There's no way of climbing up there now, and we haven't enough time to improvise one before the ship hits the water. The engines are working at full capacity to keep us aloft, but without her wings, this ship is fighting a losing battle."

Ivey looked back at the side of the cabin. The long metal ladder had been ripped away by the storm. As her gaze continued upward, she could see the trail of destruction it had left behind when it tore through the riggings. It must have been the ladder's sharp metal edges that had pierced the envelope's resilient fabric. It was hard to tell from a distance, but the hole looked to be no bigger than the span of Ivey's arms. Its ragged edges fluttered wildly as the balloon hemorrhaged its lifting gases.

"Please, Dolan, let me try. I've already been up in those riggings, and I didn't need the ladder to get down." She grabbed his arm and led him to the spot on the walkway where she'd fallen. "This is the closest point between the cables and the walkway. I can climb across to one of the legs that connect the cabin to the envelope. Once I'm there, I'll continue across the surface of the envelope until I reach the tear."

Dolan considered her words. "It's nearly three times my height to that cable. How will you reach it?"

"I can fly."

Dolan didn't blink an eye. "Well, of course . . . if you can fly up there and make a repair, I will make no effort to stop you."

Ivey reached toward him. "I need something to launch from. Put your hands together and stand like this." Ivey demonstrated by bracing herself and then lacing her fingers together, holding them out in front of her forward leg to make a foothold.

Dolan looked around at the crewmen who stared in disbelief. "Would you prefer someone with a bit more muscle?"

"It's height I need, and one of them might flinch. I have faith in your ability to remain perfectly still. It could be the difference between success and a dunk in the sea."

Dolan assumed the position. "I never flinch."

"Yes, I've noticed."

Ivey placed her right foot in his hands to find her bearings. She closed her eyes and stepped back a few paces, taking several long, deep breaths. A smile tinged her lips as she opened her eyes and focused on the cable above. She ran toward Dolan with a bounding stride. Her right foot sprung off his hands, and her left foot followed, pushing lightly against his shoulder. He barely felt her weight as she leapt forward and up.

Ivey sailed through the air and caught the cable in her hands before pulling her legs up and wrapping them securely around the metal.

She looked down and saw the crewmen cheering her on. Even Dolan couldn't resist applauding her success.

∾

"Men! What is this?"

Dolan looked over to see Captain LeClere topping the stairs. The captain quickly strode across the grated walkway and joined a knot of crewmen who were watching a lone figure climb the riggings.

LeClere shielded his eyes from the sun as he stared up. "Who is that?"

"It's Miss Thornton," Dolan replied. "She's attempting a repair."

The captain looked at him in disbelief. "What in the world? The last I heard, she was at death's door . . ." his words trailed away.

Dolan crossed his arms and sighed. "She was dead for a while, but apparently she prefers life. And it would seem she can fly, too."

With a loud groan, Officer Harwood of the Dicæon staggered up and onto the walkway.

"Captain, there's been a security breach." He rubbed the sides of his neck. "Someone overpowered me."

"Can you give a description, Officer?" the captain asked.

"Well—she was blue." The man crumpled to his knees, holding his head in his hands.

The captain waved at two crewmen. "You there. Take him to the lounge below the bridge and find him a cot." The captain slowly shook his head. "What is the world coming to? The *Monarch's* going down at sea, and one of the Dicæon's senior officers was just clocked by a blue girl."

Without warning, Dolan found himself making a comical sound.

LeClere looked at him sharply. "What was that, man?"

"I may have laughed," he replied thoughtfully.

The captain's face grew red. "This is no laughing matter. She has no business up there. We will break the water's surface in a matter of hours. Before that happens, I'll have no choice but to set off the emergency charges that separate the cabin from the rest of the ship. If she is still in those riggings, even Miss Thornton will be dead for good, and we will be left to explain that to Mrs. Fenchurche and her son, if we aren't all drowned."

"I allowed her to do so, sir, and I will take responsibility for her safety." Dolan watched Ivey's progress as he continued. "She found our way out of the storm. Who's to say that she cannot keep us out of the water? If she is successful, what are our chances of making it to land?"

"Meager, if nothing else goes wrong. As much as it would please me to watch this play out, I must return to the bridge and see what I can do to buy her more time. I leave Miss Thornton's fate in your hands."

Dolan nodded. "Yes, Captain."

While the captain disappeared down the walkway's stairs, Dolan beckoned to one of the engineers. "I want you to do something."

"Sir?"

"Go to housekeeping and get me the biggest, softest thing you can find. If Miss Thornton intends to return to us, the least we can do is to give her a safe landing." Dolan folded his hands behind his back and watched as Ivey began to scale the metal lattice of the leg far above his head.

Her slender frame was dwarfed by the enormity of the ship's envelope. At that altitude, the wind would be strong. The slightest misstep could lead to a fatal fall.

Dolan did not want to imagine facing Minnette's son with such news. Miles seemed quite taken with her, and Dolan realized the wily creature had somehow found a small spot in his own heart as well.

☙

Arvel grabbed Silas by the arm and rushed him toward the study. His mind was a blur of questions and concerns, but first, he had to make sure that no one overheard their conversation.

Inside the study, he softly closed the door and led Silas toward his desk.

"Now. Tell me everything," he said urgently.

"I'm sorry, Arvel. The *Monarch* is lost."

There was genuine compassion in Silas' voice, but the words were too painful to comprehend.

"No, that's impossible! How could such a thing happen?"

"All I can say is that the ship went down at sea."

The strength left his legs. Arvel dropped into the chair behind his desk. "I need a moment."

"Of course. Take your time," Silas spoke softly.

Arvel leaned forward, resting his head in his hands, eyes closed. In his heart, he couldn't believe that his daughter was gone.

He tried to slow his breathing and focus his mind.

"Do you need a drink?" Silas asked.

"I need silence."

Arvel took a long, slow breath and let his spirit reach out to his daughter.

The vast feeling of emptiness between the two of them was frightening, but he kept his focus on one thing—the energy of her soul.

He stayed that way a long time, searching.

His heart began to pump faster as he sensed great fear amid the turbulence of a storm. After that came a wave of grief, coupled with a strong will to survive. A bright light exploded in his mind's eye.

"Ivey!"

Arvel jumped up from his chair. "Mount a rescue. She isn't lost."

Silas sighed. "There is little reason to hope."

"Listen to me. I just sensed her. My daughter is very much alive . . . and fighting to stay that way."

"Arvel, this isn't the time for your mystical hogwash. The *Monarch* was driven off course."

"By a storm."

"That is an obvious guess, but yes, the ship was being torn apart by a squall when it disappeared. Even if there were survivors, we have no idea where to search for them."

Arvel leaned forward suspiciously. "If you don't know where this happened, how could you know they crashed?"

Silas stood. "I'm not going to quibble with a grieving father. I should go."

"Sit yourself down!" Arvel advanced toward Silas with fists clenched. "You're not leaving until you tell me what is going on."

"I've already told you. I'm sorry, but your daughter is lost."

"No, she isn't. She still exists in this world and I can prove it."

"Do that, and we'll talk."

Silas sat in his chair, with crossed his arms, waiting.

Arvel had no choice. He took a few steps closer, fastening the other man in an unflinching gaze. In his mind, Arvel envisioned a white ball of energy, whirling in the center of his being. He allowed the energy to grow until it expanded outside of his body.

As it grew in strength, Arvel saw Silas's face redden, and his breathing became rushed as he tried but failed to hoist himself out of the chair.

When Arvel stepped away and dispelled the force, Silas dropped back into his seat.

Silas raised a trembling hand to his forehead. "What is the meaning of this?"

Arvel clenched his hand before his heart. "*Pneuma biou.*"

"Is that a recognized term or a charlatan's parlor trick?"

"It is what defines us. The will to live. Our ability to reason, to feel. It is the energy of our soul."

"Explain what you did to me."

Arvel searched for an answer that Silas could comprehend. He'd learned at a young age that those who only saw the world as being brightly lit were unwilling to grasp that which lies deep within the shadows.

"I focused myself, my energy—" Arvel pointed to a place on his chest, below his heart and above his waist, "—and pushed outward." From the look on the other man's face, Arvel knew that Silas was having a hard time disbelieving him. "I projected my energy toward your body."

"Can anyone do that?"

Arvel sidestepped the question. "It's how I found my daughter. My energy reached out to hers, and I felt a response."

"Over such a distance? How can you be certain it was her energy you felt?"

"Each soul has its own unique character, as distinct as a person's voice. Ivey's is like no other."

Silas stared out the window before finally coming to his feet. "I'm terribly sorry, but you haven't proven a thing here. As always, you rely on wishful thinking, not science."

"I know you felt it, Silas. I proved my point." Arvel worked to control his temper. "My child is alive, and my connection to her can help locate the *Monarch*."

"Belief does not dictate reality, Arvel. This is false hope. Give your family my condolences."

"Wait!" Arvel grabbed the man's sleeve in an act of desperation. "There's something else you should know."

Silas pulled away. "What?"

"Fenchurche Industries is developing a shield for the *Boreas*. This innovation will give the ship the ability to disappear into its surroundings."

"Invisibility? What is your obsession with the impossible?"

"Miles Fenchurche has found a way to make it possible. The preliminary tests have been a success," Arvel lied. "You cannot afford to lose that man or his research if the *Monarch* is still out there."

"I might ask for proof, but you are clearly deranged."

"Come outside and see it with your own eyes." Arvel paused. "I will prove beyond your every doubt that invisibility is attainable."

"I've heard enough nonsense." Silas moved aside and gestured for Arvel to lead the way. "This is your last chance. If what you claim is true, I will take you to Cadenbury to show you how real scientists control energy."

Chapter Twenty

PATCHING TIME

L ucey Sue, get in here!" Minnette Fenchurche was at her wit's end. Dolan had been gone far too long, and she had not received a report on Miles' condition in hours.

"Yes, ma'am?" Her bleary-eyed maid appeared in the bedroom doorway.

"Where is Dolan? Why haven't I been escorted to the library with my son? Are any of you doing your job on this ship, or are all of you content to sit and watch the *Monarch* burn?"

"Oh dear, there's no fire, ma'am, and if there were, it wouldn't last long after we splash down in the sea . . . I don't think."

"Fortunately, it's not your job to think. Time is wasting, and I need Dolan now!"

"I am sorry, ma'am. I haven't seen Mr. Dolan since before sunrise. Should I go and look for him?"

"No," Minnette said, throwing back her covers. "I will take care of this myself."

"Ma'am, I'm sure the doctor would want you to stay in bed."

"Silence. After you help me dress, send word to the captain. I need the Dicæon officer and his lieutenant to meet me in my son's suite immediately. I will not leave my son's life in that girl's hands for one more moment. Bringing her aboard this ship was a mistake."

Ivey stopped climbing; it was time to make a decision. She'd scaled the metal anchor leg and had finally reached the network of grappling wires that spanned the underside of the envelope. The narrow cables suspended several inches above the fabric provided the ship's engineers a place to affix their climbing harnesses when performing repairs.

If Ivey were to go one direction, the climb looked to be easier, but it would take her longer. The other route led straight up, meaning she would have to traverse sideways to reach the tear. The ship's diminishing distance from the water pushed Ivey onto the quickest path.

The wires should have been taut between the metal eye bolts they were anchored to, but the loss of pressure left just enough slack for Ivey's slim legs to wrap tightly around them. She pulled herself upward, hand over hand.

The steady wind and warm rays of the sun made the climb agreeable, although it became more strenuous when the angle of her ascent began to steepen.

Ivey wiped the sweat from her eyes once she reached the point where she would have to work her way from one vertical wire to another to reach the hole.

The sea was bright blue and the air smelled especially sweet. A feeling of exhilaration swept over her. She drew a long breath and closed her eyes. The cool air filled her lungs and swirled in her head, its scent reminding her of the wildflowers in her father's garden. She was light as a feather, ready to float away on the fragrant breeze.

As she hung there, she heard an odd murmuring from somewhere far away. The sound reminded her of Arvel calling her back to the manor at the end of a long day. Ivey opened her eyes and looked down.

A tiny figure was waving up at her. It might have been Dolan, but he had two heads and was carrying on in the silliest manner. Ivey waved back and took another deep breath of the delicious air. Her ears rang, and her body tingled.

She relaxed her grip on the wire and started to lean back.

A voice whispered in her head.

Don't breathe the gasses.

Ivey jerked herself back against the envelope and held her breath. Now that she was aware of the gas's intoxication, she felt dangerously weak and reckless.

She wrapped her left arm around the wire and, with her free hand, frantically groped for her leather bag.

❧

Dolan held his breath. He couldn't make out what she was doing, but Ivey seemed to be encountering a difficulty.

A cry went up from the crew on the walkway as the girl pitched backward and fell. Rather than crashing to the platform, however, she stopped and dangled in midair.

"Mercy," Dolan muttered. "Don't tell me she can spin a web, too."

One of the engineers handed him a spyglass. "She's got a sling. Look."

Dolan raised the glass to his eye and focused. Ivey had a slender rope tied around her waist and shoulders. He followed it up and saw that it was knotted to the grappling wire. He watched as she took several deep breaths.

❧

When she felt recovered, Ivey slowly exhaled every bit of air in her lungs a few more times before filling them to their bursting point.

Arvel had once helped Ivey time herself as she held her breath underwater for over a quarter of an hour. Attempting the repair would require too much effort to last that long on a single breath. She would have to hold out as long as possible, then drop again to the fresh air before taking her next breath.

She pulled herself back up her father's rope until she was able to grab ahold of the envelope's fabric. Digging her hands into the loosened material, she crept sideways along the balloon until she reached the tether wire that ran across the tear.

What she found was discouraging. The fabric was far too tattered for a simple stitch to pull its gaping edges together. Ivey regretted her paltry attention to her mother's sewing lessons, but she did recall a time that her mother had used extra fabric from the hem to patch a hole in her father's favorite work trousers.

Ivey took a threaded needle from the satchel and held it in her teeth. She ripped open Miles' shirt and pulled it off, leaving herself clad from the waist up in nothing but a silk camisole.

Holding the shirt across the bottom of the hole, Ivey stitched quickly, tacking it in place before the gases escaping from the balloon could blow it away.

By the time she'd sewn down the first edge of the makeshift patch, her lungs were unwilling to wait any longer for fresh air. She held the rope around her waist and kicked off from the envelope. When the rope jerked her to a halt several feet down, she gasped.

After her lungs were cleared, Ivey climbed back up. There was still a rip in the envelope that needed patching. She pulled the knife from her bag and flipped it open, running the blade through the leg of Miles' trousers. After she cut the fabric from around the top of her thigh, she pulled off the leg of the pants and sliced the fabric open from top to bottom.

She retrieved another threaded needle and stitched the sturdy material across the top of the hole. When she finished, she took several shallow breaths, hoping that the gases around the patch would begin to dissipate. The air was still sweet, so she was careful not to take in too much.

Ivey cut the other leg from the trousers to sew an extra layer across the seam that joined the patches. When it was finished, she licked her finger and rubbed it across her cheek. She held her face against the fabric, slowly running her cheek across the patch. A distinct chill told her that the leaking hadn't completely stopped.

Ivey reached into the satchel, hoping that Sylvia had replaced all of its contents. When her hand closed around the tin of balm, she squeezed her eyes shut and thanked her lucky stars.

She removed the lid and rubbed the balm across the patchwork until the tin was nearly empty. The sappy substance thickened almost immediately against the brisk morning air, creating a resinous seal that penetrated the fibers of her patch.

Satisfied with her work, Ivey pushed off from the balloon. She heard another murmuring sound and looked down. The men on the walkway were cheering her success.

Ivey had never felt so wonderfully alive and free.

"Wait until Arvel hears about this!' Ivey laughed aloud, imagining her father's reaction. "A good ruckus, indeed."

She swung back to the envelope to give the *Monarch* a loving pat before climbing down.

As she made her way back along the cable above the walkway, a group of engineers stood waiting to catch her in an outstretched quilt.

Dolan held one hand across his eyes for modesty's sake. "We're ready for you, Miss Ivey."

Ivey was irked by his assumption that after everything she'd just demonstrated, he still thought she would need any help in getting down. Nevertheless, landing on their improvised trampoline looked like fun.

She tied her father's rope to the cable and dropped the remainder to the walkway so the engineers would have a way up into the riggings to work on the wings.

"Thank you, gentlemen. Hold it tight now."

"Will you not rebound?" Dolan inquired, still shielding his face.

"Your concern is touching," Ivey teased.

He shrugged and answered dryly, "I am hereby free of any blame if you take a dunk into the sea."

"Dolan, I will always remember what you did for me today. You know, I might actually learn to like you," Ivey laughed.

He cleared his throat.

"You heard the lady. Hold it tight, men."

Ivey released the cable with her legs and hung by her hands.

She gave a little swing with her legs, then dropped into a sitting position before landing on the tight surface of the blanket. Dolan and the crewmen couldn't resist watching as she landed. Just as Dolan had predicted, she bounced back into the air, almost to the height of the cable. She tucked into a somersault and landed on the walkway.

"Now you're just showing off," Dolan said.

Ivey laughed. "I suppose I am."

"Men, avert your eyes." He removed his jacket and offered it to her. "You do have a talent for underdressing."

Ivey looked down at her camisole and hacked-off trousers.

"Well, I've always said that dresses are highly overrated." Ivey slipped on the jacket. "Thank you."

"Thank you for saving this ship and her passengers once again."

"I'm afraid I only bought the crew a little more time to open the wings and give the *Monarch* some much-needed lift. I'd stay to help, but Mr. Fenchurche needs me. Good day."

Before Ivey hurried off, Dolan soberly turned to the stunned men around him. "You heard the girl; there is work to be done. This ship isn't saved yet."

❧

Chapter Twenty-One

A GRIM DISCOVERY

O n her way back into the ship, Ivey met a pair of flight crewmen running down the corridor from the bridge.

She had never seen the one who sported a head of curly hair that nearly matched his red jacket, but the older man had dined with her at the captain's table. Ivey remembered being told that he was one of the ship's senior officers.

They stopped to stare when they saw her climbing through the hatch.

Ivey calmly met their puzzled gazes. "Officer, please tell the captain that a patch is in place on the main mixing chamber. It should hold until we reach a dock."

The officer nodded silently, and the younger man gave her an awkward salute before she hurried off to share her triumphant news with Sylvia and Miles.

Upon entering the private parlor, Ivey's stomach grew strangely uneasy. Something was wrong. She skipped across the broken glass and entered the sitting room of the master suite.

Angry voices were coming from the other side of the bedroom door, the loudest of which belonged to Minnette Fenchurche. Ivey ran and flung open the door.

A Dicæon officer had Sylvia by one ankle. He was trying to yank her from the bed, but the maid's arms were tightly wrapped around one of the head posts.

"He is not to be moved!" Sylvia kicked at the officer's face to keep him away from Miles, who was lying pale and unconscious beside her. "Now stop it!"

Minnette looked apoplectic. "I gave no such orders. Get her out of here. Lock her up if you must."

Ivey rushed up to the officer who was grappling with Sylvia. "Those were my orders. Release her at once."

The man hesitated, as if confused by Ivey's odd appearance and commanding demeanor. He looked to Minnette, who was now glaring at Ivey.

"Who do you think you are?" she hissed between clenched teeth.

Ivey turned and summoned her courage. "I'm the woman your son will have to marry. You gave me the right to protect his welfare."

Minnette's eyes glittered with contempt. "You are not a Fenchurche, and you have no authority over my staff. You certainly do not speak for Miles. If you truly cared about his welfare, you wouldn't hold him prisoner while this ship crashes down around us."

"Your son is lucky to be breathing," Ivey said. "Moving him too soon could cause his heart to stop, and I doubt we could bring him back a second time."

"He will certainly die if he doesn't take shelter."

Ivey lifted her chin in determination. "No, he will not. I've repaired the *Monarch*'s envelope, and there is no need to risk his life in such a way now."

Minnette's face twisted with suspicion.

"If you don't believe me, ask Dolan," Ivey said.

"This woman is deranged. Officer Harwood, do your duty." Minnette gestured to a much bigger Dicæon officer, who'd been sitting in one of the bedroom chairs.

The brute Ivey had fought with in the restricted hallway rose stiffly from his seat.

She slowly reached for her leather bag. "No one touches Mr. Fenchurche," Ivey said with all the gravitas she could muster.

The man squared his shoulders and cracked his thick neck. "You got lucky. Trust me, I won't go down like that again."

Ivey pulled her dart gun from the satchel and pointed it at the looming officer. "Force me to use this, and you'll be down for the rest of the day."

Minnette was shaking with rage. "Do something, man! My son's life is at stake!"

"Look out!" Sylvia yelled.

The other Dicæon officer was making a leap across the foot of the bed. He caught Ivey's arm, but she got a shot off, which struck him in the leg. He jerked the dart out and threw it on the floor, but it was too late.

"Why you . . ."

Arvel's dart cartridges were spring loaded, delivering a pressurized dose of the tranquilizer that took effect on impact. The man stumbled toward Ivey before crumpling with his eyes rolled back in his head.

Ivey looked at Officer Harwood. "I didn't want to do that."

He looked at her menacingly. "Out of shots, are we?"

Ivey dropped the gun and pulled the knife from her satchel. She flipped open the blade and struck the same pose her father had taken against the beast.

"Listen carefully, you. Miles Fenchurche nearly died for me, and moving him now could be fatal. If you think otherwise, you'll have to go through me."

Minnette made a strange choking sound and grabbed her chest. Ivey glanced over; the woman's face had gone gray and she was about to collapse. "Sylvia, help her—"

Her instructions ended as everything exploded in a blinding flash of light.

❧

Ivey awoke, lying on the floor. A swirling cloud of fireflies danced above her, and a bitter odor stung her nostrils.

"That's a nice girl. Take another whiff."

Her eyes focused on the face of Ildwick Curio. He was kneeling over her waving a small vial beneath her nose.

Ivey shoved it away and started to rise, but the chemist set a firm hand on her shoulder.

"Ah-ah-ah. You may be injured."

Ivey tried to push past him.

The big Dicæon officer loomed over her. "Should I help hold her?"

"No, thank you, Harwood. I think blindsiding our bride-to-be was more than enough help."

"She attacked me in a restricted area, and this time she had a knife. What would you have done?"

"I might have verified her story with Dolan before knocking her senseless. You're lucky that she kept you from harming Mr. Fenchurche."

Ivey lifted her head and scanned the room. Sylvia and Minnette were gone, but Miles was still in his bed. It was worrisome that he hadn't moved or made a sound through all the commotion.

When she opened her mouth to ask about his condition, sharp pains shot up each side of her face, and all that came out was a garbled howl.

"Dammit, Officer Harwood. Looks like you've dislocated her jaw," Ildwick said. "I'll see what I can do to put it back in order. Miss Thornton, brace yourself." He gave the bigger man a withering look. "I'll ask you to hold her still, but do try not to break anything."

Ivey did not intend to let either one of them lay their hands on her. She put the heels of her hands under her chin and shoved upward, which was a mistake. A searing pain left her writhing in agony.

She thrashed about until the big officer finally got hold of her shoulders and pinned her down. When she gasped for air, Ildwick stuck his thumbs in her open mouth and applied a steady pressure downward on her back molars.

With a loud crack, the jaw popped into place. Ivey massaged her face in relief.

Officer Harwood, turned green before stumbling back into his chair.

Ildwick wiped his hands with a handkerchief. "Wasn't that exciting? You really ought to learn to accept help, Miss Thornton. It's much easier than bashing these things out yourself."

Ivey took several long, deep breaths to clear the pain. After a time, she looked at the chemist. "Than' you for fishen' my zhaw," she mumbled.

He nodded. "*Than'* you for leaving my thumbs intact."

Ivey worked the bottom of her mouth back and forth until it began to feel normal again.

Miles.

She sat up suddenly.

"Not so fast," Ildwick caught her sleeve. "We must make sure you haven't been given a concussion." He stuck his hand in front of her. "How many fingers do you see?"

"There will be one less if you don't get them out of my face."

Ildwick held Ivey's arm as she rose. She took a moment to steady herself.

Ildwick peered into her eyes. "Still fine?"

"Yes." Ivey pulled away and rushed to Miles' bed. "Something's wrong with him. How could he possibly sleep through all of this?"

"Not to worry." Ildwick joined her. "I stopped by to check on him while you were off saving the ship. Imagine my surprise to find a feisty little chambermaid warming the master's bed. Thankfully, your maid finally allowed me to administer a medication that will restore his blood. I also took the liberty of giving him a sleeping elixir to keep him quiet while his heart recovers." He glanced at Officer Harwood as he continued. "That is why he was able to sleep through the mayhem."

Ivey laid her hand on Miles' forehead. "He feels warmer. That's a good sign."

"Mr. Fenchurche is responding well to the medicine. So is his mother."

"What happened to her?"

"Nothing serious—a palpitation of the heart. I gave her a tonic to calm her nerves."

"And what of the doctor?" Ivey asked.

Ildwick tapped his pocket. "I had prepared the serum and was just on my way to deliver it when I was sidetracked by your latest hijinks. Dart guns, knives, and fisticuffs . . . there's never a dull moment with you, is there?"

"Go tend to Doctor Brendel. I'll take care of things here." Ivey started to adjust the covers around Miles.

Ildwick shrugged. "I suggest you leave him be until he's ready to wake up." He glanced sideways, peeking beneath Dolan's ill-fitting jacket at her lack of clothing. "Your fiancé is warming up, but if you've taken a chill," he said with a smug grin, "I'm certain that Mr. Fenchurche wouldn't mind having you snuggled back in his bed."

Ivey was tired and her head hurt. The thought of lying next to Miles and listening to his breathing was almost as comforting as it was embarrassing to imagine. She looked at the chemist in disgust.

"What possesses you to say such crude things, Mr. Curio?"

"I was in the lobby the morning we departed. If you have a habit of parading around in precious little attire and hopping in and out of the master's bed, you can hardly blame me for noticing."

"My appearance is none of your business, and neither is my concern for the health of Miles Fenchurche. Unlike you, he is a true gentleman. You would do well to learn from his example."

Officer Harwood snickered. "She's got sass."

"Hmm, well, perhaps I have spent too many years in the wild," Ildwick conceded. "From here on, I will make a special effort not to offend the refined young lady's sense of propriety."

"Don't waste your time," Ivey replied flatly, rubbing her cheek. She turned her back on the chemist and stalked over to the Dicæon officer in the chair. "Harwood?"

He nodded apprehensively.

Ivey extended her hand. "I meant no harm to you or your partner. You were only following orders. Return my knife and gun, and we'll call it even."

The man's giant paw completely engulfed Ivey's hand as they shook. "Only if you teach me how to deliver that nasty strike." He rubbed his neck.

Ivey frowned. "It's intended to disable, not dismember. You would have to promise not to break anyone's neck."

He chuckled. "You have my word as a senior officer of the Dicæon."

"My father says boxing is barbaric, but I am coming to respect the ability to throw a decent punch. Show me your moves, and I'll show you mine."

Ildwick laughed at the officer's chagrined expression. "Sounds like quite an offer, Harwood."

"Boxing lessons with a girl? You won't be happy until my reputation is completely ruined, will you?" Harwood grumbled.

"The better a fighter I am, the less it will matter that I knocked you out first."

The big man rose to his feet. "I'll consider it. It's time I returned to the bridge." He went to the officer, who was sprawled on the floor. "Come along, Lieutenant Faust!" He kicked the man's leg.

Ivey cringed. "I'm sorry. He won't be waking up for a very long time."

Harwood grumbled as he picked up his fallen comrade and threw him over his shoulder. "I know a nice cot where you can sleep this off. Then you can tell everyone about that time a blue girl took you down."

Ivey tapped his arm. "My knife and gun?" She held out her hand expectantly.

"Yeah, well, the captain has problems with passengers carrying arms."

Ivey put her hands on her hips. "Really? That knife repaired the *Monarch*'s envelope, and my gun kept Miles Fenchurche out of harm's way. How is this a problem for the captain?"

Ildwick laughed. "I think we can trust Miss Thornton to use her implements for good. Besides, I seem to remember that you shook hands on the deal. I'm afraid that you are bound by your word, sir."

Harwood dug into his pocket and returned the knife and gun, along with a stern warning: "Next time you pull one of these on my men, you're going in the brig. Girl or not."

Ivey smiled and returned the belongings to her satchel. "Fair enough."

Ildwick opened the bedroom door and waited as Harwood trudged past him.

"Mind his noggin," Ildwick warned, a split second before Faust's head banged against the doorframe. "And with that, I'm off to give the doctor our serum. Do get some rest."

"Wait," Ivey called as she hurried after him. "I've decided to go with you."

Ildwick stopped. "You should stay here." Ivey detected a change in his manner. The lightness was gone from his eyes; he was hiding something.

"And I heed orders from you because—?" Ivey taunted.

"Those were your orders, my dear. You demanded that I tend to the doctor and leave Miles in your care."

"Well, I've changed my mind," Ivey informed him. "Since you have him safely sedated, I'll find my maid and let her handle things here. I want to see what happens when you administer that serum."

"No, you don't." Ildwick took a step toward her, blocking the doorway with his arm.

"But," Ivey stammered, "you promised to share your knowledge of the leeches. Are you not bound by your word, Mr. Curio?"

There was a distinct edge to the chemist's voice when he answered. "If this serum does not work as I expect, things could get unpleasant."

"How so?"

"There may be side effects."

"Such as?"

"There's a chance it could kill the doctor, or worse."

Ivey felt her gut twist. "Worse than death?"

Ildwick lowered his voice. "You are the one who demanded discretion. Do you really mean to have this conversation with your prospective mother-in-law in the next room?"

Ivey pulled Ildwick back into the bedroom and shut the door. "You made that serum from my blood. If there's something wrong with me, I demand to know."

"Are you in need of a mirror?"

"You tried that joke before, and I'm still not laughing. Tell me what's going on." She jabbed a finger into his chest.

Ildwick looked toward the bed. "In front of Mr. Fenchurche?"

"I'm sure I can trust him with my private matters far more than I trust you."

Ildwick reached out for Ivey, and she jumped back defensively.

"I'm only after your skin," he explained. "May I have a closer look?"

Ivey reluctantly offered her right hand. Her looks had never mattered, but something like this could make her life even more complicated. "Is it permanent?"

"I don't think so, though I cannot predict how or when it will end."

"How helpful," Ivey said with a sniff. "So, why would the serum endanger the doctor?"

"Your blood is abnormal."

"In what way?"

"It contains strange elements, which probably accounts for your present complexion. The most perplexing is a potent catalyst. Do you know what that is?"

Ivey rolled her eyes. "A catalyst accelerates chemical change. Any decent scientist knows that, Mr. Curio."

"Yes, well, as I introduced ingredients into the serum, your blood altered itself in ways I have never seen before."

"But it was contaminated by the leeches and then mixed with Miles' blood. How can you say the abnormal compounds even came from me?"

"All I know is that the blood I tested could cause transformations to occur at an alarming rate."

Ivey frowned. She'd always had abnormalities, but since her exposure to the otheophainer, they seemed to be multiplying.

She raised her left hand and showed him the row of stitches marooned in her restored flesh. "Miles said the leeches would heal my wound. And they did, in one night. I think they are the source of your catalyst."

Ildwick inspected her hand. "We'll never know, because you and the leeches contaminated each other. As for who is mutating whom, that remains a mystery, but the leeches' physiology is every bit as bizarre as yours. Even after they perished, their cells continued to divide and grow for quite some time. And that is not the worst of it. Judging by their level of development, those were only infants."

Ivey shuddered at the thought.

"Yes, Miss Thornton. At the rate they were growing, we are very lucky that Mr. Fenchurche drowned them in sterilizing solution. Now, I have told you everything there is to know. Will you please stay here while I see to the doctor?"

Ivey drew her gun and a fresh dart cartridge from her satchel. She flipped open the chamber's cover and slid the dart inside. "If I were about to administer a serum that might cause a dangerous reaction, I would want someone armed with one of these at my side. Please do not underestimate me, Mr. Curio."

Ildwick replied with a wry shrug. "Only a madman would turn down an offer like that. Let's get on with it then." He opened the bedroom door. "After you."

Ivey stashed the gun in her satchel and led the way into the sitting room. She was relieved to see Minnette resting on a sofa with Sylvia sitting to the side.

Sylvia jumped up to inspect Ivey's face.

"You were out cold, you poor thing, and after all you've been through."

Ivey rubbed the side of her chin. "I thought my social calendar was going to be a dreadful bore, but it seems flying on the *Monarch* really is the adventure of a lifetime. How are you feeling?"

Sylvia held out her ankle. "I may have a few bruises, but I'm a farm girl. We're tough, too."

Ivey gave her a quick hug. "Thank you for protecting Miles. Would you please watch him while I'm away?"

Minnette staggered to her feet. "Where are you going?"

"I am glad to see you're looking better," Ivey said.

In truth, the woman looked a little loopy. Ildwick's treatment had done a fine job of softening her brittle edges.

"I would like to know what is more important than your concern for my son's welfare," Minnette said with narrowed eyes.

"Mr. Curio is going to administer a serum that may save Doctor Brendel. I'm going to assist him and find some fresh clothing." Ivey clutched the front of Dolan's jacket shut. "I realize that my appearance is less than adequate."

Minnette turned to Ildwick. "Curio? Have we met?"

Ildwick grinned at Ivey before he replied, "Of course, madam. I am the chemist who gave you some lovely medicine just a short while ago. Do we not remember?"

Minnette snapped back, "Of course I remember! I was speaking about the past. Were you ever at Ferndale?"

Ildwick shook his head. "I never had that pleasure. I've been away for some years, but recently, I have been collaborating with the Chemists' Collective at Cadenbury. You may have seen me there. Now, if you will excuse me, I must see to the doctor."

"Do." Minnette looked at Sylvia. "Take care of my son until I return. I'm going with them."

"I am afraid I cannot allow that—" Ildwick objected, but Minnette brushed past him without a word.

Ivey shrugged and followed. "I don't think she takes orders either."

"Spirits save me from these bullheaded women," he muttered as he followed her from the room.

They arrived at the guest suite to find the doctor lying unattended on the large couch. The sitting room was in shambles from the storm, and Ivey found it disturbing that there was no sign of his guard.

The lingering aura of the leeches hung in the air.

She'd always been repulsed by the pests, but this species was especially vile. Ivey was afraid that the trembling of her knees was becoming noticeable.

She removed the gun from her satchel and held it out of sight as Ildwick pulled the cover from the syringe. He glanced in her direction and she nodded, discreetly displaying the gun.

Minnette leaned over the doctor to watch.

"You will want to stand back," Ildwick said. "If this works, the doctor may experience tremendous spasms."

Minnette moved back.

Ildwick pulled up the doctor's shirt. "The muscles in his arms and legs have become hardened, so I will have to inject the serum into his belly."

Ildwick pricked the skin below the doctor's navel and, with some effort, pushed the needle in.

Ivey tensed as the dark liquid in the syringe slowly disappeared.

No one spoke or moved as they waited for a reaction.

When none came, Ildwick pressed a finger against the doctor's neck. "Well?" Minnette asked in a husky voice.

Ildwick sighed. "I am sorry." He glanced at Ivey. "Too little or too late."

Ivey put her gun away, wondering if it were her blood that had killed him.

She heaved a mournful sigh.

Ildwick reached out to put an arm around her. She leaned against him with her eyes closed, imagining for a moment that she was on her father's shoulder.

Minnette came forward to lay a hand on the doctor's arm. "You will be missed, old friend." She bent down to kiss his cheek farewell.

The moment her lips touched his skin, the doctor's eyes flew open. "—bitch!" he shouted.

The doctor knocked Minnette backward, and she fell with a scream.

Ildwick leapt over her to try and restrain Doctor Brendel while Ivey fumbled with the gun. Her hands were shaking too violently to take aim.

"It stung me!" The doctor stopped struggling with Ildwick and looked around the room in disbelief. "What in the world?"

"Do you know your name? Can you flex your arm?" Ildwick asked.

"Of course I know who I am! Who the devil are you?" Doctor Brendel flexed his arm and delivered an indignant slap across the chemist's face. "How in blazes did I get in here?"

Ildwick rubbed his reddening cheek. "Calm down, my friend, or I'll ask that girl to tranquilize you."

The doctor glanced in Ivey's direction.

"You! Is this your doing?" He stared at her blue features. "What kind of monstrosity are you?"

Ivey lowered the gun. "A relieved one. Welcome back, doctor."

"I demand to know what's going on here!" the doctor roared.

After Ivey helped Minnette up from the floor, the lady brushed herself off and returned to the doctor's side. "Really, Mathias. We've all had a bad day; you should thank them for your life."

Doctor Brendel fell back against the couch. "That's it. I've lost my mind."

Minnette gently smacked him on the shoulder. "Save your outbursts. My son needs a doctor, and you are all I have. How soon can you see him?"

"Before there is any worry of that, allow me to introduce myself." Ildwick offered his hand. "I am Ildwick Curio. I examined the leeches that attacked you and Miss Thornton. I will explain everything that happened after you were stung."

Ivey knew the leeches' noxious aura would be even stronger in her bedroom, but she was anxious to get back to Miles, and she was in terrible need of new clothes. "If you'll excuse me, I am going to get dressed."

Ildwick smiled. "I was just growing used to your jaunty sense of fashion. Would you like me to check the bedroom?"

"No. All I require is privacy, sir. I can take care of myself." She held up the dart gun in warning then jerked open the bedroom door, strode through, and slammed it shut behind her. She immediately regretted the act of bravado.

The curtains were drawn and the room was dark. The stench of blood and leeches made her spine ache with fear. Ivey forced herself to breathe slowly as she inched her way along the wall toward the window.

They're gone. Let in some light, everything will be fine.

Halfway there, her bare foot came down on something cold and slimy.

She jumped back and clapped a hand across her mouth to stifle a scream, reassuring herself that something had merely spilled during the storm.

Moving forward, her bare toe stubbed against a hard object.

Ivey jumped over the obstacle and made a dash for the drapery, hurling it back.

Sunshine spilled into the room.

She leaned her cheek against the cool glass, letting the steady hum of the ship's engines sooth her jangled nerves.

Through the window, the surface of the water still appeared frightfully close. The ship didn't look to be more than a hundred feet above the towering waves.

Crewmen were swarming the riggings and scrambling up the grappling wires to apply more patches to the damaged envelope. Once they stabilized the envelope enough to open the wings, the *Monarch* would regain some much needed lift.

Ivey turned to survey the room. Her bed was coated in dried blood and bathing salts, and the wardrobe had tipped over in the storm. One of the doors was open when it fell, propping the wardrobe up slightly. It looked like there was enough room for her to wriggle underneath the opening and retrieve some of her clothes.

On the floor next to the wardrobe, she noticed a dark streak across the rug, ending at the spot where she'd stubbed her toe.

What had tripped her was not a piece of furniture. It was a red uniform worn by the flight crew.

At first she thought it was the uniform she'd stolen from the service lockers. Then she noticed the grisly remains of a man were still inside. His flesh was shrunken and gray, as if his body had been petrified.

Run!

She started for the door, but the same paralyzing force she'd experienced on the dock overtook her. It wrapped around her, dragging her back and forcing her down on her knees beside the macabre figure.

It was impossible to stop her fingers from reaching out to the man's withered skin.

A vision of his death flooded her mind. Like the doctor, he'd been trapped in his own body as a voracious predator drained his life away.

Ivey sensed the dreadful being moving through the ship, on its way to claim her. The harder she fought to escape, the closer it drew her toward the grim corpse, until her lips were nearly touching the slain crewman's. She was grateful when her consciousness finally slipped away.

A sharp knock stirred her. The door opened a crack.

"I am aware that women can take æons to get dressed, but this is becoming quite ridiculous. Should I come in and help?" When there was no response, the tone in the voice changed. "Miss Thornton, if I am forced to enter, you had better not shoot me."

Please, hurry.

Finally the door flew open, and Ildwick charged into the room. "Ivey, what are you doing?"

He jerked her to her feet. "Get up!"

The spell was broken. She backed away, shuddering in revulsion.

"Move." Ildwick grabbed her arm and dragged her out of the room. He slammed the door shut and began shoving furniture in front it. "We have to stop whatever killed that guard."

Ivey struggled to pull a table over and help him. "Those leeches, were they . . . ?"

"Their cells were growing, but I can assure you that all three were dead before I dissected them.

In her mind, Ivey recalled seeing the jar in Doctor Brendel's hand just before she'd kicked him. "Ildwick. I think there were more than three."

"Are you certain? Doctor Brendel, how many leeches did you have with you?"

"I counted four in the jar when I retrieved it from the infirmary's cabinet," he answered.

Ivey ran to her sitting room's service button and pounded on it repeatedly.

"What is going on?" Minnette cast a fretful look toward the barricaded bedroom door.

"We have to get out of here," Ildwick answered with a sense of urgency.

The doctor tried to rise, but his muscles hadn't fully recovered from the toxin.

"Lose some weight, Mathias," Minnette scolded, as she tried to lift him.

Ildwick rushed over to assist. "The most heavily guarded area on this ship right now is the bridge. Let's go."

"Ildwick. We can't leave Sylvia and Miles behind," Ivey said as she threw open the front door of her suite.

"It's still too risky to move him." Ildwick lifted the doctor to his feet and supported his weight as they made their way to the door. "We'll have to send guards to his quarters."

"Absolutely not. I won't allow him to be unprotected for one moment," Minnette objected.

"I agree," Ivey said. "That thing devoured an armed guard, Ildwick."

"Yes," Ildwick said through gritted teeth. "It's faster and more aggressive than I anticipated."

Ivey drew her gun and headed toward the master suite. "I'll stay with them until help arrives, but please hurry."

Minnette shouted after her, "Fetch Lucey Sue. She's sleeping in my room."

Ivey nodded, calling over her shoulder, "Ildwick, have Harwood send his men to my suite. Tell him they need to be armed with every available weapon and all the bathing salts they can lay their hands on!"

Chapter Twenty-Two

THE CIPHER CONUNDRUM

Silas rushed Arvel past every guard along the entrance to the martial wing of the Cadenbury Institute. The Promacheon's offices and laboratories had always been shrouded in secrecy. Most of the scientists who worked at Cadenbury had never set foot inside this portion of the main building.

At the end of a long hallway, the two men came to the doors of a large elevator. They entered and descended in silence, deep into the bowels of the complex. The elevator car finally came to a halt, and the door slid open, revealing another long hallway, this one dimly lit.

"Where are we going?" Arvel inquired.

Silas gestured toward the open door. "After you."

The hallway ended in front of a heavily fortified door. Silas opened a cabinet and removed two pairs of tinted goggles.

"Put these on." He handed a pair to Arvel and depressed a lever beside the door. With a loud clank, an internal bolt drew back, and the door slid open.

They entered a cavernous, rock-hewn room with only enough light for Arvel to make out a colossal glass dome resting on the cavern floor.

As they drew closer, Arvel strained to see inside the glass. There was nothing but a black hole with no bottom in sight.

Around the dome, towers of machinery were manned by crews of white-coated scientists, who appeared to be working under close guard by men wearing the black uniforms of the Promacheon.

"What is all this?" Arvel asked.

Silas gestured to the operator at the closest station. "Show him."

The man obliged, opening a set of valves that released a concoction of gases into the dome. In seconds, the interior came alive with an array of colorful streaks that vibrated and danced in oscillating patterns.

Arvel drew a sharp breath. "The cosmocrene?"

"When it comes to understanding the forces of nature, you and Stanley Honeycutt haven't a clue. The Zephyr Project is nothing compared to the power that can be wielded with this planetary resource."

A strange foreboding struck Arvel as he watched the vibrations in the dome. Something wasn't right with this place.

There was a brief silence before Arvel asked, "What power do you speak of?"

"The Promacheon discovered that the cosmocrene had many promising characteristics. While Stanley's team at Cadenbury dedicated itself to the Zephyr Project, we worked in a different direction. You are aware that the energy of the cosmocrene is not static. It oscillates."

Arvel nodded.

"We began to investigate the properties of this phenomenon. The oscillation is omnipresent. Any disturbance to the oscillation's signature will travel across the cosmocrene's entire expanse.

"After some experimentation, our scientists discovered that we could transmit phemai."

"*Phemai?*"

"Messages encoded by a series of pulses." Silas waved his hand in a gratuitous fashion. "They are every bit as unique as the sound of your daughter's soul, Arvel, and I dare say more profound. Imagine a world where detailed messages need not be delivered by hand."

"How do energy pulses convey messages?"

Arvel followed Silas to another station farther around the dome.

"They can be parsed and controlled, allowing us to create a form of language that is neither written nor spoken."

Silas set his hand on the shoulder of the pallid man at the console. Arvel could see that the poor fellow hadn't been above ground for some time. "You may tell him about the cipher device."

"It's fairly rudimentary," the man said. "Cipher equipment generates a pheme, which can be detected by a corresponding piece of equipment at a remote station. That device receives and decodes the information. The team on the other end can then transmit a reply using the same process."

"Can you determine the location from which a pheme originates?" Arvel asked.

When the man nodded and turned back to his work, something in his eyes struck Arvel. He stepped closer, and loosened his shoulders. A single word came to Arvel's mind.

Trapped.

That was the source of his foreboding. It seemed that these scientists were little more than prisoners of the Promacheon.

Arvel suddenly realized that no one in his family knew where he'd gone. If he weren't careful, he could become the next hostage.

"Silas, my only concern is my daughter's safety. How does this relate to the *Monarch*?"

"A team of my men boarded the ship to test a mobile prototype of the instrument. We hadn't attempted its operation at sea yet, and the sightseeing cruise was ideal for such an event."

"So your team was sending information about the storm as it happened?" Arvel asked.

"Yes, but as the storm worsened, we lost contact with them and haven't been able to reestablish communications. That can only mean one thing."

The scientist looked up from his controls. "Not necessarily. If the *Monarch*'s course abruptly changed, it's possible that we've only lost track of her position on the map, and they've lost their bearings as well."

"Is there any way to relocate it?" Arvel asked.

Silas cocked his head. "Maybe. Let's see if you can project your energy into the cosmocrene to find your daughter."

Arvel turned to look at the dome. "I wouldn't begin to know how to do such a thing."

"Mr. Harp, what you're suggesting is not permitted by the design of this machine," the scientist interjected.

"But you see, Mr. Thornton is a living pheme," Silas mocked. "If he projects his '*pneuma biou*' into the oscillations to connect with his daughter's soul, it might help you pinpoint her position. Isn't that right, Arvel?"

Arvel tensed. If such a thing were possible, he had to try it. "I'll do anything to help my daughter," he said.

"Excuse me." The scientist rose to his feet. "I must speak with you privately about this, Mr. Harp."

Silas followed him a short distance away, where Arvel observed a heated exchange. He could not make out their words, but it was obvious that the man had severe objections to his overseer's proposition. Silas was adamant, and when they returned, the pale man sat down at the controls with an air of resignation.

"Mr. Thornton, I do not know what will come of this. If anything goes awry, you must disengage yourself immediately."

"Time is escaping." Silas shot the man a look of warning before turning back to Arvel. "Your daughter's life rides on this."

Arvel approached the dome and laid one hand against it. He let his body relax and turned his thoughts inward. Even with his eyes closed, he could see the colorful streaks of gas swirling hypnotically before him. They soon lulled him into a state of total relaxation.

In his mind's eye, he was adrift in a great void. Far away, a tiny pinpoint of light grew larger. As it approached, Arvel felt something immense bearing down on him at blinding speed. A wave of energy broke over him.

Flashes of childhood memories intertwined with bits and pieces of his past adventures and cherished moments with his family. Through a barrage of images whirling around him, a baby's hand reached out. Arvel felt the tiny fingers wrap around his.

Ivey.

The hand slipped away into the mælstrom of mental images. Arvel tried to stay focused on her. He reached out with all his heart.

Ivey. Where are you?

He could see her on the docking platform, nervously scanning the crowd that was boarding the *Monarch*.

Ivey!

She turned in surprise.

Can you hear me?

Her face pinched with fear as a shadow fell across her. She turned and ran into a spinning tunnel of darkness. Arvel followed.

Ivey, wait! It's me!

He heard her terrified panting. "Who are you?"

It's father. I'm looking for you.

Unable to recognize him, Ivey ran away. No matter how swiftly Arvel pursued, she stayed several paces ahead. He was closing in on her when a light blinded him.

Once his eyes adjusted, he found himself in her bedroom on the *Monarch*. Furniture was overturned, and the bedding was stained with blood. Ivey was leaning against the window, trembling.

Ivey, don't be afraid.

She looked in his direction and started for the door.

No. Stop running.

She slowly turned, a look of dread on her face.

I'm coming for you. Please let me help you.

Arvel reached out, and her hand drifted toward his. Before their fingers touched, the room vanished, and Arvel was beneath the glass dome, surrounded by the machine's luminous gases.

He looked up and saw Ivey floating above him. She wore a blue gown, her auburn hair blazed around her like a halo. Tendrils of energy flickered up and around her.

"Where are you, Father? I need you."

I can find you, Ivey, just show me your light.

"I'm ready to go home." Ivey threw her arms open, and the energy radiating from the pit enveloped her body. Her skin glowed with the vitality of youth, and the beating of her heart reverberated inside the glass.

Contact.

Arvel sensed something happening in the energy field below. He looked down. The beautiful waves had turned dark and choppy as they bubbled up out of the pit. The bands of energy against her gown blackened, staining the blue fabric.

Ivey struggled to escape, but she was caught like a moth in a spider's web. The sound of her heartbeat grew louder and louder until it pounded like a colossal war drum.

"Father! What do I do?"

"Break the barrier that separates us."

It was unmistakably his voice, but Arvel hadn't spoken.

In a flash, he was back outside the dome, while a perfect imitation of himself beckoned to Ivey from inside.

"Come back to me," it said. "We have another chance to be together."

Arvel hammered his fists against the glass. "Ivey. Don't go near it. It's a trick."

A gnarled limb rose from the pit and caught his daughter's leg, dragging her down into the depths.

As her face disappeared beneath the mire, he heard a coarse whisper. "Let go."

"No! Don't do it!" Arvel screamed.

In the distance, he heard a man shouting. "Mr. Thornton, stop!"

The trance ended, and Arvel's consciousness was brought back to the subterranean laboratory.

The pale scientist was shaking him by the shoulders. "Stop whatever you're doing before the dome shatters."

An ominous pounding reverberated through the cavern, as if a colossal being were smashing its way through the rock beneath his feet.

The technicians shouted above the din and frantically worked the equipment at their stations. Promacheon agents gathered around a large crack in the dome that was creeping toward the spot where Arvel was standing.

"What happened?" Arvel shouted. "What is that?"

"Lock it all down!" the pale scientist yelled at his coworkers. He turned and shoved Arvel in the direction of the exit. "Get out while you can."

Arvel resisted. "My daughter, did you see her?" He tried to peer around the man. "What is happening? Where's Silas?"

"Take this." The man shoved a piece of paper with hastily scrawled map coordinates into Arvel's hands. "We found the ship. If you want to save them, run!"

"Are you trapped, man, or is it something in there?" Arvel pointed at the dome. "What have you done?"

"Do not speak of this place or what's in that energy field. They will make you pay." The man ran back to his station.

Arvel turned to see the large metal door sliding back into place. The room was nearly sealed off.

He raced toward the shrinking opening and leapt through a moment before it slammed into place.

The pounding stopped.

Arvel set his ear against the door, but it was too thick to hear what was happening on the other side. He could feel no vibrations coming through the metal or the rock floor.

The hallway was deserted, so he turned and ran for the elevator.

On the ride up, he decided that the best course of action would be to take the pale man's advice and stay silent while he turned his attention to mounting a rescue.

If the *Monarch* was safely located, he would have to think very carefully about sharing what he'd seen in the hidden laboratory.

∾

Chapter Twenty-Three

Unexpected Catalyst

I vey burst into the master bedroom with her gun drawn. Miles was sleeping peacefully, but Sylvia jumped to her feet in alarm.

"What now?"

"When you went to my quarters, did you see a guard?"

"He helped me gather your things. Did something happen to him?"

"Yes."

Sylvia raised her hand to her mouth. "Is he like the doctor?"

Before she could answer, Lucey Sue appeared in the bedroom doorway with her arms full of bathing salts. Ivey turned to give Minnette's maid instructions.

"Empty one of the jars over the threshold to this suite, then close the door and watch it. If you see or hear anything, smother it in salt and scream for your life."

"Yes, miss."

While Lucey Sue went back to the entrance of the master suite, Ivey closed the bedroom door and spoke in a low voice, so as not to disturb Miles' sleep.

"The doctor has revived, but the man guarding him is dead. There was a fourth leech."

"The poor soul."

"I want you to take this until help arrives." Ivey offered the dart gun.

Sylvia pushed it back. "Oh, no. You're much better with it."

"Please listen," Ivey whispered. "If I become dangerous, you'll need to protect yourself and Miles."

Sylvia stared. "What?"

"Something inside me is causing mutations."

"Mutations?"

"Abnormal changes, like what's happened to my skin. Mr. Curio said it's caused by a catalyst in my blood."

"And you trust this Mr. Curio?"

"Not entirely, but if I become threatening, you may have to stop me." She offered the gun again.

Sylvia grabbed Ivey's shoulders. "Miss Ivey! Why would you say that?"

Ivey took a long breath. For everyone's sake, she had to tell the truth.

"There's always been something wrong with me. When I was little, there were times that I could not control myself. I would lose my temper and attack my family. Nothing they did could make me stop when I was like that. Only my father was able to calm me down and bring me back to normal, but he has scars from where I scratched and bit him."

"That was just a child's fits, miss. I must have given my brother more licks than I can even remember. You wouldn't hurt a soul now."

"Listen to me." She took Sylvia's arm, pulling her farther from the bed, so that Miles wouldn't overhear.

"Before I learned to love animals, I had an overpowering compulsion to hunt them. It started with the wild creatures that lived on our grounds, but then it was my sisters' pets."

Sylvia shook her head in dismay.

"I've worked hard to contain those impulses," Ivey continued. "I thought I could, but dangerous things are happening aboard this ship. If I ever lost control like that again, I might kill anyone who tried to stop me."

"That isn't true," Sylvia said.

"I can't help what's in my nature." Ivey's chin began to tremble.

"Well, I know that you're not capable of murder. You have shown me nothing but kindness and respect. And what about Mr. Miles? He was willing to die for you, and you've said the same."

Ivey's head drooped. "That was pride. I couldn't let some foolish man die for me."

"No, miss. You've warmed his heart. For the first time, he's felt love."

Ivey turned away and whispered sadly. "I hope that's not true. Our engagement is a fraud."

"What?"

"My father offered me a deal. I never intended to marry Miles. I only agreed to break him free from his mother's grasp to win my own independence."

Ivey looked toward the bed where Miles lay sleeping.

"I came here under false pretenses, and everything I've done has gone wrong. I've nearly cost you and Miles your lives, and now a man is lying dead in my room."

Sylvia frowned. "I'm sorry you feel that way, but it doesn't make any of this your fault. If we'd listened to you, those leeches would be dead. You've saved us from more than one disaster, miss, and you'll get us through this, too."

"No. Those things are far more than leeches. Even before I boarded the ship, I felt their sickening presence. They are evil and cunning creatures capable of invading the mind and body. Who knows what they might make me do if they gain control over me? I'm not strong enough to stop something like that."

The gun slipped from Ivey's grasp and dropped to the floor.

"I don't want anyone else to die like that poor guard," she gasped. "I'm afraid for all of us. I don't know what to do."

Sylvia wrapped her arms around Ivey's shoulders and rocked her in a soothing hug.

"Hush now. You were blessed with more than your share of courage. You have a heroic spirit and a loving heart. You are dear to many people on this ship, and I assure you, if you can't defend yourself, we will."

Sylvia bent down and picked up Ivey's gun. "Show me how this contraption works. I'll patrol the sitting room while you get some sleep."

"No," Ivey murmured. "I can't rest until that thing is dead."

Someone shrieked in the sitting room.

Sylvia recoiled in fear.

Ivey snatched the gun out of her maid's hand and ran from the bedroom, taking aim at a large, dark figure looming in the suite's doorway. Before she could squeeze the trigger, a deep voice boomed.

"How can I protect the women on this ship if they keep attacking me?" Officer Harwood had taken a hail of Lucey Sue's salts right to the face.

Another familiar voice chided, "Don't barge in and frighten them half to death, then. I take it everyone's all right in here?"

Ildwick squeezed past Harwood and stared at the gun in her hands.

"Whoa, Miss Thornton. Put that thing down before you do something I might regret." He squinted at her and lowered his voice. "Oh, dear."

Ivey stumbled to the sofa. Her stomach churned, and her ears were ringing. Her body felt as if it were turning to ice.

∾

Ildwick held Ivey's head in his hands, turning it sideways to get a better look at the strange shape of her ear.

Her eyelids began to flutter, as if the spell was passing.

"Get your greasy hands off her or I will break this over your head, sir."

He looked up to find Ivey's maid threatening to dash his skull with one of the few vases that had survived the storm.

Ildwick sighed and gently laid Ivey's head back against the sofa cushion.

"Do I really look like the sort of man who would take advantage of a helpless woman?"

"Yes," Sylvia and Ivey answered in perfect unison.

Ildwick stood, holding his hands out in surrender. "Apparently I am in need of a decent shave."

"What were you doing there?" Sylvia asked.

"I was only trying to let her hair down." He leaned as close to the maid as she would allow. "It would be wise if you helped her before anyone notices her ears." He discreetly inclined his head toward Harwood and Lucey Sue, who were still busy brushing salt from the large man's face and wiping his eyes.

"Step aside." Sylvia pushed past him and sat next to Ivey. Ildwick heard her gasp when she saw the misshapen cartilage and flesh.

"What is it?" Ivey's hands followed Sylvia's eyes to her ears, feeling their curious shape. "This is hideous!" She yanked at her ponytail, trying to free her hair and hide the deformity.

Sylvia grabbed Ivey's hands and squeezed them. "Allow me." She untied the green ribbon and stuck it in her apron pocket, then carefully arranged Ivey's hair against the sides of her face while Ildwick observed.

Ivey glared up at him.

"What's so damned interesting, Curio?"

"You should try to calm down."

"Don't tell me what to do." Her voice rose.

Ildwick knelt beside the couch. "I have a theory, if you care to hear it."

He waited until she finally spoke.

"What?"

"Our bodies contain chemicals that assist in carrying out the functions of life. They trigger a multitude of physiological responses, some of which are known as instincts."

"There's no need to lecture me about instincts," Ivey sniffed.

"Good. Then you clearly understand they can be quite powerful and undeniable. They've been honed by nature to help us protect ourselves and others. Why, they even make us do ridiculous things like fall in love and ensure the production of future generations."

"I hardly need such—"

"Simply put," Ildwick interrupted, "your instinct to survive has become rather problematic. It elicits the chemical responses needed to make you stronger, faster, and more resistant to pain. In turn, those responses excite the catalyst in your blood, which triggers the whole process anew. If this cycle is not interrupted, these mutations may progress at a quickening pace."

The tension on Ivey's face eased. "Thank you, Mr. Curio. I appreciate your insight. Do you believe this process could be slowed or possibly reversed if I try to calm myself?"

"I believe that is precisely what could happen. Take my advice and get some sleep."

"I will not sleep with that thing on the loose, but I will take a minute to refresh myself."

Ildwick rose to his feet and clapped his hands together. "Isn't it grand that you always know best? Before you retire, I'll need a few vials of your blood to make more antivenin."

"Is that safe?" Ivey touched the hair covering one of her misproportioned ears.

"The doctor has recovered superbly with no sign of such afflictions. We should keep a reserve for any other victims who haven't been bled dry."

"All right. But I ask that you do something for me."

Ildwick smiled. It looked like the girl was beginning to trust him.

"I am at your service, Miss Thornton. What is your wish?" He gave her a rakish bow.

"Refill my gun's cartridge with a strong dose of that sleeping elixir you gave Miles. We may need it later." She gave her maid a nod. "Sylvia, would you go and find the spent dart cartridge on the bedroom floor?"

The instant Sylvia had gone, Ivey beckoned for him. "Come here."

He stepped toward the couch.

"Closer."

When he bent down, she grabbed his shirt, pulling his face close to hers.

She was completely serious, but Ildwick had to laugh. "I thought you were an engaged woman."

"Shut up," she said in a harsh whisper. "Fill that cartridge with the deadliest poison you've got, something that could fell a beast in its tracks."

Ildwick was touched by her innocent vulnerability. "And by beast, you mean . . . ?"

Ivey's eyes locked onto his. "Anything that threatens the welfare of the *Monarch* or her passengers."

Ildwick pulled her hand from his shirt and held it a moment.

"A brave gesture, but quite unnecessary." He looked away from her frightened gaze.

"You said the mutations will get worse, and I have a violent nature. We should prepare for what might come."

"Now is not the time for such a discussion, but let me assure you, I've been to places and seen things far worse than whatever demons you harbor."

Sylvia entered the room with the empty dart in her hand.

"Not a word," Ivey warned softly.

Ildwick noticed the maid's hesitation when she saw him holding Ivey's hand.

"Here it is, sir." The wily girl rushed forward and held the cartridge just out of his reach.

When he rose to accept it, she slipped past him and took his place at Ivey's side, pulling up her mistress's sleeve.

"Let's get this over with so you can be on your way, Mr. Curio."

Lucey Sue jumped up from her station near the suite's door. "Something's coming!"

Ivey sat up and aimed her dart gun over the back of the sofa.

Harwood planted his feet and raised his gun. Over his shoulder he shouted, "Curio, get the women into the bedroom!"

Ivey's warning scowl turned in Ildwick's direction. Clearly, the lady had no intention of being herded to safety.

"Are you trying to get me killed, Harwood?" he asked dryly.

"This is my fight too, gentlemen," Ivey said.

An austere knock at the door made everyone except Lucey Sue freeze. She lowered her jar of salts and undid the latch. The door opened and Dolan entered, followed by three guards carrying canisters of food and water.

"Where's the salt to throw in *his* eyes?" Harwood mumbled.

Lucey Sue looked at Harwood with incredulity. "Why, I know Mr. Dolan's knock like the back of my hand, sir." She reached for one of the food canisters. "I'll take that. Haven't had a bite all day."

Ivey groaned and fell back onto the seat of the couch. "My skin feels like it's on fire."

"What should we do?" Sylvia asked.

"I'll get her some water," Ildwick answered as he rushed over to take a canteen from one of the guards. On the way, he slipped a hand into his front pocket and retrieved a brown glass vial.

While he was removing the stopper, Ivey handed the dart gun to her maid.

"Aim for my leg," she gasped.

"Are you sure?" Sylvia's voice trembled.

"Do it, before anything happens."

Sylvia picked up the gun and warily pointed it at her mistress.

"Sylvia! What is the meaning of this?"

Dolan rushed past while Ildwick poured the vial's contents into the canteen and gave it a slight shake.

Sylvia stood silently, staring at the gun in her hands.

"Tell him before it happens," Ivey said through clenched teeth.

"Tell me what?" Dolan asked.

"My blood . . ." Ivey wheezed.

"What is she saying? Answer me now!"

"Let me explain." Ildwick approached, holding out the canteen. "Miss Thornton is suffering a delirium brought on by her trauma. Allow me." He gestured for Dolan and Sylvia to make room. He knelt beside the couch and slid his arm under Ivey's shoulders lifting her head, and bringing the metal rim to her lips. "Here, drink this up."

She took a sip and gagged, spitting the water onto the back of the couch. "It's sour."

Ildwick took a small sip for himself and rolled it around his mouth like a fine wine. "Mmm, delicious. Your sense of taste must be off. Now drink it."

"No. It smells like vinegar." Ivey pushed it away.

Sylvia gave Ildwick an accusing look. "Vinegar?"

He coolly returned her stare and spoke with great deliberation. "If she doesn't drink this, her condition will worsen very quickly."

With a resigned sigh, Sylvia took the canteen from his hand and took a sniff before offering it to Ivey. "Smells fine, miss," she said. "Here."

Ildwick gave the maid a thankful nod when Ivey grudgingly brought her lips to the mouth of the canteen and choked down its contents. Her face puckered and her body contracted as the liquid settled in her stomach.

Dolan moved closer to the couch, wearing a worried frown. "Should I not call the doctor? She looks terrible."

"That won't be necessary," Ildwick replied. "Give her a moment to quiet down while I look for more syringes in the medical supply cabinet. I am afraid that we will need as many doses of antivenin as we can get."

"Do not go anywhere without escort." Dolan pointed at the men he'd left standing by the door. "Have those guards bring your things here." He waved his hand at a door on the near wall of the sitting room. "That is Mr. Fenchurche's study, where you'll find a work bench that will lend itself to your needs."

Ildwick patted Ivey on the arm. "Do you hear that? We're going to be roommates."

"Dolan?" Ivey lifted her wobbly head. "In my room—did they get it?"

"Not yet, but Officer Harwood's men are trained to handle situations like this. You need not worry."

"Sylvia . . . m'gun . . ." Ivey slurred. "I nee to go with . . ." Her eyes rolled back, and her head dropped mid-sentence.

"Are you sure she's all right, Mr. Curio?" Dolan asked.

"Positively. That drink was just what the doctor ordered. Sleep is her best medicine now."

"I must report back to Mrs. Fenchurche." Dolan turned to Sylvia before leaving. "If you need the doctor, send word."

As Dolan left, Ildwick felt something poking him. He turned his head to find Ivey's furious maid jamming the barrel of the dart gun into his back.

"You put sleeping elixir in that water."

"And you helped," he said.

"Only to stop those mutations. I don't like you one bit, so be warned, if you ever slip a potion into her drink again, I will be happy to shoot you."

"Be careful, Miss Feather," he teased. "I have a weakness for dangerous women." He waited a moment. "Will that be all?"

"No," Sylvia drove the barrel deeper into the fabric of his jacket. "I need you to carry her to Mr. Miles' bed."

Ildwick pretended to be shocked as he waggled his finger in her face. "Is that really any of my business?"

"They need to be where I can see both of them."

"Naturally, but I cannot forget that she took great offense when I suggested she climb beneath the master's sheets earlier this morning." Ildwick straightened his back.

"Don't make light of her feelings, Mr. Curio. Ivey and Miles were made for each other. Now get moving." Sylvia kicked at his calves.

"At once," Ildwick chuckled, tempted to linger and enjoy more of the girl's brash temperament. "Do not think for a moment that I haven't seen through your game, dear Sylvia. Your mistress is a still long way from accepting the bonds of matrimony, and it is obvious that until she does, you want me all for yourself."

Sylvia's mouth fell open. Her eyes flashed and her cheeks flushed.

"You're a bad man, Mr. Curio. A very bad man. Now get to it!" She waved the loaded gun in his face before storming into the bedroom.

Ildwick smirked. "She fancies me."

His face became serious as he lifted Ivey from the couch and started toward the bedroom.

"And you, Miss Thornton, have certainly thrown my plans into disarray. This world is coming apart at the seams, but I'll do what I can to keep you and your beloved alive. I owe that much to the house of Fenchurche."

Chapter Twenty-Four

THE LURKING THREAT

Winora awoke to find herself lying fully clothed in bed with the afternoon sun streaming through the window. She rubbed her brow, trying to recall how she had come to be sleeping in the middle of the day. Ivey's departure and Prim's arrival had made the past week tiring, but Winora rarely needed a nap.

"Mother, you will never believe what I saw." Iris burst into the room and launched herself onto the bed.

The scratches on her daughter's face took Winora back to the terrifying scene in the nursery. According to Arvel, it had been nothing more than a vision, but she snatched Iris and held her tightly, burying her nose in the girl's silky blond locks to be sure.

"You are my beautiful daughter," she sighed. Iris squirmed impatiently.

"Mother, let go. Something big and shiny just flew over the woods and landed in Father's garden."

Iris tried to wriggle away, but Winora held her tightly. "Iris, tell me who scratched your face."

"But Mother, you have to come see." Iris tried to back out of her arms.

"Not until you tell me what happened."

Iris fidgeted with the lace on her dress, trying to avoid her gaze.

"Mommy, don't make me say it," she finally whimpered, her lip quivering.

"I need to know, Iris."

"You can't be mad. She didn't mean to hurt me."

"Was it Prim?"

Iris shook her head. "No. She's a secret."

"A secret, like Ivey's creature?"

"No. She's always with me."

If it weren't for the tangible marks across the girl's face, Winora would have presumed that Iris was referring to one of her fantastical playmates. Being too young for her sisters' activities, Iris often entertained herself by coming up with games involving a host of odd characters—with foreign names and customs—whom no one but Iris could see or hear.

"Why would your friend harm you?"

"To stop me from listening to something bad."

Winora tensed. "Something bad?"

"I hear it sometimes. She told me to ignore it because it's not real, and it can't hurt me."

Winora's stomach lurched at the thought of her youngest daughter falling victim to the same strange affliction that was tormenting Prim.

Iris looked directly into her eyes and asked. "That's the truth, isn't it?"

Winora smiled bravely, putting her hand under Iris' chin and gently kissing her forehead. "It is, Iris. We shall both ignore it until it goes away."

"Darling?" Arvel appeared in the doorway, his hands full of wildflowers and herbs. "How is the most beautiful woman in the world feeling?"

"What is all that for?" She pointed at his fragrant bouquet.

"Well, I could claim that I'm a thoughtful husband, but this serves a purpose. Come here, Iris. I have a task for you."

"Yes, Father?" Iris bounced off the bed.

"Go to the middle garden and pick as many plants like these as you can find, enough to make sure that every room in the house has a vase full of them. Ask Neveah to help. Can you do all of that before dark?"

Iris grabbed his hand and gave it a tug. "Yes, but Father, something shiny and round came down from the sky and landed in your garden."

Arvel gave her a sly smile. "Wasn't it marvelous? It's my flying machine."

Iris looked at her mother in disbelief. "Can Father fly? Is it true?"

Winora nodded slowly. "If he says he can, it must be."

"Oh, Father! I want to see you fly." Iris clapped her hands in anticipation.

Arvel knelt down to give a stern warning. "You can watch me take off if you promise to stand a good distance away. That goes for every-one—especially you, my dear." Arvel smiled at his wife before turning back to Iris. "Now go and gather the plants."

Once Iris was gone, Arvel sat on the side of the bed. The look on his face was grim.

"What is it?" Winora reached for her husband's hand. "Are you leaving already?"

"There's something I have to go do. It may take a few days. While I'm away, I'd like to ask a favor, if you feel well enough."

"Of course. What is it?"

"Do you remember how we purified Thornhall when you first arrived?"

"Yes. That's why you need those plants."

"Winora, I'm beginning to fear that there is more to our daughters' strange episodes than just their exposure to the Zephyr's machinery. While I'm away, I need you to be vigilant and strong."

Winora held his hand tightly. "I know what happened in the nursery wasn't real, but in my heart, I believe something is trying to harm our children. First Ivey, then Prim, and even Iris is feeling its presence. What is this thing? How do we guard against something that exists only in illusions?"

"I hope to have answers when I return, but until then, you must keep your heart and our home full of light and love."

"That has always been my privilege." Winora stroked his cheek.

Arvel took her hand and kissed her fingers. "I've spoken to Stanley. He will work from here and help you watch for trouble." He sighed. "As much as it pains me to leave, I have to go."

"I see. Is there anything else I can do?" Winora asked.

The look in Arvel's eyes made her heart race as he leaned forward to whisper.

"I could use a kiss for luck."

"Come and claim it then." She could have lingered in his embrace forever, but someone cleared his throat.

Winora looked up. A young man in a vibrant orange waistcoat was standing in the open doorway.

"Oh, dear. I'm sorry. You asked me to tell you the minute everything was in order. I had no idea you were . . . ," he stammered, "I should have waited downstairs."

Arvel laughed. "Nicolai. This is my wife, Winora. Dear, meet Nicolai Slate."

Arvel helped Winora come to her feet. She was dizzy for a moment, but he steadied her.

"The lady's knees often go weak when we say our special goodbyes," her husband joked.

Winora blushed and smiled. "Arvel, please." Turning to the dark-eyed young man, Winora extended her hand. "I am honored to finally meet you, Nicolai. My husband tells me many wondrous things about your work."

The young man stared, failing to respond to her outstretched hand. Winora graciously withdrew, and he jumped back with an awkward bow.

"Please forgive me. I am not accustomed to socializing with such beautiful women."

Arvel coughed. "You've no one to blame but yourself, Nicolai. Come out of the lab once in a while and you might find a nice girl. Now, if you have finished charming my wife, we ought to be going."

Turning back to Winora, he added somberly, "Darling, it is very important that you take good care of yourself. When I return, we have some exciting news to discuss. Many changes are coming to Thornhall."

◑

Arvel escorted his wife and Nicolai down the staircase. Prim's husband was waiting for them in the foyer.

"Is this the one you wanted?" Stanley held out the large leather satchel that Arvel kept hanging in the study.

"Yes, thank you. It's up to you to look after my girls, Stanley, while Nicolai and I are away. And if Silas Harp or anyone from the Promacheon comes sniffing about looking for Ivey's creature. . ."

"That beast saved my wife from a nasty accident. I'll make sure they find nothing," Stanley said firmly. "Have a safe and successful trip, gentlemen. Mind the open water. Nobody yet knows how well our Zephyrs will perform over the seas."

"We shouldn't encounter any deep trenches on the way to—" Nicolai stopped himself and stuttered, "—to the coordinates." He looked down.

Arvel quickly spoke up to cover for him. "Nicolai and I have business in the Mesotomic Islands, a quaint village called—"

"Will my child die?" Winora asked in a strange and hollow voice.

Arvel tensed. "What's that you say?"

"It's going to take my baby." Her eyes glazed over and she began to sway.

Stanley gasped. "This is how it started with Prim."

"Winora?" Arvel grabbed his wife, protectively wrapping his arms around her.

Whatever she was experiencing was not only in her mind. Arvel felt it too; a terrible pressure had enveloped them. When he tried to resist it, the energy pushed back with more intensity.

Arvel did his best to relax and let the oppressive force flow around him until it finally dissipated, leaving his wife's body hanging limp against his.

Nicolai pulled back his sleeve and held out his arm for the others to see. The dark hair that ran along his forearm was standing straight up. "Did you feel that? The air is charged. The same thing happens around an unshielded otheophainer."

"Was it coming from the *Boreas*?" Stanley asked.

"It couldn't have, not when it's shielded. It must have been a disruption in the cosmocrene," Nicolai said.

Stanley looked down. "That's impossible. What could be powerful enough to cause a disturbance like that?"

Arvel knew the answer to that question.

The pulses Silas and his men transmitted through Aether's core of energy were not merely carrying messages; they were provoking an alien form of consciousness, one with the power to shake solid stone.

He'd hoped that the cipher equipment had fallen silent after his escape from the underground facility, but it appeared the machine's disruptive influence was becoming more dangerous.

"There's an instrument in my offices that may have recorded the signature of the disruption," Nicolai said. "Is there time to go to Cadenbury before we leave, Arvel?"

As he swept Winora into his arms and started for the staircase, Arvel replied, "No, I'm afraid our plans have just changed, gentlemen. I'll explain after I see to my wife."

Arvel was certain that Winora's terrible words had been a warning from whatever was lurking in the cosmocrene.

If he left to find the *Monarch* now, the entity would attack his wife and her unborn child.

॰ৄ

Chapter Twenty-Five

BRACED FOR A FIGHT

Minnette joined a small group of passengers and crewmen gathered on the bridge's loft at the request of Officer Harwood.

"When the captain sets us down, anyone who is not navigating this ship must be in the library," Harwood said.

"And what about my son?" Minnette interrupted.

"His condition has improved greatly," Doctor Brendel said. "When the time comes, I will oversee his relocation personally, madam."

"Thank you, Doctor." Minnette gave his arm a grateful tap. Mathias Brendel was one of the few people whom she held in a friendly light. "It is good to have you back on duty."

"May I continue?" Harwood interjected. "Once we hit the ground, my men will evacuate the passengers from the library. After they are moved a safe distance away, charges will be set off to demolish the ship's cabin."

"I beg your pardon?" Captain LeClere stood slowly. "Destroy the *Monarch*?"

"As a senior security officer of the Dicæon, it is my duty to terminate anything that threatens the greater good of our nation. Whatever's infesting this ship must not be let loose on the mainland. The only way to be sure it isn't is to blow this structure to smithereens and set fire to whatever remains."

The captain looked at Minnette. "Madam?"

"Very well, Officer Harwood," she conceded quietly. "Take whatever course of action you feel is necessary."

Minnette had already decided that no one in her family would set foot on the cursed ship again. Miles' condition was improving, but there was a risk that he had suffered permanent injuries. Minnette couldn't understand why her son had endangered his life for the Thornton girl, but she was determined never to let it happen again.

❧

Ildwick was watching the sun set through the portside window of the master suite when he heard Miles Fenchurche stir.

The young man stared up through the panel of glass above his bed for some time. His confused gaze fell on the wingback chair where Ildwick sat resting his crossed legs on the foot of the bed with an heirloom sword taken from a display in the suite's study lying across his lap.

Miles sat up, slowly rubbing his eyes.

Ildwick gave him a polite nod.

"We meet at last, Mr. Fenchurche."

He watched as Miles looked to his right and discovered Ivey sleeping in a man's nightshirt. Upon looking to his left, the young master found his chambermaid napping with her fingers coiled around the grip of a dart gun.

"Aren't they adorable when they're quiet?" Ildwick chuckled.

Miles blinked and looked back at him.

"I've been waiting to see that look on your face," Ildwick said with unabashed delight. "Would you believe that two of the more beautiful women on this ship insisted on bedding with you while you lay there like an aristocratic stump? I salute you, Mr. Fenchurche."

"It's a dream," Miles said softly. His eyes closed and he fell back onto the bed, startling Sylvia awake.

"Who's there?" She sat up and swept the gun across the room until her sights landed on Ildwick's chest. "What do you think you're doing?"

Ildwick lifted the sword with a grin. "Protecting your life and reputation, milady. It seemed that you and Miss Thornton were in need of a chaperone. People talk, you know."

Sylvia pushed her hair from her eyes with the back of her hand. "I didn't mean to fall asleep."

"I hope you don't mind that I moved you into the bed," Ildwick said in sincerity. "It's been a rough patch for you, my dear, and you tend to put your own needs last."

He stood. "Your master is showing signs of life, and I cannot imagine that Miss Thornton will tolerate sedation for much longer. Why don't I have the guards fetch something from the galley? You three have precious little time to regain your strength before the fun begins."

"What are you on about?" Sylvia whispered.

"In a matter of hours, if we reach the coast in one piece, the captain will perform a crash landing."

"Must this ship crash every last time I close my eyes?" Ivey grumbled from her side of the bed.

"See?" Ildwick said. "There she is now, all refreshed and hungry for the next reason to be annoyed."

"How long did I sleep?" Ivey stretched and yawned.

"Ivey?" Miles rolled over to stare at her. "Is that you?"

"Isn't it obvious?" Ivey asked. A second later, her face twisted, and she clapped her hands over her ears. "Oh no. I must look hideous."

"Not to worry, sunshine." Ildwick leaned forward. "The beauty sleep worked wonders. Your complexion is a paler shade of blue, and your ears are looking pretty again."

Ivey felt her head and inspected her arm. "So it seems."

She turned to Miles. "Enough about me. How are you feeling?"

He gave her a sappy smile. "Perfect."

Ivey peered into his eyes. "You look muddled."

Sylvia leaned in for a look. "Mr. Miles, do you know where you are?"

He sighed. "I've been to the heavens and back."

Ivey's expression silently accused Ildwick.

"He's just delighted to have woken between the two of you," Ildwick laughed. "I certainly would be."

"He wasn't like that before you came along. This had better not be the fault of your medicines," Ivey threatened. "Miles, we're still on board the *Monarch*. You nearly died during the storm. Can you remember anything that happened?"

"Yes," he pondered. "I was floating far away. Then there was a bright light that brought me back." Miles smiled dreamily at Ivey. "It was you."

"Ildwick? What's wrong with him?" Ivey demanded.

Ildwick pretended to frown. It was hard not to have a little fun her naïveté. "I'm sorry, Miss Thornton, but I'm afraid he's acquired a life-altering condition, rarely cured."

"Is there nothing we can do for him?" Ivey's lip trembled.

"You're a stinker, Mr. Curio," Sylvia scolded, catching onto his game. "He's teasing, miss. Mr. Miles is like this because he's—he's happy to be alive."

Ivey laid her hand on Miles' forehead. "I still think we should send for the doctor. Something is causing this confusion."

"Ivey. I am not confused, and I don't need a doctor." Miles pulled her right hand from his brow and laid it over his chest. "Can't you feel it? My heart is beating just as hard as yours."

"We can't be certain," Ivey argued.

Miles took her other hand and pressed it against her own heart. "Yes we can."

Her mouth dropped open and tears brimmed in her eyes.

"What's wrong?" Miles asked.

"Nothing," Ivey said. "You're alive. You're alive and happy."

Miles squeezed her hand affectionately, but Ivey snatched it away, leaving his palm resting against her chest.

Ivey froze as both of their faces turned bright red. Sylvia buried her face in her hands. Before Miles could withdraw his hand, the bedroom door flew open and Minnette's entourage swept into the room.

Ildwick snickered to himself.

"Miles!" Minnette shrieked so sharply that she nearly choked herself.

Ivey toppled backward off the bed with a cry of her own.

Minnette glowered at Dolan suspiciously. "Is this why I was being kept from my son? What kind of deplorable behavior has been going on in here?"

Armed men swarmed into the master bedroom, believing that there had been another attack. Miles was nearly smothered, and the young women were gruffly inspected for any wounds while Ildwick sat back in his chair and enjoyed the spectacle.

∾

Ivey wrestled herself free from the commotion and escaped into the privacy of Miles' bath. She meant to wash her face at the basin, but a nauseating odor coming from the crystal tub drew her attention. She knelt down and peered inside. A column of foul-looking water had backed up into the drainpipe.

She heard Sylvia enter behind her.

"I've got you some clean clothes from Mr. Miles' wardrobe," she said. "I am sorry about all this, miss. I wanted you to sleep comfortably, so I put you in one of Mr. Miles' nightshirts. I never thought his mother would come—"

"Never mind that. She could hardly think any less of me now." Ivey took the garments that Sylvia offered and rose to dress herself. "I see the ship is still on high alert. Tell me everything that has happened. And why does this bathroom smell so dreadful?"

Sylvia sniffed the air. "It seems fine to me."

"You can't smell that?"

Sylvia shook her head.

"It was worse a moment ago, coming from the drain." She looked down. The water had disappeared. "That canteen water tasted rotten, too. I'm afraid the *Monarch*'s water supplies have gone bad on us."

"I lied," Sylvia blurted out. "Mr. Curio put a sleeping elixir in your drink. I hated it, but you were having the mutations, and he said sleep would stop them."

Ivey waved her hand. "You're not to blame, Sylvia. I'd wring that man's neck if he hadn't been right. I do admit that I feel a thousand times better." She buttoned up the front of the shirt.

"What now?" Hearing raised voices, Ivey put her ear to the bathroom door and listened.

"Mother, tell Captain LeClere that I will not allow the Dicæon to destroy my ship," Miles said angrily.

"Your ship, Miles? Since when have you shown any care for the good of Fenchurche Industries and its property?"

"I care deeply about the *Monarch*, and so does Ivey."

"Don't bring that girl into this. I've had my fill of her outrageous conduct and this disaster of a voyage. My decision is final. As soon as we reach land, the captain will set us down, and we will abandon this ship before Officer Harwood detonates the cabin. Until that time, you will try to act like a gentleman and keep that poor excuse for a lady out of your bed."

Ivey heard more than one loud gasp.

"Mother! You were the one who insisted that I accept her into my marriage bed," Miles shouted. "You brought her to me. For that I owe you a debt of gratitude, but I will not allow you to disparage her character."

"Her disgraceful character is not my greatest concern," Minnette snapped back. "I have serious doubts that you will ever fill your father's shoes."

There was no response.

Ivey heard the doctor mutter something about Miles' heart.

She cracked the door open and saw that Doctor Brendel was already giving Miles an injection. "Take deep breaths, and try to stay calm until the sedative takes effect," he said, easing Miles back onto the bed.

The doctor cast an angry look at the crewmen and staff who'd accompanied Minnette to the suite.

"Would everyone get the hell out?" As they scattered, he turned to Minnette and offered his arm. "May I escort you to the bridge, madam?"

"I'm his mother. He needs me."

"Please. His heart needs peace and quiet."

Minnette spun on her heel and stormed out of the room. Doctor Brendel searched his pockets to retrieve a medicine bottle, then rushed after her.

Ivey stepped back and closed the bathroom door quietly.

"How dare she!"

"What is it, miss?" Sylvia whispered.

"That woman is going to let Harwood destroy the *Monarch*. Why would they do something so insane?"

"They've no choice, miss. The slimy little beast is every bit as wicked as you said. Since you were sleeping, two crewmen were attacked and another killed. The fiend goes through locked doors without a trace. Truth be told, I don't think the officer's men have a clue how to find it."

Ivey rolled up the sleeves of Miles' shirt. "If the *Monarch*'s fate rests upon destroying the leech before we make land, then I will hunt that creature down and kill it myself."

"What can I do to help?"

"Repack my satchel, and then go find Mr. Curio. I need him to do something for me."

"He's probably back in Mr. Miles' study," Sylvia muttered softly. "I wouldn't trust that one as far as I could throw him."

"I don't," Ivey said. "But I'll need an ally with his skills."

After Sylvia left, Ivey quickly washed up and finished outfitting herself for the task ahead. She used a pair of Miles' suspenders to hold the rolled-up trousers in place, and then she tucked her hair under one of his felt riding caps.

When Ivey emerged from the bathroom, Miles had fallen back into a deep sleep. Her satchel was sitting on a small dining table that had been brought into the bedroom and set with a meal.

"I don't have time for this," she started to argue, but Sylvia took her firmly by the arm and sat her down in one of the chairs.

"You are skin and bones, Miss Ivey. If you're determined to go after that monster, I demand that you eat a decent meal first." She held out a pair of black boots. "And you'll be needing these too."

"I can't take your shoes, Sylvia."

"Oh yes you will." Sylvia resolutely crossed her arms.

"I thought there were rules, many rules," Ivey reminded her with a smirk.

"I'll be happy to return to the old rules when we get to Ferndale, miss, but this is a matter of survival. Now eat up."

Seeing a second place set at the table, Ivey said, "At least you'll be joining me."

"No." Sylvia sighed. "That's for Mr. Curio. Even he deserves a last meal."

Ivey looked down at her lap. "So, you think it's that hopeless?"

"Not at all!" Sylvia exclaimed. "You were born for this fight, miss. That creature is not long for this world, of that I am certain." She laid her hand on Ivey's shoulder. "I just want this over with so that awful man will go away and leave us alone."

Without turning her head, Ivey spoke. "Did you hear that, Ildwick?"

"Are we on a first-name basis now?" The chemist stepped out from behind the partially opened door to the sitting room.

"All this for me, Sylvia?" He smiled as he closed the door then took a seat across from Ivey. "They say good cooking is the quickest way to a man's heart."

"Tell that to the portly fellow who's manning the galley. I only set the table."

Hunger and urgency gave Ivey an excuse to abandon polite table manners. She stuffed a large forkful of roasted potatoes into her mouth and looked up at Ildwick. "Did you do what I asked?"

"No. I'm afraid your plan has a flaw."

He pulled her spare dart cartridges from his pocket and laid them on the table.

Ivey pursed her lips. "How so? Harwood's guards aren't going to let us leave this suite."

"True, but even if I could dilute your tranquilizers to a limited dose," he jabbed his thumb at the door, "it would take every last shot to neutralize all the men in that sitting room. That would leave your friends here unprotected. Not to mention that your barrel would be empty for the big hunt."

"We'll fight our way out, then." Ivey went back to her food.

"You aren't very subtle for a lady, but then again, you eat like a man."

Ivey made a show of talking with her mouth full. "I'd love to hear the ingenious plan you've come up with."

"Miss Feather creates a diversion in the master bath, and we slip past the guards and disappear down the dark corridor. No fuss, no muss."

"Fine. Let's do it." Ivey pushed back from the table.

"Hold your horses." Ildwick took another sip of his stew. "I have something else for you." He pulled another dart from his breast pocket.

When Ivey snatched for it, he drew it back quickly. "Be careful! It took everything I had to make a cocktail that can kill what we're going up against. This is the only helping, so use it wisely." Ildwick carefully placed the dart in Ivey's hand.

She found the phosphorescent chalk in her satchel, and used it to mark the sides of the cartridge before wrapping the dart in her napkin and stowing it in the bag.

"You're not planning to load it?" he asked.

"It's wise to hold fire until you know your enemy."

"Will you ever cease to surprise me? There's more to you than pleases the eye, Miss Thornton."

Ivey loaded her gun with one of the other tranquilizer cartridges. "I was trained well, Mr. Curio, but I should warn you. These leeches have shown the ability to take control of me, so be prepared to defend yourself if needed."

"Have you always been afraid of leeches?"

Ivey's eyes narrowed. "I never said that I was afraid of them."

"You didn't have to," Ildwick stated. "May I share some advice?"

Ivey looked away.

"I will take that as a yes." Ildwick leaned forward and waited until she finally gave in and made eye contact with him. "Fear is the only thing that can control someone like you, Ivey. Master your emotions, or they will be your downfall."

"I believe what you say, but what's happening on this ship goes beyond fear," Ivey softly admitted. "I've had dreams that feel completely real; then I wake up and it's as if I'm still trapped in a dream. My nightmares are becoming reality, and I can't help but wonder if somehow it's me that is endangering the *Monarch*."

"You give yourself too much credit. The force driving this ship toward oblivion is no figment of your imagination. It existed long before you found yourself tangled in this web of unreal terrors. The danger this entity poses is grave, but you are an unexpected element in a greater equation. Keep your wits until it reveals itself. You'll know when it's time to take your shot."

Ivey sat quietly, hoping the man would reveal the depth of his knowledge on the ship's mysterious predicament.

When his attention returned to his stew, she had to ask, "So, Ildwick, where exactly do you fit into the equation? Friend or foe?"

"It is a dreadfully complicated story, and we do not have the luxury of time. By my estimate, we will be in sight of land shortly after sunrise. If we are going to save your ship, Miss Thornton, we had better get moving."

"This isn't my ship," Ivey corrected him, scooping the remaining dart cartridges into the front pocket of her satchel as she rose.

"It will be some day, Mrs. Fenchurche."

Ivey felt an odd sense of melancholy upon hearing those words. That was a future that would never come to pass, but her respect for Miles was something that she would hold for the rest of her days.

If they survived the night, she would set things straight before causing him any more grief. She walked to the bedside and touched his arm. "Miles, can you wake up? I need your help."

His eyes were closed, but his lips moved. "Destroy it, Ivey."

"I promise I won't stop until that thing is dead," she assured him.

"Listen carefully," he whispered, his hand suddenly gripping her arm. "Destroy the cipher device."

"The what?" Ivey touched his face.

A powerful life force was running through Miles' body, filling the air around her.

Ivey closed her eyes and focused on the energy.

"What?" she whispered to herself.

The mark of Miles' soul had been intermingled with an unmistakably familiar pattern. A different spirit was flowing through his body, one that she recognized.

"Father?" She grabbed his shoulders and leaned close to his face. "I can hear you."

Miles' eyes opened, and the impression of her father vanished.

"Ivey?" he mumbled.

She stepped back, repeating the words of Arvel's message in her mind, so she wouldn't forget.

"What is it?" Miles asked.

"Nothing. You were speaking in your sleep." She glanced over at Ildwick.

"A problem?" he asked, seemingly unaware.

"None." She turned back to Miles. "How do you feel?"

"Like I've slept for years."

Ivey crossed her arms, "Well, it's time to rise and shine, sir. If we're going to keep Harwood from blowing up your ship, you'll have to find me a diagram that shows every nook and cranny in which predator might be able to hide itself."

Miles squinted his drowsy eyes and frowned. "Ivey, what are you up to?"

Ivey smiled. "What I do best, Mr. Fenchurche. I am going to start a ruckus, and you are going to help me."

Chapter Twenty-Six

Wading into Battle

Prim tossed and turned in her bed. The thunder rumbling against the windowpanes startled her, which made the baby kick again. She threw back the coverlet, sat up, and searched the rug for her slippers. Not finding them, she hurried down the hall in bare feet.

Once she was inside the nursery, Prim's gaze fell upon her daughter Neveah's empty trundle. She went to Seren's bed to see if the sisters were huddling together to find comfort from the storm, but it was also barren. Prim ran to her infant's crib.

"Celeste? No!" she screamed, tearing at the empty sheets.

Hearing a faint sound from somewhere far away, she clasped both hands across her mouth and strained to make out what it was.

A child!

She raced from the nursery and down the main staircase.

"Neveah, Seren. Where did you go?" The only answer was another clap of thunder that shook the walls. "Please! Someone help me," Prim cried.

A splashing sound came from the garden room. Prim whirled and dashed toward the entrance of the atrium. "Neveah? Are you in there?"

A voice called to her, but it was muffled and distorted. Prim stopped at the top of the atrium steps. Part of her knew what would happen if she went any further, but she had to save her children. As she moved forward, every one of her steps was met with resistance. She held her breath and pushed on.

When lightning illuminated the room, Prim found herself standing waist deep in murky water. She dipped her hand into the pool and swirled it around, feeling nothing but air. A prickling sensation caused her to draw back.

Swarms of inky maggots were feeding on her hand. She looked down and saw even more of them burrowing into her pregnant belly through the bloodied fabric of her nightgown.

Prim lurched backward, clutching her stomach. She turned and stumbled toward the stairs as a dark form came churning after her. It emerged from the water and grabbed her.

This time the dream continued as Prim was dragged under the water. Unable to hold her breath in her panic, she inhaled. The cold water burned its way into her lungs like lye.

Prim's last thought was how sad it was to be leaving her family. She regretted that her baby would never know the warmth of a mother's arms.

∾

Arvel followed the sound of his youngest daughter's screams down the path to the pond. As he approached, the glow of his lamp fell upon a chilling scene. Iris was crouched on the mossy bank cradling her sister's head in her lap while a bloodied waterdog stood guard over the two.

"What happened?" he exclaimed as he knelt down and set the lantern beside Prim's sodden body.

"I don't know," Iris said softly. "Beast was howling, so I came to see what was wrong. Prim was drowning in the cove, but Beast went and got her. He's hurt too."

"Take him to the stable and stay there," Arvel said as he rolled his oldest daughter onto her side. Slipping one arm beneath her ribs, Arvel gently compressed her midsection to clear her airway. He kept at it until she spat up a dark fluid and began to choke in air.

Arvel lifted her in his arms and rushed back to the manor.

Winora followed him to Prim's bedroom and tended to her while he went for the family doctor in his new Zephyr.

∾

Winora was sitting on the edge of the bed, humming a lullaby when Prim came back to consciousness. She smiled innocently and nestled into the warmth of the bed, seemingly unaware of all that had happened.

The doctor gestured for Arvel to follow him from the room.

"She looks to be out of danger, and the baby is moving. If her lungs do not take an infection, she will be fine. I am, however, concerned by her mental state. If the young lady is trying to harm herself, we'll need to commit her to a sanitarium."

"That won't happen," Arvel said curtly.

"Arvel, with your mother's history, you can't take any chances."

Arvel took him by the arm and walked away from the bedroom door. "The reason I sent for you has nothing to do with my mother," he said.

"Nothing? Primrose was in same spot where your mother's nightgown was discovered. Are you sure your daughter doesn't know what became of Ann?"

"Doctor Swift, no one knows what happened that night. I will never believe that she took her own life." Arvel lowered his voice. "I've chosen not to burden anyone in my family with the matter. I will thank you to respect my discretion."

"I've been taking care of your family since you were a boy, Arvel. I only have your best interests at heart. Sometimes a hard choice must be made for loved ones at risk."

"Locking Prim in a cell now won't protect her from the danger she faces."

"She would have supervision day and night."

"Enough!" Arvel rarely spoke so harshly. "I will take responsibility for her well-being. You have voiced your concerns; now leave us."

The doctor quickly packed his bag and showed himself to the front door.

Winora looked up at Arvel when he reentered the bedroom.

"She's asleep."

"How are you managing?"

She laid a hand against her waist and gave him a weak smile. "I will be fine, but I'm glad you didn't have to leave us." She adjusted the covers over Prim. "I do wish Stanley were here. Prim needs her husband as much as I do."

Arvel had chosen not to tell Winora about the dangerous events befalling the *Monarch*. With Prim's affliction worsening, he couldn't put his wife's delicate condition at risk by adding any more worries to her heart.

"Why don't you go to bed? I'll sit with her."

Winora stood. "First, I want you to be honest with me, Arvel."

Arvel sighed softly. "What is it?"

"Prim's clothing was torn and there are marks on her body. Did the creature in the pond have a part in this?"

"Yes. Somehow Prim was caught in that damned tree where Ivey nearly drowned. There's no way I could have gotten to her in time, but Beast did. He saved her life."

"Are you sure?"

"Iris heard him howling. She was there when he pulled her out of those branches."

Winora rose to her feet. "Where is he?"

"In the stable with Iris. He has injuries that need tending to before he can return to the water."

"I will see to him, Arvel." Winora put a firm hand on his arm. "In my heart, I know that something evil is threatening our children. If Ivey's creature is determined to guard them, I will gratefully accept his aid."

After she left, Arvel paced the floor.

His own heart was heavy with worry and guilt. Winora was right. Something evil had set its eye on his family. His efforts to project a warning to Ivey about the cipher device had been punished with an attack on Prim. It seemed that every move he made to save his family was being countered by a force beyond his comprehension.

Once the ship is safe, that damned machine must be destroyed.

∾

"We'll only have one chance to do this, Ildwick, so don't trip over your sword."

Ivey climbed into Miles' wardrobe alongside the chemist, struggling to position herself as far away from the man as the cramped space would allow.

If everything went according to plan, the two of them would be able to slip past the unwitting Dicæon guardsmen and out into the family parlor.

"Now, Sylvia," Ivey called out before pulling the wardrobe door shut. From the master bathroom, her maid let out a blood-curdling scream.

Ivey heard the sound of the bedroom door being flung open and guards shouting orders.

"Something moved behind the tub!" Sylvia wailed convincingly.

Ivey opened the cabinet door a crack to see what was happening. When the last of the men had entered the bath, she and Ildwick crept out of the wardrobe and through the open door to the parlor.

They headed for Ivey's suite to search for any trail the creature might have left behind. As they navigated the debris that littered the dimly lit parlor, Ivey sensed a presence. She raised her hand and stopped.

Ildwick spun around, setting his back against hers, sword raised. Ivey pointed her gun at something moving along the glass garden wall.

"Who is it?"

"I didn't mean to startle you." Dolan stepped out of the shadows.

"Dolan! What are you doing wandering about the ship? You will get yourself killed," Ivey said.

"So will you, miss," he replied evenly. "I suspected that you would try as much, so I borrowed something from the captain's loft and came to offer assistance." He held up a long metal contraption.

"What is that?" Ivey hadn't seen anything quite like it. It resembled a crossbow, but the barbed shaft of its bolt was attached to a long coil of rope.

"An old whaling harpoon," Ildwick said. "And a sturdy one at that. A tad bulky for our purposes, though." Ildwick took the heavy weapon and placed it on a table. "Thank you, Dolan. We'll know where it is if we need it."

"Dolan, is anyone in my suite?" Ivey asked.

"It is under watch."

"If you want to help us, order the guards away." She glanced at Ild-wick. "See? No fuss, no muss."

"I'll tell them that they are wanted on the bridge, but that will have consequences."

"Do what you can to keep them away. After that, lie low. This might get dangerous."

"I am responsible for the safety of the passengers and this ship. If seeing that responsibility through endangers my life, then so be it."

Ivey smiled. "Please be careful. I'd hate to lose a friend."

Dolan shrugged. "No one would hate that more than I, Miss Ivey."

She embraced him, which he accepted with all the tenderness of a wooden plank.

Ivey laughed. "Does anyone in Fenchurche Industries ever express affection?"

"No," Dolan replied simply. With that, he turned and approached the door of Ivey's suite.

"If you're in need of a better hug, I'm amenable," Ildwick offered.

"I've had every bit of physical contact I care to endure with you." Ivey shuddered and crouched back against the wall.

Ildwick joined her with a righteous sniff. "I kept my word to re-main on my side of the closet. It was the sword that did not respect your—"

"Shhh," Ivey warned. The door opened, and Dolan spoke to the men inside. As they left for the bridge, he made a subtle gesture behind his back, encouraging them to make haste.

Once inside her suite, Ivey took a few deep breaths, hoping to soothe her nerves. For the time being, the catalyst in her blood seemed to be dormant. To keep it that way, she would have to stay calm.

She moved around the room, taking note of every detail, but finding nothing out of the ordinary.

"How could it get out of this room without leaving a trail?" she wondered aloud.

She turned to the bedroom door, steeling herself before pulling open the handle. To her relief, the lamp sconces were still alight inside the room. She pushed the sliding lever on the wall to increase the flow of gas, but the lights barely brightened. She fiddled with the valve lever.

"They must be conserving the fuel," Ildwick said behind her. "The last thing anyone on this ship needs now is to be left alone in the dark."

"That doesn't explain why it was so dark in here this morning." She walked toward the bed and leaned over to look up at the glass panel overhead.

It was covered in a thick, fibrous substance, not unlike an insect's cocoon.

"What in blazes is this?"

Ildwick joined her. "The little booger must be starting a family."

"You told me they were infants."

"Their life cycle may be more expedient than I imagined."

"Only one of them survived. How could it reproduce by itself?"

"Some species don't need a mate to spawn. There may already be more of them out there."

"Give me your sword." Ivey reached for it.

"I wouldn't do that." Ildwick drew back. "The little bundles of joy might drop right on our heads."

"Better to face them now then wait until they're thirsty for blood," Ivey said. "Stand back if you're squeamish."

Ildwick handed her the sword, stepping back with crossed arms. "This is on you."

Ivey raised the sword and sliced through the center of the web, jumping back before anything could fall out. It split open, exposing an empty cavity lined with fine hairs. Ivey's hand flew across her face as a malodorous cloud of dust rained down from inside the cocoon.

"Happy now?" Ildwick gagged as he waved the fouled air away from his face.

She handed Ildwick the sword and ran to the bathroom. "I'll check in here while this mess clears out."

Inside the bath, Ivey spotted a streak of black sludge leading up the leg of the crystal tub and over its side. She cautiously approached and peered down. The bottom of the tub was covered with a dark residue.

"That's a nasty ring," Ildwick said from behind her.

"Do you think it was looking for water?" Ivey asked.

There was no answer. "Ildwick?"

Ivey's vision blurred, and her ears burned. Much like when Minnette nearly fell from the landing in the private parlor, she had a strange awareness of a soul in distress.

Someone grabbed her from behind.

Ivey blinked. She was in the darkened interior of the glass garden.

A husky voice drawled in her ear, "Now darling, you didn't really think we were coming here to pick flowers, did you?"

Ivey felt her lips move as a frightened girl's voice answered. "Take me back to the library. I don't like it here."

"Don't play coy with me."

The arms around her tightened. Ivey tried to resist, but although she was aware of the girl's body, she had no control over it.

The girl managed to break free and spin around. Through her eyes, Ivey saw Paisley Fitzroy glaring down at her.

"You're quite a tease, Amelia Buxhill, but this time, you'll get everything you deserve." With that, he shoved her to the ground.

Ivey felt a sharp pain when Amelia's head struck a hard surface.

Paisley was standing over her. Then something moved in the darkness behind him.

He turned and slowly backed away as a dark form advanced out of the shadows.

What followed was a horrifying jumble of sensations. There was a low hiss and agonized screams amid the flapping wings and cries of frightened birds.

Ivey felt something rip Amelia's cheek, and the warmth of blood running down her chin.

The rush of pain ended when Ivey's senses returned to her own body. She was still standing beside the tub in her suite.

"What's wrong? You looked like you were possessed," Ildwick said.

Ivey tightened her grip on the gun in her hand. "I know where it is!" She ran from the suite and fled down the stairs toward the lobby.

When she rounded the side of the garden, Amelia Buxhill's bloody face was pressed against the glass. The only light came from the full moon outside the lobby's windows. In the gloomy atmosphere of the garden room, it was hard to make out what had Amelia pinned against the garden wall.

The girl's panicked gaze met Ivey's, pleading for help. Ivey nodded and raised her gun.

Before Ivey could take a step, Amelia's head was jerked backward violently. Her arms flew up as she fell. By the time her body hit the floor, it was as dry and shriveled as the murdered crewman's had been.

Ildwick cursed in shock and disgust.

Ivey forced herself to stay focused on killing the creature.

On the floor behind Amelia's body, a dark mass surrounded by a pool of water pulsated as if it were digesting its victim's life.

Ivey clenched her teeth and started for the vestibule door.

"No." Ildwick grabbed her sleeve. "Load the poison dart."

Ivey broke free from his grasp and jerked open the outer door of the garden entry. "We'll lose it."

"Not if we block the door."

"It doesn't use doors."

Ivey passed through the vestibule and ran into the darkness of the glass garden.

She heard something move to her right.

"Ivey," Ildwick called out from behind her, "stay next to me." He cursed again as he ran into a table.

Her eyes hadn't adjusted to the dim lighting, and it was impossible to hear over the racket that Ildwick was making.

Ivey relaxed her shoulders, closed her eyes, and felt for the creature's terrible presence. She let its powerful life force pull her forward. Keeping her eyes shut, she moved through the garden like a ghost, her feet barely touching the floor.

You're too close. Stop.

Ivey had to force her eyes open.

Something was on the garden path several paces ahead of her. It had the silhouette of a leech, but it was nearly the height of her knees. None of her father's reference books had ever described a species of this magnitude.

The surface of its hide glistened in the gloomy light, but the details of its body were hard to make out.

As it slithered through the puddle of water, two red orbs bubbled to the top and turned toward her.

Eyes?

It drew closer. Ivey was horrified by what she saw.

The water on the floor was oozing up into the creature's mass, allowing its body to stretch into the air, growing taller and taller until it was the size of a man.

It had no arms or legs, just one great mass of undulating tissue.

Below its red eyes, a dark hole opened and an articulated appendage began to emerge. Ivey recognized the Y-shaped pattern of its razor-sharp teeth.

The creature emitted a low hiss as it extended its jaws in her direction.

Ivey was overcome with terror at the sight.

Ildwick had been right. If she couldn't master her emotions, she would be the monster's next victim.

She focused her mind on the soothing sound of falling water in the stone fountain until she was able to take a step back and raise her gun.

Her hand was shaking too hard to deliver a good shot at its center, so she tried to steady her right arm with her left.

Before she could squeeze the trigger, the creature lurched forward.

A beam of moonlight fell across a grotesque replica of Amelia's face that had formed around the red eyes.

"Misfit!" its garbled voice taunted as it spat on her.

Ivey felt a paralyzing jolt as something struck her neck.

An instant before the hungry jaws reached her cheek, the flash of a polished blade passed in front of her, severing the appendage. It fell to the ground, where it whipped and coiled like an injured snake.

Ildwick grabbed her waist and pulled her backward several paces; the creature melted to the ground. It hissed in pain, sprouting two pairs of stubby arms, which it used to crawl away into the darkness.

"Are you hurt?" Ildwick asked.

Ivey couldn't speak. Ildwick dragged her back toward the vestibule. Through the glass wall, she saw bobbing lights and heard voices.

"Harwood!" Ildwick dropped her next to Amelia's body and rushed off.

"Down here! Hurry! I've got at least one dead girl on my hands."

As she lay there, Ivey felt the cold poison spreading through her body. She'd been stung.

∾

Sylvia was just clearing the dinner tray she'd brought for Miles when Ildwick kicked open the bedroom door and charged into the room with Ivey in his arms.

"How steady are your hands, Mr. Fenchurche?" Ildwick said as he laid Ivey on the bed. "Sylvia, get me his surgical kit."

Sylvia grabbed the heavy cloth case from a side table and set it on the edge of the bed, then hurried around to help Miles stand. His body trembled, but he was able to join Ildwick on the other side of the bed.

She followed, peering around Miles' shoulder. What she saw made her feel sick.

Ivey's eyes were dead and frozen open. A large thorn with a bulbous end protruded from the side of her neck.

"We have to remove the stinger," Ildwick said. "If it's barbed, it won't come out easily." He pointed to the venom sac at the end. "Put any pressure on that, and it'll kill her."

Miles opened the bag and removed a pair of large tweezers. He pulled them apart, bending the metal so they would remain partially open.

Sylvia instinctively grabbed a wad of bandage gauze and soaked it with sterilizing solution. "Here, sir."

Miles took it and wiped the tweezers. He steadied his hand and carefully lowered the tips in place, using them to push the skin back from the stinger.

"Take it out," he said to Ildwick.

At the chemist's first touch, Sylvia saw the venom sac begin to pulse.

"What did you do?" she asked.

"Dammit. It's got a trigger," Ildwick said as he pinched the base of the barb to stop the venom's flow. He yanked on the stalk, but its hooks were firmly embedded in the muscles of Ivey's neck.

"Stop. I'll have to cut it out," Miles said.

"No time," Ildwick replied through clenched teeth. "If the poison seeps into my fingers, I won't be able to hold it."

"I can drain it." Sylvia grabbed a syringe from the surgical bag, pierced the venom sac, and carefully drew the liquid out.

"Smart girl," Ildwick said. "Now, find something to tie off the base so Mr. Fenchurche can dig this thing out."

Remembering Ivey's green ribbon in her apron pocket, Sylvia pulled it out and tied it tightly around the bottom of the stinger.

Miles handed the tweezers to Ildwick, and Sylvia dug through the medical bag until she found a surgical knife. She sterilized it then handed it to Miles. "What can I do?"

"Get me more light," he said.

She ran to a side table and returned with a lamp.

While she held it close, Miles eased the tip of the knife around the stinger, freeing Ivey's tissue from its hooks. He had it out within seconds.

Sylvia cringed when Ildwick leaned down and sucked the wound, quickly spitting the poisoned blood into his handkerchief.

She sterilized another length of gauze and handed it to Miles.

"Let it bleed a minute to flush out more venom," Ildwick advised.

When the bleeding slowed, Miles cleaned the wound while Sylvia searched for the tin of balm in the satchel that was still slung across

Ivey's body. She used the remains to stop the bleeding and seal the torn skin.

"Now what?" Miles' legs were shaking. He sank down onto the side of the bed.

Ildwick reached into his breast pocket and produced a syringe of antivenin.

"We hope this works." He injected the serum into Ivey's neck. "It takes a while. Perhaps you should lie down, Mr. Fenchurche. I'll watch her."

"I'm the one who should be at her side, Mr. Curio."

Ildwick gave Sylvia a wry look. "I see we've been introduced. Have you told him everything about me?"

"You can be sure," Sylvia said with a pert nod. She'd wasted no time sharing her misgivings about the chemist.

"Well, there is more." Ildwick rubbed his eyes. "And it isn't good. Ivey was afraid of these creatures for a good reason."

"Why do you say that?" Miles asked.

"The leeches were only hosts."

"Hosts? To what?"

"I'm afraid we're dealing with some sort of asymbiant."

"What is that?" Sylvia asked.

"They are shapeless bloodsuckers, Miss Feather, that feed, grow, and adapt, borrowing whatever physical traits they fancy from their prey. Depending on whom and what they eat, they can become rather nasty."

"Things that shift shapes aren't real, Mr. Curio," Sylvia said bluntly.

"If only that were true. My work takes me to many strange locales. I've become accustomed to things that defy explanation, but I never expected to encounter asymbiants on your ship, Mr. Fenchurche. I would like to know how they ended up in the good doctor's infirmary."

Sylvia had to speak up. "If you knew about these monsters, why didn't you warn us?"

"Until I saw this one on the hunt, I had no idea it was an asymbiant. I never would have suspected one to resemble something as small and vulnerable as a leech. They tend to be great, ugly things."

Miles laid his hand on Ivey's arm. "And we forced her to submit to them."

"Luckily, you killed the ones that fed on her blood. Miss Thornton bears certain traits that we would not want an enemy to acquire."

"They will never touch her again." Miles' jaw clenched. "How do we exterminate such a monstrosity?"

"Regarding that, I have good news," Ildwick replied. "I managed to wound it before it got away. Asymbiants require time to master a complex morphology such as our own, and until it does so, it will be as vulnerable to pain and injury as we are."

"How much time do we have?" Miles asked.

"Not long. We discovered an empty nest above Ivey's bed. It's looking to reproduce, and now that it's sampled our species, it will soon fill its nest with a new generation that is all but invincible to our race."

Sylvia looked down at Ivey's petrified face. "Shouldn't your serum be working by now, Mr. Curio?"

"I would hope so."

She rubbed Ivey's cheek. "C'mon, miss. Your blood beat these things before."

"Maybe it didn't." Miles jumped to his feet. "She needs a serum made from my blood."

"You haven't been exposed to the venom," Ildwick said.

"I can be." Miles picked up the syringe Sylvia had used to drain the poison sac and handed it to Ildwick. "You know what we have to do."

∽

Chapter Twenty-Seven

On the Hunt

Ivey drifted in and out of consciousness. She felt as if she were floating along in a cool stream of water. Somewhere up ahead, she heard voices. Male voices. She was getting close enough to hear what they were saying.

"We're at the point of no return," a deep voice said.

"What do you mean?"

"Curio says this thing will be ready to lay eggs. Before it killed the girl, it was feeding on birds in the garden. What if it grows wings and escapes before we can get to the mainland and destroy this cabin?"

"Shouldn't we warn the captain?"

"No, it's too late for that. If the asymbiant makes it off this ship and starts to multiply, Cemarian citizens will be slaughtered by the thousands. The *Monarch* has to go down at sea."

"But this ship is carrying many important passengers."

"That is a sacrifice that must be made, Faust. There's no other way."

Ivey had heard that name before. In her foggy state, it took a moment to remember that he was the Dicæon officer she'd shot in the leg.

"All right," the man said. "How will we do it?"

The deeper voice was answering, but Ivey could no longer make out the words of the conversation. She continued forward into the blackness.

Ivey blinked. Concerned faces hovered above hers.

"It's starting to work," said Sylvia.

Little by little, Ivey felt her body coming back to life.

"Come on, sunshine, show us that smile," Ildwick said.

Ivey's lips worked hard to form words. "Shut up."

"There she is." Ildwick cracked his hands together and laughed.

"Is it dead?" she whispered.

His smile vanished. "No. You were right about the door. It seems to pass through solid walls. Harwood's men surrounded that garden, and the thing still escaped."

The vision of Amelia's cruel death made Ivey moan.

"Are you hurting, miss?" Sylvia asked.

"Pain is a good sign." Ildwick lifted her arm and gave it a pinch. "Does that hurt?"

Ivey took a small breath. "I can't tell."

"Give it some time," Ildwick reassured her. "You were hit with an especially noxious projectile. Our foe is perfecting its ability to hunt."

"It's a shape shifter, Miss Ivey," Sylvia added.

Ivey's questioning gaze went back to Ildwick.

"An asymbiant, actually. It can acquire physical traits from the prey it claims. This one's transforming at an incredible pace, as is its venom. Your innate resistances proved ineffective this time. Luckily, your fiancé helped us prepare a new serum."

"How?"

"I injected venom from the stinger into his blood."

"You did what?" Ivey hissed through her teeth.

Sylvia laid a hand on her arm. "Mr. Curio just mixed a bit of Mr. Miles' blood with the monster's poison to make you a new medicine. He's fine, miss."

"Where is he?" Ivey asked.

"He went to wash up and get dressed."

"In the bath?"

Ivey's mind lit up with a series of images: the dark stain in her bathtub, the pool of water around the creature, and the foul liquid in the drain of Miles' bath.

The creature had been using the drainage system to get around the ship.

Miles! It could be in there right now!

Ivey tried to jump up, but her muscles barely responded. Her panicked efforts to sit up, combined with the fear and anger she'd been fighting to contain, were enough to reactivate the catalyst in her blood. Its effects took hold almost immediately.

Sylvia jumped back as the blue hue of Ivey's skin intensified. "Do something, Ildwick. She's having the mutations."

Ildwick leaned forward. "Should I intervene?"

"No." Ivey's body shook fiercely as her muscles tensed. "I have to stand up." She struggled to right herself.

"Slow down." Ildwick tried to restrain her, but Ivey wrestled from his grip and slid to the floor. Grabbing the bedpost, she hoisted herself to her feet and lunged toward the bathroom door.

The handle turned and the door flew open. With nothing to slow her forward momentum, Ivey careened into the room and collided with Miles, who was buttoning his shirt.

He tumbled backward and fell to the floor with a startled cry. Ivey landed on top of him, knocking the wind from her lungs.

"Ivey, you're awake!" His expression went from happiness to confusion. "Did you need something from me?"

Ivey pointed at the tub.

"You wish to take a bath?"

"No . . ." she gasped and wheezed.

Miles wrapped his arms around her. "Relax and let your lungs recover."

Ivey laid her head against his chest. The steady beat of his heart had a calming effect. Ivey was finally able to take a deep breath.

Sylvia appeared in the open doorway. "Is everyone okay?"

Ivey sat up. "It's in the pipes."

"The creature?" Miles asked.

"Yes, it can move through the drainage system."

"That explains how it escaped from your suite."

"And into the garden," Ivey said.

Miles thought for a moment. "Through the fountain's drain."

Ildwick appeared in the doorway behind Sylvia. "That's a relief. If it can't pass through walls, we may actually stand a chance against it."

"No, we won't." Ivey staggered to her feet. "They're going to scuttle the ship at sea before it can escape to the mainland."

Miles jumped up. "Who said that?"

"Harwood, I think. Since they haven't been able to kill the monster, he's going to sacrifice everyone aboard the *Monarch*."

"He doesn't have the authority to do such a thing," Miles retorted.

"I'm afraid he does, Mr. Fenchurche, in the name of national security." Ildwick rubbed his temple.

"Then we'll kill the monster for him," Ivey said.

"How hard could it be?" Ildwick said with a sigh. "We have until sunrise to locate a phantom that's flowing through a maze of conduits the size of a small village."

"There's a way." Miles grabbed his jacket from the valet stand in the dressing area and threw it on. "If we flush seawater into all the drain lines, the saltiness might drive the creature out of the plumbing into the open."

"But we'd still have to track it down," Ivey said. "There's not enough time."

"What if we stopped up the drains so it couldn't get out?" Sylvia suggested. "Maybe it would die in there."

"We can't count on that," Miles countered. "There's a hydraulic repair mortar on board that sets up in seconds. If we can seal every drain on this ship—but one—then we can be ready and waiting when it comes out."

"That's a lot of drains, Mr. Fenchurche. There's no time to lose!" Ildwick gestured toward the door. "After you, ladies."

While Miles convinced the crewmen guarding the suite to escort his party to the bridge, Ivey pulled Sylvia aside.

"I'm sorry, but you'll have to stay here with Lucey Sue."

Sylvia's brow darkened. "No. If the time comes that you need help, I want to be there."

"She *has* proven herself to be more than a pretty face," Ildwick said.

"Better than any man on this ship." Ivey pointed at her maid's bare feet. "But she's given me her shoes, and I'm sure that Harwood's men won't let us into my suite. I'm sorry, Sylvia. We'll have rough going and you won't be able to keep up."

Lucey Sue bent down and unlaced her boots. "Take mine then. They're a might big, but they'll keep you off the broken glass."

Sylvia turned to her mistress, and Ivey nodded.

Once the borrowed boots were on, Ildwick looked Sylvia up and down. "Not quite there," he muttered. He hurried off to the study and returned with a rapier and a walking staff.

Sylvia reached for the sword. "I can handle a blade, sir."

"Not to offend, dear lady, but this is for Mr. Fenchurche. I've heard he's a capable swordsman." Ildwick offered her the stick. "However, you shouldn't discount what can be done with a weapon like this, Miss Feather. Asymbiants' bodies recover from small wounds quickly. You'll be able to inflict more damage with a staff than with a gun."

Sylvia accepted her weapon with a glare.

The group made their way to the bridge, where Miles began to lay out his plan for Captain LeClere.

Ivey felt someone watching her. She looked up. Minnette was sitting in the loft, flanked by the doctor and Dolan.

Toward the far side of the loft, two men in plain jackets were fiddling with a very odd-looking piece of equipment sitting on a table. The large black box was covered in dials, gauges, and switches. A bulbous glass portal at its center emitted a bluish glow. The device's table was surrounded by large cylinders of compressed gas that were connected by woven metal hoses. Ivey wondered what such a strange-looking machine had to do with the flight of an airship. The men and their device were surrounded by a perimeter of guards in the black wool uniforms of Cemaria's Promacheon.

What are they doing here?

As Ivey continued to stare at the machine, her ears became filled with a sickening sound. It made the skin along the edge of her auricles burn, and started a ringing in the back of her head.

"Careful, you are about to give yourself away," Ildwick whispered in her ear.

"What?" Ivey jumped. She hadn't noticed his approach.

"If they realize that you're on to them, those fellows will not hesitate to neutralize you."

Ivey grabbed Ildwick's sleeve and pulled him to a quiet spot closer to the bridge's hatch door.

"What are you after, Mr. Curio?"

"Nothing. I'm simply an interested bystander."

"What is your interest?"

"I only want what you want."

"Which is?"

"To protect this ship and the man who owns it."

Before she could think twice, Ivey blurted out her father's message. "Then help me destroy the cipher device before it kills us all."

Ildwick's shocked expression as he glanced toward the contraption in the loft confirmed Ivey's suspicion. That thing was the cipher, and the chemist's presence on the ship was no accident.

Clearly agitated, he tried to make light of the moment. "I must be an open book. What else do you know regarding the Cipher Program?"

"Not now, we have a problem," she whispered.

Harwood had arrived on the bridge, and Minnette was coming down from the loft to join in her son's discussion with the captain.

"Miles," Minnette spoke through tightly pursed lips, "we've finally lowered the wings and regained a decent altitude. Why in Aether would you take us back down below a hundred feet?"

"That's as far as our water tank's refill hose will reach. Flooding the *Monarch*'s drain lines with seawater is our best hope of getting the creature out into the open, where the Dicæon officers can kill it."

"It's too risky. We need to evacuate this ship as quickly as possible, and we're within hours of land."

"If we don't do this, Mother, we won't make it to land."

The captain frowned. "Are you saying that this thing could kill every man, woman, and child on this ship within a matter of hours?"

"Captain, trust me, his plan would be a waste of our time," Harwood said.

"Would you like me to tell him why, Harwood?" Ivey stepped forward defiantly. "Don't these people deserve to know the truth of what will happen to them?"

Harwood's jaw clenched even tighter than his fists. "How in the hell do you know—?"

"We haven't reached the point of no return yet," Ivey stated firmly. "Miles has a plan to destroy the creature."

"And if you can't?"

"Then we'll allow you to do what is right for Cemaria. Please, you have nothing to lose."

Harwood turned to the captain. "Very well. By the authority of the Dicæon, I am seizing control of the *Monarch*. Your crew is hereby ordered to do everything in its power to help Mr. Fenchurche rid this ship of the asymbiant before we make land."

Minnette's suspicious gaze snapped from Ivey to her son.

"Try not to get us killed, Miles."

His expression hardened. "I don't intend to, Mother."

Miles instructed the engineers to ready the siphon pumps. Meanwhile, the flight crew prepared for the delicate maneuver of lowering the crippled ship, in the dead of night, near enough to reach the water.

Amid the commotion, Ivey tried not to stare at the loft, but the noise coming from the device was impossible to ignore. No one else seemed to notice anything unusual. As it continued to intensify, her stomach twisted with the same dreadful terror she'd felt on the docking platform. Her urge to turn and flee the bridge was overpowering.

All of them dead. All of them dead.

The nightmarish voice from her dreams and visions was back in her head, accompanied by a pounding that sounded like the heartbeat of something titanic fighting for its life.

All of them dead. All of them dead. All of them dead.

"Enough!" Ivey screamed as the pounding grew louder.

Sylvia ran to her side. "What is it?"

"Can't you hear that?"

"Hear what, miss?"

"That awful sound." She covered her ears, trying to escape the unbearable pressure. Ivey doubled over, gasping in pain.

"I think—it's the *Monarch*!"

As the words left her lips, the lights flickered and died.

The hum of the ship's forward engines abruptly stopped, dousing the bridge and its occupants in a black, ominous silence. A murmur of concern rippled around the room.

A few seconds later, the crewmen began to activate the emergency lamps at their stations. The captain grabbed the horn of a speaking tube and called out for a report from the engineering bay.

He received no answer.

"Everyone, quiet!" He covered one ear and pressed the other tightly against the cone-shaped opening of the device. "All I hear is water."

"That's not water!" Miles jerked the captain away. "The creature's in the tube!"

Ildwick raised his sword. "Prepare to defend the bridge."

The men drew their weapons and aimed them at the speaking horn.

The dreadful noise and the burning in Ivey's ears stopped. She straightened and looked back at the loft.

The true enemy had been revealed.

Arvel's warning and Ildwick's cryptic comments were starting to make sense. That machine was tearing a hole through Ivey's reality. It was responsible for the voice in her head, and the energy it emitted was causing her visions and transcendental spells.

Father was right. It must be destroyed.

The Promacheon agents guarding the contraption suddenly jumped to their feet with carbines drawn. The expressions on their shadowed faces were alarming. If the machine's influence had completely engulfed their minds, Ivey feared they might open fire if she called any attention to the device.

An even darker realization struck her.

The monster had used Amelia's likeness to mock her in the garden. That was not the behavior of a simple predatory creature. An act like that was rooted in a cruel form of intelligence. Whoever controlled that device was trying to harm the ship and her passengers, and they had just called the creature to come and kill everyone on the bridge.

"Miles, you have to stop it before it gets here!" Ivey shouted.

Sylvia rushed forward with a fistful of salt from her apron pocket and pelted it into the speaking horn.

Miles grabbed a plumb weight hanging from a nearby equipment rack and jammed it into the top of the horn, forming a tight plug.

While they waited to see if it would hold, Ivey turned to the captain.

"Were either of the crewmen who died engineers?"

"Yes," he replied.

"Then it knows how to maneuver the ship."

"That's impossible. Shifters are primitive creatures who do little more than kill, eat, and assimilate," Ildwick argued.

"It used Amelia's words to mock me. It's taking a lot more than physical traits from its victims."

"Are you certain?" Ildwick asked. "Asymbiants don't have the kind of intelligence to—"

"I think this one does." Ivey subtlety tilted her head toward the cipher equipment in the loft.

Ildwick's expression became alarmed as she continued. "If the creature takes control of the bridge, we won't be able to stop it from reaching the mainland."

"In that case, we'd better hurry," he said.

Miles pointed at a crewman. "I need every available crewman and staff member to get the mortar and start sealing every last drain on this ship with patching compound—except the one in the guest suite's bathtub. We'll drive it back to its nest."

Turning to the captain, he said, "Get us as close to the water as you can."

The captain looked at Officer Harwood, who gave him a grim nod.

"I'll do what I can, but you have to work fast, Miles. The seas are rough, and we're low on fuel."

"I will, Captain. I'll take Harwood and his men to help search for the creature while my engineers restart the ship's equipment," Miles said. "Anyone with a gun must be careful not to fire into the fuel tanks or machinery. If the thing gets past us and escapes into the central drain line, we'll need the engines to position the ship and run the siphon pumps."

While Miles was organizing the search party, Ivey hurried up the steps of the loft. She avoided looking at the men gathered around the cipher device and made her way to where Minnette was sitting with Dolan and the doctor. "May I have a word?"

Minnette ignored her, but her hand arched receptively.

"Your son is a remarkable man. I'm privileged to fight beside him, and if we die, I swear it will be with honor."

When Minnette nodded, Ivey continued, leaning closer.

"But we cannot prevail without your help."

"This ship is no longer under my control."

Ivey's eyebrow rose. "That never stopped a woman with a strong sense of purpose."

Minnette glanced at her for a brief moment. "Go on."

Ivey whispered as softly as she could. "I don't know what they've told you about its function, but the machine to our side is a menace. It's responsible for every mishap this ship has suffered, and now it's being used to control the creature. If we have any hope of surviving, both of them must be destroyed. Be prepared to strike when the time comes."

Getting no response, Ivey's gaze went to Dolan. His head nodded ever so slightly, and Ivey returned the gesture as she straightened, knowing that at least he would make an attempt.

Ivey ran down the steps and fell in line between Ildwick and Sylvia as they followed Miles and his engineers down the spiral stairs below the loft.

Many of the men carried luminous globes, which cast splintered shadows around the dark stairwell.

Once everyone had reached the bottom of the stairs, they divided into two groups. Harwood and his men were going to search the water-works in the bow of the ship. If they found nothing there, they would continue on along the portside service passageway.

Miles and his group would search along the starboard passage. The two parties would work their way to the back of the ship and meet in the engine room. If the creature had escaped, Miles would set in motion his plan to flush the drainage system.

The first room Miles' party came to was used for storage. It was crowded by a jumble of crates and rows of shelving that had overturned during the storm.

"Stay on your guard. It could be hiding anywhere," he said.

"I'll feel for its presence." Ivey closed her eyes and took a slow breath.

"Watch out," Ildwick warned. "That's how she got herself stung."

Sylvia moved up and raised her staff protectively.

Ivey eyes opened. "It's not here."

They carried on with the search until they reached the ventilation control room. There was no sign of the creature or the men that should have been operating the equipment.

"We have to reactivate the central turbines," Miles said.

"Do it later, Mr. Fenchurche," Ildwick said. "Time is of the essence."

"The library is practically airtight," he explained. "If we don't get some exchange going, the passengers' air will go stale."

Ivey guarded the door while Miles and the engineers tended to the machinery. It was disturbing that they hadn't encountered any of the men who normally worked on the lower level.

Someone shouted, and a gun fired at the front of the ship. It sounded like Harwood's team had found something in the waterworks.

Realizing that she'd never loaded the poison dart, Ivey dug into her leather bag and felt for the napkin. She retrieved the cartridge and chambered it, checking the gun to be sure it was ready to fire.

"Miles, I'm going ahead—" Ivey stopped mid-sentence. The ventilation room was completely dark and empty.

The others had vanished.

"Miles? Sylvia?" her voice echoed around her.

It's happening again. Don't make a move until it passes.

"Neveah! Seren! Where did you go?"

A ghostly figure in a flowing gown ran past an open door.

"Please, someone help me!"

It was Primrose.

Ivey closed her eyes and tried to block out the sound of her sister's heartbreaking screams.

From behind her still-closed eyelids, a terrible vision appeared in Ivey's mind.

Prim's drowned body was floating below the surface of the pond, caught in the branches of the sunken tree.

All of them dead.

The nightmarish voice had returned.

"You're lying," Ivey said. "I know what you're doing now. None of this is real."

∾

Chapter Twenty-Eight

FIGHT TO THE FINISH

A rush of fresh air hit Ivey in the face. She uncovered her eyes and found herself squinting in the light of the morning sun. She was standing on the front drive at Thornhall. It couldn't be possible, yet every one of her senses told her that the setting was real.

I'm home?

Someone came up the path from the pond.

"Iris!"

The little girl looked startled.

"Don't be afraid. It's me."

Ivey saw Iris kneel on the ground beside the path. It looked like she was talking to one of her invisible playmates.

"Did you hear that, Mito?" she asked. "What is it?"

"Iris, it's me! Ivey! Please listen."

The sound of an approaching carriage brought the child to her feet, and she dashed toward it. As Iris passed, Ivey reached for her hand, but grasped only empty air. She turned and ran after her little sister.

The carriage was being driven by Prim's husband, Stanley Honeycutt.

"Stanley, don't you see me?" Ivey shouted.

Something spooked the team of horses, and Iris shrieked as the lead horse reared over her head.

"Iris, look out!" Ivey lunged forward and grabbed at her sister. For a brief instant, she felt the skin on her sister's face. Thankfully, the contact propelled the little girl away from the descending hooves.

Stanley struggled to hold back the horses. "Prim, please, get the girls out of the carriage."

The door opened, and Neveah climbed out, leading Seren and Celeste to safety. Ivey jumped inside the carriage while it was still open.

"Prim!"

Her sister stared blankly.

"Something evil is coming for you. Don't go near the pond."

Prim replied softly, "I've already drowned. Didn't you see?"

Ivey gritted her teeth.

It isn't real. It can't be real.

"Prim?" Arvel appeared in the carriage door. "Prim. Give me your hand."

"Father, I'm here!" Ivey leapt into his arms, but he was knocked backward onto the drive. Stanley was thrown from the carriage, and the horses bolted down the path toward the pond.

Ivey climbed out of the open door and clung to the side of the carriage. Something flew over her head and landed on the path in front of them.

"Beast! Help me!" she screamed. He responded to her plea by throwing his head back and letting out a mournful howl.

❧

Ivey was back in the maze of pitch-black tunnels she'd envisioned after the doctor applied the leeches. This time she heard Iris screaming for help in the distance.

"Prim, come back. Help! She's drowning!"

Whoever was lurking behind the cipher machine seemed to be fixated upon cruel tricks. While they wasted efforts creating illusions and torturing her family, Ivey's sole objective was to destroy the contraption. That gave her an advantage.

She reached inside her satchel and dug for the luminous chalk. This time she would find the way out of the maze. Ivey swung her arm to dash a large X against the stone. There was a terrible screeching sound amid an unexpected shower of sparks.

"Dammit," she cursed as the piece of flint Arvel had given her slipped from her hand. She located the chalk and scraped it along the rock wall, marking her path through the twists and turns of the labyrinth.

It felt like hours had passed when the ground beneath her feet began to feel different. She crouched down to touch the surface. It was soft and spongy.

She was at moss-covered bank of her pond.

Ivey's mind flashed back to that fateful day when she had nearly drowned at age six. She remembered the pain and panic of being trapped underwater, but her conscious memory stopped the moment her body had given up the fight to live. The lapse of time between that moment until her father had pulled her out of the tree's branches had always been a mystery.

Finally, that memory resurfaced.

Shivering and alone, she'd wandered through a series of dark tunnels for hours, until she finally found a way back.

Ivey retreated several paces, and hastily scrawled a message onto the rock wall.

She returned to the bank of the pond, plunged into the dark water, and swam toward the sunken tree.

∾

Sylvia was beside Ivey at the door to the ventilation control room. She glanced at the men working to restart the turbines.

When she looked back, Ivey had vanished.

"Mr. Miles, she's gone!"

"Then go after her," he called back.

"I can't. She's just disappeared into thin air," Sylvia stammered, hardly believing her own eyes.

Miles dropped what he was doing. "Ildwick, did you see anything?"

Ildwick shrugged, but Sylvia saw something in his eyes.

"He's lying." She went to face him directly. "What happened to Miss Ivey?"

"I can only hazard a guess."

"Go on," Miles said.

"There's a machine aboard your ship that is rupturing the horizons of this world. Your fiancée would appear to be sympathetic to its resonance."

"What machine?" Sylvia asked suspiciously.

"One I've been tracking for some time now, Miss Feather. It's part of a clandestine operation called the Cipher Program. It's using a dangerous new technology that poses a serious threat to Cemaria . . . and Aether, from what I've gleaned. For some nefarious reason, the Promacheon is testing one of their portable cipher devices on the *Monarch*."

"That black contraption in the loft?" Miles asked.

Ildwick nodded. "You know of it?"

"No. Mother made the arrangements with one of the Cemarian executive councilors."

"I can assure you that he failed to warn her of the danger this technology poses. Wherever the Promacheon has operated the device, mayhem has soon followed."

"That must be why all those Promacheon agents have been on the bridge," Miles said.

"Even so, they sorely underestimated the risks of such a test. I have no doubt the infernal contraption caused us to be caught in the storm. A short while, ago Miss Thornton realized that the cipher device is commanding the asymbiant, much like the device is attempting to control her own mind. When she resisted the machine's influence, someone eliminated her from the equation."

Sylvia caught her breath. "She's dead?"

"She may still be alive, but not in this place. I'm afraid it might have pulled her through a dimensional crack."

Sylvia turned to Miles, dumbfounded by what she was hearing. "Is he mad?"

"A device that could rupture this dimension? That's nonsense," Miles said.

"It's hardly the first nonsensical thing to take place on this ship since we departed. You don't have to believe my fantastic explanations, Mr. Fenchurche, but the fact remains that your fiancée vanished before Miss Feather's eyes."

"She did!" Sylvia gasped.

"How do we get her back?" Miles asked.

"We can't," Ildwick replied. "Her fate lies beyond our reach now. She is on her own, as are we."

"After everything Miss Ivey did for us? How can you say such a thing?" Sylvia had to stop herself from spitting in his face.

"Stiffen your spine, Miss Feather, or she will have nothing to return to. This world is on a path to ruin."

"I should believe the likes of you," Sylvia muttered under her breath.

"And what of the machine?" Miles asked.

"It has to be destroyed," Ildwick said, "but in doing so, we may seal the rift in our reality—and Miss Thornton's chance to return with it."

"No!" Sylvia choked. Tears rolled down her face.

Miles placed a gentle hand on her shoulder. "Ivey crossed the void to find me, Sylvia. She'll find a way back to us."

The look in his eyes was hopeful and comforting. Sylvia wiped her cheek. "Of course."

"That's my girl." Ildwick patted her on the other shoulder.

Sylvia wheeled and slapped his face. "Don't you dare! You knew what was happening, and you said nothing until it was too late."

She raised her hand to strike again, but Miles caught her arm. "Sylvia, please."

Sylvia bowed her head in shame. In all her years of employ, she'd never behaved in such an unacceptable manner. "I'm sorry, sir."

"You needn't be." Miles took a step closer to the chemist. "When this is over, you'll answer for keeping your silence on this matter, Mr. Curio."

A shot rang out from the aft end of the hallway.

"The engine room!" Miles cried. "They've found it!" He ran from the ventilation room, followed by Ildwick and the other men.

Sylvia struggled to keep up as she ran in her borrowed boots.

"What's happening?" Miles shouted as he approached Officer Harwood.

"Something flashed over there." The big man pointed past one of the ship's engines.

Sylvia saw the officers advancing with drawn weapons.

Miles gestured for his party to circle around the other side of the engine in an effort to trap the creature between the machinery and the wall.

After a tense wait, it became evident that whatever had drawn their fire had eluded them, but not before it had sabotaged one of the ship's main engines.

Miles performed a quick inspection of the machinery. "Hoses have been cut and bearings smashed. This could take hours to repair. We'll need to check all the engines."

Ildwick pointed at Harwood. "Better get your men moving. The stairwell to the bridge is unattended. This may have been a diversion."

While the Dicæon officers stormed off, Sylvia stayed near Miles, holding a light for the men who were working to restart one of the undamaged engines.

Ildwick's presence made her uncomfortable, so she moved closer to the sabotaged engine. In the lamplight, she saw something glowing on the wall.

Next to a shining green streak that trailed off into the darkness, a large diagonal was scratched into the wall's surface.

When Sylvia went to take a closer look, she felt a crunch beneath the toe of her boot. She knelt to pick up a piece of flint.

She followed the green streak until it ended. A message had been scrawled on the wall.

Carry on with the plan. I found a way back.

❧

Ivey dove deep into the black water of the cove.

She passed between the limbs of the ancient tree. The prickly branches ripped at her clothing and sliced into her skin, but she pressed on until the air in her lungs was stale and her body was spent. She felt a strange tug and then oblivion.

❧

"Damn it, Ivey Thornton. You will not die because of me. Give me a chance to know you. Please!"

Ivey awoke with a shallow gasp. Someone was squeezing her hand. A young man with green eyes the color of the sea lifted his head from her chest.

"Hello, Miss Thornton. I am Miles Fenchurche. It's a pleasure to finally make your acquaintance."

She stared into his eyes. It seemed so real.

Before Ivey could open her mouth to warn him about the cipher device, she sneezed.

◈

Ivey saw her father silhouetted against the sunset. He was slumped over on their special bench, with his head in his hands. She ran to him.

"Father?"

He gave no response. She knew better than to try to touch him again.

A gentle voice from behind her spoke.

"Arvel, we've come to share your pain, although we cannot fathom your grief."

Ivey turned.

Miles was coming down the garden path. A fair-haired boy holding a porcelain doll walked solemnly beside him.

Arvel looked up. "Maddox."

Ivey gaped in disbelief. Miles was the young adolescent. The man was his father, Maddox.

"I loved the girl like my own," Maddox said with great sorrow in his eyes. He patted the boy's shoulder. "Miles thought the world of her."

"I never dreamed she'd leave us like this." Arvel choked back his tears. "She always loved the pond."

"And Winora?"

"Her heart is broken. The doctors fear she will lose the baby."

Maddox took a seat on the bench beside Arvel. "When Minnette died, they said Miles was too frail to survive without a mother, but your wife proved them wrong. Winora is strong, Arvel. She will give you another child to love."

"Even so, how can I live without the one that is lost?" He looked up at the splendor of the evening sky. "She'll never see another sunset."

When Arvel turned to weep in his friend's arms, Ivey had to move away. Her father's grief was unbearable.

At the edge of the garden, young Miles had gone to lay a porcelain doll beside the cut flowers on a fresh grave.

As Ivey drew closer, she saw a tear roll down his cheek.

"Oh, Ivey. How I wish you could have lived."

She knelt beside him and whispered in his ear, "I will live, Miles."

He looked up, almost as if he'd heard. "Ivey? Ivey?"

His voice faded.

❧

Ivey's arms and legs flailed in the water until she looked up and recognized the glass panel over her crystal bathtub on the *Monarch*.

She bolted upright.

The tub was overflowing with frigid seawater. She clambered out to follow a trail of dark streaks across the wet floor.

It looked like Miles' plan to force the asymbiant out of the plumbing had worked.

Ivey crept to the door and listened. Something was moving in her bedroom. She knelt down and peered through the crack beneath the door.

A half-naked Amelia Buxhill was rummaging through a pile of Ivey's clothes pulled from beneath the overturned wardrobe.

Ivey reached into her sopping leather bag and drew her gun. Rising to her feet, she pulled the door open and took a step into the bedroom.

Amelia swiveled to face her. "Please don't hurt me, Ivey."

The shifter looked and sounded exactly like the girl it had murdered. Ivey moved forward, keeping the gun trained on its chest while she worked up her courage. "You're not Amelia. I saw you kill her."

"You're wrong. I'm still alive!"

"Not for long," Ivey said softly.

"Please," it sobbed. "I'm like you. I only want to live."

"You're nothing like me."

"Are you sure?" Anger flashed in Amelia's cold, blue eyes. "You will die a misfit."

It spat at her again, but this time Ivey dodged its poisonous projectile. The asymbiant picked up a side table and hurled it across the room.

Ivey threw her arms up, but the force of the impact knocked her backward, and the table landed on top of her. She shoved it aside and struggled to her feet, chasing the creature into the sitting room.

It ripped the front door from its frame and bolted into the private parlor with Ivey in pursuit.

"Take cover!" Harwood warned, "We've got it trapped."

Ivey saw Miles, Sylvia, Ildwick, and several armed crewmen blocking the stairs and elevator while Harwood and his officers guarded the door to the bridge.

As soon as Ivey was clear, Harwood gave the order to fire.

The first volley of bullets struck the replica of Amelia's body with a dull splatter. The creature screamed and clutched at multiple wounds oozing its tarry blood.

Before a second round could be fired, a piercing tone swelled in the parlor. This time, Ivey wasn't the only one struck by the paralyzing effects of the cipher device.

Everyone stood helpless while the asymbiant sloughed off its damaged tissue and stolen clothes and transformed into a heaving black mass.

Two thick appendages sprouted to hoist and hurl a large sofa at the parlor window. The heavy piece of furniture smashed through the weakened glass, creating a shower of tiny shards that blew into the room, sending those closest to the window crashing to the floor.

By the time Ivey had regained her senses, the shifter was forming a pair of bird's wings.

In the early dawn light, she could make out the distant peaks of the Rosman Mountains on the horizon.

Ivey started sprinting toward the creature.

"Curio! Snap out of it!" she shouted at the chemist, who'd collapsed at the top of the staircase. "It's going to escape!"

Shaking off his stupor, Ildwick retrieved the harpoon gun that was lying on the floor and came to his feet.

Ivey jumped onto a large table and vaulted over the winged beast, landing between it and the gaping hole in the side of the cabin.

The time had come to use the poisoned dart. She took careful aim at the creature's center and shouted, "It's now or never, Curio!"

He moved into position with harpoon raised.

Ivey pulled the trigger. Her dart disappeared into the oily black feathers.

The shifter let out a hideous screech and doubled over, its gelatinous body quivering from the impact.

She dropped to the floor, waiting for the harpoon's barb to strike from the other side.

"Shoot it!" Getting no response, Ivey stood and ran around the wounded creature.

Ildwick looked at her helplessly as the harpoon tumbled from his hands and he sank to the floor.

The dart had passed completely through the shifter's body and struck him in the leg.

"No!" Ivey fell to her knees. She snatched the dart from his calf, found the tourniquet in her bag, and knotted it tightly below his knee.

Miles staggered over to drop down beside her. "Your knife—I'll bleed out the poison."

She found it in her satchel and had just put it in his hand when Sylvia shouted, "Look out!"

Ivey looked back. The creature was regenerating itself again.

She jumped to her feet, and ran to intercept it before it could escape through the open window.

As the shifter lumbered closer, Ivey fumbled to find a tranquilizer dart in her bag.

It loomed over her with hideous wings spread. Ivey looked up and saw the tip of another barbed stinger emerging from its open mouth.

"Get down, Ivey!" Sylvia screamed. She clumsily snatched up the harpoon and pulled the trigger. The bolt hit the shifter in the abdomen and burst out of the other side, disappearing through the broken window.

The harpoon's rope violently passed through the creature's body until a coil caught around Sylvia's forearm yanked her forward.

The maid slammed into the shrieking creature, and they both slid to the threshold of the broken window. The asymbiant teetered on the edge before falling backward. Sylvia tried to brace herself, but the weight on the rope was pulling her over.

Ivey dived forward just in time to snatch one of Sylvia's ankles with both hands.

The floor was slippery with the creature's blood. Ivey felt herself going over the edge when Harwood's bulky body landed across her legs, pinning her to the floor.

She tightened her grip on Sylvia's boot.

"Pull us up!" she screamed.

Harwood started to drag them back to safety, but Sylvia's foot slipped out of Lucey Sue's ill-fitting boot.

Ivey heard a long scream as her friend fell.

She scrambled back to the edge and looked down. Sylvia had already disappeared into the roiling water a hundred feet below.

Miles ran up beside her. "Sylvia!"

Ivey grabbed her knife from his hand and jumped, arms outstretched, through the hole. Before she hit the water, Ivey took a long breath, drew her arms in, and arched her back, letting her feet pierce the surface first.

The cold saltwater exploded against her body, roaring in her ears and burning its way up her nose. She grabbed the strap of her satchel and held tight until the painful rush of her descent gave way to the heavy water below.

Ivey opened her eyes and began to swim.

The dawn's light was still dim. Ivey couldn't see far in front of herself, so she swam in slow circles as she descended in the water, watching for bubbles or any sign of life. Ivey knew she could last under water much longer than Sylvia, so she had to find her quickly.

Something in the water below emitted a dull sound. As she swam closer, she could see Sylvia's apron waving in the water as if it were a signal for help. A few feet down, Ivey could make out fingers gripping the apron's tie.

Ivey kicked her legs furiously until she was able to grasp the hand and pull it up.

Amelia's gruesome face rose from the depths.

The eyes flicked open, revealing sunken red orbs.

Ivey drew back, but the creature's hand dug sharp claws into her flesh. Ivey slashed at it with her knife until she'd severed the appendage. As it sank, the hand disintegrated in a plume of black blood.

Salt.

Sea brine would destroy the asymbiant's body if she could inflict enough open wounds.

The shifter reshaped into an elongated mass. A set of jaws encircled by talon-bearing limbs grew out of its center.

It lunged, but Ivey twisted and turned in the water, exactly as she had done for so many years with the beast in her pond.

She struck at the shifter again and again, shredding the surface of its hide. The monster ripped and snapped at Ivey, but with every slash of her blade, large pieces of its flesh were carved off into the sea, and soon, there was no remnant of its body left to attack.

The battle left Ivey running out of breath.

Where are you, Sylvia?

As the dark blood in the water dissipated, a beam of sunlight glinting off a metallic object on the shallow seafloor caught her eye.

It was the harpoon.

Ivey kicked her legs as hard as she could, forcing her body deeper into the water, ignoring the painful pressure in her ears.

There was no sign of Sylvia.

Ivey followed the rope to where it disappeared over the rim of an oceanic trench. When she tugged the line, there was weight on the other end.

Ivey frantically pulled the rope up until Sylvia—her arm helplessly twisted in the coil—emerged from the chasm.

Ivey cut the line and grabbed Sylvia around the waist as she pushed off from the bottom. They shot up a distance, but something dragged them back down.

Below them, Ivey saw a darkness swirling in the water. It looked like the blood and dissolved bits of the creature's carcass were reforming as an underwater vortex that was draining into the chasm.

Ivey gave everything she had to break free of the current, but her spirit had gone as far as it could, and her body was failing.

At least we won't die alone.

She hugged Sylvia tightly and closed her eyes, preparing for the end.

The best moments of her life at Thornhall passed through her mind. She savored the moment when she had first glimpsed the *Monarch* and the exhilaration of watching her father's Zephyr rise into the air. She could almost feel its radiant energy flowing throughout her body, lifting her into its bright aura.

Ivey embraced the light, letting it fill her lungs. She hoped that Sylvia could feel it, too.

Cold sea air stung Ivey's cheeks. She gasped. They were at the surface.

"There!" a voice called out from above.

She looked up. The unmistakable belly of a Zephyr hovered just above her head. A man in a bright orange vest leaned out of the craft and tossed down a white rescue ring on a line before jumping into the water.

"Sylvia, we're alive!" Ivey shouted.

There was no response.

"Hurry, she's badly hurt!" Ivey shouted.

The man reached the two of them and eased the ring over Sylvia.

"Someone will come for you, too," he said. The man held the line with one arm around Sylvia as the rescue ring was pulled up and into the vessel.

Ivey felt the otheophainer pulse when the Zephyr took off for the prow of the *Monarch*'s cabin.

The sea grew dark and choppy. The mouth of the vortex was coming to the surface.

A piece of wood from the sofa that had been thrown through the window was circling in the current. Ivey swam toward it and grabbed ahold.

She fought to keep her head above the turbulent water as the vortex grew.

There was more shouting from high above. Ivey looked up and saw a second Zephyr hovering alongside the broken glass wall of the family's parlor. The vessel's door opened and Miles leapt into the flying machine before it descended toward her.

Miles threw down a rescue ring, but the current of the whirlpool made it impossible for her to grab onto.

He slid down the rope, wrapped his legs around the ring, and reached for her.

"Hang on to me!" Miles shouted.

Ivey caught his arms and clung tightly while the Zephyr pulled them out of the water.

The pilot maneuvered the craft toward the captain's observation deck and hovered, unable to set down with two people still dangling precariously from the rescue rope.

"You have to let me go!" Ivey yelled.

"Are you sure?"

"Trust me!"

Miles released her. She fell, tumbling across the deck.

She clambered to her feet while Miles tried to free his legs from the ring. A gust of wind blew the Zephyr upward.

He slipped off and fell head first. Ivey scrambled to break his fall with outstretched arms. When he landed on her, she grabbed him and rolled forward to absorb the shock.

They lay in each other's arms, soaking wet and gasping for air.

Miles finally sat up with a groan. "Thank you for catching me."

"Thank you for dropping me. Is Ildwick alive?"

"He's holding out. What about Sylvia?"

Ivey closed her eyes. "I don't know. It's bad."

Glancing at her ripped and bloody clothing, Miles touched her arm. "And you?"

"In one piece." Ivey took a long breath and sat up. "The creature is dead, but it's not over, Miles. There's a machine in the loft—"

"Ildwick told me."

"It will keep attacking until we're dead."

Ivey dragged herself to the railing. The whirlpool was growing, and a strange thundering sound reverberated from the depths of the sea.

"How can we stop something with that much power?"

"There's a way," Miles said, "but first I have to get it off my ship."

Ivey found Miles' confidence reassuring. "Can I help you?"

"Yes," he replied. "There are explosive charges on the service walkway. I'll need to get them. Are you ready?"

He offered Ivey a hand, and she wearily rose.

When they entered the bridge, the man who'd saved Sylvia was helping the doctor apply a splint to her left arm.

"Nicolai. Come with me," Miles said.

Sylvia moaned in pain.

The man looked up. "I'm sorry, Miles, but this lady needs me."

Ivey knelt down to take his place. "I'll take care of her. Go."

He looked at her wet hair and blue face. "You're Arvel's daughter."

"Yes."

Miles glanced out the window. "Storm clouds are gathering. Nicolai, we have to go."

The man laid a hand on Sylvia's quaking shoulder. "Don't give up, miss. I promise we'll get you to a hospital." He stood and ran after Miles.

Ivey held the supports in place while Doctor Brendel wrapped bandages around the splint. Sylvia's body contracted. She coughed up a mixture of blood and seawater.

Minnette rushed toward them with an armful of blankets. "I found these. Will she live, Mathias?"

"I delivered her into this world, and I'll be damned if she departs it while I'm on duty," he said.

Ivey took the blankets and tucked them around Sylvia. "I should never have turned my back on that thing."

"What in all of Aether?" Minnette said.

Ivey rose, looking toward where Minnette pointed. Beyond the bridge's main window, a waterspout had broken the ocean's surface. It reached skyward toward a wall of clouds directly in the *Monarch*'s path.

"Retract the wings, and bring her about!" Captain LeClere yelled.

The flight crew jumped into action, throwing levers and spinning handwheels.

An alarm sounded. Ivey heard the whine of the winch rotors.

Everyone on the bridge grabbed for a handhold as the ship swayed sharply.

The *Monarch* began to maneuver away from the growing column, but with only one engine, she was having a hard time pulling free.

Ivey looked up. The men guarding the cipher machine were at the loft's rail, distracted by the spectacle. Dolan was still in the sitting area to their side. He caught her eye. Rising to his feet, he inconspicuously moved toward the captain's collection of nautical artifacts displayed along the loft's back wall. Absent the antique harpoon, the only suitable weapon was an ancient wooden oar.

As he reached for the oar, Ivey slipped her hand into the satchel. Her knife had been lost somewhere on the seafloor, but she still had her gun and tranquilizer darts. Dolan wouldn't stand a chance without help.

Minnette's gaze went from Ivey to Dolan. She started toward the loft.

"Don't." Ivey grabbed her arm. "They'll kill you."

Minnette shook her off. "You'll need time to reload. Do not waste it."

Ivey pulled the darts from her bag and lined them up on a map table behind a tall console. Her hand brushed against a piece of thin fabric at the bottom of her satchel.

Impossible.

She clearly recalled having dropped the napkin on the floor of the ventilation room after loading her poisoned dart, yet somehow, when she withdrew her hand, she was holding the square of white linen. She closed her eyes and hoped for a miracle as she squeezed it.

Her eyes opened wide. She unfolded the layers of fabric to uncover the poison cartridge marked with luminous chalk.

I was already in an altered reality—it never happened here!

Knowing that Ildwick would not die by her hand gave her a surge of hope. All could be set right once they sent that infernal device to the bottom of the sea and transported Sylvia to a hospital.

Ivey leaned out from behind the console and aimed her gun at the loft.

Minnette was approaching the four Promacheon agents. She shouted at them, pretending to be panicked by the approaching squall, flailing her arms and bumping into their table.

They attempted to drag her back to her chair in the loft, but she clutched her chest, collapsing into the arms of the guard closest to her.

Doctor Brendel snapped to his feet and started toward the loft to help her.

Ivey shot at the agent farthest from Minnette, hitting him squarely in the chest with the first dart. He looked down. Fortunately, the sedative took its effect before he could alert his comrades. He fell backward, unnoticed.

Ivey crouched behind the console to load the next shot. She peeked out and set her sights upon the second agent. She tagged him in the arm, but he managed to grab the fellow next to him on his way down.

That agent reacted quickly, drawing his gun and scanning the bridge. Ivey ducked behind the console and reloaded.

When she leaned out the agent had his gun aimed in her direction.

Dolan struck him from behind with the oar, sending him to the floor.

That left only one agent, the one holding Minnette.

Dolan rushed forward, but the man used Minnette's body as a shield and fired his gun.

The shot knocked Dolan backward, and the oar slipped from his hand as he fell.

The agent took aim at Dolan's head, but Minnette bit his hand and delivered a sharp elbow to his groin.

Amid the struggle, the two men operating the cipher device jumped to their feet. Doctor Brendel dived into the fray just before Ivey fired, causing her dart to miss its mark.

One of the cipher operators attacked the doctor, while Ivey reloaded and fired another round that took down his companion.

There were no more tranquilizer darts on the map table, so Ivey loaded the poison dart and ran for the loft.

When she reached the top of the stairs, the Promacheon agent had Minnette in a chokehold, while Doctor Brendel was being pummeled by the operator.

Ivey pointed her gun at the agent. "Let her go, or I'll kill you."

The agent tightened his grip on Minnette and trained his weapon on the doctor's back.

"Please." Ivey pointed at the cyclone. "It's trying to kill us. Why are you protecting it?"

For a fleeting moment, the agent looked as though he was considering her words, but a chilling expression washed over his face.

She pulled the trigger, and the agent fell to the floor, convulsing violently as the poison spread through his body.

Ivey turned her attention to the cipher operator, who was savagely beating Dr. Brendel.

She threw herself onto the operator's back, trying to position herself for a strike at the man's neck, but he backhanded her with his arm, nearly knocking her over the loft's railing.

Ivey recovered and took a swing at his face. The man caught her arm and jerked her into the air. He lifted her high, then slammed her to the ground with tremendous force.

For a moment, Ivey was lost in a haze of pain. Her ears were ringing, and her body had gone numb.

She saw Miles appear at the top of the stairs, his eyes furious and his fists raised.

The operator threw the first punch.

Miles ducked, driving his shoulder into the man's abdomen and knocking him to the floor. Miles struck the operator's face. The man kicked him off and grabbed one of the agent's guns, which had fallen to the floor. He lifted it toward Miles.

"No!" Ivey screamed, helpless to stop it.

Minnette whacked the man soundly on the skull with the oar. He crashed to the floor.

"No one threatens my son." She kicked the gun away from his hand.

Miles picked up the pistol and handed it to a crewman coming up the stairs.

"Detain these men." He looked around the loft. "Where's Ivey?"

"Over here," she groaned. "I'm hurt." Her voice had a strange echo.

"Where is she?"

Ivey heard the panic in Miles' voice, but her senses were dimming.

"She was just here." Minnette pointed at the dead Promacheon agent. "She saved my life."

"Dammit, it's taken her again!"

Miles' voice sounded far away.

A sense of peace came over Ivey as she was swept off into the black clouds bearing down on the *Monarch*.

∽

Chapter Twenty-Nine

Breaking the Illusion

All the pain and fear had gone. Ribbons of light lapped around Ivey as she floated through a colorful aurora toward the bright light above.

It's beautiful, but I'm not ready to die.

"You don't have to."

Ivey looked down and saw Arvel standing beside the grave where the young version of Miles had left a porcelain doll.

He reached up for her. "Come back to me. We have another chance to be together."

Ivey smiled sadly. "I know this isn't real."

"It will be if you go back."

"Back to where?"

"The cove. I promise that this time I will find you before it's too late. You'll grow up with Miles, and Maddox will dance at your wedding. We can all be together, darling."

Ivey's heart leapt. If this was another reality, it was a happier one for Miles and his father, with an empty spot—which she could fill—in the Thornton family.

Although it was tempting to accept the invitation, the fear of causing her true family grief and leaving Miles alone in his sadness held her back.

"What about the people who care for me in my world?"

"You'll have to forget them." Arvel seemed anxious. "Come with me now and live in happiness."

"But, Father—"

"Ivey, it's the only choice. If you want to live, make the leap while the barrier is still broken."

Ivey thought for a moment before answering, "I can't leave without telling Miles goodbye."

"He won't hear you. There's no time." Arvel's voice was strident.

"Please, Father . . . it's the only way I'll be able to let go."

In a flash, Ivey was lying back on the observation deck, where she and Miles had dropped from the Zephyr.

Harwood burst through the hatch door carrying the cipher machine. Ivey sat up. "Harwood!"

The officer ran past her, taking no notice. He set the device down in front of Nicolai, and the two men began to wrap it in a net. Several red canisters were tied to the net with green ribbons.

The ship's envelope was folding toward the raging waterspout as the lone operational engine strained at full capacity to pull away.

"Arm the charges," Harwood yelled.

Nicolai took a small brass key from one of his front vest pockets and reached for one of the canisters.

Miles jumped through the hatch opening. "No, not yet!"

"Do it!" Harwood yelled above the wind. "We won't last much longer."

"Ivey's coming back." Miles dropped to his knees beside the device. "I can feel her."

Even though it made her heart ache, Ivey knew what had to be done. She ran to his side and wrapped her arms around his neck; they passed through his body like vapor.

"Please save them, Miles," she whispered in his ear. "It's the right choice. Trust me."

Miles took a sharp breath, almost as if he'd heard. "Very well, Nicolai. I'll do it."

Arvel appeared at the railing. "Now, Ivey. We have to jump before they close the rift!"

Taking the key from Nicolai's hand, Miles inserted it into one of the canisters and gave a half-turn. With teary eyes, he uttered, "Break the seal."

Nicolai pulled a cord attached to the canister.

Arvel gestured wildly to Ivey. "Run!"

Ivey raced alongside Harwood as he carried the machine to the railing.

He swung his arms back and launched the device overboard.

Ivey grasped the front of Arvel's jacket.

"My father would never tell me to forget the people I love. Be gone, monster!"

She shoved him over the railing. He and the device disappeared into the water below.

The canisters detonated, sending a plume of seawater skyward, followed by a billowing tower of thick black smoke. As it rose over her head, Ivey recognized it as the same ghoulish cloud that had descended over her and Prim on the *Monarch*'s docking platform.

"Miles! Don't let it take me!" She turned and ran toward him.

"Ivey?" He rose to his feet and started in her direction.

He stopped short when she struck his chest and wrapped her arms around his waist.

This time she could feel the solid warmth of his body. In his eyes, Ivey saw the reflection of her hair whipping in the wind. The destruction of the machine was dissolving its grip on her.

"No!" Miles held her tightly as the black cloud of swirling smoke engulfed their bodies and dragged them toward the railing.

They would have been pulled over if Harwood hadn't set his back against a spyglass mount and spread his arms to block their path.

Nicolai dropped and flattened himself against the deck as the black mass swept over him toward the empty Zephyr. The flying machine began to rock, then lifted up and was carried off into the cyclone.

"This is the end," Miles said as the great ship pitched toward the wall of clouds. He turned Ivey away to shield her from the destructive force for as long as possible.

Ivey saw movement from above. A circular flying machine was descending toward the midsection of the cabin. "What is that?"

Miles looked up. "It's the *Boreas*!" he shouted. "Your father's ship!"

"Arvel? I knew he'd come for me!" Ivey's heart skipped with joyous relief.

The craft came to bear against the cabin's hull. Its engines roared as the *Boreas* pushed the airship back from the funnel of water.

The black cloud and its raging winds were sucked into the open chasm beneath the *Monarch*, and seawater rushed to fill the void.

It was over.

The clear morning sky was as blue as the glimmering water below.

The *Boreas* rose to the observation deck, where it hovered effortlessly. A door on the side of the vehicle opened.

"Father!" Ivey waved wildly until she saw Stanley Honeycutt appear in the doorway.

"More help is on the way." He gestured toward the coast, where a formation of Zephyrs was flying before the second largest airship in the Fenchurche fleet, the *Regent*. It was a glorious sight, but Ivey's face fell.

"What is it?" Miles asked

"This can't be real," she cried.

"What?"

"Never in a million years would my life be saved by Stanley Honeycutt."

Miles laughed and rocked her in his arms. "Our reality is changing."

Ivey looked up at him. "Sylvia—"

The smile disappeared from Miles' face.

"Stanley, hold tight," he shouted. "We have injured who need to be taken to Spirehaven's hospital."

Ivey dashed through the cabin's hatch and down the steps to the bridge. Nicolai and the crewmen were already preparing Sylvia for evacuation. She barely made a whimper as they lifted her onto a canvas cot. Ivey leaned over to kiss her pale cheek.

"A farm girl is tough enough to survive this. I expect you back at work, Miss Feather."

Sylvia's eyelids opened slightly. "Yes, miss," she murmured.

Nicolai directed the process of hoisting the cot up onto the deck and into the hovering craft. He jumped in after it and reached back for Ivey.

"Are you coming?"

"No, others have injuries worse than mine. Will you please stay with her until I get there?"

"You can count on it," he replied.

Ivey raced back to the loft, where Minnette was tending to Doctor Brendel's broken nose while Miles packed tea towels around the bullet wound in Dolan's shoulder. His condition appeared to be every bit as serious as Sylvia's.

Miles and the crewmen used a blanket to lower Dolan over the loft's rail. From there, he was taken to the observation deck, where he joined the injured on the *Boreas*.

Ivey stayed behind in the loft. All but one of the Promacheon agents had already been carried out. She knelt down and touched the man's face. There was no trace of life.

She had also experienced the overpowering energy that the cipher device emitted. The poor man stood little chance of resisting its control. She bowed her head and begged forgiveness from the loved ones who would never see his face again.

Miles appeared beside her.

"Mother told me what happened."

"The dart that hit Ildwick was only a sedative. I used the poison against this man," she paused. "I did it without blinking."

"What can we do?"

She shook her head. "Nothing. I tried to escape it, but I've always known that I was destined to kill."

Miles put his arm around her shoulder. "Ivey, you saved so many lives. I would have done the very same for my mother—for you. There's no other choice when someone threatens the life of a person you . . ." He paused, as if searching for the right word.

A voice called up from below.

"Should we put Mr. Curio on the *Boreas*?" Harwood's men had carried him from the parlor.

"If there's space," Miles answered. "If not, he can sleep it off on the *Regent*."

"Oh, no! The tourniquet!" Ivey rushed down the loft stairs. She pulled up Ildwick's pant leg and untied the cord around his calf. The restriction of his circulation had produced swelling and a worrisome discoloration of the skin.

"How bad is it, Miles?"

He joined her, and felt for a pulse in the main artery.

"The blood has stagnated, he could lose his leg. We've got to get his circulation moving." Miles started massaging the muscles.

"Let me." Ivey laid her palm on each side of Ildwick's calf. As she rubbed the muscles she visualized her healing energy surging life back into his damaged tissues.

After a few moments, blood started to ooze from the wound left by the dart, and Ildwick stirred. His eyes cracked open.

"Sunshine?"

Ivey looked up and smiled. "Shut up."

"She adores me," Ildwick mumbled to a crewman before falling back into unconsciousness.

Miles patted him on the arm. "Go ahead and take him."

Harwood's men carried Ildwick up the stairs, and once he was on the *Boreas*, Stanley took off for Spirehaven at the craft's top speed.

After the *Regent* had come alongside the *Monarch*, an emergency gangplank had been extended between the two airships. The haggard passengers and personnel were evacuated while fresh crewmen came aboard to man the crippled ship.

A man wearing the uniform of a fleet captain entered the bridge.

Miles offered his hand. "Your ship is a sight for sore eyes, Captain McEvoy." He turned to Ivey. "Please allow me to introduce my friend, Ivey Thornton."

The captain blinked a few times. "Do pardon me, Miss Thornton. I didn't realize I was in the presence of a lady."

He graciously bowed over Ivey's hand in spite of her frightful appearance.

"Your father is the one who located the *Monarch*. A suite has been prepared for you, and one of Spirehaven's finest physicians will attend to your . . . needs." He tried not to stare at her bloodied blue hand.

Ivey turned to Miles. "Are you leaving the *Monarch*?"

"I have to oversee the transfer of auxiliary gas from the *Regent* to restore our envelope."

"Then I will stay and help you," Ivey volunteered.

Captain McEvoy raised a hand. "I apologize, Miss Thornton, but this ship is now closed to everyone except authorized personnel. The executive council is sending a team from Spirehaven to investigate what happened here. It's certainly no place for a fragile, young . . ." His voice trailed off as Ivey tightened her mouth and clenched her fists.

Captain LeClere chuckled. "You should know, Frederic, that there is nothing fragile about this young woman, and there's no use in telling her what not to do."

"And I believe you promised me a flying lesson, Captain LeClere. I'd like to begin once we're under way," Ivey added crisply.

Miles laughed at the other captain's befuddlement.

"A flying lesson?" McEvoy asked incredulously. "But the fleet protocol—"

"She's earned her place on my bridge. I think we can classify her as a temporary part of the crew." LeClere gave her an approving nod.

"Really, Captain?" Ivey's eyes lit up. "Do I get my own uniform?"

"You already stole one," Miles teased. "We both need to clean up and find something to eat. Then we should go see how your patch on the envelope is holding up."

"Oh, Miles." She held out her left hand, showing the frayed surgical thread on her palm. "Before we do that, could you help me remove these stitches?"

"I would love to."

On their way off the bridge, Ivey heard the two captains conferring.

"What in Aether is going on here, Ernst?"

"Well," LeClere replied, "you know what a peculiar young man Mr. Fenchurche can be?"

"I do."

"It seems he's met his match."

Because Ivey's suite had been sealed for the investigation, Miles invited her to use the master suite for the remainder of the flight while he stayed in his mother's quarters. He also offered to let her take another uniform from the lockers, but after hearing that a dozen crewmen and engineers were still unaccounted for, she'd felt it would be disrespectful.

After a long and soothing bath, Ivey was content to dress in Miles' clothes, which had a pleasant scent and were quite comfortable.

She was ready to leave the suite when there was a knock at the front door. Ivey checked her reflection in the dressing mirror and hurried to open it.

"I don't know about you, but I'm starving—" Ivey stopped. A group of serious-looking men were gathered in the parlor. "May I help you?"

"We represent the Cemarian executive council of Archons. They've sent us to open an investigation of the deadly events that took place on this ship."

Ivey noticed that the men were exceptionally well built for a group of politicians.

A burly man in front flashed an identifying credential and then quickly returned it to his breast pocket. "I'm Undersecretary Peel. Are you Ivey Thornton?"

"Yes." Ivey's heart started beating faster.

"I need to ask you some questions."

Ivey gestured toward the parlor. "Shall we?"

The man gave her a look that felt vaguely menacing.

"Your privacy is of the utmost importance in this matter," he said.

When he pushed past her into the room, she moved away, and the others followed him inside. The last one in shut the door and stood in front of it with his arms crossed.

Secretary Peel gestured toward a sitting room chair. "Please have a seat."

Ivey took a few steps back. "No, thank you. What do you want to know?"

Peel took a small notebook from one of his front pockets and referred to it. "We've spoken with members of the crew who claim you were stung by an asymbiant."

"Yes?"

"How did you survive?"

"A chemist on board made an antivenin. It was used to save other passengers as well."

"We've also been told that during a struggle on the bridge, you killed an agent of the Promacheon."

"I had to. He was trying to kill Minnette Fenchurche."

"We haven't found any direct witnesses to that event."

"Oh." Ivey blinked. "They've all been taken to the hospital."

"I see. And the color of your skin? How do you explain that?"

"Doctor Brendel used leeches to treat an infected wound I suffered. We believe their venom caused the discoloration."

"May we see this wound?"

"No. It's healed now," Ivey stammered. "But that's because of the leeches. They were the asymbiants."

Pointing at the scratches and cuts on her arms and face, Peel asked, "How did you get those?"

"I fought with one of the asymbiants."

"The crewmen told us that they saw this asymbiant after it had taken the form of a young woman it attacked. Did you witness such a thing?"

"Yes. We were trying to kill it."

"And did you?"

"It fell into the ocean. I jumped in to save my friend and it attacked me. I used a knife to slice it apart in the seawater. It was destroyed, so the threat is—"

"Was it destroyed?" the undersecretary asked sharply.

"What do you mean?"

"Who's to say that Ivey Thornton isn't lying dead at the bottom of the sea, and you have stolen her shape? We've heard you possess many uncanny qualities."

"Miles Fenchurche and Captain LeClere can verify my identity. You have to question them about the events. Ask them about the cipher machine and what it did to me."

Peel glanced at one of his colleagues in surprise.

"We have a security risk."

That man stepped forward and held up an official-looking badge. "We have been tasked directly by the Archon of War to protect this nation from creatures like you," he said.

"What?" Ivey gasped.

"You've displayed violent behavior, and you admitted that you killed a man," Peel coolly replied, returning the notebook to his pocket.

"Talk to Minnette Fenchurche," Ivey pleaded. "She'll tell you that I stopped him from murdering her in cold blood. I am not an asymbiant."

"Then why do you behave like one?"

Ivey gasped in disbelief. "I don't."

"By the time we reach Spirehaven, you will." Peel gave a business-like nod.

Two men jumped forward to grab Ivey by the arms, while a third plunged a hypodermic needle into her shoulder.

꩜

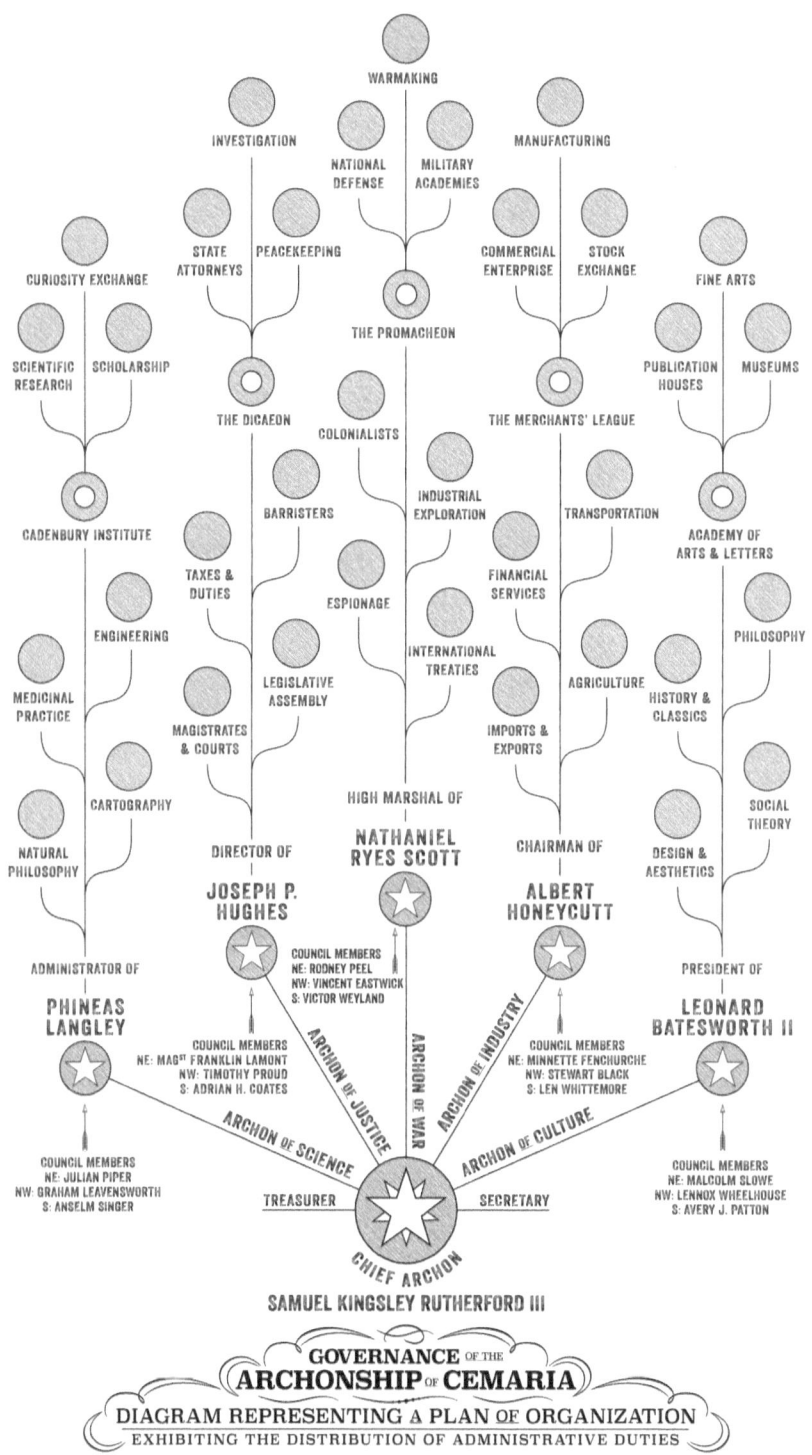

WARMAKING

INVESTIGATION

MANUFACTURING

NATIONAL
DEFENSE

MILITARY
ACADEMIES

STATE
ATTORNEYS

PEACEKEEPING

COMMERCIAL
ENTERPRISE

STOCK
EXCHANGE

CURIOSITY EXCHANGE

FINE ARTS

THE PROMACHEON

SCIENTIFIC
RESEARCH

SCHOLARSHIP

PUBLICATION
HOUSES

MUSEUMS

THE DICAEON

COLONIALISTS

THE MERCHANTS' LEAGUE

CADENBURY INSTITUTE

BARRISTERS

INDUSTRIAL
EXPLORATION

TRANSPORTATION

ACADEMY OF
ARTS & LETTERS

TAXES &
DUTIES

FINANCIAL
SERVICES

ENGINEERING

ESPIONAGE

PHILOSOPHY

MEDICINAL
PRACTICE

LEGISLATIVE
ASSEMBLY

INTERNATIONAL
TREATIES

AGRICULTURE

HISTORY &
CLASSICS

MAGISTRATES
& COURTS

CARTOGRAPHY

IMPORTS &
EXPORTS

SOCIAL
THEORY

NATURAL
PHILOSOPHY

HIGH MARSHAL OF

DESIGN &
AESTHETICS

DIRECTOR OF

NATHANIEL
RYES SCOTT

CHAIRMAN OF

ADMINISTRATOR OF

JOSEPH P.
HUGHES

ALBERT
HONEYCUTT

PRESIDENT OF

COUNCIL MEMBERS
NE: RODNEY PEEL
NW: VINCENT EASTWICK
S: VICTOR WEYLAND

PHINEAS
LANGLEY

LEONARD
BATESWORTH II

COUNCIL MEMBERS
NE: MAGᵗ FRANKLIN LAMONT
NW: TIMOTHY PROUD
S: ADRIAN H. COATES

COUNCIL MEMBERS
NE: MINNETTE FENCHURCHE
NW: STEWART BLACK
S: LEN WHITTEMORE

ARCHON OF JUSTICE

ARCHON OF WAR

ARCHON OF INDUSTRY

COUNCIL MEMBERS
NE: JULIAN PIPER
NW: GRAHAM LEAVENSWORTH
S: ANSELM SINGER

ARCHON OF SCIENCE

ARCHON OF CULTURE

COUNCIL MEMBERS
NE: MALCOLM SLOWE
NW: LENNOX WHEELHOUSE
S: AVERY J. PATTON

TREASURER

SECRETARY

CHIEF ARCHON

SAMUEL KINGSLEY RUTHERFORD III

GOVERNANCE OF THE
ARCHONSHIP OF CEMARIA

DIAGRAM REPRESENTING A PLAN OF ORGANIZATION
EXHIBITING THE DISTRIBUTION OF ADMINISTRATIVE DUTIES

Chapter Thirty

Escape from Panacea

Days had passed since Stanley and Nicolai set off in the *Boreas* to search for the *Monarch*. The morning after the two departed, Prim and Winora's visions had abruptly ended, and the dismal cloud over Thornhall lifted.

Soon after, Arvel had shared his discovery of the new baby with his wife. The joyful news filled their hearts with hope for a long and happy future with their growing family.

He hadn't heard a word from Silas or his men since the frightening event he'd witnessed in the Promacheon's hidden cipher laboratory. Arvel assumed that the machine had gone silent for some reason, but he suspected that Silas had other such installations hidden across Cemaria.

As soon as word arrived that Ivey was safely settled in at Ferndale, Arvel planned to do what he could to uncover the truth of the Cipher Program.

He sat at his desk, flipping through the pages of an old academic treatise written by his friend, Maddox Fenchurche. He was hoping to find some explanation for the unnatural happenings in Prominence and aboard the *Monarch*.

Not all of Maddox's ambitious ideas had won him favor with the rest of Cadenbury's scientific fellowship. Even Arvel had been dismissive of the eccentric claims about dimensional rifts that Maddox made in his last publications, but now, the extraordinary events befalling the Thornton family drove Arvel to reexamine the troubling texts.

He jumped to his feet when he heard a distinct pulsing sound coming from behind the manor.

"The *Boreas*."

To be safe, he grabbed the powerful dart rifle from his expedition bag and slipped out a side door.

Peering around the side of the building, he spotted a stranger in a blue Dicæon uniform striding up the path from Thornhall's gardens. He was headed toward the tree where Iris was pushing Prim's daughters in the swing.

Arvel raised the gun and set his sights on the man. Something lifted him from behind, sending the dart into a flowerbed and leaving his feet dangling in the air. He struggled to break away, but a pair of massive arms tightened around his chest.

A deep voice boomed in his ear. "Easy, Mr. Thornton. Your daughter would kill me if I break you."

"Who are you?"

"A friend of Ivey's."

"She doesn't have friends."

"She's got the finest lot I've ever seen. I'll put you down if we can talk about it."

"Yes," Arvel agreed. The hulking man set him down on the grass. "Where is she?"

Arvel had lied. He spun around to attack the stranger, but the giant man threw up his arms, blocking the disabling strike at his neck.

The man chuckled. "So that's where she learned it. Forgive me for the ambush. They may be watching your home."

"Who exactly?" Arvel stepped back as the big man reached into his pocket and produced a folded note embossed with the Fenchurche coat of arms.

"First, an introduction." He offered the note.

Arvel cast a wary glance toward the other uniformed man, who was standing uncomfortably close to the children. He unfolded the paper and read.

The Monarch *is safe. Urgent business is still at hand. Please trust those who have come to assist you. I am doing everything in my power to keep my oath. ~Miles Fenchurche.*

The big man offered his hand. "I'm Harwood, a senior officer of the Dicæon. Mr. Fenchurche and I met aboard the *Monarch*."

Arvel hesitated. "Where is Ivey now?"

Harwood grimaced. "She's been detained in Spirehaven."

"Detained? Why?" Arvel felt his temper rising.

"The Promacheon is holding her on an official directive. She killed one of Silas Harp's agents."

Arvel's shoulders sank. He could only imagine his daughter's distress at being confined for taking a life. "Will she be released?"

"We're not sure," he said. "The agent was strangling Minnette Fenchurche at the time. She had no choice. The Fenchurche barristers are working on the case, but she hasn't been allowed any visitors."

"Why not? It was justified."

"There were asymbiants on board the *Monarch*. Three were killed in their primary form. A fourth escaped, and things became ugly. Your daughter was able to kill it, but the physicians in Spirehaven believe that she may have been contaminated. They say she's dangerous."

Arvel needed no further explanation of the situation's dire nature. "Take me to her."

The officer raised his hand. "There are other matters."

"Nothing is more important to me than my daughter's well-being."

Harwood looked at the little girls on the swing.

"The only asymbiants in this country were kept in the Curiosity Exchange at Cadenbury, Mr. Thornton. I should not have to convince you of the risk posed to every son and daughter in Cemaria if any more of them are missing. Mr. Fenchurche thinks you might have information that can help us. I need you to come with me."

"He's not going anywhere." Winora was standing at the corner of the manor with a gun trained on the officer. "Leave now, or so help me, I will shoot."

The officer looked back at Arvel in exasperation. "These bloody dart guns . . ."

Arvel grimaced at his wife. "Darling, that isn't a dart gun."

Winora glanced at the weapon in her hands. "It's not? Good heavens, take this from me before someone gets hurt." She held it out for Arvel.

The man extended his hand. "Mrs. Thornton, I presume? I am Officer Harwood of the Dicæon."

Winora crossed her arms. "Why have you accosted my husband?"

Arvel explained, "It was a misunderstanding. Miles sent Officer Harwood. He's a friend of Ivey's."

Winora's face brightened. "How is she? Was her voyage pleasant?"

"It was astonishing," the officer said. "Now, if you would be so kind, I must speak with your husband privately."

"She should hear what you have to say. Let's go inside." Arvel pointed at the other man. "And what about him?"

"Lieutenant Faust's assignment is to guard your children."

"I beg your pardon?" Winora said. "You can't come on to our property without—"

"Your husband and daughter have made some powerful enemies, madam. My men will be staying here to keep watch over your family."

Winora frowned. "I am not accustomed to having strangers on the premises."

"Our orders came from the Archon of Justice. You are under the Dicæon's protection whether you like it or not."

"I see," she answered curtly. "And who will protect your men from me?"

"I'm sorry?"

"One word, and he meets his end." She pointed at the other officer. "Beast, show yourself."

The man on the path shrieked and fell backward as the snarling waterdog appeared, standing in front of the girls. Little Seren clapped her hands and squealed, while Iris hugged the ferocious creature's neck.

"If anyone sets a finger on my children, I will respond forcefully. I may be in a delicate condition, but I will not be trifled with. Consider yourself warned." Winora finished her threat with a gracious smile. "Now, may I offer some refreshments while we talk?"

Officer Harwood rubbed his neck. "You Thorntons are a curious lot," he finally muttered.

❧

Miles and his mother rushed down a long hallway in the secure ward of Panacea Hospital, trailed by several legal officials. They stopped at a door barricaded by an armed contingency of Promacheon agents who'd arrived from Prominence.

"The Promacheon has no claim on this patient," Minnette informed the agent who looked to be in charge. Turning to a small man holding an official-looking document, she said, "Show him."

The man thrust the paper in the agent's face.

"This order has been signed by Chief Magistrate Lemont under the direction of Archon Albert Honeycutt, and it bears the official seal of Cemaria's executive council. Step aside so that we may see her," he proclaimed.

Minnette glared imperiously at the agent.

His response was a terse, "No visitors."

Miles stepped forward. "Gentlemen, let's be reasonable. We have gone through all the proper channels. If she is not being tried under the War Act, you have no legal jurisdiction over her, and we have the right to visit her."

"No one but our specialists may enter this room until we determine whether the girl's exposure to asymbiants has caused any dangerous alterations. There is still a chance she might become one of those monsters herself. Either way, she is a threat to the greater good and must be moved to a secure location."

"I can assure you that she is Ivey Thornton through and through." Miles felt his jaw clench. Things weren't going as well as he'd imagined. "Where are you taking her?"

The man looked away, refusing to respond.

Miles took a step forward, tempted to shake an answer out of the fellow, but his mother shot him a look of warning.

She gestured to the lawyers. "Well, do not just stand there. Resolve this."

While the barristers stepped forward and argued their case, Miles cast a nervous glance back at the hallway behind him.

He was relieved to see an elderly doctor with a pronounced limp, approaching as scheduled. Miles discreetly looked away as the doctor presented his credentials to the guards and was admitted into the room.

∾

Once inside the cell, Ildwick removed the thick spectacles of his disguise and tucked them into a breast pocket on his white medical jacket.

He slowly approached the bed. Ivey lay in a dingy hospital gown with both of her arms chained to the bed's iron frame, her face turned to the wall.

What have they done to her?

From the dark blue color of her skin, he knew her condition was dire. At the moment, she appeared to be sleeping. He crept closer, reaching out for the place on her wrist where the shackles had torn into her flesh.

Before his fingers even touched her skin, Ivey arched her back and howled. The chains jerked so violently that he jumped back in fear.

She wrenched around to look in his direction, causing Ildwick to draw a sharp breath at the sight of her feral appearance.

"It's me, sunshine." He mustered a smile.

She stopped fighting and stared into his eyes.

"That's my girl," Ildwick said. "We haven't much time, so listen carefully. I have a medicine to make this stop. Please do not fight it. Go to sleep, and when you awake you'll see the moon in that window—" he pointed to a small casement sealed by thick bars, "—and then you must act quickly. Use this." He pulled a key from his pocket and showed it to her.

"This will free you from the shackles."

When he tried to push it underneath her back, she recoiled with a snarl.

"I know it hurts to be touched, but it must be hidden in a place that you can reach."

He tried again, and although she shuddered, she allowed his hand to slide the key under her waist.

"Good. Once you are free, break the glass."

"Doctor."

A tall man in a Promacheon uniform had entered the chamber and was standing behind Ildwick.

"What's that you're doing?"

"Sedating the patient."

"I am Major Aden Landers, the ranking officer overseeing this girl's quarantine and relocation. There were no orders for her sedation. Stop it at once."

"If you plan on moving her at daybreak, you will have one hell of a time." He muttered in a gravelly tone, inspired by Doctor Brendel's surly gripes.

"What is your name?"

". . . Barndale."

There was a long pause as the man scanned a piece of paper in his hands. "There's no Barndale on my list."

"I have been practicing at this hospital since you were in diapers. Now, shall I do my job, or would you rather deal with the thrashings of a rabid animal?"

Landers strode over to the bed. "She doesn't look so tough."

Ildwick held out a small vial. "Then maybe you'd prefer to give this to her."

The officer snatched it from his hand. He leaned down and pinched Ivey's nose shut, causing her mouth to fly open. The liquid was down her throat in the blink of an eye.

"Decent effort," Ildwick said.

"Anyone with an ill child knows that trick," the Promacheon officer bragged.

Hiding a smile because the man had failed to realize he'd administered the unauthorized medication himself, Ildwick limped toward the door.

"I have other patients to deal with." He went through and pushed his way into the crowded hallway.

Miles Fenchurche grabbed his arm.

"Doctor, I am this patient's fiancé," he said with an anxious frown. "They will not allow any visitors, so I need you to give her this gift on my behalf." Miles handed Ildwick a crystal vase stuffed full of the most expensive flowers available in Spirehaven.

"Do I look like a delivery boy to you?" Ildwick snatched the vase and hobbled back toward the room, muttering, "Damned Fenchurches think they own the world."

At the door, a young-looking agent blocked his path. "Stop where you are, Doctor. No unauthorized items can be taken into this room."

"Are you blind, man? These flowers are from her betrothed over there," he said. "For pity's sake, from what I've heard, he will never see his love again. Have a heart."

Luckily, the young man was susceptible to Ildwick's romantic plea. He took the flowers and carefully inspected the clear glass vase. Its slender neck was tied up with a green ribbon. The opening of the vase was small and tightly packed with the flower stems. He tilted it to pour a bit of the water into his hand, gingerly touching the liquid to his tongue.

"I will take this to her if you clear the rabble from this hallway."

Ildwick harrumphed loudly, "So, now I'm a common doorman? We used to teach respect for our elders."

Miles approached the agent. "We will leave, sir. But please, give her the flowers, and tell her that their beauty in the moonlight will reveal the depth of my affection."

A sympathetic expression hung on the man's face. "I am sorry for your loss." He turned and disappeared into the cell.

∾

Late in the night, Ivey awoke. Her mind felt clear, but she had little memory of what had transpired before Ildwick's arrival in her cell. There were dim visions of being dragged off the airship, and then of doctors forcing her into a strange room. She had no idea how or when she'd come to be manacled to a bed.

In the darkness of her cell, Ivey tried to remember Ildwick's hurried instructions. A ray of light shone through the small window in the corner of the room, illuminating an arrangement of flowers sitting on a shoddy table.

The moon. What was I supposed to do?

She reached beneath her back, searching until her fingers found the cold, hard edge of the key. She looked around to ensure no one was watching her from outside the cell door's grated window.

Ivey contorted her shoulders until the key fit into the lock on the left side of the bed. She twisted the key until she felt the tumbler click. As soon as her arm was free, she unlocked the other chain and crawled toward the moonlight streaming through the dirty windowpane.

Break the glass!

The window was high, and her legs were wobbly. She slowly pulled herself up and grabbed hold of one of the metal bars that protected the glass, giving it a yank.

It was solid. Breaking the pane would do no good if she were not able to pass through the tight bars. Ivey slid down against the wall, searching her memory for the missing piece of the escape plan.

The young man who entered with the flowers had said something about the moon as well.

The flowers in the moonlight . . .

She turned to the vase on the table and noticed the green ribbon.

Miles!

On the glass beneath the ribbon, something glowed in the light coming from the window. Ivey crawled over and found a message written in luminous chalk.

Break this.

She carried the vessel to the bed and wrapped it in the sheets to muffle the sound. Lifting one of the heavy shackles over her head, she brought it down swiftly.

There was a soft crunch, and a dark stain from the water spread across the fabric.

When Ivey folded back the bedding, she discovered a small red capsule hidden among the shattered glass and flower stems. She held it up in the shadowy light coming from the corridor. Inserted into the capsule's narrow tip was a small key. It looked a smaller version of the explosive charge that she had seen Miles and Nicolai use to destroy the cipher device.

Ivey looked back toward the window, dizzied by a sensation that the moon was bobbing up and down. She moved closer, holding her hand before her eyes to block out the glare from the orb of light.

It wasn't the moon. A Zephyr was hovering close to her window, waiting for her to escape.

∽

Panacea Hospital's night watchman was growing wary. A group of Zephyrs had arrived on schedule from Cadenbury earlier in the day, but nothing in his orders explained why this particular flying machine was hovering near the secure wing of the hospital, waving a bright light at one of the windows.

The guard blew his whistle seconds before an explosion tore through the side of the building, nearly knocking the Zephyr to the ground.

∽

Ivey had taken cover beneath her overturned bed after arming the explosive capsule and placing it against the window casement.

She pushed the mattress off and stumbled across the debris toward the rough hole left by the blast.

The Zephyr had disappeared. As she drew closer, she saw that it had dropped far below the level of her cell.

She noticed that a section of the wall separating the outside corner of her room from the next room was missing. Through the opening, Ivey saw the silver hair of an old woman. The woman was bound in a canvas jacket that held her arms tightly against her sides.

The head lifted, and a face that looked not much older than her own appeared beneath the tangled gray hair.

"Tell them to free me. I'm not mad," the woman said in a dry-throated whisper.

"Who are you?"

"Autumn—"

"You there!"

The cell door burst open, and guards poured into the room.

Ivey darted through the break in the outer wall, onto a narrow stone ledge that ran high along the side of the building. She teetered on the crumbling ledge for a moment before catching her balance and shuffling to a more stable section.

With her back pressed to the wall, she steadied herself and looked down. She was far too high in the air to make a jump, but the Zephyr was rising below her.

A uniformed man climbed through the hole beside her. He put his back to the wall and side-stepped the damaged section of the ledge. As he advanced, Ivey inched herself toward the corner of the building where the ledge ended.

He snatched at her hospital gown, but Ivey leaned away.

"Don't be a fool," he shouted. "Give me your hand."

"I'll die first."

"No one will hurt you," the man cajoled. "We need you alive."

Ivey looked down. She couldn't bear the thought of being caged for a moment longer. She raised her arms and prepared to jump.

"Stanley, get under her!" Miles screamed as Ivey flung herself from the ledge.

She hit the top of the glass cabin and bounced off, falling past the door before he could get it open.

Ivey grabbed for the Zephyr's landing rail. Missing it, she disappeared into the darkness below.

Miles threw the door open and stepped out onto the landing rail, refusing to believe that she had fallen. He reached for the spotlight that Nicolai had configured to run from the power of the otheophainer and swept it across the stone courtyard below.

There was no sign of a body, but several agents of the Promacheon were racing to their Zephyrs and would soon be in pursuit.

"Ivey?" Miles called.

"Miles! Help me!" Her voice answered from somewhere below the Zephyr's belly.

He knelt down and held on to the rail to peer beneath the ship.

Ivey was clinging to the end of a short rope ladder that he and Stanley had affixed to the rail.

"Have you got a good grip?" he cried.

"Yes!" she shouted back.

"Then hang on. We have to outrun the agents chasing us."

Miles extinguished the light and set it back inside the cabin. The Zephyr disappeared into the darkness as it raced over the rooftops of Spirehaven.

"We have her, Stanley. Get to the rendezvous!" Miles called out before kneeling down again.

"Stanley Honeycutt?" Ivey asked in complete bewilderment. "What's happening?"

"We're taking you to a safe hiding place. You'll be in good hands."

"With you?"

"No, I have to go back to Spirehaven."

"Miles? I want—"

"I have to clear your name," he insisted. "Please, Ivey, promise to stay put until I come for you."

"What's happened?"

"We can't talk now. Things are going to get bumpy. Hold tight," Miles said as he climbed back into the Zephyr.

Ivey tightened her grip as the vessel abruptly changed direction, making the ladder sway. She looked back and saw the Zephyrs in pursuit.

After several evasive maneuvers and a daring rush through a grove of trees, they emerged into the open countryside.

Miles leaned down and pointed at a lonely stretch of road where a wooden wagon was being pulled a pair of plodding workhorses. "There's your ride. Get ready to drop."

"We're going too fast."

"Stanley will slow down for you," Miles said. "There's hay in the wagon, so dig down and cover yourself. Stay hidden until it stops and a tall, funny-looking fellow calls your name."

"Miles, wait."

"You can trust him. His name is Basil, and you know his sister. Now, jump!"

Chapter Thirty-One

THE FEATHERS

Arvel had never been called into the private offices of the Archon of Sciences, Phineas Langley.

An executive aide opened the door. "You may enter."

Inside, Arvel and Officer Harwood found an illustrious group of councilors sitting around a table with Langley.

Among them was the Archon of Industry and Stanley's great-uncle, Albert Honeycutt. Albert had the distinction of being Cemaria's longest-serving archon. At the far end of the table, sat the newly appointed secretary of war, Victor Weyland.

Arvel did not recognize every face in the room, but the tall gentleman with snow-white hair and a handlebar mustache was undoubtedly the Chief Archon of Cemaria himself, Samuel Kingsley Rutherford III.

"Gentlemen," Arvel nodded respectfully as he took an empty seat. Harwood remained on his feet.

"Your report, please, officer." Langley's tone implied the anticipation of bad news.

"The Cipher Program has done it again," Harwood stated. "Things that defy explanation happened on the *Monarch*. We nearly crashed in two raging storms. An asymbiant ran amok, killing a passenger and two of the crew, as well as wounding many others."

The councilors' mouths fell open as Harwood continued. "There are critically injured victims in Panacea Hospital, and a dozen crewmen are still missing. If it weren't for Mr. Thornton and his daughter, everyone on that ship would be dead."

Samuel Rutherford looked at Arvel. "You were on the ship?"

"No, sir. Only my daughter."

"Then what role did you play in stopping this disaster?"

"The *Monarch* transmitted a message of distress through the cipher equipment. Silas Harp informed me of their situation, and I intervened to organize a rescue."

"Silas Harp came to you for help?" Phineas Langley sounded incredulous. "What exactly did you do?"

"I assisted in determining the ship's location."

The council members exchanged worried glances.

Victor Weyland was the first to speak. "And who knows about this, Mr. Thornton?"

Sensing a conflict within the group, Arvel chose not to mention the message he'd communicated to Ivey through Miles.

"Officer Harwood alone."

"How were you able to determine the *Monarch*'s location at sea?" Albert Honeycutt asked.

Arvel tensed. "That cannot be explained in any established terms. This cipher technology transcends boundaries we can barely comprehend. The link between the two devices allowed me to contact the ship. During that brief contact, the *Monarch*'s map coordinates were made visible and were recorded by an operator at the cipher facility."

Victor Weyland leaned back in his chair. "Well, it appears that this technology saved the *Monarch*."

Arvel turned to look at Weyland. The man seemed sincere, but if anyone understood the deadly ramifications of the Cipher Program, it would be a senior aide to the Archon of War.

"Sir," Harwood addressed Weyland soberly. "It was a criminal act for Silas Harp to put that receiver on a ship full of unwitting passengers."

Harwood crossed his arms and looked around the room. "We have yet to explain how hazardous specimens from the Curiosity Exchange found their way into the *Monarch*'s medical closet. And had she been told of the Cipher Program's history, Minnette Fenchurche would never have taken such a risk."

"None of that proves that testing of the cipher equipment caused any of the disastrous events," Weyland argued.

Arvel rose to his feet. He had to speak up, even though there was a risk that he would not be believed.

"There's something else you should know. When I engaged the device, I encountered something in the cosmocrene, something animate. I witnessed it attempt to take my daughter's life."

The chief archon leaned forward. "There's life in the cosmocrene?"

Arvel thought for a moment. "I can't define what I experienced in those terms, but I can assure you of this—I'm not the only person who's experienced its malicious effects."

Harwood spoke up. "You can count me in that number."

"That is why we've come here to warn you," Arvel continued. "It seems the cipher technology is allowing this dangerous force a means to reach into our world."

There was a long, ominous silence before Phineas Langley asked. "Where is this facility you speak of?"

Arvel was shocked that the archon didn't know. "Why, it's below your feet, sir, in a cavern excavated beneath this building's foundations."

Phineas rose from his seat. "Gentlemen, I suggest that we pay Silas and his project a visit."

Samuel Rutherford stood as well. "If Harp cannot convince us that these machines played no role in the disasters on board the *Monarch*, the project will be terminated at once."

"Please wait!" Arvel burst out. "There is another urgent matter. My daughter needs your help."

✋

Ivey waited until Stanley had her positioned directly above the wagon. She let go and fell backward into a thick pile of newly mown hay.

The Zephyr had pulled up and sped away by the time she had concealed herself. Moments later, she heard the sound of other Zephyrs passing overhead. Stanley had proven to be an excellent flyer, but she hoped for Miles' sake that he was the best pilot in the air that night.

She might have enjoyed the hayride on a late summer evening if her situation hadn't been so desperate. The stars shone above, and a warm breeze wafted through the sweet-smelling fodder piled around her. She tried to relax, but it seemed like an eternity had passed before the wagon stopped and she heard footsteps approaching her.

"Miss Ivey, we're here. You can come out now."

She sat up, expecting to discover the tall man that Miles had described. Instead, a short and pudgy adolescent boy gaped at her.

"Who are you?" Ivey asked warily.

"I'm Basel," he said innocently enough.

"No, you aren't," she said. "Miles said Basil is tall."

"That he is." The boy spoke simply. "But I'm not Bah-zul, I'm Bay-sul."

Ivey scowled. "I was told that Basil was a tall, funny-looking fellow."

A lanky young man with dark hair and familiar-looking hazel eyes appeared beside the wagon. "That I am. Well, not that *funny-lookin'* part. Glad to meet you, miss. I'm Basil Feather." He stuck out his hand in greeting. "My big sis says you're somethin' special."

"Sylvia! How is she?" Ivey seized his hand and pumped it up and down enthusiastically.

"All banged up, but we Feathers are made of tough stuff. She'll be back from the hospital soon, and the doctors reckon she'll be fit as a fiddle in no time at all."

"That's wonderful. Are you related to Sylvia too?" Ivey asked the other boy.

"Not yet," he said with a gleam in his eye.

"Not yet?"

"He's just an idiot stable boy; pay him no mind," Basil laughed.

The young lad batted his eyelashes flirtatiously. "Basel Stone is my name, but a pretty girl can call me whatever she likes! Dashin', darin' . . . darlin'!"

Ivey smiled at his antics. "Basil will do."

"I'm not Bah-zul." He pointed at his friend. "He is."

"Haven't you two got the same name?"

"Not at all. He's Basil with an *i*, I'm Basel with an *e*."

Ivey's forehead knotted into a small, perplexed crease. "Strange."

"Let's go in," Basil suggested. "Mær'll have us a good hot meal. Yer skinny as a filly off her feed."

"Who's an idiot now?" little Basel chided. "You'll never get a girl to kiss you if you tell 'em they look like hungry horses!"

"Oh, gee, I'm sorry, miss." Basil thumped himself on the forehead. "I'm an idiot, too."

Ivey patted his hand. "Never mind that. I've been told that I eat like a horse, and quite frankly, I can't remember the last time I was fed."

Sylvia's brother lifted Ivey out of the hay and set her on the ground. She stepped out from behind the wagon and into view of a cottage with glowing windows and the shadowy outline of a large barn in the background.

The trio had just started up the path to the house when the front door opened and a merry little woman with apple-colored cheeks bustled onto the front porch to greet her.

"Miss Ivey! Welcome to our humble home."

"Mrs. Feather?"

"Only to strangers, dear. My name is Beatrice. Call me Bea." She put her hands to her cheeks and clucked in dismay as she took in Ivey's ragged clothing, bare feet, and ratted hair.

"Poor little lamb, you've had nothin' but misery." She put a motherly arm around Ivey and grinned. "That's all over now, miss. We've got a warm house and a hot meal waitin' for you. Boys, put the horses up and make yourselves presentable for dinner. We don't want to keep the lady waitin'," she giggled.

The cheer radiating from the woman was infectious, and Ivey's natural reserve began to thaw until something rustled in the darkness beside the house.

Ivey broke away from Bea and dropped to a crouch, her hands raised defensively. She sucked air through her teeth, making a loud hissing sound.

Little Basel nearly jumped into his friend's arms. "Here it comes!"

"Calm down, you little sissy," Basil teased nervously. "It's just the Pær."

A bear of a man carrying a pitchfork stepped into the light.

"Don't be upset, dearie. It's only my husband, Benjamin," Bea said kindly.

"Didn't mean to spook you, miss. I was just makin' sure no one followed the boys. I promised Mr. Miles that we would protect you like one of our own. He said Sibby would be gone from us if it weren't for you." He turned to the young men. "You heard the Mær. Get the team put up before anyone comes snoopin.'"

He smiled warmly and offered Ivey his arm. "Come on in now, sis."

Ivey stepped back. The Promacheon's drugs hadn't completely worn off, and the fright of hearing something in the dark had her heart racing with a primal instinct to escape.

"You can trust us," he coaxed. "You're one of the family now."

The sweetness of his tone eased Ivey's anxiety. She slowly reached for his arm and went with him.

Inside, the cottage was neat as a pin. It was filled with simple, well-made furniture and decorations. The rooms were small with plastered walls and low-hanging wooden ceilings, but Ivey found the tight space surprisingly comfortable.

Seeing Ivey in the light, the Feathers' cheerful expressions faded.

She rushed to explain. "Yes, my skin . . . I was bitten by something on the *Monarch*, but I swear, I am not like them. I would never hurt any of you."

Bea sighed. "Of course not, sweet child." She reached for Ivey's wrist, where the lacerations from the manacles were still open. "I'd have half a mind to go to Spirehaven and give those bad men a whippin' myself."

"We wouldn't even treat an animal like that," her husband agreed. "But we'll leave those scoundrels to Mr. Miles." He grinned at Ivey. "Sibby says you're the best medicine that mother of his ever gave him."

Ivey stared at her grubby feet.

"Oh, Ben, you stop that, now. Come along, dear, let's tidy you up. Sibby's bed is all made up for you."

Bea took Ivey's hand and led her to a neat little bedroom. "There's hot water in the washbowl, and I laid out some of Sibby's things for you. They'll be a might bit big, but they're clean and awfully soft."

❧

The group of men packed tightly into the car of the elevator and descended the long shaft toward the Promacheon's cipher laboratory. Harwood had sent a party ahead to ensure the safety of the executive figures venturing into what he warned might be hostile territory.

Harwood and the rest of his officers rode in the front, gripping their weapons as they listened for any sounds of trouble coming from below.

When the door opened, the officers stepped out and scanned the hallway before motioning for Arvel and the rest of the group to exit. They hurried down the long hallway that led to the reinforced door at the cavern's entrance.

It had been driven from its track and was hanging precariously. Harwood held up his hand, ordering the men back while he spoke to an officer who emerged from the opening.

"It's scrubbed clean, sir. They knew we were coming."

"I'm not surprised. If Harp has a receiver in Spirehaven, he would have been warned long before we arrived at Cadenbury."

Arvel moved forward, trying to peer through the doorway.

"May I?"

Harwood nodded, and Arvel stepped through.

The only light in the cavern came from the globes that had been carried in by the first group of officers. Arvel picked one up and moved forward, stepping carefully as he searched for the edge of the pit.

The further he walked, the more perplexed Arvel became. The rock floor was completely solid all the way to the laboratory's far wall. He followed the wall for a distance then turned and walked back across the center of the cavern to be certain.

The pit had vanished, along with every trace of the dome and the towers of equipment that had surrounded it.

Phineas Langley and the executive council members entered the space. Many of them picked up lighted globes and walked about in silence, studying the area.

Victor Weyland nervously rubbed his forehead. "There must be a mistake. This can't be the installation you spoke of."

"What do you make of this, Arvel?" Albert Honeycutt asked.

"Either the facility that Silas showed me was an illusion, or a cipher device is capable of transporting more than messages."

Weyland looked at Arvel sharply. "Mr. Thornton's word is all he has to prove his assertions."

"Not quite." Harwood stepped forward. "Mr. Thornton's daughter appeared out of thin air on the *Monarch*'s deck."

"It is unwise to make hasty conclusions," Weyland insisted. "We are in a time of crisis, and there is much confusion, Mr. Harwood."

"I'm a senior officer of the Dicæon, sir, and I saw what the cipher device did with my own two eyes. There is no confusion about the men who disappeared from the belly of the ship. The *Monarch* barely escaped destruction, and its owners were almost killed by agents of the Promacheon."

Harwood turned to the chief archon with a blunt question. "Do these occurrences seem coincidental to you, sir?"

Rutherford shook his head in dismay. "This must stop. Find Silas, and put an end to the Cipher Program immediately."

❧

Chapter Thirty-Two

TURNABOUT IS FAIR PLAY

Nearly a fortnight had passed since Sylvia's release from Panacea Hospital and return to her old room at the Feather family farm. Bea had planned to let her guest sleep in Basil's empty room, but Ivey insisted on making use of a simple cot beside Sylvia's bed while she recuperated.

"Time to wake up!" Ivey burst into the room carrying a tray of Bea's sausage biscuits with peppered gravy and jam. She set the tray on a table and threw open the window shutters.

"I'll never get used to this." Sylvia rubbed the sleep from her eyes and stretched. "Ow!" she yelped, clutching the plaster cast protecting her broken arm.

"Easy there." Ivey adjusted Sylvia's pillows. "How's that?"

Sylvia reached out and gave her hand a squeeze. "It's wonderful. I always wished I had a sister to share my room."

"Your father says we're one big family now, so you have me plus four more sisters in Prominence! Eat up, there. You'll want to be ready when your gentleman caller arrives."

Sylvia blushed. "Ivey. He's only pretending."

Nicolai Slate had been a constant visitor to Sylvia's room in the hospital, so it aroused no suspicion for him to make routine visits to the Feathers' farmhouse. His discrete purpose was to keep Ivey informed of the legal proceedings of her case and carry words of encouragement from Miles, but Ivey suspected that he held another particular interest in calling every day.

"Pretending?" She laughed. "Oh, I've seen this sort of nonsense before, Sylvia Feather! The secretive holding of hands, the longing gaze into bashful eyes, and the sweet sorrow of every good-bye. That man's dumbstruck in love, and if he isn't, I'd say he's an actor of great talent!"

"Indeed," Sylvia said softly, "to be so kind to an old maid like me."

"Old maid? What a dreadful expression. You're hardly older than me, Miss Feather. And besides, marriage isn't the only thing we girls are good for."

Sylvia shook a finger at Ivey. "Don't you start with that again."

"I will start. You know I have no intention of getting married at any age."

"But Mr. Miles—"

"When things calm down, I will settle the matter with him."

"You can't fool me," Sylvia chided. "I've seen how you miss him. You hang on every word Nicolai reads of his reports."

"Well, of course I do. If Miles doesn't succeed, I'll either spend the rest of my life in hiding or being used as a test subject in one of the Promacheon's laboratories."

"And you trust him to do that because you have feelings for him. Don't you?"

Ivey glanced off as she responded, "Not those kind."

"Look me in the eye and say that," Sylvia challenged.

Without flinching, Ivey met her friend's gaze and spoke firmly. "I have great admiration for the man. I trust him with my life, which is a lot more than I ever expected from our arrangement. I simply have no interest in marriage.

"And look at me." Ivey gestured to her discolored skin. "Who could think for one moment that Minnette Fenchurche would ever allow her son to bring a real blue-blood into the family?"

"You won't feel that way forever. I know it in my heart."

"I hope that Miles and I will always be friends, but honestly, why can't I enjoy life on my own?"

Sylvia smiled sadly. "Because it's lonely. Didn't you ever wonder what it must be like to spend all your days and nights with someone you love?"

"No. I've seen what that claptrap did to three of my sisters. Once the ring goes on your finger, you belong to your husband. His wants and needs come before yours—and then there are the babies." Ivey shuddered. "I say no thank you, miss, but if you like the sound of it, why don't you get married?"

Sylvia looked up with a rueful expression. "No one's ever asked me."

"Then ask for yourself."

"Ivey, you say the strangest things," Sylvia laughed.

"Turnabout is fair play. If you want to be Nicolai's wife, then let him know."

Sylvia's eyes clouded. "A gentlemen like him desires proper ladies, not their maids."

Ivey sat down and gently lifted Sylvia's chin with her hand. "If that's true, then Nicolai is a very poor gentleman."

Ivey stood and rubbed her hands together. "Now—you saved my life, and that means I have a responsibility to look after yours. So, either you say something to him, or I will."

"Please don't! I would die—" A harsh knock at the door startled them into silence.

"Hide," Sylvia whispered.

Ivey glanced around and saw that the only escape was the window. She was halfway through the opening when a grumpy voice sputtered from the other side of the door.

"I don't have all day, ladies."

Ivey rolled her eyes at Sylvia and mouthed the words, "Doctor Brendel."

Every one of the doctor's visits to the farm brought another unpleasant treatment for Ivey. Minnette expected the poor man to restore her complexion, but none of his remedies had shown any sign of success.

Ivey sighed and climbed back into the room. If Miles could restore her liberty, she would resign herself to a secluded life with blue features and avoid doctors altogether.

She opened the door. "Good morning to you, Doctor."

"If you insist." He whisked past her and went to Sylvia's bedside. "Have you been resting?"

Sylvia nodded meekly.

"Sleeping well? Keeping a bland diet?"

Sylvia hid a smile as Ivey snuck the breakfast tray from the bedside table and set it out of sight on a chair.

"Yes, sir."

"Good. Then it's time to get up and start moving around."

Sylvia's eyes lit up. "At last."

"Slowly," he said emphatically. "Do not exert yourself. Begin by walking around the house, and when you recover more strength, you may go outdoors—if someone stays by your side. A fall could put you back in a hospital bed under my watch again."

"Thank you, Doctor. I will do exactly as you say." Sylvia beamed at Ivey.

"That's good news," she agreed. "What about Autumn, Doctor? Have you found her yet?"

"No. I've told you before, the girl doesn't exist."

"I saw her as clear as day. She begged me for help."

"The drugs you were given are meant to cause hallucinations. There is no record of any girl named Autumn being kept as a patient of Panacea, nor is she listed as a resident of Spirehaven."

"She was real, Doctor. You've heard how the Promacheon treated its prisoners. No one deserves that."

"Trust me, their private ward has been emptied, and the ruffians will never gain access to our facilities again. Those of us on the hospital board will make certain of that." Doctor Brendel's gruff demeanor softened as he reached for Ivey's hand.

"I am sorry to bring you bad news, Miss Thornton. We've exhausted every possible remedy to no avail, and your affliction does not appear to be resolving itself. You may have to accept that your skin will never return to normal."

Ivey put on a brave face. "Sylvia's recovery is all that matters to me." She leaned close to inspect his face. "And I have to say, your nose is healing nicely."

He rubbed it and sniffed delicately. "It is askew. I think it adds character." He almost smiled. "It was my first brawl, you know."

"You were mighty brave to tangle with ruffians like those." Ivey smiled kindly, knowing that the men would have likely finished him off if she and Minnette hadn't intervened.

"Yes," he answered somberly. "I am sworn to do no harm, but I will not stand idly by while any man threatens a lady."

Ivey stared at her hands, caught in one of those awful moments when her mind flashed back to killing the agent.

"You both saved us," Sylvia spoke up. "I'm sure that Mrs. Fenchurche is grateful. I know Mr. Miles is."

"Yes, he certainly is," said a soft voice from the doorway.

"Miles?" Ivey ran across the room and threw herself into the young man's arms.

He patted her back.

Ivey pulled away and hung her head, to hide the crush of conflicting emotions behind her eyes.

"Well?" Sylvia finally asked on her behalf. "Is it over?"

"Yes, and this makes it official." Miles handed Ivey a document on fine letterhead.

She looked down and skimmed the opening paragraph. Her eyes caught upon a sentence bearing her name in bold script.

The Promacheon, under direction of Archon Ryes Scott, its officers and secretaries, and the whole of its agents are to immediately relinquish any claim of custody over

Ms. Ivey Thornton of Prominence,

whose deadly actions against Sgt. Griffith Page aboard the airship Monarch on the 27th day of the 9th month constituted no violation of Cemarian High Law, and whose Bill of Health has been found to pose no danger to the governance of the nation and safety of its citizens.

She looked up at Miles, unable to control the quivering of her chin. "I'm free then?"

"Yes. All claims against you have been declared null and void. Sadly, the conspirators of your escape from Panacea might face charges, but they remain at large . . . though Fenchurche Industries has offered a generous donation to repair the damage to the hospital building," he added with a sly grin.

Ivey looked up into his eyes. "Really? There's nothing dangerous in my blood now?"

Miles gave her an apologetic shrug. "I can't say." He held out his arm. "The two of us are closely matched, so when our Doctor Barndale presented samples to the hospital's superintendent he found perfectly normal blood with no characteristics of an asymbiant."

"Barndale?" Doctor Brendel grumbled. "Who the devil is that?"

Ivey couldn't stop herself from smirking. "A true curmudgeon of a healer. He almost reminds me of someone else," she added, before turning back to Miles. "How is the *doctor*?"

Miles shook his head. "He's off on mysterious business, but his leg will be fit in no time."

"I've no time for chitchat. Here is my advice, Miss Thornton," Doctor Brendel interrupted. "Things went to hell in a handbasket the moment you arrived. Now that this matter has been put to rest, I do hope you will try to settle down and act like a lady. And for pity's sake, let the rest of us catch our breath."

He turned to Sylvia. "And you—don't try to keep up with her antics, or it really will be the death of you, my dear."

In spite of his irritated tone, Ivey caught a glint of pride in the doctor's eyes.

"Farewell, Doctor Brendel," she said with a slight curtsey.

"Indeed." With that, he stomped from the room.

Miles smiled. "Now, there's something else we need to discuss."

Ivey's mind flooded with questions she'd been waiting to ask. "That can wait. I've been patient, but now I have to know—what was Stanley Honeycutt doing with my father's ship? Why wasn't Arvel part of the *Monarch*'s rescue? And where was he the night you helped me escape from Panacea? He hasn't even come to see how I was doing here. My father would never sit by while I was in danger or in need. Is anything wrong?"

Miles stared at his feet. "He's been dealing with certain matters."

"What are you not telling me? Did something happen to him?"

Miles looked up quickly. "Not him. The cipher device was also affecting Primrose."

Ivey put a hand over her mouth as another memory flashed through her mind. "I knew something bad was going to happen." She looked at Miles in terror. "Did my sister drown and no one told me?"

Miles took her by the shoulders and looked directly into her eyes. "No. There was an accident, but trust me, she and the baby she's carrying are fine now. Your father had to stay and protect her, though, and he trusted Stanley and me to help you."

"I see." Ivey couldn't shake her sense of apprehension. "Once Sylvia's recovered, I'm free to go see my family at Thornhall and live wherever I wish to. Is that right?"

"On my word, it is." Miles laid a hand across his heart.

His conviction gave Ivey a great sense of relief until she realized that she no longer knew where she belonged. Despite the harrowing series of events since she'd left Thornhall, both the *Monarch* and the Feathers' farmhouse had begun to feel like home. Her first taste of independence was sweet, and it would be impossible to resume life under her mother's rules.

"Before you decide where you're headed next, I have something for you." Miles reached into his breast pocket and handed her an ornate envelope.

Ivey carefully removed the card inside. On the top she saw a beautifully rendered picture of the *Monarch*. It pained her to recall that last sight she'd caught of the broken and battered ship as the Promacheon agents were dragging her away.

Basil and Basel claimed that the nearby village of Shadydale was spinning with rumors that the *Monarch* was being torn down at the maintenance dock in Spirehaven.

She opened the card and began to read. Ivey's jaw dropped open.

"What is it?" Sylvia asked impatiently.

"An invitation." Ivey turned to her and read:

The pleasure of your company is requested upon the night of the harvest equinox to rededicate the Airship Monarch and honor the heroic crew who brought her safely home. The ceremony will be followed by a masked ball and nightlong cruise open to all distinguished guests.

"The *Monarch* lives!" She grinned at Miles. "This is perfect! Sylvia will be back on her feet just in time."

"Miss Ivey, stop!" Sylvia said, mortified. "That invitation is yours . . . a serving girl cannot go to the ball," she stammered.

Miles gave a lighthearted shrug. "I see. I suppose I'll have to discard this one." He pulled another invitation from his pocket. "It was addressed to a Miss Sylvia Feather, who I believe played an unmistakable role in saving my life and my ship."

Sylvia looked miserable. "Oh, sir. I really cannot. I've nothing to wear. I'd have to buy a dress."

"That's already been arranged," he assured her.

"Oh, no. I wouldn't know how to . . . I mean, I've never . . ."

"Sylvia. I would never underestimate your ability to masquerade," Miles said with a wink.

"Masked balls are great silly things," Ivey acknowledged. "But haven't you ever wondered what it would be like to spend all night dancing in the arms of someone special?" Ivey lifted her brow at Sylvia.

"Not yet!" Sylvia squealed.

"I do hope you will reconsider." Miles hung his head with a guilty smile. "You see, poor Nicolai could find no one to escort, and it's possible that I might have encouraged him to take you."

Sylvia disappeared like a tortoise into its shell under the quilt on her bed.

"She accepts!" Ivey proclaimed.

"And you, Ivey?" Miles turned to her with great earnestness as he asked, "May I have the honor of escorting my fiancée?"

Ivey's stomach did a flip. He'd spoken as if those words had meaning. "Your what?"

"Well, we never formally announced our engagement, and this ball would be the perfect setting."

"Perfect setting? Miles, look at me." Ivey held out her discolored arms. "What will all those people think?"

"They will be in costumes and masks, you will stand out no more or no less than Sylvia."

Ivey swallowed hard. "May we speak as friends?"

Miles took her arm and led her away from where Sylvia was still hiding under the covers.

"Please do."

"Prim told me that you didn't want to enter this arrangement any more than I did. Your mother's feelings are very clear. And no one knows what will happen with my condition. Why do we have to plan a future that isn't—"

"I only wish to celebrate life and anticipate our future, whatever it may be." Miles moved closer. "All I ask is that we share a dance, Miss Thornton. I don't expect you to do anything ridiculous, like . . ."

His gaze drifted down to her lips.

Ivey's heart was beating wildly.

"Please say yes?" Miles leaned closer.

Ivey tugged at the collar of her borrowed dress as a drop of perspiration rolled down her back.

"She accepts," Sylvia answered from beneath the covers.

"Sylvia!" Ivey jumped away from Miles, covering her cheeks to hide her extreme embarrassment.

"Turnabout is fair play." Sylvia threw the quilt from her face. "Miss Ivey and I would be honored to attend your ball, Mr. Miles."

At a loss for words, the only thing that Ivey could think to do was snatch the tray from the chair and back out of the room, mumbling something about Sylvia's breakfast going cold.

❧

Chapter Thirty-Three

A MISFIT

W here did a lady like you learn to scrub so well?" Bea Feather bent down and admired her spotless kitchen floor.

"Oh, I've had plenty practice," Ivey said with a laugh. She dropped her bristle brush into the pail of sudsy water and rose to her feet, wiping her wet hands on the legs of her trousers. "From an early age, my sisters and I were given daily chores."

Ivey set her hands on her hips and surveyed her work as she continued, "Twice a year, my mother cleans the whole manor from top to bottom. It's a big house, so she's lucky to have five daughters to help."

"Your mother cleans her own house?"

"She says it's a wife's duty to make an inviting home for her husband."

"Now, that's good common sense," Bea exclaimed.

"Hardly. I agree that cleaning is good exercise and is uplifting for the soul, but tell me, why wouldn't such a thing benefit a man equally well?"

Bea tapped a finger against her chin. "Sibby said you have an odd way of lookin' at things."

"I find it odd that anyone considers cleaning to be a woman's work."

Bea's brow furrowed. "Oh me, hope I didn't offend, miss."

"Not at all." Ivey put her arm around Bea. "It's my pleasure to help you prepare for guests."

"They'll be arriving soon. I'll put things away while you get ready."

"I am ready," Ivey answered nonchalantly. Because Sylvia's dresses didn't fit, she'd taken to wearing old work clothes borrowed from little Basel, and was set on adopting the style of dress for good.

"Oh, Miss Ivey, you say the funniest things." Bea waved her away with a laugh. "Now, scoot!"

ॐ

The *Monarch* ball was days away, and the whirlwind of final preparations had the Feather household in a tizzy. Sylvia and Ivey were scheduled to have a fitting for their masquerade costumes before lunch, and a dancing lesson was on the agenda not long after.

Shortly before midday, an elegant Fenchurche carriage pulled up in front of the farmhouse. Sylvia was out on her daily walk with Nicolai, and Bea was busy in the kitchen, so it fell upon Ivey to answer the sharp knocking at the door and greet the tailor.

"It's you?" she blurted out, surprised to discover Paisley Fitzroy leaning against the porch rail. Ivey had hoped that Minnette's pet designer would have been too occupied dressing the socialites of Spirehaven to bother with her costume.

"Such manners." Paisley took a disdainful sniff. "Trust me, darling, I'd rather be anywhere but here."

Chenille Foxton emerged through the open carriage door and climbed down unassisted while Paisley strutted past Ivey into the farmhouse.

He cast a look around the front room. "Good lump, some people really live like this?"

"I'd say they live better than most," Ivey said, keeping a wary eye on the man.

In the chaos surrounding her detainment at Spirehaven, Ivey'd never had an opportunity to tell any officials that Paisley Fitzroy was partially responsible for Amelia's death on the *Monarch*. Even if she had tried, it would have been impossible to prove the horrors she'd witnessed through the poor girl's eyes.

She was still confident that Paisley's reaction to the details of her testimony could implicate him in the matter, but it had to be delivered in the right time and place. For now, she would have to be civil.

"Mr. Fitzroy, welcome."

"I must say, you look even worse than I heard . . . and what are you dressed in?" Paisley gave her a scorching look from head to toe.

When she failed to take the bait, he continued, "Well, fortunately for you, I've constructed another gown that will conceal your feminine flaws and accentuate your most colorful assets."

"How nice," Ivey muttered through clenched teeth.

She turned to Chenille, who'd followed him into the living room. "It's good to see you again, Miss Foxton. Is Mr. Fitzroy treating you as nicely as he did Miss Buxhill?"

Paisley took a menacing step in her direction. "Why Ivey Thornton, are you playing with me? You should know, I play for keeps."

"And," Ivey responded firmly, "you should know that I am capable of winning."

"Yes, tell me, how is jail these days?"

Bea's cheerful entrance with a tray of drinks kept Ivey from having to answer that question.

"Oh, Mr. Fitzroy, it's such an honor to have you in my home!"

Bea giggled like a girl as Paisley bowed and kissed her hand.

"The honor is mine, madam."

His smile and tone were so convincing that Ivey could have thought this display of respect was genuine.

"And what a charming little hovel you've got here," Paisley exclaimed. "I had no idea life in the country was so . . . bucolic."

Beatrice beamed. "I can't wait to see what you're fixing for our Sibby!"

Her eyes grew watery. "We thought she was lost, you know, and now here she is, off to a real ball on the finest ship that ever flew—and wearin' one of your dresses!"

"Dear lady, these are no mere dresses. I craft works of art that can have no price."

"Don't be so modest, Paisley," Ivey interjected. "They're worth at least half of what people pay you."

Chenille tried to stifle a short laugh, but Paisley's dark glare turned toward her.

"Do something useful for a change. Go and fetch the gowns," he said with an arrogant toss of the head.

Chagrin written all over her face, the girl started toward the door.

Ivey started after her. "I'll help you," she offered.

"I can do it myself." Chenille turned on her heel and stomped off.

"Chenille, wait." Ivey followed her outside and spoke softly. "That man is dangerous. Please go back to Prominence before you end up like Amelia."

Chenille eyed her with suspicion. "You really are mad, aren't you? Everyone knows that Amelia was killed by a monster. Paisley had nothing to do with it."

"But he did. Paisley took her to the garden room and knocked her to the ground. Then the coward ran away, leaving Amelia alone with that creature."

"Why would I believe a thing you say?" Chenille continued as she climbed into the carriage. "Have you looked in a mirror lately? You're every bit as monstrous as the thing that killed her. I should hope they put you back in a cage soon, Ivey Thornton."

The carriage door slammed shut. A second later, it reopened and two large dress boxes tumbled out and landed in the dirt. Chenille leaned forward to glare at Ivey. "You were never worthy of a Fenchurche. Go back home and let a suitable lady have a turn at him."

Ivey took a breath. "I'm only trying to warn you, Chenille. Before things with Paisley Fitzroy go wrong, you need to get away."

"Humph," the girl scoffed. Seeing Nicolai and Sylvia approaching, Chenille shut the carriage door and closed the curtains.

Nicolai hurried over and knelt to pick up one of the boxes. "These must be your dresses, ladies."

"These are no mere dresses," Ivey said as she dropped down beside him. "They're torturous, overpriced abominations."

Sylvia giggled at Nicolai's stunned expression. "She's only joking. Open the box, and let's have a peek."

Nicolai read the label on the box in his hands. "This one is yours, Sylvia." He stood and lifted the lid for her.

Sylvia folded back the paper, revealing a gown made of a multicolored, iridescent fabric. When she lifted the top of the dress, the fabric at the shoulders unfurled.

"It has wings—butterfly wings!" Sylvia cried. "I've never held a garment this finely crafted."

"Look at this." Nicolai reached into the box to remove a jeweled, wing-shaped mask fashioned to accompany the dress. He pulled on the stretchable strap across the back. "It's made to wear, so you won't have hold it all night."

"You'll be the belle of the ball in this, Miss Feather!" Ivey exclaimed.

She looked down and frowned at the other box lying on the ground in front of her. "I suppose this one is for me."

Ivey tossed the lid aside and ripped open the tissue paper. The silky fabric inside was streaked with green, deep purple, and a shade of blue that nearly matched her skin.

"A colorful asset indeed," Ivey muttered.

With a sigh of resignation, she picked up the dress and stood, holding it high to inspect the design.

The gown had a long, elaborate train made of fabric and feathers, but the sparse amount of substance on the top made it nearly impossible to tell the back from the front.

While she and Sylvia held it one way and then another, trying to make sense of the risqué bodice, Nicolai coughed in embarrassment.

"Mr. Fitzroy!" Ivey shouted at the open door of the cottage. "What makes you think I would ever be caught dead in something like this?"

∽

Ivey endured a miserable fitting process during which Paisley repeatedly stuck her with long pins while marking the areas that she felt needed more fabric.

After he'd checked the nearly perfect fit of Sylvia's costume, he and his sulking companion had finally departed.

Bea served a late lunch on the back porch, and Ivey was helping clear the dishes when she heard a second carriage coming up the drive.

"They're here now!" Ivey exclaimed. She plopped down the plates she was carrying and raced through the house to greet Miles and his mother's assistant, who were scheduled to give Sylvia, Nicolai, and herself a lesson in ballroom dancing.

The carriage door opened and out stepped Dolan. She hadn't seen the man since his evacuation—in a deathly condition—from the *Monarch*. A sling under his open jacket was evidence that his shoulder had yet to heal from the gunshot wound, but he looked to be in remarkably fine shape.

"Dolan! Oh, Dolan, how are you?"

"Very well, Miss Ivey," he replied, taking note of her cross-dressed attire. "Still charming gentlemen out of their clothing, I see."

"I've missed you," she laughed.

"And I you, Miss Ivey."

While Ivey offered him a gentle hug, she couldn't resist peeking around him through the open door.

The carriage was empty.

She straightened. "Where's Miles?"

"Well . . . something's come up. Business affairs—last minute. He sends his regrets."

Dolan was adept at many things, but lying wasn't one of them.

For some reason, Miles hadn't visited the farm since the day he'd delivered her invitation to the ball. There could be no doubt that he was avoiding her.

Ivey tried to hide her disappointment with a casual shrug. "I see. Then how will we take our dancing lesson?"

"I am certain that Nicolai can manage two partners," Dolan said with a comforting pat on the shoulder.

"No need, Mr. Dolan." Basil Feather strode up, followed by the rest of his clan. "I'll dance with her," he said, wearing a goofy grin.

Ben held out a well-worn fiddle. "And I'll play us all some dancin' tunes. The old barn's a fine spot for fancy footwork, ain't it, Mær?" He smiled at his wife, who nodded enthusiastically.

Everyone made their way to the barn, and the dancing lesson commenced. The Feathers were in high spirits, but Ivey was frustrated by her inability to follow Dolan's instructions. The only dancing she'd ever done was standing on her father's feet during her sisters' social events. She found it difficult to keep track of the repetitive patterns and follow Basil's meandering lead. He was an eager partner, but his legs tangled easily, and he kept stepping on her toes.

Little Basel finally cut in to give Ivey's feet a break. His dancing was markedly more competent. His hand, however, had a way of slipping down the back of her waist, forcing Ivey to pull it back up to where it belonged.

The lesson would have been completely miserable if Sylvia's happiness wasn't so infectious. Even with her injuries, she fit perfectly in Nicolai's arms and easily followed his lead.

Her parents were bursting with pride, and Ivey recognized the look in Bea's eyes. It was the same one her mother had whenever there was a wedding to be planned.

Before leaving for town that evening, Nicolai offered to fly Sylvia to the ball in his Zephyr. Ivey heartily encouraged her to accept the offer, but Sylvia declined, explaining that she planned to ride alongside her friend in the carriage Miles would send for them.

∾

That night, Ivey tossed and turned on her cot. No matter how hard she tried, she couldn't get Chenille's words out of her head.

I should hope they put you back in a cage soon, Ivey Thornton.

The Feathers had welcomed her presence on their family's farm. Cemarian high society, on the other hand, would not be as willing to overlook her blue skin and unconventional ways.

Miles had won her freedom from the Promacheon's imprisonment, but what if other government agencies in Prominence decided that she still posed a threat?

I would rather die than live in a cell.

As her fears of confinement rose, Sylvia's bedroom began to feel tight and stuffy. Ivey finally gathered up her blankets and crept out to sleep in an open field.

She gazed up at the stars, trying to envision the path of her future.

There was no joy in imagining what lay next in her relationship with Miles. The chill of his absence made Ivey realize how much she missed being around him. She worried that he had stayed away so there would be no opportunity for her to talk him out of publicly announcing their engagement at the *Monarch* ball.

Ivey was certain that marriage and children were not in her future. Regardless of her own feelings, she had little doubt that a clumsy union between them would ruin Miles' prospects to find happiness in both his career and home.

It was imperative that she speak to Miles before the ball and convince him not to make such a mistake. If he resisted, then she would have to leave so he might find someone else to fulfill that role in his life.

As she finally drifted off to sleep, Ivey wondered whether the only place in Aether where she could find a happy sanctuary was at Thornhall, by her father's side.

∾

Chapter Thirty-Four

THE MONARCH BALL

O n the afternoon of the harvest equinox, a crystal coach grand-
er than anything the Feathers had ever seen came to collect
Ivey and Sylvia for the ball.

Basil was driving the carriage, wearing a coachman's uniform borrowed from the stable master at Ferndale. As Basel loaded the overnight
trunks, Basil jumped down to offer a hand as the girls, dressed in their
masquerade gowns with masks in hand, climbed into the empty coach.

On the road to Spirehaven, Ivey got her first good look at the landscape west of Cemaria's largest city. Among the patchwork of farmland
settlements, there were several beautiful estates situated in the foothills
of the Rosman Mountains. As she stared out the window, Ivey wondered how these opulent properties compared to Ferndale Manor.

"What's wrong, Ivey?" Sylvia asked.

"Nothing in particular."

"You've barely said a word, and you almost look miserable."

"That may be," Ivey replied.

"Why?"

"It's my nature to be selfish . . . and I'm going to miss you."

"Miss me? Why would you say that?"

Ivey sighed. "I don't want to spoil the surprise."

"Oh, miss, please do," Sylvia implored, "I'm not going anywhere."

"Yes, you are," Ivey argued. "I will be happy for you, though."

"Ivey Thornton, tell me what is going on in that head of yours, or
you'll spoil the whole ball for me."

Ivey finally relented. "Someone's going to have a proposal for you
tonight."

"A proposal? You don't mean . . ." Sylvia fidgeted with the sling
around her plaster cast. "Nicolai is an important scientist. He can't go
marrying a common maid."

"He won't," Ivey explained. "You'll be a proper lady, and your new calling will be to make him endlessly happy."

"No," Sylvia argued. "My job is to care for you. I wouldn't desert you, Ivey."

"Then I'll desert you," Ivey said softly. "We'll always be friends, Sylvia, but I can look after myself—and I can't let you miss a chance for your dreams of romance to come true."

"Well then." Sylvia's expression became defiant. "You should be warned. I intend to do the same thing for you, Ivey Thornton."

"See?" Ivey laughed. "You've already proved my point. No Fenchurche servant would ever take that tone with her mistress. You never were a common maid, Sylvia Feather, and you're not going to be an old maid."

Ivey's heart was torn as she leaned forward to lay her gloved hand over Sylvia's.

"I'm happy to have helped make that possible," she continued bravely, "but I think it's time for me to go home."

Sylvia caught her breath. "No. Ivey, please tell me you're joking."

Ivey squeezed Sylvia's hand. "You are my dearest friend, and your family is wonderful, but I'm missing my own."

Sylvia's bottom lip quivered. "I can be selfish too, you know. I don't want you to leave. Not yet. You promised to show me how to fly," she patted her sling. "And I can't learn with a broken wing."

"Take your time to heal. Someday I'll be back to share my best secrets."

"At least come see Ferndale before you go. I promise you won't be bored. It has secret rooms and passageways . . . and mysterious visitors . . . and—"

"Really?" Ivey straightened in her seat. "Secrets and mysteries?"

"Servants aren't allowed to gossip." Sylvia narrowed her eyes. "You'll have to see for yourself, miss."

The carriage rolled to a stop in front of the *Monarch's* docking platform.

"Now, you insisted that I come with you and be part of this masked silliness," Sylvia said. "Why not try to have a little fun?"

Nicolai was waiting for them on the dock. He rushed over, reaching the carriage before Basil had time to climb down and open the door.

"No need, lad, I'll do it," Nicolai called up to him.

"They're all yours then," Basil replied.

Sylvia laughed as Nicolai opened the door. He was dressed in a flowing golden robe and pointed conjurer's hat. In one hand, he held a staff affixed with illuminated glass orbs.

"What in Aether are you supposed to be?"

"I am the wizard of time and space, of all things past, present, and future," he said, giving her a deep bow.

Sylvia's eyes lit up. "Really? Can you see my future?"

"I certainly hope so." He offered his arm to help her down from the carriage step. "Rather—perhaps, we might discuss such things later."

Ivey nudged Sylvia in the ribs and whispered in her ear. "Looks like I can predict the future too."

"What did she say?" Nicolai asked.

"Oh, it's nothing sensible." Sylvia quickly took his arm and climbed down the step.

She turned her back to him. "Nicolai, would you mind fastening my wings? They wouldn't fit through the carriage door."

Nicolai snapped the pliable supports into place, allowing the wings on the back of her gown to float in the air.

"And now this?" Sylvia held her mask over her shoulder.

Nicolai helped slip the butterfly mask over Sylvia's beautifully coiffed hair.

Sylvia faced him and asked, "How do I look?"

"Like something I could only dream of . . ."

Ivey gathered her skirt to exit the carriage. When Nicolai turned to help, she could tell that he was trying very hard not to gaze at her exposed collarbones.

If there had been any other options, Ivey would never have allowed Paisley to dress her as one of the elegant peafowl that roamed the grounds of Ferndale.

The dress was striking, however. She had to give him that.

The saturated colors of the fabric were hand-painted with rows of overlapping feathers, and the gown fit her like a glove. The corseted bodice had been devised to allow a deep neckline in the front, and a dauntless open back that revealed the lines of Ivey's blue spine all the way to where a train of long peacock feathers emerged from her waist.

Ivey's demand that he cover the swaths of exposed skin in the front and back were met when Paisley returned the dress two days later with only a fine blue netting to disguise the strange pigmentation of her flesh. The mesh insets began at the waist and continued up until they crossed her shoulders, reaching to the top of her neck.

The gown's billowing sleeves were fashioned from a sheer green fabric and were tucked into golden gloves that completed her disguise. Ivey's mask was made of feathers, and when she slipped it over her head, her entire face was hidden, except for her turquoise eyes and painted red lips.

She felt a gaze upon her.

Across the platform, in the *Monarch*'s open entryway, stood Miles— wrapped in the purple cloak of an ancient scholar.

Seeing him silhouetted against the restored vessel caused Ivey's heart to skip.

The moment their eyes met, he turned and disappeared into the crowded lobby.

What?

Ivey felt her knees begin to tremble. A part of her wanted to turn and run.

After watching Miles' retreat, Ivey turned to see that her friend had been watching her.

"Would you be kind enough take us in, sir?" Sylvia asked, giving Nicolai a gentle push, prompting him to offer his other arm to Ivey.

"Shall we? This will be a night to remember," Nicolai said with a hopeful smile aimed in Ivey's direction.

Not wanting to spoil his evening with Sylvia, Ivey took his arm and returned the smile.

They entered the airship's lobby, which was already teeming with costumed guests.

Across the cavernous room, an ensemble of chamber musicians played in the midst of a barren expanse.

Ivey's beloved glass garden was gone.

The winding stairway to the third level rose starkly from a strange, dark floor that hid any evidence that the botanical wonder ever existed.

To their right, the grand staircase to the second floor had been festooned with garlands and orchid-shaped tea lights, but they paled in comparison to the floral masterpiece that had once been the heart and soul of the *Monarch's* lobby.

Ivey's stomach twisted. In this incarnation of the ship, she was a stranger.

A tall, thin figure outfitted as a royal court jester approached. Even before she noticed the telltale bandage immobilizing his wounded shoulder, Ivey recognized Dolan's ramrod posture.

She laughed heartily. "Well! I never imagined I'd see those legs in tights!"

"It seems that Mr. Fitzroy has a sense of humor." He inspected her up and down. "You're looking remarkable, as always, Miss Ivey."

"I'd trade costumes with you in a heartbeat," Ivey grumbled.

"Heaven forbid. Blue is not my best color."

Ivey laughed. "Dolan, that was a fine joke!"

"Well, I am the jester," he replied dryly. "And as always, I'm on a tight schedule, so if you and Miss Feather would find your seats, we will begin the memorial ceremony." He gestured toward a row of chairs at the foot of the staircase.

"Before that, I must speak with Mr. Fenchurche," Ivey said firmly. "It is important."

"He's asked me to relay that he will be unavailable until after the ceremony."

"Is that so?" Ivey felt a growing sense of unease. She pointed her finger and stuck out her chin.

"Then go tell him if he doesn't have the time to hear me out before making a public announcement, I will have no choice but to leave his ship."

"To think I actually missed this." Dolan shook his head and hurried off to deliver her threat.

"Now, now, sunshine . . ."

Ivey spun around. "Ildwick?"

"I'm glad to see you haven't lost that spine of steel . . . which, by the way, is looking quite nice from where I stand." The man couldn't resist chuckling at his own joke while he held out his arms.

Ivey might have considered hugging him, but was inclined to merely offer her hand.

He bowed and kissed her glove.

She stared at his costume: a long-tailed black suit with a full cape and a tall black hat. Below his half-mask, he sported a curled mustache.

"And who are you supposed to be?" Ivey asked.

"A thief!"

"Ah," she said. "I'd have guessed a mortician."

"Yes, well, I have been robbing graves."

Ildwick looked at Sylvia. "And who is this voluptuous social butterfly? Could it really be you, my dear Sylvia?"

"Please keep to yourself, sir." Sylvia shrank back against Nicolai's side.

"Goodness, have you already forgotten those two long nights we spent together? I do hope this handsome gentleman hasn't stolen all of your affection."

Nicolai's mouth gaped, but before he could respond, Ivey stepped between them. "Pay this rat bag no attention, Nicolai. He's only trying to stir things up."

"Guilty as charged," Ildwick admitted before turning back to Ivey. "Now, be a good little peahen and get your tail feathers into the seat of honor that's waiting for you over there."

"You're lucky I haven't got my gun," Ivey muttered.

"You've shot me once, sunshine. Isn't that sufficient?"

Ivey looked down at his leg. "It appears you've recovered."

"Save me a dance, and I will show you."

"I am in no dancing mood, and if Miles doesn't make an appearance right now, I will be leaving."

Ildwick leaned down and spoke softly in her ear.

"Listen here, you little realize how much is at stake this evening. If you spoil my plans by throwing a tantrum, I will not hesitate to turn you over my knee and spank you."

"Dammit, Ildwick!" Ivey said. "Must you insult me with more riddles?"

"You know you love it." He smiled and pointed to the second-floor landing of the lobby's grand staircase, where Miles and the other speakers for the evening were assembling.

"Go find the seat with your name on it. Things are about to get interesting."

While Nicolai ushered the two of them across the lobby, Ivey noticed that Ildwick gave Miles a small salute before disappearing into the crowd.

The musicians stopped playing when Captain LeClere stepped forward onto the stairway's landing.

First, he paid homage to the service staff who'd put their lives at risk while caring for the passengers and flight crew. Then he spoke of the crewmen who remained at their posts during disaster after disaster, fighting to keep the ship aloft.

Finally, he delivered a heartfelt tribute to those who had perished. A large painting was unveiled above the staircase with the portraits of the missing and lost crewmen depicted below the *Monarch*'s envelope.

"And now," he spoke in a voice heavy with emotion, "may we all take time to reflect on the tragic events and acts of courage that took place aboard this vessel."

Ivey clutched Sylvia's hand and fought back tears as her own fateful moment in the loft overtook her mind again.

The silence was broken when Minnette stepped forward on the landing, wearing a look of consternation.

"Thank you, Captain," she said before turning her attention to the crowd below. "Fenchurche Industries can never repay our exemplary crew for the sacrifices they made in service of the *Monarch*.

"The events that took place here were unimaginable, and the suffering of our passengers cannot be forgotten either. We respectfully mourn the loss of Amelia Buxhill, who was not safely returned to her family. And to all those with the grace and resilience to join us here tonight, we thank you for your courage and willingness to forgive.

"Although this evening is meant to lift the spirits, Fenchurche Industries does not take lightly the horrendous events that occurred and the lives that were lost on one of our ships. So, due to the tragic nature of her last voyage, the *Monarch* will be taken out of the passenger service fleet, and a new ship, the *Matriarch*, will be made the flagship of the Fenchurche luxury line. Please, enjoy the *Monarch's* final act of hospitality."

The crowd erupted with shock and confusion.

Minnette gave Miles a nod before she turned and walked away.

Ivey's heart sank. It made no sense to have restored the ship only for Minnette to announce its dismissal.

"Please . . . ladies and gentlemen," Miles spoke over the raised voices. "I have a happier announcement."

"I cannot stay here," Ivey said as she began to rise from her seat.

Sylvia gripped her arm tightly. "Yes you can. If you respect Miles, do him the honor of listening to what he has to say."

Ivey relented, sinking back into her chair and bracing herself.

"Thank you." Miles acknowledged the quieting of his guests as he descended the stairs.

"We are here tonight to partake in an old Cemarian tradition. The farce of your disguises and warmth of your merriment will stand in defiance of the tragic disaster that many of those here tonight survived.

"Like the masked balls of our ancestors, through centuries of plague and war, tonight's celebration will assert the undying will of our people's spirit to emerge from calamity and greet tomorrow with hopeful laughter."

Miles turned to the group of costumed guests sitting in the chairs of honor.

"Our survival, although miraculous, did not come as a gift of happenstance. In spite of the crew's every effort, the *Monarch* would have been lost if it were not for the heroic acts of certain passengers and employees aboard the ship."

He approached a plump woman dressed as a black and white cat, sitting in the first chair.

"Lucey Sue Stilwell, you were steadfast in the face of danger, proving that you are well worth your salt. In recognition of your exemplary service, you will be rewarded with a cottage home and garden of your own on the grounds of Ferndale."

Miles waited for the applause to die down before he gestured toward a portly knight in a mock suit of armor sitting in the next seat.

"Doctor Mathias Brendel, it would seem that you are both a healer and a warrior. We were blessed to have someone with your dedication in our deadliest hour. In your name and honor, Panacea Hospital will be given a new wing—where your precious gift of healing can be shared with everyone in this community."

The next figure in the line of chairs was an enormous Audelian judge in a powdered wig that covered most of his face. Miles gave him a crisp salute.

"Officer Harwood, you broke many protocols in the interest of saving lives on board the ship and protecting our nation. It was not within your orders, but it was nevertheless right, and Cemaria is well served by such an officer. In support of your efforts to protect all citizens, Fenchurche Industries will sponsor the development of a new generation of larger flight engines, which shall be named the Notus, for the exclusive use of the Dicæon."

Miles continued down the line. "Ildwick Curio, when things looked their darkest, you delivered us from great peril by sharing your many talents as a chemist and a swordsman. Fenchurche Industries is forever in your debt, and in return for your assistance, you will be permitted unfettered access to all of our experimental facilities as you further your research."

Ivey's heart hammered against her ribs as Miles drew closer to her chair.

"Gustavo Dolan Wyndham, it was once said that you have no life outside of your position as my mother's personal assistant, yet you were willing to give that life defending her and this vessel. Your composure in the face of danger is inspirational, and to ensure that you may heal in peace, the company has decided to send you on a well-earned vacation to anywhere you desire, accommodated in the master suite of the *Regent.*"

The smile faded from Miles' face as he came to the trembling butterfly next in line.

"And now, to someone who deserves very special recognition. I asked her to play a vital role on this voyage, and she exceeded every one of my expectations. Her intelligence, loyalty, and generosity of spirit are beyond description. She breathed the life back into me, and in a moment of crisis, it was her courage that finally rid this ship of its wicked intruder. She in turn suffered great injury and will need much time to heal. It is with sadness I report that my dear friend, Sylvia Feather, will no longer serve my family at Ferndale."

The crowd gasped.

"What does that mean?" Sylvia buried her masked face in Ivey's sleeve. "Am I fired?"

"No—that's not possible." Ivey stared through her own mask at Miles, who carefully avoided her piercing gaze.

When she started to rise, he hurried to finish.

"Sylvia's next appointment, should she choose to accept it, is as the second in command to the new owner of the *Monarch.*"

The crowd reacted with cheers and confused mumblings.

Miles' eyes finally turned to Ivey.

She was on the verge of panic, but her feet were rooted to the spot as he continued his speech.

"Which brings us to our final heroine, the one soul truly responsible for the miracle of our survival. She came aboard this ship a young girl sent against her will, but her strength of purpose and fearless devotion to the well-being of this vessel and its passengers proved beyond any doubt that this young woman's rightful place is at its helm.

"It is her destiny to ride the winds of Aether from her home in the clouds. Ladies and gentlemen, it is with pleasure that I introduce you to the new mistress of the *Monarch*, Miss Ivey Thornton."

Miles withdrew a parchment scroll from inside his robe and held it out to her. "I offer you this deed. Will you accept it?"

There was a long silence as Ivey struggled to find any words with which to respond.

Ildwick finally leaned forward and whispered, "Say yes."

Ivey couldn't move or speak, fearful that she would awaken from what had to be the strangest and best dream of her life.

She heard Sylvia's voice. "We accept! You do . . . don't you?" Sylvia squeezed her hand.

Ivey finally found her voice. "What do you mean by this?"

"The *Monarch* is yours to do with as you please."

"It's too much for one person. How would I manage it?"

"A trust has been set up in your name to maintain the ship and pay the expenses of her crew. If you don't take it, the *Monarch* will be discarded."

"Why me?"

"Every person on board would have died if it weren't for you, Ivey. You love this ship more than anyone, and it offers you the freedom to go wherever your heart leads you. It would be my honor to give you that which you have rightfully earned. Please, will you accept this deed?"

Ivey took a deep breath and slowly approached, taking the parchment from his hand. "I will."

The crowd applauded wildly, and to Ivey's great surprise, several voices were cheering her name.

Miles took her hand and held it high.

"Ladies and gentlemen, if you may," he called them to order. "It's time for Miss Thornton to perform her first official duty! Please join us on the docking platform for the rededication and blessing of this vessel."

Ivey was numb with joy as he walked her through the boisterous crowd in the lobby and out onto the dock.

In the warm glow of the setting sun, she was handed a bottle of sparkling wine to celebrate the rebirth of her ship.

"According to tradition," Miles explained, "a ship can be renamed at the time of its dedication. You may call her whatever you want."

Without hesitation, Ivey raised the bottle. "All hail the *Monarch*—the greatest vessel to ever rule the skies of Aether! Long may she sail in peace!" She smashed the glass against the bow while the crowd cheered.

After the ceremony, the delighted guests returned to the lobby, where they were treated to endless glasses of spirits. The masked revelers toasted the maiden voyage of the reborn *Monarch* as she lifted off and sailed into the western sky.

When they reached the cruising altitude, the dark floor that had replaced the glass garden began to glow with a projected image of the ground below.

As the guests gathered around to stare in wonder, Miles invited them onto the crystal ballroom floor to enjoy the best view.

When the last vestige of daylight had faded, taking the view of the countryside below with it, filaments in the floor lit up in undulating patterns of the constellations beneath the guests' feet. The crowd moved back to watch, and the musicians raised their instruments, waiting for their cue.

Miles walked Ivey to the center of the floor and turned to face her. "May I have the first dance with the mistress of the ball?"

With the warmth of the bubbling wine tickling her nose and a powerful sense of freedom flowing in her blood, Ivey was delighted by the prospect of dancing in his arms but reluctant to make herself the center of the crowd's attention.

She stood on her toes and whispered into his ear, "I'm sorry. It seems that I have two left feet when it comes to this sort of thing."

Miles took her firmly into his arms. "I'm quite proficient. Just follow me."

Ivey was skeptical. "Following has never been my strong suit."

"Then read my mind. You'll know every move I'm going to make before I do." He nodded at the musicians, who began to play.

"Start with your left foot forward," Miles said leaning toward her ear. "Then sidestep and close."

Ivey did her best to follow his instructions and avoid stepping on his toes.

"Good. Now, repeat with the right foot: forward, sidestep, close. And again with the left."

Ivey giggled as they smoothly moved in one direction.

"Isn't it about time to reverse?" she asked.

"You read my mind, Miss Thornton! I think you've got it."

To her surprise, as they glided across the floor, Ivey's feet naturally mirrored his, and following his lead was much easier than she had expected. She gradually relaxed into his arms and found that she enjoyed dancing.

All too soon, the first song was over.

Nicolai and Sylvia joined them on the dance floor, followed by the other guests, for a spirited traditional dance that sent couples whirling among each other in lines and spirals. Nicolai was mindful not to keep Sylvia on her feet for too long, but Ivey felt that she could have danced all night.

As the evening wore on, the music softened, inviting a more intimate style of dance. Nicolai held Sylvia closely while Ivey and Miles carried on with a long conversation in each other's arms, unaware as each song blended into the next.

After questioning Miles about her confinement in Panacea and all that had happened since then, Ivey turned her attention back to the *Monarch*.

"This floor . . . it's magical, but why did you remove the glass garden?"

"To make sure the asymbiant left no venomous residues behind, the *Monarch*'s entire pipeworks had to be torn out and destroyed," Miles explained. "The garden floor was pulled up in the process, and it seemed like a change was in order.

"Someone once taught me that wild creatures weren't meant to live in such a cage, so I set them free."

Remembering her words about the dying songbird, Ivey's eyes glistened beneath her mask. "You are a quick study, Mr. Fenchurche."

He leaned close. "You are a fascinating subject, Miss Thornton."

"Tell me more—" she glanced away, "—about the reconstruction, I mean."

"Most of the damage from the storm has been repaired, but there's still work to be done inside. It's actually something I would like to talk about when the time is right."

Ivey's curiosity was instantly piqued. "Now is fine. Please, go on."

"Fenchurche Industries has been asked to join an alliance of scientists dedicated to studying the cosmocrene and its possible threats to this world."

"Isn't that what Cadenbury does?"

"If it hasn't been compromised."

"So—" Ivey looked at Miles sharply. "Is that what Ildwick was doing on this ship?"

"Yes."

"Does his alliance have a name?"

"The Affiliation of Independent Researchers."

"And what does that have to do with me?"

"Our affiliation will need a secure research center, and Ildwick has presented me with an intriguing idea— if you are agreeable, of course. What would you think of replacing part of the passenger decks with laboratories, so that scientists can travel around the world to share their findings?"

"An airborne scientific research facility?" Ivey bounced on the tips of her toes as they danced. "That's brilliant! We have so much work to do. Oh—wait! Would this alliance be willing to work with someone like me?"

"If the facility was on this ship, I'd imagine the owner would set those rules."

"I see." Ivey pondered for a moment. "Then here's the first rule. Any capable woman who wishes to participate will always be welcome on my ship." Ivey lifted her chin and stared into Miles' eyes. "What do you think of that?"

Miles returned her gaze. "I think that Aether needs every bright mind it has on the front lines if we are to defeat what threatens us."

"The Cipher Program?"

"Let us leave that for later," Miles offered kindly. "I would rather we simply enjoy ourselves tonight."

"All right, but may I ask you one more question?"

Miles nodded. "Of course."

"How does your mother feel about all this?"

"When the ship returned to Spirehaven, she meant to scrap it and be done, but when I proposed deeding the ship to you, she agreed that it was the right thing to do. So, once again, it was your destiny to save the *Monarch*."

"Why didn't she stay for the ball?"

"She's unhappy, but about something else. Captain LeClere resigned from her service this afternoon."

"Really? Why?"

"It seems that he wishes to work under fewer rules and regulations. He is your captain now, Ivey."

"Miles, you must do something." Ivey held out her arm.

"Yes?"

"Pinch me as hard as you can."

"Do what?"

"What if this is all an illusion, and I'm still in that horrible little cell?"

"I vowed to be your champion. It's my duty to keep breaking you out until it becomes reality."

"Oh!" A joyful thought struck Ivey. "If my father joins the alliance, he and I will be able to work together!"

"Yes, but the *Monarch* will have to remain docked in Spirehaven until the refitting is completed. In the meantime, I was hoping you'd come with me to Ferndale. I could use your help on something of great importance."

"Really? What is it?"

"Harwood managed to secure highly classified documents that will help Nicolai and I construct a machine to simulate the cipher device's mode of operation. It may allow us to determine the nature of the effect it had upon you. If we are successful, we may discover a way to keep you and anyone else from being harmed by it again.

"Such an experiment could result in the type of dangerous events we experienced on our voyage. This could put you at risk more than anyone, and I'll understand if you'd rather not be involved."

"Miles, if there's any way to bring those missing crewmen home, you have to try."

"So, you're willing to help us?"

"With all my heart." She laid her head against his chest with a sigh. "Thank you, Miles. Thank you for letting me follow my dreams."

Miles held her a little tighter. "Thank you, Ivey, for giving me that chance."

The music stopped, and Miles glanced at their feet. "Look, we landed on the Five Sisters."

"What?" Ivey looked down.

"Your constellation." He stepped away and pointed at the pentacle glowing in the glass floor beneath them. "The Five Sisters."

"The Five Sisters?" Ivey stared. "Are you sure that's a constellation?"

"Didn't your father tell you a story about five princesses and the evil spirit that stole their queen?"

Ivey shook her head in bewilderment. "No. Never."

"Are you certain?"

Ivey laughed. "Miles, this is the first I've heard of it."

Miles frowned as the next song began. "How strange. I guess it was only a dream. It seemed so real."

"Maybe it was real, in another place and another time," Ivey replied. "Our awareness only scratches the surface of our existence, but that machine was taking us deeper."

Miles reached for her, and they began to dance.

He was quiet for some time. Ivey sensed that he was struggling to say something.

"Was there anything else?" she finally asked.

"I was wondering if your parents ever spoke of my father."

"Yes. They've said many kind things about him."

"Would you happen to know if he visited Thornhall shortly before he died?"

Ivey leaned back so abruptly, she nearly broke Miles' hold on her.

"The answer to that question is serious . . . I'd rather not discuss it here."

"Of course, I'm sorry. I've arranged a private dinner later. Perhaps then." Miles drew her closer.

"I believe this is the last number. Let's enjoy the music and dance."

Ivey nodded agreeably, but she had spied Ildwick from across the floor, waltzing with a petite woman dressed as a black spider.

There was something uncanny about the lady's appearance. The stylized web draped across the red hourglass on the back of her costume was occupied by a large, violet-colored arachnid. Ivey assumed that it was merely a decoration, but somehow its legs waved in time with the music.

"Who in the world is that?"

"What?"

"Look over there. The spider lady with Ildwick." Ivey pointed.

"I've no idea, although something has been occupying a good deal of his time lately."

"Really?" Ivey leaned away from Miles' arms. "I'm going to find out who she is."

Miles pulled her back. "Hold on. I'm the one leading tonight, remember?"

Ivey craned her neck to look around him.

Ildwick caught her staring and whispered into his partner's ear. The woman stopped dancing and turned to look straight at Ivey. The many eyes of her headpiece covered most of her face, but a single wisp of silver hair hung in the center of her forehead.

She gave Ildwick a kiss on the cheek before disappearing into the crowd that surrounded the dance floor.

Before Ivey could go after the mysterious woman, a dark-robed figure with an executioner's hood tapped Miles on the shoulder, indicating a desire to cut in. Without waiting for a response, the man brushed Miles aside and clutched Ivey in a tight hold, forcing her around the floor in a manner that had very little to do with dancing.

"Please." Ivey resisted. "Take your hands off me."

"Come on, now," The man's voice was low and husky, and through the mask his breath smelled of spirits. "You owe me the last dance, darling."

Ivey's eyes flashed in anger. "I owe you nothing, Mr. Fitzroy!"

"The lips say no, but the dress says come and get me," he drawled.

"By whose design?" Ivey snapped.

"It got you an airship, didn't it? Showing skin is how girls get what they fancy from rich men, but darling, there's always a price to pay. I can assure you that young Mr. Fenchurche is expecting a return on his investment this evening."

He reached down the back of her gown and grabbed her dress where it fit against her hips. "I hope you're ready to make good on the bargain."

"I don't know what Minnette Fenchurche sees in you. You're nothing more than a pompous ass." Ivey struggled to push him off.

"I believe that'll be your role tonight."

Before she could wrestle away, Paisley jerked a spring-loaded trigger built into the train of the dress that caused the feathers of the skirt to rise and fan out above her head.

The uncomfortably brief undergarment which the gown had obliged her to wear came into clear view of the nearest dancers. Ivey could hear their shocked reactions and feel a cool breeze across her exposed blue legs.

"Oh, mercy!" She struggled to force the feathers back down, but the mechanism had locked in place, and her flailing only drew more attention from those around her.

She looked around and saw Ildwick and Miles pushing their way through the crowd.

"What in Aether? Give me your cape, man," Miles shouted at Ildwick.

"You only see something like that once in a blue moon," Ildwick cackled, before handing it over.

Ivey started to dash toward the winding stairway that led to the private parlor. Changing her mind, she spun and ran back to the dance floor with her gloved fist tightly balled.

She swung at Paisley with all her might, knocking the man to his rear.

"Nice hook." Harwood rushed up and caught Paisley by the scruff of the neck, dragging him to his feet.

"I'm working on it," Ivey said. "Detain this man until we dock—and then throw him off my ship."

With that, she turned and took flight up the staircase, with Miles in pursuit.

"Ivey, wait!" Miles stumbled up the steps, tripping over his scholar's robe.

Ivey dreaded imagining what he must have been able to see from behind her. She ran faster, hoping that her overnight trunk had already been delivered to her suite.

At the top of the stairs, Ivey skidded to a halt. She hardly recognized the parlor. The glass wall of the garden was gone, as was her entire suite. In its place was a much smaller glass enclosure. There were no birds or butterflies, but it was filled with flowering plants and small trees.

A spiral staircase in the center of the garden disappeared through an opening in the ceiling.

Miles staggered up from behind Ivey and threw his arms around her.

"Miles? What are you doing?" She jumped forward in shock.

"I was trying to cover your . . . um . . . uh . . . your tail," Miles stammered.

Ivey grabbed the cape from Miles and wrapped it around her waist.

"Let us be clear. I do not ever again, for any reason, for the rest of my life, want to so much as look at a dress designed by Paisley Fitzroy."

"I'm so sorry," Miles apologized. "My mother commissioned him to make something appropriate for the ball."

"I hardly think your mother expected him to booby-trap my gown."

"What? He did this on purpose?"

"This isn't all he's done. I need to get out of this wretched garment. Where are my things?"

Miles gestured toward the master suite. "Where they belong."

"In your room?"

"Oh." Miles took a long breath. "As the owner of the *Monarch*, you belong in the master suite, not me. I'm staying in the passenger section. I'm sorry if you—"

"No. I'm sorry for acting like an ungrateful fool. I know better."

Ivey sank onto the closest chair and leaned forward, pulling the mask from her face.

"It's just that Paisley made a crude comment." She gestured toward the new garden room. "And this is so unexpected and confusing."

"The guest suite had to be completely removed, so I took the liberty of designing a private garden in its place. I thought you'd like it."

"I do—I just need a moment to collect myself and get out of this miserable dress."

"We both need a change of clothes. Would you mind if I show you to your door?" Miles asked hesitantly.

"Yes . . . I mean, no, I wouldn't mind a bit. Please forgive me, Miles. You've been a perfect gentleman, and by my heart, I trust you completely."

Miles helped her to her feet, and they crossed the parlor. He opened the master suite's door. Ivey took a breath, then peeked inside.

"At least this looks familiar." She laughed self-consciously.

"You can make as many renovations as you like. All I wish is for you to have a place where you will always feel safe and comfortable."

"Miles, you shouldn't have done all this. I certainly don't deserve it."

"The work we are going to do here will serve Aether well. But let's not get ahead of ourselves. You should find everything you need in the wardrobe. When you're ready, will you meet me at the top of your garden stairs?"

"Are there any more surprises?" Ivey asked sheepishly.

"Perhaps one or two." Miles looked down bashfully.

Ivey backed her tail feathers through the door, and Miles closed it behind her. Before she changed out of her gown, Ivey couldn't resist taking a look around.

I'm home.

The workbench in the study was empty, but a few books had been left for her on the desk. She saw Maddox's leather journal lying open to the essay about dimensional rifts. She closed the book and ran her finger over the face on the cover.

"I wish you were here to see the things your son has accomplished," she said softly. "You would be so proud of him."

Ivey went to the bedroom and opened the wardrobe. She'd begrudgingly left Basel's work clothes back at the farm, so she pawed through the dresses that Bea had borrowed from a friend's daughter. Something hanging at the far end of the rack caught her eye.

She pushed the other clothes aside and discovered a green jacket piped with black braid and dotted with rows of gleaming brass buttons. It was similar in style to the red uniforms worn by the *Monarch*'s flight crew, but the waistline was clearly tailored for a woman's body.

"He couldn't have," Ivey whispered, lifting the hanger from the rack. Behind it she discovered a pair of matching trousers.

"I don't believe it!"

She snatched the slacks from the hanger and held them against her body. The length was just right. Of all the honors Miles had paid her, this was the most unexpected and the most significant. She raced to the dressing area of the bathroom and ripped Paisley's gown from her body in pieces.

Once she was dressed in the uniform, Ivey studied her reflection in the full-length mirror beside the vanity. She'd never worn trousers that weren't cinched at the waist and rolled up at the cuff.

Even with blue skin, the effect was quite pleasing to her eye as Ivey turned to observe herself. She stuck her hands into the jacket's front pockets and felt something in the bottom of one of them. She pulled it out.

In her hand was a green engineering ribbon.

There you are, old friend.

Ivey tied her hair back and retrieved a pair of flat slippers from the wardrobe, then set off to find the young man who would be waiting at the top of the garden stairs.

She opened the door and stepped inside the enclosure of her new garden. There were a few benches beside the moss-covered bank of a small glass pond.

A place for Beast.

The night air was sweet, rushing down the garden's open stairway. She looked up at the starlit sky peeking out from behind the envelope of the *Monarch*.

Is this really my airship?

Everything in Ivey's world had changed. She finally had the freedom to travel, study the mysteries of nature, and reinvent herself in ways she'd never even imagined.

When offered the key to her gilded cage, Miles Fenchurche had been brave enough to let her prove that she was capable of living independently. With his support, she had surpassed her own expectations, and for that she would be eternally grateful.

She climbed the stairs and stepped out onto a large wooden platform. "Miles?"

She had arrived first. The gas lighting on the deck was low. To her left, she could see hooded deck chairs. Next to them, a small candlelit dining table was set with covered dishes. Having been too nervous to eat before the ball, Ivey's stomach was now rumbling.

All thoughts of food vanished, however, when she spied a gleaming object perched on the far side of the deck. She ran over to inspect the Zephyr.

It bore an engraved nameplate that read "*Eleutheria II.*"

"The second? So there's more than one of you?" Ivey wondered aloud.

"There should always be at least two," a voice answered. "If one gets into trouble, the other will come to its aid."

She looked back. Miles was at the top of the stairway behind her.

"You think I will get into trouble?" Ivey laughed.

Miles tilted his head and smiled. "I've noticed a pattern."

He stepped onto the deck, and Ivey rushed to join him.

"You found the uniform."

"Oh Miles, I love it! How did you get such a good fit?" She turned so he could appreciate the full effect.

"I have an excellent tailor."

"It puts Paisley Fitzroy to shame. It is perfection!"

"Not yet. There's still one thing that it's missing." Miles held out her leather satchel, which had been confiscated by the Promacheon agents in Spirehaven. "You're not fully dressed without this."

"I thought I'd never see it again."

"Everything's there, except your knife. When we get to Ferndale, I can teach you how to make a new one."

"It is too good to be true." Ivey snatched it into her arms and hugged it tightly. The leathery scent took her back to the day that Arvel had given her the unlikely engagement gift. Even he couldn't have engineered a brighter future than the one Miles Fenchurche was offering.

She felt a pang of guilt. After so many of Miles' heartfelt gestures, she had nothing to offer in return.

She had promised to let Miles prove himself worthy, but when it came to love and marriage, Ivey knew that she could never be domesticated. Somehow, she'd allowed Miles to get caught up in a romantic fantasy. It was cruel. She rubbed her brow in shame.

"Are you all right?"

"Yes. No." Ivey's voice trembled. "I never expected this."

"What?"

"The effect you've had on me. You've given me so much."

"It pales in comparison to what you've given me," Miles said softly.

Tears started to roll down her cheeks. "Miles, I know your feelings changed, but mine haven't. I cannot give you the family you deserve.

"Father asked me to show you how to enjoy your life. Once I did, I'd have his blessing to go home," Ivey cried. "Our engagement was a lie from the beginning."

Miles took in a long breath. His expression was painful and troubling, but she pressed on.

"You will always have a place in my heart. I want you to be happy, but I never intended to marry you. I tried not to mislead you, and now I would rather die than hurt you. I'll go back to Thornhall if it is too much to bear." Ivey broke into sobs.

Miles took her by the shoulders. "Ivey, may we speak as friends?"

She nodded through her tears.

"Since that day at the farm, I've done a great deal of thinking, and I came to the same conclusion. This arrangement was doomed from the start. We were both pushed into it, but I will be eternally grateful for having the chance to know you. I would never do anything to hurt you either."

He let go of her shoulders and gently took her by the hands. "I propose we call the engagement off."

"I can't—" Ivey looked up and sniffed. "What did you say?"

Miles pulled out a handkerchief and offered it to her. "Let's end the arrangement—as friends."

Ivey gasped. "You'd do that for me?"

"There may be one or two conditions," Miles said with a playful smile as she dabbed at her eyes. "I'd like to start this phase of our relationship on new terms."

"What are the terms?"

"Well, I've been wondering what it would be like to court someone properly. Is there any way a fellow could try such a thing with you?"

Ivey gave a nervous laugh. "Why waste your time courting a misfit like me? You're an incredible person, Miles. You should pursue the things that make you happy."

"Who says I'm not?"

Miles led her to the railing, where a finely made telescope was pointed toward the night sky.

"Take a look," he said, "and tell me what you see."

Ivey brought her cheekbone to rest against the ocular lens. In the telescope's field of vision, she saw a familiar constellation.

"The Firedog."

"Yes. Now look below it. Do you see those five bright stars in the shape of a pentacle, like the ones on the dance floor?"

"No . . . wait, yes! There they are. I never noticed them before."

"That's because they weren't there until now. I've checked every one of Aether's celestial charts. They didn't exist, and yet, there they are, exactly the way you showed me in that dream I mentioned. I'm only now beginning to understand what it all meant."

"Tell me," Ivey said, her voice barely above a whisper.

"We were on the observation deck after you saved the songbird. You persuaded me to let you stay and watch the sunset by telling me the legend of the five sisters. You said it was your destiny to change this world, but you couldn't do it until you had someone at your side. Someone who could pull you back if you went too far.

"If I were lucky enough to be that person, I would do everything in my power to keep you safe and make you happy for as long as I live."

"Oh, Miles—"

"All I'm asking is that you give me a chance."

"I don't know how. What if I hurt you?"

"I'll take that risk."

Miles took her by the arms. "Let me show you how I feel and see what happens."

Ivey looked up through her tears. His green eyes were spellbinding. It was as if she had glided out of her body, and all she could do was watch in curious fascination as Miles caressed her cheek, then gently lifted her face to his.

His mouth softly descended, and when his lips tasted hers, she surrendered to a haunting sense of pleasure. He pulled her closer. For a breathless, timeless moment, they were lost in each other's embrace.

When he released her, Ivey whispered.

"What was that?"

"Our first kiss," he answered softly. "It was better than I ever dreamed. What did you think?"

Ivey's head was spinning. Something had awoken within her.

The catalyst!

Ivey gasped, then disappeared into darkness.

∾

She was lighter than air, completely at peace, while a warm hand gripped hers.

"Ivey, try to open your eyes. You have to see something."

She looked up and saw the *Monarch*'s dark envelope. She glanced around and found herself lying on a deck chair with Miles sitting beside her.

"I'm back."

Miles laughed softly. "You never left. You fainted, Miss Thornton." He lifted her pale hand in the moonlight. "But look what's happened. Your complexion has returned to normal."

Ivey sat up and touched her face. "It has? Everywhere?"

"It appears so."

She pulled up her sleeve and the leg of her trousers, uncovering more pale skin.

"Why now?"

Miles touched her cheek. "Ildwick was right. We have good chemistry."

"Ildwick? You've lost me."

"Our kiss started a chemical reaction that triggered the catalyst. You began to shake, and your skin—it was almost luminous. Then it stopped, and you were restored. It was truly incredible. How do you feel?"

"Like I want to do it again!" Ivey grabbed Miles by the arms.

"What?" Miles pulled away in surprise. "I'm not sure that's wise."

"Why not?"

"Well, um," Miles stammered. "For one thing, I wasn't prepared for such a reaction."

"Neither was I," Ivey said with sigh. "If I'm to understand how this chemistry works, we need to kiss again."

She closed her eyes and lifted her chin. When nothing happened, she sat straight and gave him a quizzical look. "What are you waiting for?"

Miles ran a hand through his hair and looked around. "Well . . ." He pointed at the little dining table. "You just fainted. Maybe you should eat something. Why don't I have another meal sent up? I'm sure the food's gone cold." He started to rise, but Ivey grabbed his arm.

"Miles, don't you want to kiss me again?"

"I do, but to be honest, you have me confused, and it's obvious that you're not thinking clearly either."

"What does thinking have to do with this?"

"You said it yourself. You're overwrought. It's been a very eventful evening, and you were drinking wine. In a proper courtship, a gentleman should never take advantage of a lady under such circumstances."

"But I never imagined kissing would be so sweet and exciting. I want to feel it again."

Miles smiled self-consciously. "I completely agree, but Ivey, I'm worried. If we take things too quickly, it could get complicated."

"Yes, well, now you have me confused," Ivey said plaintively. "We just experienced an intense chemical reaction. Don't you want to see what happens next?"

"I want to kiss you and hold you in my arms for the rest of my life—as your husband."

"But Miles—"

"Sorry."

"When did you get so stubborn?" Ivey huffed.

"It's called strength of purpose." Miles gave her a provocative smile. "I swore an oath of honor to your father, and I will keep it or die trying."

"Never mind that, you just kissed me!"

"As an appropriate part of courtship," Miles explained. "When a gentleman escorts a lady for the evening, he is allowed to bid her a proper farewell, and once she is safely back home, he leaves."

"Fine. Then you may retire." Ivey crossed her arms. "I'm sleeping here."

"This lounge is for daytime use only. No one sleeps outside the cabin. Captain's rules," Miles said firmly.

"Honestly? I believe I hold the deed to this ship now, so I will make the rules." Ivey smirked. "I will be sleeping here tonight."

"Fine." He dragged another deck chair over and patted it. "Then I will too.

"It's getting chilly. I'll go get some quilts and a midnight snack, just for you." As he started to leave, Ivey grabbed his hand.

"Wait. I want to be clear. If I let you court me, and we spend an evening together—when it's over, do you promise to bid me another proper farewell?"

"I most certainly do." Miles' eyes smoldered as he stared at her pursed lips.

"Very well. The courtship begins tomorrow."

"Duly noted."

"Good. I shall look forward to the pleasure of your company, Mr. Fenchurche."

"And I to yours, Miss Thornton."

As Miles disappeared down the stairwell, Ivey threw herself back onto the chair and looked up at the stars above. The night air was invigorating, and Ivey had never felt so vibrantly alive.

"Poor Miles has no idea who he's dealing with," she said aloud. "As if I'd have half a mind to marry any man—" Her frustrated thought continued—*and make him kiss me every day for the rest his life.*

Chapter Thirty-Five

New Rules of Engagement

Ivey awoke from a deep and dreamless sleep. She sat up and looked around. Apart from the neatly folded blankets on the other chair, there was no sign of Miles. The morning air was cold, but the deck was aglow with dewy sunlight, and she was warm beneath the down quilts on her chair.

When she rolled over to go back to sleep, something fluttering on the dining table caught her eye. Ivey sprang out of the chair and ran for the table.

It was a note from Miles, inviting her to a farewell breakfast at the captain's table before the ship docked in Spirehaven. On the horizon, the tall skyline of the city was already coming into view.

She raced down the spiral stairs to her new suite. Her green uniform had wrinkled during the night, but Ivey had no intention of trading it in for a dress.

Reaching for the handle of the bathroom door, she recalled bursting through it and crashing into Miles. Even though it seemed silly, she knocked before opening the door. The room was empty, but a fresh green suit, identical to the one she was wearing, was hanging on the valet stand.

After washing up and dressing, Ivey fixed her hair by pulling it back tightly with the green ribbon, then wrapping it into a plain knot.

The chattering in the dining hall hushed when Ivey entered. She wasn't sure whether the guests were silenced by her strange apparel or the return of her fair skin.

She laughed as she made her way across the room to the captain's table. Most of these people would never board the *Monarch* again, so she hoped they were getting a good eyeful.

"Ivey! Look at you!" Sylvia rose to her feet and rushed to embrace her.

Ivey cocked her head. "Look at those rosy cheeks! What have you been up to, Miss Feather? I guessed right, didn't I?"

Sylvia nodded and held out the cast, wiggling her fingers to display a sparkling gemstone.

"Have you seen my cows?"

"Your cows?"

"That's how a farm girl tells her friends she's engaged. I'm engaged, Ivey!"

Ivey grinned. "And I'm not! This really is perfect."

Sylvia's mouth turned down at the corners. "Oh no, you didn't break it off, did you?"

"I didn't, but he did!" Ivey clapped and laughed, to Sylvia's dismay.

"Don't make that face, Sylvia. We have a new arrangement now. He may court me so long as I get a proper goodnight kiss in the bargain. Marriage may not be for me, but did you know that kissing can be quite wonderful? And I think I'm fairly good at it. I know Miles is."

Sylvia coughed and lowered her voice. "Ivey, you really do say the strangest things." Then she leaned close and whispered. "Nicolai is good too."

"We're quite lucky! What are your plans? Will he take you back to Prominence until we take possession of the *Monarch*?"

"No! I'm coming with you to Ferndale. He and Miles have an important project to work on."

"Of course." Ivey looked at the table. "Where is Miles?"

"I don't know, but come sit down. I'm sure he'll be here soon." She led Ivey to her seat and whispered, "I still can't believe I've got a seat at the captain's table."

"This is our table now, Miss Feather," Ivey whispered back.

"Ladies." Captain LeClere rose to his feet, along with Nicolai and Ildwick.

"Gentlemen." She nodded deferentially and firmly removed Ildwick's hand from the back of her chair. "I can seat myself, thank you."

"Suit yourself." He crossed his arms with a smirk. "And speaking of suits, I trust you had an enjoyable evening. Good chemistry, indeed."

Ivey tried to be nonchalant, but she felt her face turning pink. "I have no complaints."

"Of course not," Ildwick insisted. "You've been stuck in a surly blue mood since the night I met you, but I knew young Master Fenchurche was bound to awaken your amorous side. I do hope he's braced for what's ahead though. Try to be gentle with him, won't you, sunshine?"

Ivey immediately drove the topic away from her own private affairs.

"Why, Ildwick, aren't you the one who should be careful? Female spiders are known to devour their mates."

"You must mean my . . . niece," Ildwick said innocently.

"Your niece? The two of you seemed awfully close."

"The girl does love me to death." He chuckled nervously.

"Will you be bringing her to Ferndale?"

"Who says I'm going to Ferndale?"

"What else will you do until the new research facility is ready?"

"This and that, and that and this, but mostly I will thank you dearly for keeping your nose out of my business."

Ivey shook her head and turned her attention to the captain.

"Captain LeClere, I cannot tell you how happy I am to have you back on the bridge of the *Monarch*. I want you to teach me everything there is to know about this ship. Additionally, there are some modifications I'd like to make while she's in dock."

"Such as?" The captain's brow rose.

"We'll need a secondary access to the riggings, and every cable must be reinforced."

"I see. Will that be all?"

"Not in the slightest. I want to increase the capacity of the reserve fuel tanks, and this ship needs much more lift. I'll see what Miles can do to incorporate otheophainers into the cabin, and let's look at altering the envelope's surface design to give us more speed."

The captain nodded dubiously. "Working under your employ is sure to be quite an experience."

"Please, Captain, I want you to work beside me. An airship can only have one hand on the helm," Ivey stated, "and I am hardly ready to assume that role yet!"

Ildwick patted the captain's shoulder. "Yet? Isn't that reassuring!"

Miles entered the dining room, followed by Harwood. Ivey instantly noticed that Miles appeared shaken.

She jumped up. "What's happened?"

"It was nothing."

There was something off about the way he held his right hand in his front pocket. She pulled it free. His knuckles were wrapped in a bloody handkerchief.

"Miles, did you cut yourself?" Ivey asked.

Miles' jaw clenched. "Not at all. I simply had a little accident helping Paisley Fitzroy prepare to disembark the ship."

Harwood nodded. "He's got a fat lip to go with the black eye you gave him."

Ivey tilted her head appreciatively. "Miles, you didn't have to do that for me."

"I did it for me." He squared his shoulders. "And I should have done it long ago."

"Well, it seems that someone has awoken your ferocious side, my good man."

Ildwick reached into one of his pockets and pulled out a tin of ointment and a roll of bandages. "Let's get this cleaned up. You wouldn't want to catch anything nasty from Mr. Fitzroy."

~

After breakfast, Ivey took a last walk around the *Monarch* before the ship docked. The guests had all departed by the time she ended up below the portrait in the lobby.

Looking up at the faces of the lost crewmen, she recognized the young man with curly red hair who'd saluted her after she repaired the

Monarch's envelope. The name below his picture read, *Rowan James*.

A sudden chill ran through her when she realized it was his uniform that she'd stolen. Somehow that knowledge made her feel painfully close to this poor soul.

"You'll soon know what it feels like to hold responsibility for others' lives and deaths."

Ivey turned to find Minnette, dressed in her traveling cloak and hat. Ivey hung her head. "I'm afraid I already do."

Minnette folded her arms.

A strange expression crossed the woman's face. Ivey couldn't tell if she was sad or angry. There was an uncomfortable silence until Minnette finally spoke.

"I owe you an apology for some of the things I said in the midst of disaster. Without your intervention, my son would not be alive today."

Ivey opened her mouth to speak, but Minnette held up her hand.

"There's more. About the man you killed—it was my life or his. You simply realized that before he did." She cleared her throat. "That is why I led the fight for your release and agreed to give you this ship . . . it was my way of thanking you, Miss Thornton."

"You're welcome." The lump in Ivey's throat preventing her from saying more.

Minnette stared at her a long time before she asked, "Where will you go from here?"

"I haven't decided. Miles and I will be working together at Ferndale, and from there, we'll see where the wind takes the two of us."

"The two of us? My son has given you everything you need to start a new life on your own. Do you care at all for what he needs?"

"I want Miles to finally be happy." Ivey tried not to look away from Minnette's steely gaze.

"There is a difference between what a person wants and what he needs, Miss Thornton. Miles is the last of an extraordinary bloodline. He needs a wife that will give him strong sons and dutiful daughters to ensure his legacy. Nothing has made me believe that you are that person."

Ivey couldn't stop her chin from rising a bit. "There's more to life than inherited duties. Why shouldn't Miles be allowed to enjoy himself?"

The expression on Minnette's face hardened. "This is no time for frivolous distractions. Imagine the creatures that infested this ship rampaging across Cemaria. How long could our people fight off such an invasion?"

"For as long as we live and breathe," Ivey said with resolution.

"What if that struggle lasts beyond the time of your generation? This company will play a vital role in protecting Aether, and Fenchurche heirs may be its only hope of salvation. I trust you will think carefully before wasting Miles' time or his life."

Ivey had to glance away. She mustered her defiance before looking back. "You will have to excuse me. Your son is waiting, and I would never waste his time. I'll see you at Ferndale."

Minnette nodded coolly and left.

Ivey hurried back to her suite to pack her things, robbed of the elation that had come with the *Monarch*'s deed. Even climbing aboard her new Zephyr and watching Miles prepare to take off wasn't as thrilling as it should have been.

"Don't let her upset you," Miles remarked, while he tested the gauges of the flight panel.

"Did you know your mother was going to speak with me?"

Miles looked surprised. "No, I didn't. That's odd."

Ivey glanced at him sideways. "Can you tell what I'm thinking right now?"

He stared at her a moment. "I imagine that you'd like to trade places with me and pilot the *Eleutheria*."

Ivey burst out in laughter. "What a fantastic idea! May I?"

Miles pointed up at the *Monarch*'s envelope looming above them. "Your lessons will begin at Ferndale, where there's more room to make a mistake."

"Aren't you willing to take a risk for me?" Ivey teased.

Miles' gaze searched her face, ending on her lips. "Only if it pays off at the end of the day."

The tenacious look in his eyes sent a strange feeling rushing through Ivey's veins. She sat up straight and took a deep breath.

"Right then, let's get on with it."

Miles released the otheophainer's activation lock, and the machine came to life, pulsing with a steady heartbeat of its own.

"Do you feel anything out of the ordinary?" he asked.

"Yes," Ivey mused, "but I don't think it's the machine."

Ivey had dreamed of this moment for as long as she could remember. Rising from the deck of the *Monarch* and launching off into the clear autumn skies above Spirehaven was beyond anything she'd ever imagined as a child.

Miles was an experienced pilot, and once they reached the open countryside, he showed off for Ivey, performing simple ærial tricks that made her stomach drop in the most delightful way.

As they passed over an old barn Ivey jumped from her seat.

"That's the Feathers' place! Are we close to Ferndale?"

Miles grinned. "We've been flying over it for some time now."

Scanning the horizon, Ivey saw nothing but a lush valley dotted with farms.

"Where?"

"It's most of the land that you see. The manor is on the other side of that outcropping of rock." He pointed ahead.

"You own all of this?"

As they topped the ridge, a thick forest covered the foothills until it gave way to the meadows and dells on the floor of the neighboring valley.

Ahead, a magnificent home sat amid a labyrinth of gardens. It was larger than Thornhall, but not as ostentatious as she'd expected.

"Oh, Miles. Ferndale is lovely."

"Hmm? That's not the manor, that's the hut."

"The hut, you call that a hut?"

"Actually, it's the hermit's hut."

"You have a hermit?" Ivey's face was pressed against the glass as they passed over it. "Who is he?"

"He is a she."

"Miles, why does a hermit woman live on your property?"

"All I know is that she wishes to be left alone. You'll have to respect her privacy, Ivey."

"How can I do that if I don't who she is and why she's there?"

"I think you'll manage."

They cleared the treetops, and stretched out before them was Ferndale Manor, a structure of legendary proportions. The sprawling edifice had multiple wings with steep copper roofs lined by stone buttresses and gargoyles. There were turrets, balconies, domes, and too many massive windows to count. On one side of the building, a tall tower with a glass observatory soared high into the sky.

A cobbled driveway circled a massive fountain in front of the manor's colonnaded entrance.

"This isn't a house, it's a c-castle," Ivey said.

"It is a bit dramatic, but we call it home."

As they landed, Ivey saw Dolan standing among a large detachment of people dressed in starched uniforms and lined up beneath the entryway.

"What is he doing?"

"It is traditional for the servants to come out and welcome a new . . . well . . . they don't know you're not my fiancée anymore. I'm sorry. Would you mind going through the motions with me? Mother will be upset if they don't follow protocol."

"Protocol?"

"Just shake their hands, smile, and nod. You don't have to talk to them."

"I don't mind talking to them."

"I know. It's just that they aren't allowed to converse with you. Mother doesn't believe in public displays of familiarity with servants."

"What? How can anyone live like that?"

"If they break Mother's house rules, there are consequences."

"Oh dear, I'll probably get someone sent to the dungeon."

"Not if you follow my lead."

"I don't know. Maybe I should go back to the *Monarch*."

Miles powered down the Zephyr's engines and reached for her hand. "Ivey, I want you here, working with me."

"But Miles, you know how I am."

"Yes I do. I gave you the *Monarch* so you can live by your own rules. However, this is my mother's home, and she is set in her ways. If you can be patient until things are settled, it will make life much easier for everyone."

Ivey's brow furrowed as she looked at the row of stoic faces before the fortress looming in front of her.

"This won't be easy."

"I'm afraid not. But try to imagine her life for a moment. I am all that she has in this world. If I'm lucky enough to win your heart, we will live wherever you want. Before that can happen, I have to help my mother let go of me. I owe that to her."

Ivey sighed. Miles' kindness toward his mother was touching. He gave her a hopeful smile, and his sweet, sad eyes sealed her fate.

"All right, the staff is watching. I will be a proper gentleman and open the door for the gracious young lady that I now have the honor of courting. Can you play along with me?"

Ivey's eyebrow went up.

"Let me show you how I feel." She lunged forward and, in front of all the manor's attendants, gave the young master a lingering kiss.

Before he could stop her, Ivey jumped out of the Zephyr and curtsied to the dumbstruck servants, then turned back to offer Miles her hand.

"Come along, Mr. Fenchurche. I can't wait to see what happens next."

Glossary

Asymbiant – (ə-SIM-bē-ant) – A mysterious, shape-shifting parasite

Boreas – (BŌR-ē-ˈəs) – Arvel Thornton's enhanced Zephyr

Cosmocrene – (KÄZ-mō-krēn) – Aether's core of perfect energy

Eleutheria – (el-yü-THE-rē-a) – The assigned name of the *Monarch*'s dedicated Zephyrs

Gelthinium – (gel-THIN-ē-ˈəm) – A mineral repelled by the cosmocrene

Lunial – (LÜ-nē-ˈəl) – A mineral attracted to the cosmocrene

Notus – (NŌ-təs) A line of Zephyrs to be designed for the Dicæon

Otheophainer – (ō-THĒ-ō-fī-nər) – The device on a Zephyr that produces its lift

Pheme – (fēm) *pl.* **Phemai** (FĒ-mī) – Messages sent through the cosmocrene by the cipher device

Pneuma biou – (NÜ-ma bē-YÜ) – Archaic term for the soul

Zephyr – (ZE-fər) – A flying machine whose lift is generated by the cosmocrene

❧

Acknowledgments

This book wouldn't exist without the love, support, and creativity of my family. I wouldn't exist without Richard and Phyllis Ammeter, who gave me many gifts, including a love of language.

I'm grateful for my first audiences, my husband Rick Owen, who listened many long nights as I spun this tale, and for Etta Owen and Gladys Kitchens who enjoyed the original recording of the book, my initial editor, April Ammeter Sakane, and Rick Sakane for setting up my early social media sites. Their efforts were joined by the friends and family who read, reviewed, advised, and cheered me on: Gary and Phyllis Ammeter, Crystal Ammeter, Shelly Stanford, Linda Young, Soozy Martin, Tanya and Ludmila Murray, Laura Woodward, Marian Schiff, Elizabeth Dail, Bob Lavallee, Fred Holmes, Jim Rowley, Rachel Schnitzius Rouse, Alyx Kasmer, Sheena Gordon, Jaye Restivo, Becky Burks, Linda Sladovnik, Katelyn Rogers, Cheryl Kimberley, Penny Young, Todd and Helen Hosfelt Schump, Bridget Lachner, Dicia Ames, Grant James and Juli Erickson, Karla Zemler, Michele Mattia, and to the LeClere and McEvoy families for letting me borrow their names for my airship captains.

Special thanks to my mom across the alley, Ruth Montgomery, for her constant encouragement and support, to John Galt, who convinced me many years ago that I was a writer, which put me on the path to a writing career at Radio Disney, and to Bob Evans who opened the door for me at *Barney & Friends* - where I wrote scripts for a pair of talented girls named Demi Lovato and Selena Gomez.

A tip of the hat to my first book signing fan, Ben Schwartz, to Molly Grogan and The Dallas Academy's Ivey League fan club, June Weber, Carolyn Renz and Kyra Fick Concalves, M.E. Sutton Clary, and to my first international fan, Jade Kops.

Here's to other cheerleaders near and far: Jean and Blair Leggett, Steve Taft and Theatre UNI, Katy Massingill Manck, Amy Grundmeyer, Sheryl Betenbender, Rae Ann Dighton Holub, Scot and Hannah Berko Violette, Lauren Shambeck, Margie Herbert, Amber Martin,

Karen Kitchen, Jordan Mathews, Jared Dimick and Pinja Friström, Kristy Blacklund, Patti Smith, Amanda Alexander, Kim Kelley-Wagner and her talented daughters Lily and Meiko, Colby Bladow, Denise Crowell, Sarah Gengler, Diane Knott, Barb Cook, Judy Isaacson, and all the ladies of the Coggon book club.

Tremendous credit goes to Blair Gauntt for his design work on the first edition and its promotion, and for shooting the author's photo, to Annette Maxberry-Carrara for mentoring the first edition of *Ivey and the Airship* at Wisdom House Publishing, and to Erik Christopher of Ugly Dog Digital for the eBook design and distribution.

A resounding huzzah to the talented crew at Pantala Press for getting the revised edition off the ground: Shanette Eckols, who helped redefine the characters and edit the story, Deanne Lachner, my trusty CMS editor and continuity guardian, Jenn Oliver, eagle-eyed proofreader, and the extremely gifted illustrator Wylie Beckert, who brought Ivey Thornton to life in her cover art.

And finally, my undying gratitude goes to my creative director, writing consultant, book designer, and illustrator, Bob West. His meticulous and inspirational work on every aspect of the Aether's Edge series and its branding has been the wind beneath my airship's wings.

࿂

REVIEWS

Cheryl Ammeter's writing is fresh, inventive, and cinematic. I could easily visualize all the airships, monsters, and friends of the family. Ivey's pet monster—the often invisible, ferocious 'waterdog'—is a boffo creation. Ivey and the Airship really has everything: adventure, romance, humor, large metaphors . . . and I loved the ending!"

—**Jane Howle**, founder of Baskerville Publishers, Inc.

"Ivey and the Airship is the first book in our library catalog with the subject heading 'Steampunk,' but I hope it won't be the last."

—**Amy Grundmeyer**, District Librarian, North Linn Schools

"Welcome to the steampunk world of Aether, where a young lady's social skills are far more valued than her intelligence, where a good marriage is a barometer of success, and where Ivey Thornton is determined to do things differently."

—**Katy Manck**, MLS Librarian-at-large & independent book reviewer

"This is a wonderful book that engages the reader. It is written with beautiful descriptions and imaginative details that take you to new and special places—and I wish such an airship existed!"

—**Jill Sayre**, author of *The Fairies of Turtle Creek*

"I could NOT put this book down! Original and witty, the characters are so realistic that I felt like I was part of their world and the story. Cheryl Ammeter knocked it out of the ballpark on her first book."

—**Janae Marshall**

"I must say I haven't been so utterly consumed by an author's ability to develop a world and characters in . . . well . . . never. I seldom one-shot a book, but this was an epic story that deserves your full attention. You won't be disappointed!"

—K. M. Smith

"I so much enjoy finding a book centered on an interesting and complex female character; here, Ivey does not want to be forced into a loveless marriage, and she isn't so sure about a potentially love-filled marriage if it will turn her into an insipid mother-woman, so she embarks on a fascinating journey aboard an airship in a fantastical realm."

—Becca W.

"As you read this book, you can't help but fall a little bit in love with Ivey and her world. It is sharp and witty, believable, and just plain fun. Once you start, you won't want to put it down."

—Loves to Travel

"It reads a bit like the first Harry Potter book, but set in a science fiction steampunk universe that reminds me of *The Girl who Heard Dragons* by Anne McCaffrey."

—Jason A. Miller

"I was so sad when I found myself on the last page and the adventure was at an end . . . for now. I am delighted to hear that book two is in the works."

—Victoria W.

"If I had a stack of these signed by the author, I could easily see the investment out-performing my stock portfolio. Good Job!"

—Lisa Carnahan

☙

ABOUT THE AUTHOR

Cheryl Ammeter grew up on a dairy farm in Iowa and currently lives in Pacifica, California with her husband, children, and two miscreant cats that came with the property.

She is best known as an award-winning scriptwriter for over seven seasons of the globally acclaimed children's program, *Barney & Friends*. At Radio Disney, she wrote and performed in a variety of Disney features including *Generation Girl Theatre*, where she adapted a series of Barbie® books into episodic radio plays for Mattel and Golden Books.

After years of adhering to production budgets and schedules, her larger-than-life imagination has finally been set free in the adventurous world of Science Fiction Fantasy. *Ivey and the Airship* is the first in five-book series called *Aether's Edge*. Cheryl is currently at work on the second book in the series, *Masters of Misfortune*.

ॐ

www.ingramcontent.com/pod-product-compliance
Lightning Source LLC
Chambersburg PA
CBHW022239020726
47496CB00004B/981